The Wheat Princess

Jean Webster

If you leave the city by the Porta Maggiore and take the Via Prænestina, which leads east into the Sabine hills, at some thirty-six kilometers' distance from Rome you will pass on your left a grey-walled village climbing up the hillside. This is Palestrina, the old Roman Præneste; and a short distance beyond—also on the left—you will find branching off from the straight Roman highway a steep mountain road, which, if you stick to it long enough, will take you, after many windings, to Castel Madama and Tivoli.

Several kilometers along this road you will see shooting up from a bare crag above you a little stone hamlet crowned by the ruins of a mediaeval fortress. The town—Castel Vivalanti—was built in the days when a stronghold was more to be thought of than a water-supply, and its people, from habit or love, or perhaps sheer necessity, have lived on there ever since, going down in the morning to their work in the plain and toiling up at night to their homes on the hill. So steep is its site that the doorway of one house looks down on the roof of the house below, and its narrow stone streets are in reality flights of stairs. The only approach is from the front, by a road which winds and unwinds like a serpent and leads at last to the Porta della Luna, through which all of the traffic enters the town. The gate is ornamented with the crest of the Vivalanti—a phoenix rising out of the flame, supported by a heavy machicolated top, from which, in the old days, stones and burning oil might be dropped upon the heads of the unwelcome guests.

The town is a picturesque little affair—it would be hard to find a place more so in the Sabine villages, it is very, very poor. In the march of the centuries it has fallen out of step and been left far behind; to look at it, one would scarcely dream that on the clear days the walls and towers of modern Rome are in sight on the horizon. But in its time Castel Vivalanti was not insignificant. This little hamlet has entertained history within its walls. It has bodily outfaced robber barons and papal troops. It has been besieged and conquered, and, alas, betrayed—and that by its own prince. Twice has it been razed to the ground and twice rebuilt. In one way or another, though, it has weathered the centuries, and it stands to-day grey and forlorn, clustering about the walls of its donjon and keep.

Castel Vivalanti, as in the middle ages, still gives the title to a Roman prince. The house of Vivalanti was powerful in its day, and the princes may often be met with—not always to their credit—in the history of the Papal States. They were oftener at war than at peace with the holy see, and there is the story of one pope who spent four weary months watching the view from a very small window in Vivalanti's donjon. But, in spite of their unholy quarrels, they were at times devout enough, and twice a cardinal's hat has been worn in the family. The house of late years has dwindled somewhat, both in fortune and importance; but, nevertheless, Vivalanti is a name which is still spoken with respect among the old nobles of Rome.

The lower slopes of the hill on which the village stands are well wooded and green with stone-pines and cypresses, olive orchards and vineyards. Here the princes built their villas when the wars with the popes were safely at an end and they could risk coming down from their stronghold on the mountain. The old villa was built about a mile below the town, and the gardens were laid out in terraces and parterres along the slope of the hill. It has long been in ruin, but its foundations still stand, and the plan of the gardens may easily be traced. You will see the entrance at the left of the road—a massive stone gateway topped with moss-covered urns and a double row of cone-shaped cypresses bordering a once stately avenue now grown over with weeds. If you pause for a moment—and you cannot help doing so—you will see, between the portals at the end of the avenue, some crumbling arches, and even, if your eyes are good, the fountain itself.

Any contadino that you meet on the road will tell you the story of the old Villa Vivalanti and the 'Bad Prince' who was (by the grace of God) murdered two centuries ago. He will tell you—a story not uncommon in Italy—of storehouses bursting with grain while the peasants were starving, and of how, one moonlight night, as the prince was strolling on the terrace contentedly pondering his wickednesses of the day, a peasant from his own village up on the mountain, creeping behind him, quiet as a cat, stabbed him in the back and dropped his body in the fountain. He will tell you how the light from the burning villa was seen as far as Rocca di Papa in the Alban hills; and he will add, with a laugh and a shrug, that some people say when the moon is full the old prince comes back and sits on the edge of the fountain and thinks of his sins, but that, for himself, he thinks it an old woman's tale. Whereupon he will cast a quick glance over his shoulder at the dark shadow of the cypresses and covertly cross himself as he wishes you, 'A rivederla.'

You cannot wonder that the young prince (two centuries ago) did not build his new villa on the site of the old; for even had he, like the brave contadino, cared nothing for ghosts, still it was scarcely a hallowed spot, and lovers would not care to stroll by the fountain. So it happens that you must travel some distance further along the same road before you reach the gates of the new villa, built anno domini 1693, in the pontificate of his Holiness Innocent XII. Here you will find no gloomy cypresses: the approach is bordered by spreading plane-trees. The villa itself is a rambling affair, and, though slightly time-worn, is still decidedly imposing, with its various wings, its balconies and loggia and marble terrace. The new villa—for such one must call it—faces west and north. On the west it looks down over olive orchards and vineyards to the Roman Campagna, with the dome of St. Peter's a white speck in the distance, and, beyond it, to a narrow, shining ribbon of sea. On the north it looks up to the Sabine mountains, with the height of Soracte rising like an island on the horizon. For the rest, it is surrounded by laurel and ilex groves with long shady walks and leafy arbors, with fountains and cascades and broken statues all laid out in the stately formality of the seventeenth century. But the trees are no longer so carefully trimmed as they were a century ago; the sun rarely shines in these green alleys, and the nightingales sing all day. Through every season, but especially in the springtime, the garden-borders are glowing with colour. Hedges of roses, oleanders and golden laburnum, scarlet pomegranate blossoms and red and white camellias, marguerites and lilies and purple irises, bloom together in flaming profusion. And twice a year, in the spring and the autumn, the soft yellow walls of the villa are covered with lavender wistaria and pink climbing roses, and every breeze is filled with their fragrance.

It is a spot in which to dream of old Italy, of cardinals and pages and gorgeous lackeys, of gallant courtiers and beautiful ladies, of Romeos and Juliets trailing back and forth over the marble terrace and making love under the Italian moon. But if there have been lovers, as is doubtless the case, there have also been haters among the Vivalanti, and you may read of more than one prince murdered by hands other than those of his peasants. The walls of the new villa, in the course of their two hundred years, have looked down on their full share of tragedies, and the Vivalanti annals are grim reading withal.

And now, having pursued the Vivalanti so far, you may possibly be disappointed to hear that the story has nothing to do with them. But if you are interested in learning more of the family you can find his Excellency Anastasio di Vivalanti, the present prince and the last of the line, any afternoon during the season in the casino at Monte Carlo. He is a slight young man with a dark, sallow face and many fine lines under his eyes.

Then why, you may ask, if we are not concerned with the Vivalanti, have we lingered so long in their garden? Ah—but the garden does concern us, though the young prince may not; and it is a pleasant spot, you must acknowledge, in which to linger. The people with whom we are concerned are (I hesitate to say it for fear of destroying the glamour) an American family. Yes, it is best to confess it boldly—are American millionaires. It is out— the worst is told! But why, may I ask in my turn, is there anything so inherently distressing in the idea of an American family (of millionaires) spending the summer in a seventeenth-century Italian villa up in the Sabine hills—especially when the rightful heir prefers trente-et-un at Monte Carlo? Must they of necessity spoil the romance? They are human, and have their passions like the rest of us; and one of them at least is young, and men have called her beautiful—yes, in this very garden.

CHAPTER I

It was late and the studio was already well filled when two new-comers were ushered into the room—one a woman still almost young, and still (in a kindly light) beautiful; the other a girl emphatically young, her youth riding triumphant over other qualities which in a few years would become significant. A slight, almost portentous, hush had fallen over the room as they crossed the threshold and shook hands with their host. In a group near the door a young man—it was Laurence Sybert, the first secretary of the American Embassy—broke off in the middle of a sentence with the ejaculation: 'Ah, the Wheat Princess!'

'Be careful, Sybert! She will hear you,' the grey-haired consul-general, who stood at his elbow, warned.

Sybert responded with a laugh and a half-shrug; but his tones, though low, had carried, and the girl flashed upon the group a pair of vivid hazel eyes containing a half-puzzled, half-questioning light, as though she had caught the words but not the meaning. Her vague expression changed to one of recognition; she nodded to the two diplomats as she turned away to welcome a delegation of young lieutenants, brilliant in blue and gold and shining boots.

'Who is she?' another member of the group inquired as he adjusted a pair of eye-glasses and turned to scrutinize the American girl—she was American to the most casual observer, from the piquant details of her gown to the masterly fashion in which she handled her four young men.

'Don't you know?' There was just a touch of irony in Sybert's tone. 'Miss Marcia Copley, the daughter of the American Wheat King—I fancy you've seen his name mentioned in the papers.'

'Well, well! And so that's Willard Copley's daughter?' He readjusted his glasses and examined her again from this new point of view. 'She isn't bad-looking,' was his comment. 'The Wheat Princess!' He repeated the phrase with a laugh. 'I suppose she has come over to marry an Italian prince and make the title good?'

The originator of the phrase shrugged anew, with the intimation that it was nothing to him who Miss Marcia Copley married.

'And who is the lady with her?'

It was Melville, the consul-general, who replied.

'Her aunt, Mrs. Howard Copley. They live in the Palazzo Rosicorelli.'

'Ah, to be sure! Yes, yes, I know who they are. Her husband's a reformer or a philanthropist, or something of the sort, isn't he? I've seen him at the meets. I say, you know,' he added, with an appreciative smile, 'that's rather good, the way the two brothers balance each other. Philanthropist and Wheat King!'

An English girl in the group turned and studied the American girl a moment with a critical scrutiny. Marcia Copley's appearance was daintily attractive. Her hat and gown and furs were a burnished brown exactly the colour of her hair; every little accessory of her dress was unobtrusively fastidious. Her whole bearing, her easy social grace, spoke of a past in which the way had been always smoothed by money. She carried with her a touch of imperiousness, a large air of commanding the world. The English girl noted these things with jealous feminine eyes.

'Really,' she said, 'I don't see how she has the audacity to face people. I should think that every beggar in the street would be a reproach to her.'

'There were beggars in Italy long before Willard Copley cornered wheat,' Melville returned.

'If what the *Tribuna* says is true,' some one ventured, 'Howard Copley is as much implicated as his brother.'

'I dare say,' another laughed; 'millionaire philanthropists have a way of taking back with the left hand what they have given with the right.'

Sybert had been listening in a half-indifferent fashion to the strictures on the niece, but in response to the implied criticism of the uncle he shook his head emphatically.

'Howard Copley is no more implicated in the deal than I am,' he declared. 'He and his brother have had nothing to do with each other for the last ten years. His philanthropy is honest, and his money is as clean as any fortune can be.'

The statement was not challenged. Sybert was known to be Howard Copley's friend, and he further carried the reputation of being a warm partizan on the one or two subjects which engaged his enthusiasm—on those which did not engage it he was nonchalant to a degree for a rising diplomat.

The two—Sybert and the consul-general—with a nod to the group presently drifted onward toward the door. The secretary was bent upon departure at the earliest possible opportunity. Teas were a part of the official routine of his life, but by the simple device of coming late and leaving early he escaped as much of their irksomeness as possible. Aside from being secretary of the Embassy, Sybert was a nephew of the ambassador, and it was the latter calling which he found the more onerous burden of the two. His Excellency had formed a troublesome habit of shifting social burdens to the unwilling shoulders of the younger man.

They paused at Mrs. Copley's elbow with outstretched hands, and were received with a flattering show of cordiality from the aunt, though with but a fleeting nod from the niece; she was, patently, too interested in her officers to have much attention left.

'Where is your husband?' Sybert asked.

The lady raised her eyebrows in a picturesque gesture.

'Beggars,' she sighed. 'Something has happened to the beggars again.' Mr. Copley's latest philanthropic venture had been the 'Anti-Begging Society.' Bread-tickets had been introduced, the beggars were being hunted down and given work, and as a result Copley's name was cursed from end to end of Rome.

The men smilingly murmured their commiserations.

'And what are you two diplomats doing here?' Mrs. Copley asked. 'I thought that Mr. Dessart invited only artists to his teas.'

Sybert's gloomy air, as he eyed the door, reflected the question. It was Melville who answered:

'Oh, we are admirers of art, even if we are not practitioners. Besides, Mr. Dessart and I are old friends. We used to know each other in Pittsburg when he was a boy and I was a good deal younger than I am now.'

His gaze rested for a moment upon their host, who formed one of the hilarious group about Miss Copley. He was an eminently picturesque young fellow, fitted with the usual artist attributes—a velveteen jacket, a flowing necktie, and rather long light-brown hair which constantly got into his eyes, causing him to shake his head impatiently as he talked. He had an open, frank face, humorous blue eyes and the inestimable, eager air of being in love with life.

The conversation showing signs of becoming general, the officers, with visible reluctance, made their bows and gave place to the new-comers. The girl now found time to extend a cordial hand to Melville, while to the secretary she tossed a markedly careless, 'Good afternoon, Mr. Sybert.' If Miss Marcia's offhand manner conveyed something a trifle stronger than indifference, so Sybert's half-amused smile as he talked to her suggested that her unkindness failed to hurt; that she was too young to count.

'And what is this I hear about your moving out to a villa for the spring?' he inquired, turning to Mrs. Copley.

'Yes, we are thinking of it, but it is not decided yet.'

'We still have Uncle Howard to deal with,' added the girl. 'He was the first one who suggested a villa, but now that exactly the right one presents itself, we very much suspect him of trying to back out.'

'That will never do, Miss Marcia,' said Melville. 'You must hold him to his word.'

'We are going out to-morrow to inspect it, and if Aunt Katherine and I are pleased——'
She broke off with a graceful gesture which intimated much.

Sybert laughed. 'Poor Uncle Howard!' he murmured.

The arrival of fresh guests called their host away, and Mrs. Copley and Melville, turning aside to greet some friends, left Miss Copley for the moment to a tête à tête with Sybert. He maintained his side of the conversation in a half-perfunctory fashion, while the girl allowed a slight touch of hostility to creep beneath her animation.

'And where is the villa to be, Miss Marcia—at Frascati, I suppose?'

'Farther away than Frascati; at Castel Vivalanti.'

'Castel Vivalanti!'

'Up in the Sabine hills between Palestrina and Tivoli.'

'Oh, I know where it is; I have a vivid recollection of climbing the hill on a very hot day. I was merely exclaiming at the locality; it's rather remote, isn't it?'

'Its remoteness is the best thing about it. Our object in moving into the hills is to escape from visitors, and if we go no farther than Frascati we shan't do much escaping.' This to the family's most frequent visitor was scarcely a hospitable speech, and a smile of amusement crept to the corners of Sybert's mouth.

Apparently just becoming aware of the content of her speech, she added with slightly exaggerated sweetness: 'Of course I don't mean you, Mr. Sybert. You come so often that I regard you as a member of the household.'

The secretary apparently had it on his tongue to retort, but, thinking better of it, he maintained a discreet silence, while their host approached with the new arrivals—a lady whose name Miss Copley did not catch, but who was presented with the explanatory remark, 'she writes,' and several young men who, she judged by their neckties, were artists also. The talk turned on the villa again, and Miss Copley was called upon for a description.

'I haven't seen it myself,' she returned; 'but from the steward's account it is the most complete villa in Italy. It has a laurel walk and an ilex grove, balconies, fountains, a marble terrace, a view, and even a ghost.'

'A ghost?' queried Dessart. 'But I thought they were extinct—that the railroads and tourists had driven them all back to the grave.'

'Not the ghost of the "Bad Prince"; we rent him with the place—and the most picturesque ghost you ever dreamed of! He hoarded his wheat while the peasants were starving, and they murdered him two hundred years ago.' She repeated the story, mimicking in inimitable fashion the gestures and broken English of Prince Vivalanti's steward.

A somewhat startled silence hung over the close of the recital, while her auditors glanced at each other in secret amazement. The question uppermost in their minds was whether it was ignorance or mere bravado that had tempted her into repeating just that particular tale. It was a subject which Miss Copley might have been expected to avoid. Laurence Sybert alone was aware that she did not know what a dangerous topic she was venturing on, and he received the performance with an appreciative laugh.

'A very picturesque story, Miss Copley. The old fellow got what he deserved.'

Marcia Copley assented with a smiling gesture, and the woman who wrote skilfully bridged over a second pause.

'You were complaining the other day, Mr. Dessart, that the foreigners are making the Italians too modern. Why do you not catch the ghost? He is surely a true antique.'

'But I am not an impressionist,' he pleaded.

'Who is saying anything against impressionists?' a young man asked in somewhat halting English as he paused beside the group.

'No one,' said Dessart; 'I was merely disclaiming all knowledge of them and their ways. Miss Copley, allow me to present Monsieur Benoit, the last Prix de Rome—he is the man to paint your ghost. He's an impressionist and paints nothing else.'

'I suppose you have ghosts enough in the Villa Medici, without having to search for them in the Sabine hills.'

'Ah, oui, mademoiselle; the Villa Medici has ghosts of many kinds—ghosts of dead hopes and dead ambitions among others.'

'I should think the ghost of a dead ambition might be too illusive for even an impressionist to catch,' she returned.

'Perhaps an impressionist is better acquainted with them than with anything else,' suggested Dessart, a trifle unkindly.

'Not when he's young and a Prix de Rome,' smiled the woman who wrote.

Mrs. Copley requiring her niece's presence on the other side of the room, the girl nodded to the group and withdrew. The writer looked after her with an air of puzzled interest.

'And doesn't Miss Copley read the papers?' she inquired mildly.

'Evidently she does not,' Sybert rejoined with a laugh as he made his adieus and withdrew.

Half an hour later, Marcia Copley, having made the rounds of the room, again found herself, as tea was being served, in the neighbourhood of her new acquaintance. She dropped down on the divan beside her with a slight feeling of relief at being for the moment out of the current of chatter. Her companion was a vivacious little woman approaching middle age; and though she spoke perfect English, she pronounced her words with a precision which suggested a foreign birth. Her conversation was diverting; it gave evidence of a vast amount of worldly wisdom as well as a wide acquaintance with other people's affairs. And her range of subjects was wide. She flitted lightly from an artistic estimate of some intaglios of the Augustan age, that had just been dug up outside the Porta Pia, to a comparison of French and Italian dressmakers and a prophecy as to which cardinal would be the next pope.

A portfolio of sketches lay on a little stand beside them, and she presently drew them toward her, with the remark, 'We will see how our young man has been amusing himself lately!'

There were a half-dozen or so of wash-drawings, and one or two outline sketches of figures in red chalk. None of them was at all finished, but the hasty blocking in showed considerable vigour, and the subjects were at least original. There was no Castle of St. Angelo with a boatman in the foreground, and no Temple of Vesta set off by a line of scarlet seminarists. One of the chalk drawings was of an old chestnut woman crouched over her charcoal fire; another was of the octroi officer under the tall arch of the San Giovanni gate, prodding the contents of a donkey-cart with his steel rod. There were corners of wall shaded by cypresses, bits of architectural adornment, a quick sketch of the lichen-covered elephant's head spouting water at Villa Madama. They all, slight as they were, possessed a certain distinction, and suggested a very real impression of Roman atmosphere. Marcia examined them with interest.

'They are extremely good,' she said as she laid the last one down.

'Yes,' her companion agreed; 'they are so good that they ought to be better—but they never will be.'

'How do you mean?'

'I know Paul Dessart well enough to know that he will never paint a picture. He has talent, and he's clever, but he's at everybody's service. The workers have no time to be polite. However,' she finished, 'it is not for you and me to quarrel with him. If he set to work in earnest he would stop giving teas, and that would be a pity, would it not?'

'Indeed it would!' she agreed. 'How pretty the studio looks this afternoon! I have seen it only by daylight before, and, like all the rest of us, it improves by candle-light.' Her eyes wandered about the big room, with its furnishings of threadbare tapestry and antique carved chairs. The heavy curtains had been partly drawn over the windows, making a pleasant twilight within. A subtle odour of linseed oil and cigarette smoke, mingled with the fresh scent of violets, pervaded the air.

4

Paul Dessart, with the Prix de Rome man and a young English sculptor of rising fame, presently joined them; and the talk drifted into Roman politics—a subject concerning which, the artists declared with one accord, they knew nothing and cared less.

'Oh, I used to get excited over their squabbles,' said the Englishman; 'but I soon saw that I should have to choose between that and sculpture; I hadn't time for both.'

'I don't even know who's premier,' put in Dessart.

'A disgraceful lack of interest!' maintained the American girl. 'I have only been in Rome two months, and I am an authority on the Triple Alliance and the Abyssinian war; I know what Cavour wanted to do, and what Crispi has done.'

'That's not fair, Miss Copley,' Dessart objected. 'You've been going to functions at the Embassy, and one can absorb politics there through one's skin. But I warn you, it isn't a safe subject to get interested in; it becomes a disease, like the opium habit.'

'He's not so far from the truth,' agreed the sculptor. 'I was talking to a fellow this afternoon, named Sybert, who—perhaps you know him, Miss Copley?'

'Yes, I know him. What about him?'

'Oh—er—nothing, in that case.'

'Pray slander Mr. Sybert if you wish—I'll promise not to tell. He's one of my uncle's friends, not one of mine.'

'Oh, I wasn't going to slander him,' the young man expostulated a trifle sheepishly. 'The only thing I have against Sybert is the fact that my conversation bores him.'

Marcia laughed with a certain sense of fellow-feeling.

'Say anything you please,' she repeated cordially. 'My conversation bores him too.'

'Well, what I was going to say is that he has had about all the Roman politics that are good for him. If he doesn't look out, he'll be getting in too deep.'

'Too deep?' she queried.

It was Dessart who pursued the subject with just a touch of malice. Laurence Sybert, apparently, was not so popular a person as a diplomat should be.

'He's lived in Rome a good many years, and people are beginning to wonder what he's up to. The Embassy does very well for a blind, for he doesn't take any more interest in it than he does in whether or not Tammany runs New York. All that Sybert knows anything about or cares anything about is Italian politics, and there are some who think that he knows a good sight more about them than he ought. He's in with the Church party, in with the Government—first friends with the Right, and then with the Left.'

'Monsieur Sybert is what you call an eclectic,' suggested Benoit. 'He chooses the best of each.'

'I'm not so sure of that,' Dessart hinted darkly. 'He's interested in other factions besides the Vatican and the Quirinal. There are one or two pretty anarchistic societies in Rome, and I've heard it whispered——'

'You don't mean——' she asked, with wide-open eyes.

The woman who wrote shook her head, with a laugh. 'I suspect that Mr. Sybert's long residence in Rome might be reduced to a simpler formula than that. It was a very wise person who first said, "Cherchez la femme."'

'Oh, really?' said Marcia, with a new note of interest. Laurence Sybert was not a man whom she had ever credited with having emotions, and the suggestion came as a surprise.

'Rumour says that he still takes a very strong interest in the pretty little Contessa Torrenieri. All I know is that nine or ten years ago, when she was Margarita Carretti, he was openly among her admirers; but she naturally preferred a count—or at least her parents did, which in Italy amounts to the same.'

The girl's eyes opened still wider; the Contessa Torrenieri was also a frequent guest at the palazzo. But Dessart received the suggestion with a very sceptical smile.

'And you think that he is only waiting until, in the ripeness of time, old Count Torrenieri goes the way of all counts? I know you are the authority on gossip, madame, but, nevertheless, I doubt very much if that is Laurence Sybert's trouble.'

'You don't really mean that he is an anarchist?' Marcia demanded.

'I give him up, Miss Copley.' The young man shrugged his shoulders and spread out his hands in a gesture purely Italian.

'Are you talking politics?' asked Mrs. Copley as she joined the group in company with Mr. and Mrs. Melville.

'Always politics,' laughed her niece—'or is it Mr. Sybert now?'

'They're practically interchangeable,' said Dessart.

'And did I hear you calling him an anarchist, Miss Marcia?' Melville demanded.

She repudiated the charge with a laugh. 'I'm afraid Mr. Dessart's the guilty one.'

'Here, here! that will never do! Sybert's a special friend of mine. I can't allow you to be accusing him of anything like that.'

'A little applied anarchy wouldn't be out of place,' the young man returned. 'I feel tempted to use some dynamite myself when I see the way this precious government is scattering statues of Victor Emmanuel broadcast through the land.'

'If you are going to get back into politics,' said Mrs. Copley, rising, 'I fear we must leave. I know from experience that it is a long subject.'

The two turned away, escorted to the carriage by Dessart and the Frenchman, while the rest of the group resettled themselves in the empty places. The woman who wrote listened a moment to the badinage and laughter which floated back through the open door; then, 'Mr. Dessart's heiress is very attractive,' she suggested.

'Why Mr. Dessart's?' Melville inquired.

'Perhaps I was a little premature,' she conceded—'though, I venture to prophesy, not incorrect.'

'My dear lady,' said Mrs. Melville impressively, 'you do not know Mrs. Copley. Her niece is more likely to marry an Italian prince than a nameless young artist.'

'She's no more likely to marry an Italian prince than she is a South African chief,' her husband affirmed. 'Miss Marcia is a young woman who will marry whom she pleases—though,' he added upon reflection, 'I am not at all sure it will be Paul Dessart.'

'She might do worse,' said his wife. 'Paul is a nice boy.'

'Ah—and she might do better. I'll tell you exactly the man,' he added, in a burst of enthusiasm, 'and that is Laurence Sybert.'

The suggestion was met by an amused smile from the ladies and a shrug from the sculptor.

'My dear James,' said Mrs. Melville, 'you may be a very good business man, but you are no match-maker. That is a matter you would best leave to the women. As for your Laurence Sybert, he hasn't the ghost of a chance—and he doesn't want it.'

'I'm doubting he has other fish to fry just now,' threw out the sculptor.

'Sybert's all right,' said Melville emphatically.

The woman who wrote laughed as she rose. 'It will be an interesting matter to watch,' she announced; 'but you may mark my words that our host is the man.'

CHAPTER II

A carriage rumbled into the stone-paved courtyard of the Palazzo Rosicorelli a good twenty minutes before six o'clock the next evening, and the Copleys descended and climbed the stairs, at peace with Villa Vivalanti and its thirty miles. Though it was still light out of doors, inside the palace, with its deep-embrasured windows and heavy curtains, it was already quite dark. As they entered the long salon the only light in the room came from a seven-branch candlestick on the tea-table, which threw its reflection upon Gerald's white sailor-suit and little bare knees as he sat back solemnly in a carved Savonarola chair. At the sound of their arrival he wriggled down quickly and precipitated himself against Mrs. Copley.

'Oh, mamma! Sybert came to tea, an' I made it; an' he said it was lots better van Marcia's tea, an' he dwank seven cups, an' I dwank four.'

A chorus of laughter greeted this revelation, and a lazy voice called from the depths of an easy chair, 'Oh, I say, Gerald, you mustn't tell such shocking tales, or your mother will never leave me alone with the tea-things again.' And the owner of the voice pulled himself together and walked across the room ta shake hands with the new-comers.

Laurence Sybert, as he advanced toward his hostess, threw a long thin shadow against the wall. He had a spare, dark, clean-shaven face with deep-set, sullen eyes; he was a delightfully perfected type of the cosmopolitan; it would have taken a second, or very possibly a third, glance to determine his nationality. But if the expression of his face were Italian, Oriental, anything you please, his build was undoubtedly Anglo-Saxon. Further, a certain wiriness beneath his movements proclaimed him, to any one familiar with the loose-hung riders of the plains, unmistakably American.

'Your son slanders me, Mrs. Copley,' he said as he held out his hand; 'I didn't drink but six, upon my honour.'

'Hello, Sybert! Anything happened in Rome to-day? What's the news on the Rialto?' was Mr. Copley's greeting.

Marcia regarded him with a laugh as she drew off her gloves and lighted the spirit-lamp.

'We've been away since nine this morning, and here's Uncle Howard thirsting for news already! What he will do when we really get out of the city, I can't imagine.'

'Oh, and so you've taken the villa, have you?'

Marcia nodded.

'And you should see it! It looks like a papal palace. This is the first time that Prince Vivalanti has ever consented to rent it to strangers; it's his official seat.'

'Very condescending of him,' the young man laughed; 'and do you accept his responsibilities along with the place?'

'From the fattore's account I should say that his responsibilities rest but lightly on the Prince of Vivalanti.'

'Ah——that's true enough.'

'Do you know him?'

'Only by hearsay. I know the village; and a more desperate little place it would be hard to find in all the Sabine hills. The people's love for their prince is tempered by the need of a number of improvements which he doesn't supply.'

'I dare say they are pretty poor,' she conceded; 'but they are unbelievably picturesque! Every person there looks as if he had just walked out of a water-colour sketch. Even Uncle Howard was pleased, and he has lived here so long that he is losing his enthusiasms.'

'It is a pretty decent sort of a place,' Copley agreed, 'though I have a sneaking suspicion that we may find it rather far. But the rest of the family liked it, and my aim in life——'

'Nonsense, Uncle Howard! you know you were crazy over it yourself. You signed the lease without a protest. Didn't he, Aunt Katherine?' 'I signed the lease, my dear Marcia, at the point of the pistol.'

'The point of the pistol?'

'You threatened, if we got a mile—an inch, I believe you said—nearer Rome, you would give a party every day; and if that isn't the point of a pistol to a poor, worn-out man like me, I don't know what is.'

'It would certainly seem like it,' Sybert agreed. And turning to Marcia, he added, 'I am afraid that you rule with a very despotic hand, Miss Marcia.'

Marcia's eyebrows went up a barely perceptible trifle, but she laughed and returned: 'No, indeed, Mr. Sybert; you are mistaken there. It is not I, but Gerald, who plays the part of despot in the Copley household.'

At this point, Granton, Mrs. Copley's English maid, appeared in the doorway. 'Marietta is waiting to give Master Gerald his supper,' she announced.

Gerald fled to his mother and raised a cry of protest.

'Mamma, please let me stay up to dinner wif you to-night.'

For a moment Mrs. Copley looked as if she might consent, but catching sight of Granton's relentless face, she returned: 'No, my dear, you have had enough festivity for one evening. You must have your tea and go to bed like a good little boy.'

Gerald abandoned his mother and entrenched himself behind Sybert. "Cause Sybert's here, an' I like Sybert,' he wailed desperately.

But Granton stormed even this fortress. 'Come, Master Gerald; your supper's getting cold,' and she laid a firm hand on his shoulder and marched him away.

'There's the real despot,' laughed Copley. 'I tremble before Granton myself.'

Pietro appeared with a plate of toasted muffins and the evening mail. Mr. Copley settled himself in a wicker chair, with a pile of letters on the arm at his right; and, as he ran his eyes over them one by one, he tore them in pieces and formed a new pile at his left. They were begging letters for the most part. He received a great many, and this was his usual method of answering them: not that he was an ungenerous man; it was merely a matter of principle with him not to be generous in this particular way.

As he sat disposing of envelope after envelope with vigorous hands, Copley's appearance suggested a series of somewhat puzzling contrasts: seriousness and humour; sensitiveness and force—an active impulse to forge ahead and accomplish things, a counter-impulse to shrug his shoulders and wonder why. He was a puzzle to most of his friends; at times even one to his wife; but she had accepted his eccentricities along with his millions, and though she did not always understand either his motives of his actions, she made no complaint. To most men a fortune is a blessing. To Copley it was rather in the nature of a curse. He might have amounted to almost anything had he had to work for it; but for the one field of activity which a fortune in America seems to entail upon its owner—that of entering the arena and doubling and tripling it—he was singularly unfitted both by temperament and inclination. In this he differed from his elder brother. And there was one other point in which the two were at variance. Though their father had been in the eyes of the law a just and upright man, still, in the battle of competition, many had fallen that he might stand, and the younger son had grown up with the knowledge that from a humanitarian standpoint the money was not irreproachable. He had the feeling—which his brother characterized as absurd—that with his share of the fortune he would like, in a measure, to make it up to mankind.

Howard Copley's first move in the game of benefiting humanity had been, not very originally, an attempt at solving the negro problem; but the negroes were ever a leisurely race, and Copley was a man impatient for results. He finally abandoned them to the course of evolution, and engaged in a spasmodic orgy of East Side politics. Becoming disgusted, and failing of an election, he looked aimlessly about for a further object in life. It was at this point that Mrs. Copley breathlessly suggested a year in Paris for the sake of Gerald's French; the child was only four, but one could not, as she justly pointed out, begin the study of the languages too early. Her husband apathetically consenting, they embarked for Paris by the roundabout route of the Mediterranean, landed in Naples, and there they stayed. He had found a fascinating occupation ready to his hand—that of helping on the work of good government in this still turbulent portion of United Italy. After a year the family drifted to Rome, and settled themselves in the piano nobile of the Palazzo Rosicorelli with something of an air of permanence. Copley was at last thoroughly contented; he had no racial prejudices, and Rome was as fair a field of reform as New York—and infinitely more diverting. If the Italians did not always understand his motives, still they accepted his services with a fair show of gratitude.

As for Mrs. Copley, she had by no means intended their sojourn to be an emigration, but she reflected that her husband had to be amused in some way, and that reforming Italian posterity was perhaps an harmless a way as he could have devised. She settled herself very contentedly to the enjoyment of the somewhat shifting foreign society of the capital, with only an occasional plaintive reference to her friends in New York and to Gerald's French.

Marcia, leaning back in her chair, watched her uncle dispose of his correspondence with a visible air of amusement. He had a thin nervous face traced with fine lines, a sharply cut jaw, and a mouth which twitched easily into a smile. To-night, however, as he ripped open envelope after envelope, he frowned oftener than he smiled; and presently, as he unfolded one letter, he suppressed a quick exclamation of anger.

'Read that,' he said shortly, tossing it to the other man.

Sybert perused it with no visible change of expression, and leaning over, he dropped it into the open grate.

Marcia laughed outright. 'Your mail doesn't seem to afford you much satisfaction, Uncle Howard.'

'A large share of it's anonymous, and not all of it's polite.'

'That is what you must expect if you will hound those poor old beggars to death.'

The two men shot each other a look of rather grim amusement. The letter in question had nothing to do with beggars, but Mr. Copley had no intention of discussing its contents with his niece.

'I find that the usual reward of virtue in this world is an anonymous letter,' he remarked, shrugging the matter from his mind and settling himself comfortably to his tea.

The guest refused the cup proffered him.

'I haven't the courage,' he declared, 'after Gerald's revelations.'

'By the way, Sybert,' said Copley, 'I have been hearing some bad stories about you to-day. My niece doesn't like to have me associate with you.'

Marcia looked at her uncle helplessly; when he once commenced teasing there was no telling where he would stop.

'I am sorry,' said Sybert humbly. 'What is the trouble?'

'She has found out that you are an anarchist.'

Both men laughed, and Marcia flushed slightly.

'Please, Miss Marcia,' Sybert begged, 'give me time to get out of the country before you expose me to the police.'

'There's no cause for fear,' she returned. 'I didn't believe the story when I heard it, for I knew that you haven't energy enough to run away from a bomb, much less throw one. That's why it surprised me that other people should believe it.'

'But most people have a better opinion of me than you have,' he expostulated.

'No, indeed, Mr. Sybert; I have a better opinion of you than most people. I really consider you harmless.'

The young man laughed and bowed his thanks, while he turned his attention to Mrs. Copley.

'I hope that Villa Vivalanti will prove more successful than the one in Naples.'

Mrs. Copley looked at him reproachfully. 'That horrible man! I never think of him without wishing we were safely back in America.'

'Then please don't think of him,' her husband returned. 'He is where he won't trouble you any more.'

'What man?' asked Marcia, emerging from a dignified silence.

'Is it possible Miss Marcia has never heard of the tattooed man?' Sybert inquired gravely.

'The tattooed man! What are you talking about?'

'It has a somewhat theatrical ring,' Mr. Copley admitted.

'It is nothing to make light of,' said his wife. 'It's a wonder to me that we escaped with our lives. Three years ago, while we were in Naples,' she added to her niece, 'your uncle, with

9

his usual recklessness, got mixed up with one of the secret societies. Our villa was out toward Posilipo, and one afternoon I was driving home at about dusk—I had been shopping in the city—and just as we reached a lonely place in the road, between two high walls——'

Mr. Copley broke in: 'A masked man armed to the teeth sprang up in the path, with a horrible oath.'

'Not really!' Marcia cried, leaning forward delightedly. 'Aunt Katherine, did a masked man——'

'He wasn't masked, but I wish he had been; he would have looked less ferocious. He came straight to the side of the carriage, and taking off his hat with a very polite bow, he said that unless we left Naples in three days your uncle's life would no longer be safe. His shirt was open at the throat, and there was a crucifix tattooed upside down on his breast. You can imagine what a desperate character he must have been—here in Italy of all places, where the people are so religious.'

The two men laughed at the climax.

'What did you do?' Marcia asked.

'I was too shocked to speak, and Gerald, poor child, screamed all the way home.'

'And did you leave the city?'

'As it happened, we were leaving anyway,' her uncle put in; 'but we postponed our departure long enough for me to hunt the fellow down and put him in jail.'

'You may be thankful that they had the decency to warn you,' Sybert remarked.

'It's like a dime novel!' Marcia sighed. 'To be mixed up with murders and warnings and tattooed men and secret societies——Why didn't you send for me, Uncle Howard?'

'Well, you see, I didn't know that you had grown up into such a charming person—though I am not sure that it would have made any difference. I had all that I could do to take care of one woman.'

'That's the way,' she complained. 'Just because one's a girl one is always shut up in the house while there's anything exciting going on.'

'If you are so fond of bloodshed,' Sybert suggested, 'you may possibly have a chance of seeing some this spring.'

'This spring? Is the Camorra making trouble again?'

'Oh, no; not the Camorra. But unless all signs fail, there is a prospect of some fairly exciting riots.'

'Really? Here in Rome?'

'Well, no; probably not in Rome—there are too many soldiers. More likely in the Neapolitan provinces. I am sorry,' he added, 'since you seem to find them so entertaining, that we can't promise you a riot on your own door-step; but I dare say, when it comes to the point, you'll find Naples near enough.'

'I give you fair warning, Uncle Howard,' she said, 'if there are any riots in Naples, I'm going down to see them. What is the trouble? What are they rioting about?'

'If there are any riots,' said her uncle, 'you, my dear young lady, will amuse yourself at Villa Vivalanti until they are over,' and he abruptly changed the subject.

The talk drifted back to the villa again. Mrs. Copley afforded their guest a more detailed description.

'Nineteen bedrooms aside from the servants' quarters, and room in the stable for thirty horses!' she finished.

'The princes of Vivalanti must have kept up an establishment in their pre-Riviera days.'

'Mustn't they?' agreed Marcia cordially. The new villa was proving an unexpectedly soothing topic. 'We'll keep up an establishment too,' she added. 'We're going to give a house-party when the Roystons come down from Paris, and—I know what we'll do! We'll give a ball for my birthday—won't we, Uncle Howard? And have everybody out from Rome, and the ilex grove all lighted with coloured lamps!'

'Not if I have anything to say about it,' said Mr. Copley.

'But you won't have,' said Marcia.

'The only reason that I consented to take this villa was that I thought it was far enough away to escape parties for a time. You said——'

'I said if you got nearer Rome we'd give a party every day, while as it is I'm only planning one party for all the three months.'

'Sybert and I won't come to it,' he grumbled.

'Perhaps you and Mr. Sybert won't be invited.'

'I don't know where you'd find two such charming men,' said Mrs. Copley.

'Rome's full of them,' returned Marcia imperturbably.

'Who are the Roystons, Miss Marcia?' Sybert inquired.

'They are the friends I came over with last fall. You know Mr. Dessart?'

'The artist? Yes, I know him.'

'Well, Mrs. Royston is his aunt, and she has two daughters who——'

'Are his cousins,' suggested Mr. Copley.

'Yes; to be sure, and very charming girls. They spend a great deal of time over here—at least Mrs. Royston and Eleanor do. Margaret has been in college.'

'And Mr. Royston,' asked Copley, 'stays in America and attends to his business?'

'Yes; Mrs. Royston and Eleanor go over quite often to keep him from getting lonely.'

'Very generous of them,' Sybert laughed.

'They've spent winters in Cairo and Vienna and Paris and a lot of different places,' pursued Marcia. 'Eleanor,' she added ruminatingly, 'has been out nine seasons, and she has had a good deal of—experience.'

'Dear, dear!' said her uncle; 'and you are proposing to expose all Rome——'

'She's very attractive,' said Marcia, and then she glanced at Sybert and laughed. 'If she should happen to take a fancy to you, Mr. Sybert——'

The young man rose to his feet and looked about for his hat. 'Goodness!' he murmured, 'what would she do?'

'There's no telling.' Marcia regarded him with a speculative light in her eyes.

'A young woman who has been practising for nine seasons certainly ought to have her hand in,' Copley agreed. 'Perhaps, after all, Sybert, it is best we should not meet her.'

Sybert found his hat and paused for a moment.

'You can't frighten me that way, Miss Marcia,' he said, with a shake of his head. 'I have been out thirteen seasons myself.'

CHAPTER III

'May I come in for tea, Cousin Marcia?' Gerald inquired, with a note of anxiety in his voice, as they climbed the stone staircase of the Palazzo Rosicorelli. They had been spending the afternoon in the Borghese gardens, and the boy's very damp sailor-suit bore witness to the fact that he had been indulging in the forbidden pleasure of catching goldfish in the fountain.

'Indeed you may not,' she returned emphatically. 'You may go with Marietta and have some dry clothes put on before your mother sees you.'

Gerald, realizing the wisdom of this course, allowed himself to be quietly spirited off the back way, in spite of the fact that he heard the alluring sound of Sybert's voice in the direction of the salon. Marcia went on in without waiting to take off her hat, and she met the Melvilles in the ante-room, on the point of leaving.

'Good afternoon. Why do you go so early?' she asked.

'Oh, we are coming back later; we are just going home to dress. Your uncle is giving a dinner to-night—a very formal affair.'

'Is that so?' she laughed. 'I have not been invited.'

'You will be; don't feel hurt. It's a general invitation issued to all comers.'

Marcia found no one within but her aunt and uncle and Mr. Sybert.

'What is this I hear about your giving a dinner to-night, Aunt Katherine?' she asked as she settled herself in a wicker chair and stretched out her hand for a cup of tea.

'You must ask your uncle. I have nothing to do with it,' Mrs. Copley disclaimed. 'He invited the guests, and he must provide the menu.'

'What is it, Uncle Howard?'

'Merely a little farewell dinner. I thought we ought to put on a bright face our last night, you know.'

'One would think you were going to be led to execution at dawn.'

'We will hope it's nothing worse than exile,' said Sybert.

'Who are your guests, and when were they invited?'

'My guests are the people who dropped in late to tea; I did not think of it early enough to make the invitation very general. The list, I believe, includes the Melvilles, Signora Androit and the Contessa Torrenieri, Sidney Carthrope the sculptor, and a certain young Frenchman, a most alluring youth, who called with him, but whose name for the moment escapes me.'

'Adolphe Benoit,' said Sybert.

'The Prix de Rome?' asked Marcia. 'Oh, I know him! I met him a few weeks ago at a tea; he's very entertaining. I suppose,' she added, considering the list, 'that he will fall to my share?'

'Unless you prefer Mr. Sybert.'

'An embarrassing predicament, Miss Marcia,' Sybert laughed. 'If it will facilitate matters we can draw lots.'

'Not at all,' said Marcia graciously, 'I know the Contessa would rather have you; and as she is the guest I will let her choose. I hope your dinner will be a success,' she added to her uncle, 'but I can't help feeling that you show a touching faith in the cook.'

'Thank you, my dear; I am of an optimistic turn of mind, and François has never failed me yet.—How did the Borghese gallery go?'

'Very well. I met Mr. Dessart there—and I met the King outside.'

'Ah, I hope His Majesty was enjoying good health?'

'He seemed to be. I didn't stop to speak to him, but there was a boy in a group of seminarists near us who called out, "Viva il papa," just as he passed.'

'And what happened?' Sybert inquired. 'Did the King's guard behead him on the spot, or did they only send him to the galleys for life?'

'The King's guard fortunately had eyes only for the King, and the old priest gathered his flock together and scuttled off down one of the side paths, as frightened as a hen who sees a hawk.'

'And with good reason—but wait till the lads grow up, and they'll do something besides shout and run.'

There was an undertone in Sybert's voice different from his usual listless drawl. Marcia glanced up at him quickly and Dessart's insinuations flashed through her mind.

'Do you mean you would rather have Leo XIII king instead of Humbert?' she asked.

'Heavens, no! No one wants the temporal power back—not even the Catholics themselves.'

'I should think that when the Italians have gone through so much to get their king, they might be satisfied with him. They ought to have more patience, and not expect the country to be rich in a minute. Everything can't be done all at once; and as for blaming the government because the African war didn't turn out well—why, no one could foresee the result. It was a mistake instead of a crime.'

Sybert was watching her lazily, with an amused smile about his lips. 'Will you pardon me, Miss Marcia, if I ask if those are your own conclusions, or the opinions of our young friend the American artist?'

'He does not plot against the King, at any rate!' she retorted.

'Please, Miss Marcia,' he begged, 'don't think so badly of me as that. Really, I'm not an anarchist. I don't want to blow His Majesty up.'

'Go home and dress, Sybert,' Copley murmured, taking him by the arm. 'I have to go and interview the cook, and I don't dare leave you and my niece together. There's no telling what would happen.'

'She's a suspicious young woman,' Sybert complained. 'Can't you teach her to take your friends on trust?'

'For the matter of that, she doesn't even take her uncle on trust.'

'And no wonder!' said Marcia. 'I forgot to tell you my other adventure, just as the carriage turned into the Corso we got jammed in close to the curb and had to stop. I looked up and saw a man standing on the side-walk, glaring at me over the top of a newspaper—simply glaring—and suddenly he jumped to the side of the carriage and thrust the paper in my hands. He said something in Italian, but too fast for me to catch, and before I could move, Marietta had snatched it up and dashed it back in his face. The paper was named the Cry of the People; I just caught one word in it, and that was—' she paused dramatically—'Copley! Now, Uncle Howard,' she finished, 'do you think you ought to be trusted? When it gets to the point that the people in the street——'

She stopped suddenly. She had caught a quick glance between her uncle and Sybert. 'What is it?' she asked. 'Do you know what it means?'

'It means damned impudence!' said her uncle. 'I'll have that editor arrested if he doesn't keep still,' and the two men stood eyeing each other a minute in silence. Then Copley gave a short laugh. 'Oh, well,' he said, 'I don't believe the Grido del Popolo can destroy my character. Nobody reads it.' He looked at his watch. 'You'd better go and dress, Marcia. My party begins promptly at eight.'

'You needn't use any such clumsy method as that of getting rid of me,' she laughed. 'I'm not going to stay where I'm not wanted. All I have to say,' she called back from the doorway, 'is that you'd better stop badgering those poor old beggars, or you'll be getting a warning to leave Rome as well as Naples.'

Marcia rang for Granton.

'Have you time to fix my hair now?' she inquired as the maid appeared, 'or does Mrs. Copley need you?'

'Mrs. Copley hasn't begun to dress yet; she is watching Master Gerald eat his supper.'

'Oh, very well, then, there is time enough; I'll get through before she is ready for you. Do my hair sort of Frenchy,' she commanded as she sat down before the mirror. 'What dress do you think I'd better wear?' she continued presently. 'That white one I wore last week, or the new green one that came from Paris yesterday?'

'I should think the white one, Miss Marcia, and save the new one for some party.'

'It would be more sensible,' Marcia agreed; 'but,' she added with a laugh, 'I think I'll wear the new one.'

Granton got it out with an unsmiling face which was meant to convey the fact that she could not countenance this American prodigality. She had lived ten years with an elderly English duchess, and had thought that she knew the ways of the aristocracy.

The gown was a filmy green mousseline touched with rose velvet and yellow lace. Marcia put it on and surveyed herself critically. 'What do you think, Granton?' she asked.

'It's very becoming, Miss Marcia,' Granton returned primly.

'Yes,' Marcia sighed—'and very tight!' She caught up her fan and turned toward the door. 'Don't be hurt because I didn't take your advice,' she called back over her shoulder. 'I never take anybody's, Granton.'

She found her uncle alone in the salon, pacing the floor in a restless fashion, with two frowning lines between his brows. He paused in his walk as she appeared, and his frown gave place, readily enough, to a smile.

13

'You look very well to-night,' he remarked approvingly. 'You—er—have a new gown, haven't you?'

'Oh, yes, Uncle Howard,' she laughed. 'It's all the gown. Send your compliments to my dressmaker, 45 Avenue de l'Opéra. I thought I would wear it in honour of Mr. Sybert; it's so seldom we have him with us.'

Mr. Copley received this statement with something like a grunt.

'There! Uncle Howard, I didn't mean to hurt your feelings. Mr. Sybert is the nicest man that ever lived. And what I particularly like about him, is the fact that he is so genial and expansive and thoughtful for others—always trying to put people at their ease.'

Mr. Copley refused to smile. 'I am sorry, Marcia, that you don't like Sybert,' he said quietly. 'It's because you don't understand him.'

'I dare say; and I suppose he doesn't like me, for the same reason.'

'He is a splendid fellow; I've never known a better one—and a man can judge.'

Marcia laughed. 'Uncle Howard, do you know what you remind me of? An Italian father who is arranging a marriage for his daughter, and having chosen the man, is recommending him for her approval.'

'Oh, no; I don't go to the length of asking you to fall in love with him—though you might do worse—but I should be pleased if you would treat him—er——'

'Respectfully, as I would my father.'

'More respectfully than you do your uncle, at any rate. He may not be exactly what you'd call a lady's man——'

'A lady's man! Uncle Howard, you make me furious when you talk like that; as if I only liked men with dimples in their chins, who dance well and get ices for you! I'm sorry if I don't treat Mr. Sybert seriously enough; but really I don't think he treats me seriously, either. You think I don't know anything, just because I can't tell the difference between the Left and the Right. I've only just come to Rome, and I don't see how you can expect me to know about Italian politics. You both of you laugh whenever I ask the simplest question.'

'But you ask such exceedingly simple questions, dear.'

'How can I help it when you give me such absurd answers?'

'I'm sorry. We'll try to do better in the future. I suppose we've both of us been a little worried this spring, and you probe us on a tender point.'

'But who ever heard of a man's being really worried over politics—that is, unless he's running for something? They should be regarded as an amusement to while away your leisure. You and Mr. Sybert are so funny, Uncle Howard; you take your amusements so seriously.'

'"Politics" is a broad word, Marcia,' he returned, with a slight frown; 'and when it stands for oppression and injustice and starving peasants it has to be taken seriously.'

'Is it really so bad, Uncle Howard?'

'Good heavens, Marcia! It's awful!'

She was startled at his tone, and glanced up at him quickly. He was staring at the light, with a hard look in his eyes and his mouth drawn into a straight line.

'I'm sorry, Uncle Howard; I didn't know. What can I do?'

'What can any of us do?' he asked bitterly. 'We can give one day, and it's eaten up before night. And we can keep on giving, but what does it amount to? The whole thing is rotten from the bottom.'

'Can't the people get work?'

'No; and when they can, their earnings are eaten up in taxes. The people in the southern provinces are literally starving, I tell you; and it's worse this year than usual, thanks to men like your father and me.'

'What do you mean?'

For a moment he felt almost impelled to tell her the truth. Then, as he glanced down at her, he stopped himself quickly. She looked so delicate, so patrician, so aloof from everything

14

that was sordid and miserable; she could not help, and it was better that she should not know.

'What do you mean?' she repeated. 'What has papa been doing?'

'Oh, nothing very criminal,' he returned. 'Only at a time like this one feels as if one's money were a reproach. Italy's in a bad way just now; the wheat crop failed last year, and that makes it inconvenient for people who live on macaroni.'

'Do you mean the people really haven't anything to eat?'

'Not much.'

'How terrible, Uncle Howard! Won't the government do anything?'

'The government is doing what it can. There was a riot in Florence last month, and they lowered the grain tax; King Humbert gave nine thousand lire to feed the people of Pisa a couple of weeks ago. You can do the same for some other city, if you want to play at being a princess.'

'I thought you believed in finding them work instead giving them money.'

'Oh, as a matter of principle, certainly. But you can't have 'em dying on your door-step, you know.'

'And to think we're having a dinner to-night, when we're not the slightest bit hungry!'

'I'm afraid our dinner wouldn't go far toward feeding the hungry in Italy.'

'How does my dress look, my dear?' asked Mrs. Copley, appearing in the doorway. 'I have been so bothered over it; she didn't fix the lace at all as I told her. These Italian dressmakers are not to be depended upon. I really should have run up to Paris for a few weeks this spring, only you were so unwilling, Howard.'

Marcia looked at her aunt a moment with wide-open eyes. 'Heavens!' she thought, 'do I usually talk this way? No wonder Mr. Sybert doesn't like me!' And then she laughed. 'I think it looks lovely, Aunt Katherine, and I am sure it is very becoming.'

The arrival of guests precluded any further conversation on the subject of Italian dressmakers. The Contessa Torrenieri was small and slender and olive-coloured, with a cloud of black hair and dramatic eyes. She had a pair of nervous little hands which were never still, and a magnetic manner which brought the men to her side and created a tendency among the women to say spiteful things. Marcia was no exception to the rest of her sex, and her comments on the contessa's doings were frequently not prompted by a spirit of charitableness.

To-night the contessa evidently had something on her mind. She barely finished her salutations before transferring her attention to Marcia. 'Come, Signorina Copley, and sit beside me on the sofa; we harmonize so well'—this with a glance from her own rose-coloured gown to Marcia's rose trimmings. 'I missed you from tea this afternoon,' she added. 'I trust you had a pleasant walk.'

'A pleasant walk?' Marcia questioned, off her guard.

'I passed you as I was driving in the Borghese. But you did not see me; you were too occupied.' She shook her head, with a smile. 'It will not do in Italy, my dear. An Italian girl would never walk alone with a young man.'

'Fortunately I am not an Italian girl.'

'You are too strict, contessa,' Sybert, who was sitting near, put in with a laugh. 'If Miss Copley chooses, there is no reason why she should not walk in the gardens with a young man.'

'A girl of the lower classes perhaps, but not of Signorina Copley's class. With her dowry, she will be marrying an Italian nobleman one of these days.'

Marcia flushed with annoyance. 'I have not the slightest intention of marrying an Italian nobleman,' she returned.

'One must marry some one,' said her companion.

Mr. Melville relieved the tension by inquiring, 'And who was the hero of this episode, Miss Marcia? We have not heard his name.'

Marcia laughed good-humouredly. 'Your friend Mr. Dessart.' The Melvilles exchanged glances. 'I met him in the gallery, and as the carriage hadn't come and Gerald was playing in the fountain and Marietta was flirting with a gendarme (Dear me! Aunt Katherine, I didn't mean to say that), we strolled about until the carriage came. I'm sure I had no intention of shocking the Italian nobility; it was quite unpremeditated.'

'If the Italian nobility never stands a worse shock than that, it is happier than most nobilities,' said her uncle. And the simultaneous announcement of M. Benoit and dinner created a diversion.

It was a small party, and every one felt the absence of that preliminary chill which a long list of guests invited two weeks beforehand is likely to produce. They talked back and forth across the table, and laughed and joked in the unpremeditated way that an impromptu affair calls forth. Marcia glanced at her uncle once or twice in half perplexity. He seemed so entirely the careless man of the world, as he turned a laughing face to answer one of Mrs. Melville's sallies, that she could scarcely believe he was the same man who had spoken so seriously to her a few minutes before. She glanced across at Sybert. He was smiling at some remark of the contessa's, to which he retorted in Italian. 'I don't see how any sensible man can be interested in the contessa!' was her inward comment as she transferred her attention to the young Frenchman at her side.

Whenever the conversation showed a tendency to linger on politics, Mrs. Copley adroitly redirected it, as she knew from experience that the subject was too combustible by far for a dinner-party.

'Italy, Italy! These men talk nothing but Italy,' she complained to the young Frenchman on her right. 'Does it not make you homesick for the boulevards?'

'I suffered the nostalgie once,' he confessed, 'but Rome is a good cure.'

Marcia shook her head in mock despair. 'And you, too, M. Benoit! Patriotism is certainly dying out.'

'Not while you live,' said her uncle.

'Oh, I know I'm abnormally patriotic,' she admitted; 'but you're all so sluggish in that respect, that you force it upon one.'

'There are other useful virtues besides patriotism,' Sybert suggested.

'Wait until you have spent a spring in the Sabine hills, Miss Copley,' Melville put in, 'and you will be as bad as the rest of us.'

'Ah, mademoiselle,' Benoit added fervently, 'spring-time in the Sabine hills will be compensation sufficient to most of us for not seeing paradise.'

'I believe, with my uncle, it's a kind of Roman fever!' she cried. 'I never expected to hear a Frenchman renounce his native land.'

'It is not that I renounce France,' the young man remonstrated. 'I lofe France as much as ever, but I open my arms to Italy as well. To lofe another land and peoples besides your own makes you, not littler, but, as you say, wider—broader. We are—we are—— Ah, mademoiselle!' he broke off, 'if you would let me talk in French I could say what I mean; but how can one be eloquent in this halting tongue of yours?'

'Coraggio, Benoit! You are doing bravely,' Sybert laughed.

'We are,' the young man went on with a sudden inspiration, 'what you call in English, citizens of the world. You, mademoiselle, are American, La Signora Contessa is Italian, Mr. Carthrope is English, I am French, but we are all citizens of the same world, and in whatever land we find ourselves, there we recognize one another for brothers, and are always at home; for it is still the world.'

The young man's eloquence was received with an appreciative laugh. 'And how about paradise?' some one suggested.

'Ah, my friends, it is there that we will be strangers!' Benoit returned tragically.

'Citizens of the world,' Sybert turned the stem of his wine glass meditatively as he repeated the phrase. 'It seems to me, in spite of Miss Marcia, that one can't do much better than that.

If you're a patriotic citizen of the world, I should think you'd done your duty by mankind, and might reasonably expect to reap a reward in Benoit's paradise.'

He laughed and raised his glass. 'Here's to the World, our fatherland! May we all be loyal citizens!'

'I think,' said Mrs. Melville, 'since this is a farewell dinner and we are pledging toasts, we should drink to Villa Vivalanti and a happy spring in the Sabine hills.'

Copley bowed his thanks. 'If you will all visit the villa we will pledge it in the good wine of Vivalanti.'

'And here's to the Vivalanti ghost!' said the young Frenchman. 'May it lif long and prosper!'

'Italy's the place for such ghosts to prosper,' Copley returned.

'Here's to the poor people of Italy—may they have enough to eat!' said Marcia.

Sybert glanced up in sudden surprise, but she did not look at him; she was smiling across at her uncle.

CHAPTER IV

The announcement that a principe Americano was coming to live in Villa Vivalanti occasioned no little excitement in the village. Wagons with furnishings from Rome had been seen to pass on the road below the town, and the contadini in the wayside vineyards had stopped their work to stare, and had repeated to each other rumours of the fabulous wealth this signor principe was said to possess. The furniture they allowed to pass without much controversy. But they shook their heads dubiously when two wagons full of flowering trees and shrubs wound up the roadway toward the villa. This foreigner must be a grasping person—as if there were not trees enough already in the Sabine hills, that he must bring out more from Rome!

The dissection of the character of Prince Vivalanti's new tenant occupied so much of the people's time that the spring pruning of the vineyards came near to being slighted. The fountainhead of all knowledge on the subject was the landlord of the Croce d'Oro. He himself had had the honour of entertaining their excellencies at breakfast, on the occasion of their first visit to Castel Vivalanti, and with unvarying eloquence he nightly recounted the story to an interested group of loungers in the trattoria kitchen: of how he had made the omelet without garlic because princes have delicate stomachs and cannot eat the food one would cook for ordinary men; of how they had sat at that very table, and the young signorina principessa, who was beautiful as the holy angels in paradise, had told him with her own lips that it was the best omelet she had ever eaten; and of how they had paid fifteen lire for their breakfast without so much as a word of protest, and then of their own accord had given three lire more for mancia]. Eighteen lire. Corpo di Bacco! that was the kind of guests he wished would drop in every day.

But when Domenico Paterno, the baker of Castel Vivalanti, heard the story, he shrugged his shoulders and spread out his palms, and asserted that a prince was a prince all over the world; and that the Americano had allowed himself to be cheated from stupidity, not generosity. For his part, he thought the devil was the same, whether he talked American or Italian. But it was reported, on the other hand, that Bianca Rosini had also talked with the forestieri when she was washing clothes in the stream. They had stopped their horses to watch the work, and the signorina had smiled and asked if the water were not cold; for her part, she was sure American nobles had kind hearts.

Domenico, however, was not to be convinced by any such counter-evidence as this. 'Smiles are cheap,' he returned sceptically. 'Does any one know of their giving money?'

No one did know of their giving money, but there were plenty of boys to testify that they had run by the side of the carriage fully a kilometre asking for soldi, and the signore had only shaken his head to pay them for their trouble.

17

'Si, si, what did I tell you?' Domenico finished in triumph. 'American princes are like any others—perhaps a little more stupid, but for the rest, exactly the same.'

There were no facts at hand to confute such logic.

And one night Domenico appeared at the Croce d'Oro with a fresh piece of news; his son, Tarquinio, who kept an osteria in Rome, had told the whole story.

'His name is Copli—Signor Edoardo Copli—and it is because of him'—Domenico scowled—'that I pay for my flour twice the usual price. When the harvests failed last year, and he saw that wheat was going to be scarce, he sent to America and he bought all the wheat in the land and he put it in storehouses. He is holding it there now while the price goes up—up—up. And when the poor people in Italy get very, very hungry, and are ready to pay whatever he asks, then perhaps—very charitably—he will agree to sell. Già, that is the truth,' he insisted darkly. 'Everybody knows it in Rome. Doubtless he thinks to escape from his sin up here in the mountains—but he will see—it will follow him wherever he goes. Maché! It is the story of the Bad Prince over again.'

Finally one morning—one Friday morning—some of the children of the village who were in the habit of loitering on the highway in the hope of picking up stray soldi, reported that the American's horses and carriages had come out from Rome, and that the drivers had stopped at the inn of Sant' Agapito and ordered wine like gentlemen. It was further rumoured that the principe himself intended to follow in the afternoon. The matter was discussed with considerable interest before the usual noonday siesta.

'It is my opinion,' said Tommaso Ferri, the blacksmith, as he sat in the baker's doorway, washing down alternate mouthfuls of bread and onion with Vivalanti wine—'it is my opinion that the Signor Americano must be a very reckless man to venture on so important a journey on Friday—and particularly in Lent. It is well known that if a poor man starts for market on Friday, he will break his eggs on the way; and because a rich man has no eggs to break, is that any reason the buon Dio should overlook his sin? Things are more just in heaven than on earth,' he added solemnly; 'and in my opinion, if the foreigner comes to-day, he will not prosper in the villa.'

Domenico nodded approvingly.

'Si, si, Tommaso is right. The Americano has already tempted heaven far enough in this matter of the wheat, and it will not be the part of wisdom for him to add to the account. Apoplexies are as likely to fall on princes as on bakers, and a dead prince is no different from any other dead man—only that he goes to purgatory.'

It was evident, however, that the foreigner was in truth going to tempt Fate; for in the afternoon two empty carriages came back from the villa and turned toward Palestrina, obviously bound for the station. All the ragazzi of Castel Vivalanti waited on the road to see them pass and beg for coppers; and it was just as Domenico had foretold: they never received a single soldo.

The remarks about the principe Americano were not complimentary in Castel Vivalanti that night; but the little yellow-haired principino was handled more gently. The black-haired little Italian boys told how he had laughed when they turned somersaults by the side of the carriage, and how he had cried when his father would not let him throw soldi; and the general opinion seemed to be that if he died young, he at least had a chance of paradise.

CHAPTER V

Meanwhile, the unconscious subjects of Castel Vivalanti's 'apoplexies' were gaily installing themselves in their new, old dwelling. The happy hum of life had again invaded the house, and its walls once more echoed to the ring of a child's laughter. They were very matter-of-fact people—these Americans, and they took possession of the ancestral home of the Vivalanti as if it were as much their right as a seaside cottage at Newport. Upstairs Granton and Marietta were unpacking trunks and hampers and laying Paris gowns in antique Roman clothes-chests; in the villa kitchen François was rattling copper pots and kettles, and anxiously trying to adapt his modern French ideas to a mediaeval Roman stove; while from every room in succession sounded the patter of Gerald's feet and his delighted squeals over each new discovery.

For the past two weeks Roman workmen and Castel Vivalanti cleaning-women had been busily carrying out Mrs. Copley's orders. The florid furniture and coloured chandeliers of the latter Vivalanti had been banished to the attic (or what answers to an attic in a Roman villa), while the faded damask of a former generation had been dusted and restored. Tapestries covered the walls and hung over the balustrade of the marble staircase. Dark rugs lay on the red tile floors; carved chests and antique chairs and tables of coloured marble, supported by gilded griffins, were scattered through the rooms. In the bedrooms the heavy draperies had been superseded by curtains of an airier texture, while wicker chairs and chintz-covered couches lent an un-Roman air of comfort to the rooms.

In spite of his humorous grumbling about the trials of moving-day, Mr. Copley found himself very comfortable as he lounged on the parapet toward sunset, smoking a pre-prandial cigarette, and watching the shadows as they fell over the Campagna. Gerald was already up to his elbows in the fountain, and the ilex grove was echoing his happy shrieks as he prattled in Italian to Marietta about a marvellous two-tailed lizard he had caught in a cranny of the stones. Copley smiled as he listened, for—Castel Vivalanti to the contrary—his little boy was very near his heart.

Marcia in the house had been gaily superintending the unpacking, and running back and forth between the rooms, as excited by her new surroundings as Gerald himself.

'What time does Villa Vivalanti dine?' she inquired while on a flying visit to her aunt's room.

'Eight o'clock when any of us are in town, and half-past seven other nights.'

'I suppose it's half-past seven to-night, alors! Shall I make a grande toilette in honour of the occasion?'

'Put on something warm, whatever else you do; I distrust this climate after sundown.'

'You're such a distrustful person, Aunt Katherine! I can't understand how one can have the heart to accuse this innocent old villa of harbouring malaria.'

She returned to her own room and delightedly rummaged out a dinner-gown from the ancient wardrobe, with a little laugh at the thought of the many different styles it had held in its day. Perhaps some other girl had once occupied this room; very likely a young Princess Vivalanti, two hundred years before, had hung silk-embroidered gowns in this very wardrobe. It was a big, rather bare, delightfully Italian apartment with tall windows having solid barred shutters overlooking the terrace. The view from the windows revealed a broad expanse of Campagna and hills. Marcia dressed with her eyes on the landscape, and then stood a long time gazing up at the broken ridges of the Sabines, glowing softly in the afternoon light. Picturesque little mountain hamlets of battered grey stone were visible here and there clinging to the heights; and in the distance the walls and towers of a half-ruined monastery stood out clear against the sky. She drew a deep breath of pleasure. To be an artist, and to appreciate and reproduce this beauty, suddenly struck her as an ideal life. She smiled at herself as she recalled something she had said to Paul Dessart in the gallery the day before; she had advised him—an artist—to exchange Italy for Pittsburg!

Mr. Copley, who was strolling on the terrace, glanced up, and catching sight of his niece, paused beneath her balcony while he quoted:—

'"But, soft! what light through yonder window breaks?
It is the east, and Juliet is the sun."'

Marcia brought her eyes from the distant landscape to a contemplation of her uncle; and then she stepped through the glass doors, and leaned over the balcony railing with a little laugh.

'You make a pretty poor Romeo, Uncle Howard,' she called down. 'I'm afraid the real one never wore a dinner-jacket nor smoked a cigarette.'

Mr. Copley spread out his hands in protest.

'For the matter of that, I doubt if Juliet ever wore a gown from—where was it—, Avenue de l'Opéra? How does the new house go?' he asked.

'Beautifully. I feel like a princess on a balcony waiting for the hunters to come back from the chase.'

'I can't get over the idea that I'm a usurper myself, and that the rightful lord is languishing in a donjon somewhere in the cellar. Come down and talk to me. I'm getting lonely so far from the world.'

Marcia disappeared from the balcony and reappeared three minutes later on the loggia. She paused on the top step and slowly turned around in order to take in the whole affect. The loggia, in its rehabilitation, made an excellent lounging-place for a lazy summer morning. It was furnished with comfortably deep Oriental rush chairs, a crimson rug and awnings, and, at either side of the steps, white azaleas growing in marble cinerary urns.

'Isn't this the most fun you ever had, Uncle Howard?' she inquired as she brought her eyes back to Mr. Copley waiting on the terrace below. 'We'll have coffee served out here in the morning, and then when it gets sunny in the afternoon we'll move to the end of the terrace under the ilex trees. Villa Vivalanti is the most thoroughly satisfying place I ever lived in.' She ran down the steps and joined him. 'Aren't those little trees nice?' she asked, nodding toward a row of oleanders ranged at mathematical intervals along the balustrade. 'I think that Aunt Katherine and I planned things beautifully!'

'If every one were as well pleased with his own work as you appear to be, this would be a contented world. There's nothing like the beautiful enthusiasm of youth.'

'It's a very good thing to have, just the same,' said Marcia, good-naturedly; 'and without mentioning any names, I know one man who would be less disagreeable if he had more of it.'

'None of that!' said her uncle. 'Our pact was that if I stopped grumbling about the villa being so abominably far from Rome, you were not to utter any—er——'

'Unpleasant truths about Mr. Sybert? Very well, I'll not mention him again; and you'll please not refer to the thirty-nine kilometres—it's a bargain. Gerald, I judge, has found the fountain,' she added as a delighted shriek issued from the grove.

'And a menagerie as well.'

'If he will only keep them out of doors! I shall dream of finding lizards in my bed.'

'If you only dream of them you will be doing well. I dare say the place is full of bats and lizards and owls and all manner of ruin-haunting creatures.'

'You're such a pessimist, Uncle Howard. Between you and Aunt Katherine, the poor villa won't have a shred of character left. For my part, I approve of it all—particularly the ruins. I am dying to explore them—do you think it's too late to-night?'

'Far too late; you'd get malaria, to say nothing of missing dinner. Here comes Pietro now to announce the event.'

As the family entered the dining-room they involuntarily paused on the threshold, struck by the contrast between the new and the old. In the days of Cardinal Vivalanti the room had been the chapel, and it still contained its Gothic ceiling, appropriately redecorated to its new uses with grape-wreathed trellises, and, in the central panelling, Bacchus crowned with vines. The very modern dinner-table, with its glass and silver and shaded candles, looked ludicrously out of place in the long, dusky, vaulted apartment, which, in spite of its rakish frescoes, tenaciously preserved the air of a chapel. The glass doors at the end were thrown wide to a little balcony which overlooked the garden and the ilex grove; and the room was flooded with a nightingale's song.

Marcia clasped her hands ecstatically.

'Isn't this perfect? Aren't you glad we came, Aunt Katherine? I feel like forgiving all my enemies! Uncle Howard, I'm going to be lovely to Mr. Sybert.'

'Don't promise anything rash,' he laughed. 'You'll get acclimated in a day or two.'

Gerald, in honour of the occasion, and because Marietta, under the stress of excitement, had forgotten to give him his supper, was allowed to dine en famille. Elated by the unwonted privilege and by his new surroundings, he babbled gaily of the ride in the cars and the little boys who turned 'summelsorts' by the roadside, and of the beautiful two-tailed lizard of the fountain, whose charms he dwelt on lovingly. But he had missed his noonday nap, and though he struggled bravely through the first three courses, his head nodded over the chicken and salad, and he was led away by Marietta still sleepily boasting, in a blend of English and Italian, of the bellissimi animali he would catch domane morning in the fountain.

'It is a pity,' said Marcia, as the sound of his prattle died away, 'Gerald hasn't some one his own age to play with.'

'Yes, it is a pity,' Copley returned. 'I passed a lonely childhood myself, and I know how barren it is.'

'That is the chief reason that would make me want to go back to New York,' said his wife.

Her husband smiled. 'I suppose there are children to be found outside of New York?'

'There are the Kirkups in Rome,' she agreed; 'but they are so boisterous; and they always quarrel with Gerald whenever they come to play with him.'

'I am not sure, myself, but that Gerald quarrels with them,' returned her husband. However fond he might be of his offspring, he cherished no motherly delusions. 'But perhaps you are right,' he added, with something of a sigh. 'It may be necessary to take him back to America before long. I myself have doubts if this cosmopolitan atmosphere it the best in which to bring up a boy.'

'I should have wished him to spend a winter in Paris for his French,' said Mrs. Copley, plaintively; 'but I dare say he can learn it later. Marcia didn't begin till she was twelve, and she has a very good accent, I am sure.'

Mr. Copley twisted the handle of his glass in silence.

'I suppose, after all,' he said finally, to no one in particular, 'if you manage to bring up a boy to be a decent citizen you've done something in the world.'

'I don't know,' Marcia objected, with a half-laugh. 'If one man, whom we will suppose is a decent citizen, brings up one boy to be a decent citizen, and does nothing else, I don't see that much is gained to the world. Your one man has merely shifted the responsibility.'

Mr. Copley shrugged a trifle. 'Perhaps the boy might be better able to bear it.'

'Of course it would be easier for the man to think so,' she agreed. 'But if everybody passed on his responsibilities there wouldn't be much progress. The boys might do the same, you know, when they grew up.'

Mrs. Copley rose, 'If you two are going to talk metaphysics, I shall go into the salon and have coffee alone.'

'It's not metaphysics; it's theology,' her husband returned. 'Marcia is developing into a terrible preacher.'

'I know it,' Marcia acknowledged. 'I'm growing deplorably moral; I think it must be the Roman air.'

'It doesn't affect most people that way,' her uncle laughed. 'I don't care for any coffee, Katherine. I will smoke a cigarette on the terrace and wait for you out there.'

He disappeared through the balcony doors, and Marcia and her aunt proceeded to the salon.

Marcia poured the coffee, and her aunt said as she received her cup, 'I really believe your uncle is getting tired of Rome and will be ready to go back before long.'

'I don't believe he's tired of Rome, Aunt Katherine. I think he's just a little bit—well, discouraged.'

'Nonsense, child! he has nothing to be discouraged about; he is simply getting restless again. I know the signs! I've never known him to stay as long as this in one place before. I only hope now that he will not think of any ridiculous new thing to do, but will be satisfied to go back to New York and settle down quietly like other people.'

'It seems to me,' said Marcia, slowly, 'as if he might do more good there, because he would understand better what the people need. There are plenty of things to be done even in New York.'

'Oh, yes; when he once got settled he would find any amount of things to take up his time. He might even try yachting, for a change; I am sure that keeps men absorbed.'

Marcia sipped her coffee in silence and glanced out of the window at her uncle, who was pacing up and down the terrace with his hands in his pockets. He looked a rather lonely figure in the half-darkness. It suddenly struck her, as she watched him, that she did not understand him; she had scarcely realized before that there was anything to understand.

Mrs. Copley set her cup down on the table, and Marcia rose. 'Let's go out on the terrace, Aunt Katherine.'

'You go out, my dear, and I will join you later. I want to see if Gerald is asleep. I neglected to have a crib sent out for him, and the dear child thrashes around so—what with a bed four feet high and a stone floor——'

'It would be disastrous!' Marcia agreed.

She crossed the loggia to the terrace and silently fell into step beside her uncle. It was almost dark, and a crescent moon was hanging low over the top of Guadagnolo. A faint lemon light still tinged the west, throwing into misty relief the outline of the Alban hills. The ilex grove was black—gruesomely black—and the happy song of the nightingales and the splashing of the fountain sounded uncanny coming from the darkness; but the white, irregular mass of the villa formed a cheerful contrast, with its shining lights, which threw squares of brightness on the marble terrace and the trees.

Marcia looked about with a deep breath. 'It's beautiful, isn't it, Uncle Howard?' They paused a moment by the parapet and stood looking down over the plain. 'Isn't the Campagna lovely,' she added, 'half covered with mist?'

'Yes, it's lovely—and the mist means death to the peasants who live beneath it.'

She exclaimed half impatiently:

'Uncle Howard, why can't you let anything be beautiful here without spoiling it by pointing out an ugliness beneath?'

'I'm sorry; it isn't my fault that the ugliness exists. Look upon the mist as a blessed dew from heaven, if it makes you any happier.'

'Of course I should rather know the truth, but it seems as if the Italians are happy in spite of things. They strike me as the happiest people I have ever seen.'

'Ah, well, perhaps they are happier than we think.'

'I'm sure they are,' said Marcia, comfortably. 'Anglo-Saxons, particularly New Englanders, and most particularly Mr. Howard Copley, worry too much.'

'It's at least a fault the Italians haven't learned,' he replied. 'But, after all, as you say, it may be the better fortune to have less and worry less—I'd like to believe it.'

CHAPTER VI

On the morning after their arrival, Marcia had risen early and set out on horseback to explore the neighbourhood. As Castel Vivalanti, accordingly, was engaged in its usual Saturday-morning sweeping, a clatter of horses' hoofs suddenly sounded on the tiny Corso (the paving is so villainous that a single horse, however daintily it may step, sounds like a cavalcade), and running to the door, the inhabitants of the village beheld the new signorina Americana gaily riding up the narrow way and smiling to the right and left, for all the world like the queen herself. The women contented themselves with standing in the doorways and staring open-mouthed, but the children ran boldly after, until the signorina presently dismounted and bidding the groom hold her horse, sat down upon a door-step and talked to them with as much friendliness as though she had known them all her life. She ended by asking them what in the world they liked best to eat, and they declared in a single voice for 'Cioccolata.'

Accordingly they moved in a body to the baker's, and, to Domenico's astonishment, ordered all of the chocolate in the shop. And while he was excitedly counting it out the signorina kept talking to him about the weather and the scenery and the olive crop until he was so overcome by the honour that he could do nothing but bob his head and murmur, 'Si, si, eccelenza; si, si, eccelenza,' to everything she said.

And as soon as she had mounted her horse again and ridden away, with a final wave of her hand to the little black-eyed children, Domenico hurried to the Croce d'Oro to inform the landlord that he also had had the honour of entertaining the signorina Americana, who had bought chocolate to the amount of five lire—five lire! And had given it all away! The blacksmith's wife, who had followed Domenico to hear the news, remarked that, for her part, she thought it a sin to spend so much for chocolate; the signorina might have given the money just as well, and they could have had meat for Sunday. But Domenico was more ready this time to condone the fault. 'Si, si,' he returned, with a nod of his head: 'the signorina meant well, no doubt, but she could not understand the needs of poor people. He supposed that they lived on chocolate all the time at the villa, and naturally did not realize that persons who worked for their living found meat more nourishing.

When Marcia returned home with the announcement that she had visited Castel Vivalanti, her uncle replied, with an elaborate frown, 'I suppose you scattered soldi broadcast through the streets, and have started fifty young Italians on the broad road to Pauperism.'

'Not a single soldo!' she reassured him. 'I distributed nothing more demoralizing than a few cakes of chocolate.'

'You'll make a scientific philanthropist if you keep on,' Mr. Copley laughed, but his inner reflections coincided somewhat with those of the blacksmith's wife.

Marcia's explorations were likewise extended in other directions, and before the first week was over she had visited most of the villages from Palestrina to Subiaco. As a result, the chief article of diet in the Sabine mountains bade fair to become sweet chocolate; while Domenico, the baker, instead of being grateful for this unexpected flow of custom, complained to his friends of the trouble it caused. No sooner would he send into Rome for a fresh supply than the signorina would come and carry the whole of it off. At that rate, it was clearly impossible to keep it in stock.

By means of largesses of chocolate to the children, or possibly by a smile and a friendly air, Marcia had established in a very short time a speaking acquaintance with the whole neighbourhood. And on sunny mornings, as she rode between the olive orchards and the wheat fields, more than one worker straightened his back to call a pleased 'Buona passeggiata, signorina,' to the fair-haired stranger princess, who came from the land across the water where, it was rumoured, gold could be dug from the ground like potatoes and every one was rich.

All about that region the advent of the foreigners was the subject of chief interest—especially because they were Americani, for many of the people were thinking of becoming Americani themselves. The servants of the villa, when they condescended to drink a glass of wine at the inn of the Croce d'Oro, were almost objects of veneration, because they could talk so intimately of the life these 'stranger princes' led—the stranger princes would have been astonished could they have heard some of the details of these recitals.

And so the Copley dynasty began at Castel Vivalanti. The life soon fell into a daily routine, as life in even the best of places will. Three meals and tea, a book in the shadiness of the ilex grove to the tune of the splashing fountain, a siesta at noon, a drive in the afternoon, and a long night's sleep were the sum of Vivalanti's resources. Marcia liked it. Italy had got its hold upon her, and for the present she was content to drift. But Mr. Copley, after a few days of lounging on the balustrade, smoking countless cigarettes and hungrily reading such newspapers as drifted out on the somewhat casual mails, had his horse saddled one morning and rode to Palestrina to the station. After that he went into Rome almost every day, and the peasants in the wayside vineyards came to know him as well as his niece; but they did not take off their hats and smile as they did to her, for he rode past with unseeing eyes. Rich men, they said, had no thought for such as they, and they turned back to their work with a sullen scowl. Work at the best is hard enough, and it is a pity when the smile that makes it lighter is withheld; Howard Copley would have been the last to do it had he realized. But his thoughts were bent on other things, and how could the peasants know that while he galloped by so carelessly his mind was planning a way to get them bread?

Marcia spent many half-hours the first few weeks in loitering about the ruins of the old villa. It was a dream-haunted spot which spoke pathetically of a bygone time with bygone ideals. She could never quite reconcile the crumbling arches, the fantastic rock-work, and the grass-grown terraces with the 'Young Italy' of Monte Citorio thirty miles away. To eyes fresh from the New World it seemed half unreal.

One afternoon she had started to walk across the fields to Castel Vivalanti, but the fields had proved too sunny and she had stopped in the shade of the cypresses instead. Even the ruins seemed to be revivified by the warm touch of spring. Blue and white anemones, rose-coloured cyclamen, yellow laburnum, burst from every cranny of the stones. Marcia glanced about with an air of delighted approval. A Pan with his pipes was all that was needed to make the picture complete. She dropped down on the coping of the fountain, and with her chin in her hands gazed dreamily at the moss-bearded merman who, two centuries before, had spouted water from his twisted conch-shell. She was suddenly startled from her reverie by hearing a voice exclaim, 'Buon giorno, signorina!' and she looked up quickly to find Paul Dessart.

'Mr. Dessart!' she cried in amazement. 'Where in the world did you come from?'

'The inn of Sant' Agapito at Palestrina. Benoit and I are making it the centre of a sketching expedition. We get a sort of hill fever every spring, and when the disease reaches a certain point we pack up and set out for the Sabines.'

'And how did you manage to find us?'

'Purely chance,' he returned more or less truthfully. 'I picked out this road as a promising field, and when I came to the gateway, being an artist, I couldn't resist the temptation of coming in. I didn't know that it was Villa Vivalanti or that I should find you here.' He sat down on the edge of the fountain and looked about.

'Well?' Marcia inquired.

'I don't wonder that you wanted to exchange Rome for this! May I make a little sketch, and will you stay and talk to me until it is finished?'

'That depends upon how long it takes you to make a little sketch. I shall subscribe to no carte-blanche promises.'

He got out a box of water-colours from one pocket of his Norfolk jacket and a large pad from the other, and having filled his cup at the little rush-choked stream which once had fed the fountain, set to work without more ado.

'I heard from the Roystons this morning,' said Marcia, presently, and immediately she was sorry that she had not started some other subject. In their former conversations Paul's relations with his family had never proved a very fortunate topic.

'Any bad news?' he inquired flippantly.

'They will reach Rome in a week or so.'

'Holy Week—I might have known it! Miss Copley,' he looked at her appealingly, 'you know what an indefatigable woman my aunt is. She will make me escort her to every religious function that blessed city offers; it isn't her way to miss anything.'

Marcia smiled slightly at the picture; it was lifelike.

'I shall be stopping in Palestrina when they come,' he added.

She let this observation pass in a disapproving silence.

'Oh, well,' he sighed, 'I'll stay and tote them around if you think I ought. The Bible says, you know, "Love your relatives and show mercy unto them that despitefully use you."'

Marcia flashed a sudden laugh and then looked grave.

Paul glanced up at her quickly. 'I suppose my aunt told you no end of bad things about me?'

'Was there anything to tell?'

He shrugged his shoulders. 'I've committed the unpardonable sin of preferring art in Rome to coal in Pittsburg.'

He dropped the subject and turned back to his picture, and Marcia sat watching him as he industriously splashed in colour. Occasionally their eyes met when he raised his head, and if his own lingered a moment longer than convention warranted—being an artist, he was excusable, for she was distinctly an addition to the moss-covered fountain. The young man may have prolonged the situation somewhat; in any case, the sun's rays were beginning to slant when he finally pocketed his colours and presented the picture with a bow. It was a dainty little sketch of a ruined grotto and a broken statue, with the sunlight flickering through the trees on the flower-sprinkled grass.

'Really, is it for me?' she asked. 'It's lovely, Mr. Dessart; and when I go away from Rome I can remember both you and the villa by it.'

'When you go away?' he asked, with an audible note of anxiety in his voice. 'But I thought you had come to live with your uncle.'

'Oh, for the present,' she returned. 'But I'm going back to America in the indefinite future.'

He breathed an exaggerated sigh of relief.

'The indefinite future doesn't bother me. Before it comes you'll change your mind—everybody does. It's merely the present I want to be sure of.'

Marcia glanced at him a moment with a half-provocative laugh; and then, without responding, she turned her head and appeared to study the stone village up on the height. She was quite conscious that he was watching her, and she was equally conscious that her pale-blue muslin gown and her rosebud hat formed an admirable contrast to the frowning old merman. When she turned back there was a shade of amusement in her glance. Paul did not speak, but he did not lower his eyes nor in any degree veil his visible admiration. She rose with a half-shrug and brushed back a stray lock of hair that was blowing in her eyes.

'I'm hungry,' she remarked in an exasperatingly matter-of-fact tone. 'Let's go back and get some tea.'

'Will Mrs. Copley receive a jacket and knickerbockers?'

'Mrs. Copley will be delighted. Visitors are a godsend at Villa Vivalanti.'

They passed from the deep shade of the cypresses to the sun-flecked laurel path that skirted the wheat field. As they strolled along, in no great hurry to reach the villa, they laughed and chatted lightly; but the most important things they said occurred in the pauses when no words were spoken. The young man carried his hat in his hand, carelessly switching the branches with it as he passed. His shining light-brown hair—almost the colour of Marcia's own—lay on his forehead in a tangled mass and stirred gently in the wind. She noted it in an approving sidewise glance, and quickly turned away again lest he should look up and catch her eyes upon him.

In the ilex grove they paused for a moment as the sound of mingled voices reached them from the terrace.

'Listen,' Marcia whispered, with her finger on her lips; and as she recognized the tones she made a slight grimace. 'My two enemies! The Contessa Torrenieri and Mr. Sybert. The contessa has a villa at Tivoli. This is very kind of her, is it not? Nine miles is a long distance just to pay a call.'

As they advanced toward the tea-table, placed under the trees at the end of the terrace, they found an unexpectedly august party—not only the Contessa Torrenieri and the secretary of the Embassy, but the American consul-general as well. The men had evidently but just arrived, as Mrs. Copley was still engaged with their welcome.

'Mr. Melville, you come at exactly the right time. We are having mushroom ragoût to-night, which, if I remember, is your favourite dish—but why didn't you bring your wife?'

'My wife, my dear lady, is at present in Capri and shows no intention of coming home. Your husband, pitying my loneliness, insisted on bringing me out for the night.'

'I am glad that he did—we shall hope to see you later, however, when Mrs. Melville can come too. Mr. Sybert,' she added, turning toward the younger man, 'you can't know how we miss not having you drop in at all hours of the day. We didn't realize what a necessary member of the family you had become until we had to do without you.'

Marcia, overhearing this speech, politely suppressed a smile as she presented the young painter. He was included in the general acclaim.

'This is charming!' Mrs. Copley declared. 'I was just complaining to the Contessa Torrenieri that not a soul had visited us since we came out to the villa, and here are three almost before the words are out of my mouth!'

Pietro, appearing with a trayful of cups, put an end to these amenities; and, reinforced by Gerald, they had an unusually festive tea-party. Mr. Copley had once remarked concerning Paul Dessart that he would be an ornament to any dinner-table, and he undoubtedly proved himself an ornament to-day.

Melville, introducing the subject of a famous monastery lately suppressed by the government, gave rise to a discussion involving many and various opinions. The contessa and Dessart hotly defended the homeless monks; while the other men, from a political point of view, were inclined to applaud the action of the premier. Their arguments were strong, but the little contessa, two slender hands gesticulating excitedly, stanchly held her own; though a 'White' in politics, her sympathies, on occasion, stuck persistently to the other side. The church had owned the property for five centuries, the government for a quarter of a century. Which had the better right? And aside from the justice of the question—Dessart backed her up—for ascetic reasons alone, the monks should be allowed to stay. Who wished to have the beauties of frescoed chapels and carved choir-stalls pointed out by blue-uniformed government officials whose coats didn't fit? It spoiled the poetry. Names of cardinals and prelates and Italian princes passed glibly; and the politicians finally retired beaten. Marcia, listening, thought approvingly that the young artist was a match for the diplomats, and she could not help but acknowledge further that whatever faults the contessa might possess, dullness was not among them.

It was Gerald, however, who furnished the chief diversion that afternoon. Upon being forbidden to take a third maritozzo, he rose reluctantly, shook the crumbs from his blouse, and drifted off toward the ilex grove to occupy himself with the collection of lizards which he kept in a box under a stone garden seat. The group about the tea-table was shortly startled by a splash and a scream, and they hastened with one accord to the scene of the disaster. Mr. Copley, arriving first, was in time to pluck his son from the fountain, like Achilles, by a heel.

'What's the matter, Howard?' Mrs. Copley called as the others anxiously hurried up.

'Nothing serious,' he reassured her. 'Gerald has merely been trying to identify himself with his environment.'

Gerald, dripping and sputtering, came out at this point with the astounding assertion that Marietta had pushed him in. Marietta chimed into the general confusion with a volley of Latin ejaculations. She push him in! Madonna mia, what a fib! Why should she do such a thing as that when it would only put her to the trouble of dressing him again? She had told him repeatedly not to fall into the fountain, but the moment her back was turned he disobeyed.

Amid a chorus of laughter and suggestions, of wails and protestations, the nurse, the boy, and his father and mother set out for the house to settle the question, leaving the guests at the scene of the tragedy. As they strolled back to the terrace the contessa very adroitly held Sybert on one side and Dessart on the other, while with a great deal of animation and gesture she recounted a diverting bit of Roman gossip. Melville and Marcia followed after, the latter with a speculative eye on the group in front, and an amused appreciation of the fact that the young artist would very much have preferred dropping behind. Possibly the contessa divined this too; in any case, she held him fast. The consul-general was discussing a criticism he had recently read of the American diplomatic service, and his opinion of the writer was vigorous. Melville's views were likely to be both vigorously conceived and vigorously expressed.

'In any case,' he summed up his remarks, 'America has no call to be ashamed of her representative to Italy. His Excellency is a fine example of the right man in the right place.'

'And his Excellency's nephew?' she inquired, her eyes on the lounging figure in front of them.

'Is an equally fine example of the right man in the wrong place.'

'I thought you were one of the people who stood up for him.'

'You thought I was one of the people who stood up for him? Well, certainly, why not?' Melville's tone contained the suggestion of a challenge; he had fought so many battles in Sybert's behalf that a belligerent attitude over the question had become subconscious.

'Oh, I don't know,' said Marcia vaguely. 'Lots of people don't like him.'

Melville struck a match, lit a cigar, and vigorously puffed it into a glow; then he observed: 'Lots of people are idiots.'

Marcia laughed and apologized—

'Excuse me, but you are all so funny about Mr. Sybert. One day I hear the most extravagant things in his praise, and the next, the most disparaging things in his dispraise. It's difficult to know what to believe of such a changeable person as that.'

'Just let me tell you one thing, Miss Marcia, and that is, that in this world a man who has no enemies is not to be trusted—I don't know how it may be in the world to come. At for Sybert, you may safely believe what his friends say of him.'

'In that case he certainly does not show his best side to the world.'

'He probably thinks his best side nobody's business but his own.' And then, as a thought re-occurred to him, he glanced at her a moment in silence, while a brief smile flickered across his aggressively forceful face. She could not interpret the smile, but it was vaguely irritating, and as he did not have anything further to say, she pursued her theme rough-shod.

'When you see a person who doesn't take any interest in his own country; whose only aim is to be thought a cosmopolitan, a man of the world; whose business in life is to attend social functions and make after-dinner speeches—well, naturally, you can't blame people for not taking him very seriously.' She finished with a gesture of disdain.

'You were telling me a little while ago, Miss Marcia, about some of the people in Castel Vivalanti. You appear to be rather proud of your broad-mindedness in occasionally being able to detect the real man underneath the peasant—don't you think you might push your penetration just one step further and discover a real man, a personality, beneath the man of the world? Once in a while it exists.'

'You can't argue me into liking Mr. Sybert,' she laughed; 'Uncle Howard has tried it and failed.'

Mr. and Mrs. Copley returned shortly to their guests; and the contessa, bemoaning the nine miles, announced that she must go. Mr. Copley suggested that nine miles would be no longer after dinner than before, but the lady was obdurate and her carriage was ordered. She took her departure amid a graceful flurry of farewell. The contessa had an unerring instinct for effect, and her exits and her entrances were divertingly spectacular. She bade Mrs. Copley, Marcia, and the consul-general good-bye upon the terrace, and trailed across the marble flagging, attended—at a careful distance from her train—by the three remaining men. Sybert handed her into the carriage, Dessart arranged the lap-robe, while Copley brought up the rear, gingerly bearing her lace parasol. With a gay little tilt of her white-plumed hat toward the group on the terrace and an all-inclusive flash of black eyes, she was finally off, followed by the courtly bows of her three cavaliers.

Marcia, with Sybert and Dessart on either hand, continued to stroll up and down the terrace, while her aunt and uncle entertained Melville amid the furnished comfort of the loggia. Sybert would ordinarily have joined the group on the loggia, but he happened to be in the middle of a discussion with Dessart regarding the new and, according to most people, scandalous proposition for levelling the Seven Hills. The two men seemed to be diametrically opposed to all their views, and were equally far apart in their methods of arguing. Dessart would lunge into flights of exaggerated rhetoric, piling up adjectives and metaphors until by sheer weight he had carried his listeners off their feet; while Sybert, with a curt phrase, would knock the corner-stone from under the finished edifice. The latter's method of fencing had always irritated Marcia beyond measure. He had a fashion of stating his point, and then abandoning his adversary's eloquence in mid-air, as if it were not worth his while to argue further. To-day, having come to a deadlock in the matter of the piano regolatore, they dropped the subject, and pausing by the terrace parapet, they stood looking down on the plain below.

Dessart scanned it eagerly with eyes quick to catch every contrast and tone; he noted the varying purples of the distance, the narrow ribbon of glimmering gold where sky and plain met the sea, the misty whiteness of Rome, the sharply cut outline of Monte Soracte. It was perfect as a picture—composition, perspective, colour-scheme—nothing might be bettered. He sighed a contented sigh.

'Even I,' he murmured, 'couldn't suggest a single change.'

A slight smile crept over Sybert's sombre face.

'I could suggest a number.'

The young painter brought a reproachful gaze to bear upon him.

'Ah,' he agreed, 'and I can imagine the direction they'd take! Miss Copley,' he added, turning to Marcia, 'let me tell you of the thing I saw the other day on the Roman Campagna: a sight which was enough to make a right-minded man sick. I saw—' there was a tragic pause—a McCormick reaper and binder!'

Sybert uttered a short laugh.

'I am glad that you did; and I only wish it were possible for one to see more.'

'Man! Man! You don't know what you are saying!' Paul cried. There were tears in his voice. 'A McCormick reaper, I tell you, painted red and yellow and blue—the man who did it should have been compelled to drink his paint.'

Marcia laughed, and he added disgustedly: 'The thing sows and reaps and binds all at once. One shudders to think of its activities—and that in the Agra Romana, which picturesque peasants have spaded and planted and mowed by hand for thousands of years.'

'Not, however, a particularly economical way of cultivating the Campagna,' Sybert observed.

'Economical way of cultivating the Campagna!' Dessart repeated the words with a groan. 'Is there no place in the world sacred to beauty? Must America flood every corner of the habitable globe with reapers and sewing-machines and trolley-cars? The way they're sophisticating these adorably antique peasants is criminal.'

'That's the way it seems to me,' Marcia agreed cordially. 'Uncle Howard says they haven't enough to eat; but they certainly do look happy, and they don't look thin. I can't help believing he exaggerates the trouble.'

'An Italian, Miss Copley, who doesn't know where his next meal is coming from, will lie on his back in the sunshine, thinking how pretty the sky looks; and he will get as much pleasure from the prospect as he would from his dinner. If that isn't the art of being happy, I don't know what is. And that is why I hate to have Italy spoiled.'

'Well, Dessart, I fancy we all hate that,' Sybert returned. 'Though I am afraid we should quarrel over definitions.' He stretched out his hand toward the west, where the plain joined the sea by the ruins of Ostia and the Pontine Marshes. It was a great, barren, desolate waste; unpeopled, uncultivated, fever-stricken.

'Don't you think it would be rather a fine thing,' he asked, 'to see that land drained and planted and lived on again as it was perhaps two thousand years ago?'

Marcia shook her head. 'I should rather have it left just as it is. Possibly a few might gain, but think of the poetry and picturesqueness and romance that the many would lose! Once in a while, Mr. Sybert, it seems as if utility might give way to poetry—especially on the Roman Campagna. It is more fitting that it should be desolate and bare, with only a few wandering shepherds and herds, and no buildings but ruined towers and Latin tombs—a sort of burial-place for Ancient Rome.'

'The living have a few rights—even in Rome.'

'They seem to have a good many,' Dessart agreed. 'Oh, I know what you reformers want! You'd like to see the city full of smoke-stacks and machinery, and the Campagna laid out in garden plots, and everybody getting good wages and six per cent. interest; with all the people dressed alike in ready-made clothing instead of peasant costume, and nobody poor and nobody picturesque.'

Sybert did not reply for a moment, as with half-shut eyes he studied the distance. He was thinking of a ride he had taken three days before. He had gone out with a hunting-party to one of the great Campagna estates, owned by a Roman prince whose only interest in the land was to draw from it every possible centesime of income. They had stopped to water their horses at a cluster of straw huts where the farm labourers lived, and Sybert had dismounted and gone into one of them to talk to the people. It was dark and damp, with a dirt floor and rude bunks along the sides. There, fifty human beings lived crowded together, breathing the heavy, pestilential air. They had come down to bands from their mountain homes, searching for work, and had sold their lives to the prince for thirty cents a day.

The picture flashed across him now of their pale, apathetic faces, of the dumb reproach in their eyes, and for a second he felt tempted to describe it. But with the reflection that neither of the two before him would care any more about it than had the landlord prince, he changed his expression into a careless shrug.

'It will be some time before we'll see that,' he answered Dessart's speech.

'But you'd like it, wouldn't you?' Marcia persisted.

'Yes; wouldn't you?'

'No,' she laughed, 'I can't say that I should! I decidedly prefer the peasants as they are. They are far more attractive when they are poor, and since they are happy in spite of it, I don't see why it is our place to object.'

Sybert eyed the pavement impassively a moment: then he raised his head and turned to Marcia. He swept her a glance from head to foot which took in every detail of her dainty gown, her careless grace as she leaned against the balustrade, and he made no endeavour to conceal the look of critically cold contempt in his eyes. Marcia returned his glance with an air of angry challenge; not a word was spoken, but it was an open declaration of war.

CHAPTER VII

The Roystons approached Rome by easy stages along the Riviera, and as their prospective movements were but vaguely outlined even to themselves, they suffered their approach to remain unheralded. Paul Dessart, since his talk with Marcia, had taken a little dip into the future, with the result that he had decided to swallow any hurt feelings he might possess and pay dutiful court to his relatives. The immediate rewards of such a course were evident. One sunny morning early in April (he had been right in his forecast of the time: Palm Sunday loomed a week ahead) a carriage drew up before the door of his studio, and Mrs.

Royston and the Misses Royston alighted, squabbled with the driver over the fare, and told him he need not wait. They rang the bell, and during the pause that followed stood upon the door-step, dubiously scanning the neighbourhood. It was one of the narrow, tortuous streets between the Corso and the river; a street of many colours and many smells, with party-coloured washings fluttering from the windows, with pretty tumble-haired children in gold ear-rings and shockingly scanty clothing sprawling underfoot. The house itself presented a blank face of peeling stucco to the street, with nothing but the heavily barred windows below and an ornamental cornice four stories up to suggest that it had once been a palace and a stronghold.

Mrs. Royston turned from her inspection of the street to ring the bell again. There was, this time, a suggestion of impatience in her touch. A second wait, and the door was finally opened by one of the fantastic little shepherd models, who haunt the Spanish steps. He took off his hat with a polite 'Permesso, signore,' as he darted up the stairs ahead of them to point the way and open the door at the top. They arrived at the end of the five flights somewhat short of breath, and were ushered into a swept and garnished workroom, where Paul, in a white blouse, his sleeves rolled to the elbows, was immersed in a large canvas, almost too preoccupied to look up. He received his relatives with an air of delighted surprise, stood quite still while his aunt implanted a ponderous kiss upon his cheek, and after a glance at his cousins, kissed them of his own accord.

Mrs. Royston sat down and surveyed the room. It was irreproachably workmanlike, and had been so for a week. Visibly impressed, she transferred her gaze to her nephew.

'Paul, you are improved,' she said at length.

'My dear aunt, I am five years older than I was five years ago.'

'Well,' with a sigh of relief, 'I actually believe you are!'

'Paul, I had no idea you were such a desirable cousin,' was Margaret's frank comment, as she returned from an inspection of the room to a reinspection of him. 'Eleanor said you wore puffed velveteen trousers. You don't, do you?'

'Never had a pair of puffed velveteen trousers in my life.'

'Oh, yes, you did!' said Eleanor. 'You can't fib down the past that way. Mamma and I met you in the Luxembourg gardens in broad daylight wearing puffed blue velveteen trousers, with a bottle of wine in one pocket and a loaf of bread in the other.'

'Let the dead past bury its dead!' he pleaded. 'I go to an English tailor on the Corso now.'

'Marcia Copley wrote that she was very much pleased with you, but she didn't tell us how good-looking you were,' said Margaret, still frank.

Paul reddened a trifle as he repudiated the charge with a laughing gesture.

'Don't you think Miss Copley's nice?' pursued Margaret. 'You'd better think so,' she added, 'for she's one of our best friends.'

Paul reddened still more, as he replied indifferently that Miss Copley appeared very nice. He hadn't seen much of her, of course.

'I hope,' said his aunt, 'that you have been polite.'

'My dear aunt,' he objected patiently, 'I really don't go out of my way to be impolite to people,' and he took the Baedeker from her hand and sat down beside her. 'What places do you want to see first?' he inquired.

They were soon deep in computations of the galleries, ruins, and churches that should be visited in conjunction, and half an hour later, Paul and Margaret in one carriage, with Mrs. Royston and Eleanor in a second, were trotting toward the Colosseum; while Paul was reflecting that the path of duty need not of necessity be a thorny one.

During the next week or so Villa Vivalanti saw little more of Marcia than of her uncle. She spent the greater part of her time in Rome, visiting galleries and churches, with studio teas and other Lenten relaxations to lighten the rigour of sight-seeing. Paul Dessart proved himself an attentive cicerone, and his devotion to duty was not unrewarded; the dim crypts and chapels, the deep-embrasured windows of galleries and palaces afforded many chances for stolen scraps of conversation. And Paul was not one to waste his opportunities. The spring was ideal; Rome was flooded with sunshine and flowers and the Italian joy of being alive. The troubles of Italy's paupers, which Mr. Copley found so absorbing, received, during these days, little consideration from his niece. Marcia was too busy living her own life to have eyes for any but happy people. She looked at Italy through rose-coloured glasses, and Italy, basking in the spring sunshine, smiled back sympathetically.

One morning an accident happened at the villa, and though it may not seem important to the world in general, still, as events turned out, it proved to be the pivot upon which destiny turned. Gerald fell over the parapet, landing eight feet below—butter-side down—with a bleeding nose and a broken front tooth. He could not claim this time that Marietta had pushed him over, as it was clearly proven that Marietta, at the moment, was sitting in the scullery doorway, smiling at François. In consequence Marietta received her wages, a ticket to Rome, and fifty lire to dry her tears. A new nurse was hastily summoned from Castel Vivalanti. She was a niece of Domenic, the baker, and had served in the household of Prince Barberini at Palestrina, which was recommendation enough.

As to the broken tooth, it was a first tooth and shaky at that. Most people would have contented themselves with the reflection that the matter would right itself in the course of nature. But Mrs. Copley, who perhaps had a tendency to be over-solicitous on a question involving her son's health or beauty, decided that Gerald must go to the dentist's. Gerald demurred, and Marcia, who had previously had no thought of going into Rome that afternoon, offered to accompany the party, for the sake—she said—of keeping up his courage in the train. As they were preparing to start, she informed Mrs. Copley that she thought she would stay with the Roystons all night, since they had planned to visit the Forum by moonlight some evening, and this appeared a convenient time. In the Roman station she abandoned Gerald to his fate, and drove to the Hôtel de Londres et Paris.

She found the ladies just sitting down to their midday breakfast and delighted to see her. It developed, however, that they had an unbreakable engagement for the evening, and the plan of visiting the Forum was accordingly out of the question.

'No matter,' said Marcia, drawing off her gloves; 'I can come in some other day; it's always moonlight in Rome'; and they settled themselves to discussing plans for the afternoon. The hotel porter had given Margaret a permesso for the royal palace and stables, and being interested in the domestic arrangements of kings, she was insistent that they visit the Quirinal. But Mrs. Royston, who was conscientiously bent on first exhausting the heavier attractions set forth in Baedeker, declared for the Lateran museum. The matter was still unsettled when they rose from the table and were presented with the cards of Paul Dessart and M. Adolphe Benoit.

Paul's voice settled the question: the city was too full of pilgrims for any pleasure to be had within the walls; why not take advantage of the pleasant weather to drive out to the monastery of Tre Fontane? But the matter did not eventually arrange itself as happily as he had hoped, since he found himself in one carriage and Marcia in the other. At the monastery the monks were saying office in the main chapel when they arrived, and they paused a few minutes to listen to the deep rise and fall of the Gregorian chant as it echoed through the long, bare nave. The dim interior, the low, monotonous music, the unseen monks, made an effective whole. Paul, awake to the possibilities of the occasion, did his best to draw Marcia into conversation, but she was tantalizingly unresponsive. The guide-book in Mrs. Royston's hands and the history of the order appeared to absorb her whole attention.

Fortune, however, was finally on his side. Mrs. Royston elected to stop, on their way back to the city, at St. Paul's without the Walls, and the whole party once more alighted. Within the basilica, Mrs. Royston, guide-book in hand, commenced her usual conscientious inspection, while Eleanor and the young Frenchman strolled about, commenting on the architecture. Margaret had heard that one of the mosaic popes in the frieze had diamond eyes, and she was insistently bent on finding him. Marcia and Paul followed her a few minutes, but they had both seen the church many times before, and both were at present but mildly interested in diamond-eyed popes.

The door of the cloisters stood ajar, and they presently left the others and strolled into the peaceful enclosure with its brick-flagged floor and quaintly twisted columns. It was tranquil and empty, with no suggestion of the outside world. They turned and strolled down the length of the flagging, where the shadow of the columns alternated with gleaming bars of sunshine. The sleepy, old-world atmosphere cast its spell about them; Marcia's tantalizing humour and Paul's impatience fell away. They walked on in silence, until presently the silence made itself awkward and Marcia began to talk about the carving of the columns, the flowers in the garden, the monks who tended them. Paul responded half abstractedly, and he finally broke out with what he was thinking of: a talk they had had that afternoon several weeks before in the Borghese gardens.

'Most men wouldn't care for this,' he nodded toward the prim little garden with its violets and roses framed in by the pillared cloister and higher up by the dull grey walls of the church and monastery. 'But a few do. Since that is the case, why not let the majority mine their coal and build their railroads, and the very small minority who do care stay and appreciate it? It is fortunate that we don't all like the same things, for there's a great variety of work to be done. Of course,' he added, 'I know well enough I'm never going to do anything very great; I don't set up for a genius. But to do a few little things well—isn't that something?'

They had reached the opposite end of the cloisters, and paused by one of the pillars, leaning against the balustrade.

'You think it's shirking one's duty not to live in America?' he asked.

'I don't know,' Marcia smiled vaguely. 'I think—perhaps I'm changing my mind.'

'I only know of one thing,' he said in a low tone, 'that would make me want to be exiled from Italy.'

Marcia had a quick foreboding that she knew what he was going to say, and for a moment she hesitated; then her eyes asked: 'What is that?'

Paul looked down at the sun-barred pavement in silence, and then he looked up in her face and smiled steadily. 'If you lived out of Italy.'

Marcia received this in silence, while she dropped her eyes to the effigy of a dead monk set in the pavement and commenced mechanically following the Latin inscription. There was still time; she was still mistress of the situation. By a laugh, an adroit turn, she could overlook his words; could bring their relations back again to their normal footing. But she was by no means sure that she wished to bring them back to their normal footing; she felt a sudden, quite strong curiosity to know what he would say next.

'Hang it! Marcia,' he exclaimed. 'I suppose you want to marry a prince, or something like that?'

'A prince?' she inquired. 'Why a prince?'

'Oh, it's what you women are always after—having a coronet on your carriage door, with all the servants bowing and saying, "Si, si, eccelenza," every time you turn around.'

'It would be fun,' she agreed. 'Do you happen to know of any desirable unmarried princes?'

'There aren't any.'

'No? Why, I met one the other day that I thought quite charming. His family is seven hundred years old, and he owns two castles and three villages.'

'He wouldn't stay charming. You'd find the castles damp, and the villages dirty, and the prince stupid.' He dropped his hand over hers where it rested on the balustrade. 'You'd better take me, Marcia; in the long run you'll find me nicer.'

Marcia shook her head, but she did not draw away her hand. 'Really, Paul, I don't know— and there's nothing I hate so much in the world as making up my mind. You shouldn't ask such unanswerable things.'

'Look, mamma! aren't the cloisters lovely?' Margaret's voice suddenly sounded across the little court. 'Oh, there are Marcia and Paul over there! We wondered where you had disappeared to.'

'Oh, the deuce!' Paul exclaimed as he put his hands in his pockets and leaned back against the pillar. 'I told you,' he added, with a laugh, 'that my family always arrived when they were not wanted!'

They all strolled about together, and Marcia scarcely glanced at him again. But her consciousness was filled with his words, and it required all her self-possession to keep up her part of the conversation. As they started on, Mrs. Royston suggested that they stop a second time at the English cemetery just within the gate. Marcia, looking at her watch, saw with a feeling of relief that she would have to go straight on if she were to catch Mrs. Copley and Gerald in time for the six o'clock train. Bidding them good-bye at the Porta San Paolo, she hastily and emphatically refused Paul's proposition to drive to the station with her.

'No, indeed, Mr. Dessart,' she called out, as he was making arrangements with Mrs. Royston to meet later at the hotel, 'I don't want you to come with me; I shouldn't think of taking you away. My aunt will be at the station, and I am perfectly capable of getting there alone. Really, I don't want to trouble you.'

He put his foot on the carriage-step.

'It's no trouble,' he smiled.

'No, no; I would rather go alone. I shall really be angry if you come,' she insisted in a low tone.

The young man shrugged and removed his foot from the step.

'As you please,' he returned in a tone which carried an impression of slightly wounded feelings. The driver looked back expectantly, waiting for his directions. Paul hesitated a moment, and then turned toward her again as if inquiring the way. 'Is there any hope for me?' he said.

She looked away without answering.

'There's no other man?' he added quickly.

Marcia for a second looked up in his face. 'No,' she shook her head, 'there's no other man.'

He straightened up, with a happy laugh. 'Then I'll win,' he whispered, and he shook her hand as if on a compact.

'Stazione,' he called to the driver. And as the carriage started, Marcia glanced back and nodded toward the Roystons, with a quick smile for Paul.

CHAPTER VIII

'Ah, Sybert, you're just the man I wanted to see!' Melville came up the walk of the palazzo occupied by the American ambassador as Sybert, emerging from the door, paused on the top step to draw on his gloves.

'In that case,' the latter returned, 'it's well you didn't come five minutes later, or I should have been lost to the world for the afternoon. What's up?'

'Nothing serious. Can you spare me a few moments' talk? I won't take up your time if you are in a hurry.'

'Not in the least. I'm entirely at your disposal. Nothing on for the afternoon, and I was preparing to loaf.'

The two turned back into the house and crossed the hall to the ambassador's private library. Melville closed the door and regarded his companion a trifle quizzically. Sybert dropped into a chair, indicated another, and pushed a box of cigars and some matches across the table; then he looked up and caught Melville's expression.

'Well, what's up?' he asked again.

The consul-general selected a cigar with some deliberation, bit off the end, and regarded it critically, while his smile broadened. 'I have just returned from the mass meeting of the foreign residents,' he remarked.

'That should have been entertaining.'

'It was,' he admitted. 'There was some spirited discussion as to the best way of suppressing the riots.'

'And how did they decide to do it?'

'They have appointed a committee.'

'Of course a committee!' Sybert laughed. 'And what is the committee to do? Wait on the ministers and invite them to reconstruct their morals? Ask the King to spend a little less money on the soldiers' uniforms and a little more on their rations?'

'The Committee,' said Melville, 'is to raise money for food, and to assist the government as far as possible in quieting the people and suppressing the agitators.'

'Ah!' breathed Sybert.

'And,' he added, with his eye on the young man, 'I have the honour of informing you that you were made chairman.'

'Oh, the devil!'

'This is not an official notification,' he pursued blandly; 'but I thought you'd like to hear the news.'

'Who's at the bottom of this? Why, in heaven's name, didn't you stop them?'

'I couldn't very well; I was chairman of the meeting.'

Sybert's usual easy nonchalance had vanished. He rose to his feet and took one or two turns about the room.

'I don't see why I should be shoved into it—I wish some of these officious fools would go back home, where they belong. I won't serve on any such committee; I'll be hanged if I will! I'll resign.'

'Nonsense, Sybert; you can't do that. It would be too marked. People would think you had some reason for not wanting to serve. It was very natural that your name should have occurred for the position; you have lived in Rome longer than most of us, and are supposed to understand the conditions and to be interested in good government.'

'It puts me in a mighty queer position.'

'I don't see why.' The elder man's tone had grown cool. 'They naturally took it for granted that you, as well as the rest of us, would want to have the riots suppressed and choke off any latent tendencies toward revolution in this precious populace.'

'It was the work of a lot of damned busybodies who wanted to see what I would do.'

Melville suppressed a momentary smile. 'However,' he remarked, 'I see no reason why you should be so reluctant about serving in a good cause—I don't suppose you wish to see a revolution any more than the rest of us.'

'Heavens, no! It wouldn't do any good; the government's got the army to back it; the revolutionists would only be sent to the galleys for their trouble, and the police oppression would be worse than ever.'

He swung up and down the room a couple of times, and then pausing with his hands in his pockets, stared moodily out of the window. Melville smoked and watched him, a shade of uneasiness in his glance. Just what position Laurence Sybert occupied in Rome—what unofficial position, that is—was a mystery to the most of his friends. Melville understood him as well as any one, with the exception of Howard Copley; but even he was at times quite unprepared for the intimate knowledge Sybert displayed in affairs which, on the surface, did not concern him. Sybert was distinctly not a babbler, and this tendency toward being close-mouthed had given rise to a vast amount of speculative interest in his movements. He carried the reputation, among the foreign residents, of knowing more about Italian politics than the premier himself; and he further carried the reputation—

whether deserved or not—of mixing rather more deeply than was wise in the dark undercurrent of the government.

And this particular spring the undercurrent was unusually dark and dangerously swift. Young Italy had been sowing wild oats, and the crop was ripening fast. It was a period of anxiety and disappointment for those who had watched the country's brave struggle for unity and independence thirty years before. Victor Emmanuel, Cavour, and Garibaldi had passed away; the patriots had retired and the politicians had come in. A long period of over-speculation, of dishonesty and incompetence, of wild building schemes and crushing taxes, had brought the country's credit to the lowest possible ebb. A series of disgraceful bank scandals, involving men highest in the government, had shaken the confidence of the people. The failure of the Italian colony in Africa, and the heart-rending campaign against King Menelik and his dervishes, with thousands of wounded conscripts sent back to their homes, had carried the discontent to every corner of the kingdom. And fast on the heels of this disaster had come a failure in the wheat crop, with all its attendant horrors; while simultaneously the corner in the American market was forcing up the price of foreign wheat to twice its normal value.

It was a time when priests were recalling to the peasants the wrongs the church had suffered; a time when the socialist presses were turning out pamphlets containing plain truths plainly stated; a time when investors refused to invest in government bonds, and even Italian statesmen were beginning to look grave.

To the casual eyes of tourists the country was still as picturesquely, raggedly gay as ever. There were perhaps more beggars on the church steps, and their appeal for bread was a trifle more insistent; but for people interested only in Italy's galleries and ruins and shops the changes were not marked. But those who did understand, who cared for the future of the nation, who saw the seething below the surface, were passing through a phase of disillusionment and doubt. And Laurence Sybert was one who both understood and cared. He saw the direction in which the country was drifting even better perhaps than the Italians themselves. He looked on in a detached, more remote fashion, not so swept by the current as those who were in the stream. But if he were detached in fact—by accident of his American parentage and citizenship—in feelings he was with the Italians heart and soul.

The consul-general remained some minutes silently studying the younger man's expressive back—irritation, obstinacy, something stronger, appeared in every line of his squared shoulders—then he rose and walked across to the window.

'See here, Sybert,' he said bluntly, 'I'm your friend, and I don't want to see you doing anything foolish. I know where your sympathies are; and if the rest of us looked into the matter with our eyes open, it's possible ours would be on the same side. But that's neither here nor there; we couldn't do any good, and you can't, either. You must think of your own position—you are secretary of the American Embassy and nephew of the ambassador. In common decency it won't do to exhibit too much sympathy with the enemies of the Italian government. You say yourself that you don't want to see a revolution. Then it's your duty, in the interests of law and order, to do all you can to suppress it.'

'Oh, I'm willing to do all I can toward relieving the suffering and quieting the people; but when it comes to playing the police spy and getting these poor devils jailed for twenty years because they've shouted, "Down with Savoy!" I refuse.'

Melville shrugged. 'That part of the business can be left to the secret police; they're capable of handling it.'

'I don't doubt that,' Sybert growled.

'Your business is merely to aid in pacifying the people and to raise subscriptions for buying food. You are in with the wealthy foreigners, and can get money out of them easier than most.'

'I suppose that means I am to bleed Copley?'

'I dare say he'll be willing enough to give; it's in his line. Of course he's a friend, and I don't like to say anything. I know he had nothing to do with getting up the wheat deal; but it's all in the family, and he won't lose by it. The corner is playing the deuce with Italy, and it's his place to help a bit.'

'What is playing the deuce with Italy is an extravagant government and crushing taxes and dead industries. The wheat famine is bad enough; but that isn't the main trouble, and you know it as well as I do.'

'The main trouble,' his companion broke in sharply, 'is the fact that the priests and the anarchists and the socialists and every other sort of meddling malcontent keep things so stirred up that the government is forced into the stand it takes.'

Sybert whirled around from the window and faced him with black brows and a sudden flaring of passion in his eyes. He opened his mouth to speak, and then controlled himself and went on in a quiet, half-sneering tone—

'I suppose the socialists and priests and the rest of your malcontents forced our late premier into office and kept him there. I suppose they yoked Italy with the Triple Alliance and drove the soldiers into Abyssinia to be butchered like hogs. I suppose they were at the bottom of the bank scandals, and put the charity money into official pockets, and let fifteen thousand peasants go mad with hunger last year—fifteen thousand!——' His voice suddenly broke, and he half-turned away. 'Good Lord, Melville, the poverty in Italy is something appalling!'

'Yes, I dare say it is—but, just the same, that's only one side of the question. The country is new, and you can't expect it to develop along every line at once. The government has committed some very natural blunders, but at the same time it has accomplished a vast amount of good. It has united a lot of chaotic states, with different traditions and different aims, into one organic whole; it has built up a modern nation, with all the machinery of modern civilization, in an incalculably short time. Of course the people have had to pay for it with a good many deprivations—in every great political change there are those who suffer; it's inevitable. But the suffering is only temporary, and the good is permanent. You've been keeping your eyes so closely on passing events that you're in danger of losing your perspective.'

Sybert shrugged his shoulders, with a quick resumption of his usual indifference.

'We've had twenty-five years of United Italy, and what has it accomplished?' he demanded. 'It's built up one of the finest standing armies in Europe, if you like; a lot of railroads it didn't need; some aqueducts and water-works, and a postal and telegraph system. It has erected any number of gigantic public buildings, of theatres and arcades and statues of Victor Emmanuel II; but what has it done for the poor people beyond taxing them to pay for these things? What has it done for Sicily and Sardinia, for the pellagra victims of the north, for the half-starved peasants of the Agra Romana? Why does Sicily hold the primacy of crime in Europe; why has emigration reached two hundred thousand a year? Parliament votes five million lire for a palace of justice, and lets a man be murdered in prison by his keepers without the show of a trial. The government supports plenty of universities for the sons of the rich, but where are the elementary schools for the peasants? Certainly Italy's a Great Power—if that's all you want—and her people can take their choice between emigrating and starving.'

'Yes, it's bad, I know; but that it's quite as bad as you would have us believe, I doubt. You're a pessimist by conviction, Sybert. You won't look at the silver linings.'

'The silver linings are pretty thin,' he retorted. 'Italian politics have changed since the days of Victor Emmanuel and Cavour.'

'That's only natural. You could scarcely expect any nation to keep up such a high pitch of patriotism as went to the making of United Italy—the country's settled down a bit, but the elements of strength are still there.'

36

'The country's settled down a good bit,' he agreed. 'Oh, yes, I believe myself—at least I hope—that it's only a passing phase. The Italian people have too much inherent strength to allow themselves to be mastered long by corrupt politicians. But that the country is in pretty low water now, and that the breakers are not far ahead, no one with his eyes open can doubt. The parliament is wasteful and senseless and dishonest, the taxes are crushing, the public debt is enormous, the currency is debased. If such a government can't take care of itself, I don't see that it's the business of foreigners to help it.'

'That is just the point, Sybert. The government can take care of itself and it will. The foreigners, out of common humanity, ought to help the people as much as they can.'

Sybert appeared to study Melville's face for a few moments; then he dropped his eyes and examined the floor.

'This is a time for those in power to choose their way very carefully. There are a good many discontented people, and the government is going to have more of a pull than you think to hold its own—there's revolution in the air.'

Melville faced him squarely.

'For goodness' sake, Sybert, I don't know how much influence you have, or anything about it, but do what you can to keep things quiet. Of course the government has made mistakes—as what government has not? But until there's something better to be substituted there's no use kicking. Plainly, the people are too ignorant to govern themselves, and the House of Savoy is the only means of salvation.'

Sybert waved his hand impatiently.

'I haven't been trying to undermine the government, I assure you. I know well enough that for a good many years to come Italy won't have anything better to offer, and all my influence with the Italians—which naturally isn't much—has been advice of the same nature. I know very well that if any radical change were attempted, only anarchy would result; so I counsel these poor starving beggars "patience" like a skulking coward.'

'Very well; I don't see then why you have any objection to keeping on with your counsel, and at the same time give them something to eat.'

'It's the looks of the thing—standing up openly on the side of the authorities when I'm not with them in sympathy.'

'It's a long sight better for a person in your position than standing up openly against the authorities.'

'Oh, as for that, I'm thinking of resigning from the legation, and then I'll be free to do as I please.'

Melville laid his hand on the younger man's shoulder.

'Sybert, you may resign from the legation, but you're still your uncle's nephew. You can't resign from that. Whatever you did would cast discredit on him. He's an old man, and he's fond of you. Don't be a fool. An American has no business mixing up in these Italian broils; Italy must work out her own salvation without the help of foreigners. Garibaldi was right—"Italia farà da se."'

'"Italia farà da se,"' he repeated. 'I suppose it's true enough. Italy must in the end do for herself, and no outsider can be of any help—but I shall at least have tried.'

'My dear fellow, if you will let me speak plainly, the best thing you can do for yourself and your family, for America and Italy, is, as you say, to resign from the legation—and go home.'

'Go home!' Sybert raised his head, with a little laugh, but with a flash underneath of the real self which he kept so carefully hidden from the world. 'I was born in Italy; I was brought up here, just as little Gerald Copley is being brought up. I have lived here all my life, except for half a dozen years or so while I was being educated. All my interests, all my sympathies, are in Italy, and you ask me to go home! I have no other home to go to. If you take Italy away from me, I'm a man without a country.'

37

'I'm in earnest, Sybert. Whether you like it or not, you're an American, and you can't get away from it if you live here a hundred years. You may talk Italian and look Italian, but you cannot be Italian. A man's nationality lies deeper than all externals. You're an American through and through, and it's a pity you can't be a little proud of the fact. The only way in which there's going to be any progress in the world for a good long time to come is for Italians to care for Italy and Americans for America. We aren't ready just yet to do away with national boundaries; and if we were, we should run up against racial boundaries, which are still more unchangeable. America is quite as good a country to care about as Italy—there are some who think it's better; it depends on the point of view.'

'Oh, that's true enough,' Sybert returned, with a short laugh. 'Everything in the world depends on one's point of view; the worst place is all right if you only choose to think so. I dare say hell would be pleasurable enough to a salamander, but the point is—I'm not a salamander.'

Melville shrugged his shoulders helplessly and turned back to his seat.

'There's no use arguing with you, I know that. You're wasting your ability where it isn't appreciated, but I suppose it's nobody's business but your own. Some day you'll see the truth yourself; and I hope it won't be too late. But now as to this committee business—for your uncle's sake you ought to carry it through. I will tell you frankly—I imagine it isn't news—that the Italian government has its eye on you; and if you manage to get yourself arrested, rightly or wrongly, for stirring up sedition, it will make an ugly story in the papers. The editor and staff of the Grido del Popolo were arrested this morning. The police are opening telegrams and letters and watching suspicious persons. You'd better step carefully.'

Sybert laughed, with a gesture of dissent. 'There's no danger about me. The enthusiastic head of the Foreign Relief Committee is safe from government persecution.'

'You'll act then?'

'Oh, I don't know—I'll think it over. It's a deuced hole to have got into; though I suppose it is, as you say, about the only way to help. No doubt I can raise money and distribute bread as well as another.'

'Appoint Copley on a sub-committee. He'll be glad to give.'

'I don't like to ask him. He doesn't go in for alms; he's all for future—though in a time like this——'

'In a time like this we're all willing to step aside a bit. I'm glad you've decided to work on the side of the government. It is, as things stand, the only sensible thing to do.'

'I haven't decided yet. And I do not, as I told you before, care a rap what becomes of the government. It's the people I'm helping.'

'It amounts to the same thing.'

'Not in Italy.'

'Oh, very well. You're incorrigible. At least keep your opinions to yourself.'

'I'm not likely to shout them abroad under the present régime. And as to this infernal committee—oh, well, I'll think about it.'

'Very well; think favourably. It's the only way to help, remember—and very good policy into the bargain. Some day, my boy, maybe you'll grow sensible. Good-bye.'

Sybert paced up and down the room for five or ten minutes after Melville had left, and then picked up his hat and started out again. Turning toward the Piazza Barberini, he strode along, scowling unconsciously at the passers-by. He bowed mechanically to the people who bowed to him. Along the Corso he met the procession of carriages going toward the Pincio. Ladies nodded graciously; they even half-turned to look after him. But he was quite unaware of it; his thoughts were not with the portion of Roman society which rode in carriages. He traversed the Corso and plunged into the tangle of more or less dirty streets on the left bank of the Tiber. Here the crowds who elbowed their way along the narrow sidewalks were more poorly dressed. After some twenty minutes' walking he turned into a narrow street in the region of the grimy ruins of the theatre of Marcellus, and paused before the doorway of a wine-shop which bore upon its front the ambitious title, 'Osteria del Popolo Italiano—Tarquinio Paterno.' With a barely perceptible glance over his shoulder, he stepped into the dingy little café which opened from the street. The front room, with its square wooden tables and stiff-backed chairs, was empty, except for Madame Tarquinio Paterno, who was sweeping the floor. Sybert nodded to her, and crossing the room to the rear door, which opened into the cucina, knocked twice. The door opened a crack for purposes of examination, and then was thrown wide to admit him.

The room which was revealed was a stone-walled kitchen, lighted in the rear by a small-paned window opening on to a gloomy court-yard. 'Lighted' is scarcely the word to use, for between the dirt on the panes and the dimness of the court, very little daylight struggled in. But the interior was not dreary. A charcoal fire blazing on the high stone hearth shot up fiercely every now and then, throwing grotesque high lights on the faces of the men grouped about the room.

Sybert paused on the threshold and glanced about from face to face. Three or four men were sitting on low benches about a long table, drinking wine and talking. The one who was in the act of speaking as Sybert appeared in the door paused with his mouth still open. The others, recognizing him, however, called out a cordial 'Buona sera, Signor Siberti,' while Tarquinio hastened to place a chair and bring a tall rush-covered flask of red Frascati wine. Sybert returned their salutations, and sat down with a glance of inquiry at the excited stranger. Tarquinio ceremoniously presented him as Girolamo Mendamo of Naples, and he ended his introduction with the assurance, 'Have no fear; he is a good fellow and one of us,' and left it to be conjectured as to whether the compliment referred to Sybert or the Neapolitan. The latter took it to refer to Sybert, and after a momentary hesitation picked up his discourse where he had dropped it.

'Ah, and when the poor fishermen are sickening for a little salt and try to get it from the sea water without paying, what do the police do? They throw them into prison. The Camorra used to protect people from the police, but now the Camorra no longer dares to lift its head and the people have no protectors. It used to be that when the police wanted more money it satisfied them to raise the taxes, but now they must raise the price of bread and macaroni as well.'

He had commenced in a low tone, but as he proceeded his voice rose higher and higher.

'And last week a great crowd broke open the bakeries and carried off the flour, and the police were frightened and put down the price—but not enough. Then the people threatened again, and ecco! all the tax was taken off. That is the way to deal with the police; they are cowards, and it is only fear that makes them just.'

The man laughed hoarsely and looked around for approval. The others nodded.

'Già, he speaks the truth. It is only fear that makes them just.'

'They are cowards—cowards,' repeated the Neapolitan. 'If all the people in every city of Italy would do the same, there would soon be no more taxes and no more police.'

'I am afraid that you are mistaken there, my friend,' Sybert broke in. 'There will always be taxes and always be police. But it's true, as you say, that the taxes are too heavy and the police are unjust. The time hasn't come, though, when you can gain anything by rioting and revolutions. The government's backed by the army, and it's too strong for you. You may possibly frighten it into lowering the wheat tax for a time, but it will be at a mighty heavy cost to the ones who are found out.'

'Who are you?' the man demanded suspiciously.

'I am an American who would like to see Italy as happy and prosperous and well governed as the United States.' Sybert smiled inwardly at the ideal he was holding up.

'Ah—you're a spy!' the man cried, with a quick scowl.

'I am so far from being a spy that I have come to warn you that, if you don't want to spend the next few years of your lives in prison, you must be very careful to cheer the House of Savoy on the first of May. The police spies are keeping both eyes open just now.'

The others nodded their heads pacifically, but the Neapolitan still scowled. He suddenly leaned forward across the table and scanned Sybert with eyes that glittered fiercely in the firelight. Then he burst out again in low guttural tones—

'It is easy for you to talk, Signor Whatever-your-name-is. You have bread to eat. But if you worked all day from sunrise to sunset—worked until you grew so tired you couldn't sleep, and then got up and worked again—and then if the police came and took away all the money in taxes and didn't even leave enough to buy your family food, and the work gave out so you must either steal or die, and you couldn't find anything to steal—then you would sing another song. Wait, wait, you say. It's always wait. Will better times ever come if we sit down and wait for them? Who will give us the better times? The King, perhaps? Umberto?' The man broke off with a harsh laugh.

'Ah—we shall die waiting, and our children after us. And when we are dead the good God will keep us waiting outside of paradise because there is no money to pay for masses. No one cares for those who do not care for themselves. It's the poor people, who haven't enough to eat, who buy the gold braid on the King's clothes and pay for the carriages of his ministers. In my opinion, we would do better to buy bread for our children first.'

Sybert looked back in the man's burning face, and his own caught fire. He knew that every word he said was true, and he knew how hopeless was his remedy. What could these passionate, ignorant peasants, blazing with rage, do with power if they had it? Worse than nothing. Their own condition would only be rendered more desperate than ever. He glanced about the table from one face to another. They were all leaning forward, waiting for his answer. The fierce eagerness in their eyes was contagious. A sudden wave of hopeless pity for them swept him off his feet, and for a moment he lost himself.

'My God! men,' he burst out, 'I know it's true. I know you're starving while others spend your money. There's no justice for you, and there never will be. The only thing I want in the world is to see Italy happy. I am as ready to die for it as you are, but what can I do? What can any one do? The soldiers are stronger than we are, and if we raise our hands they will shoot us down like dogs, and there it will end.' He paused with a deep breath, and went on in a quieter tone. 'Patience is poor food to offer to starving men, but it's the one hope now for you and for Italy. The only thing you can do is to go to the polls and vote for honest ministers.'

'Ministers are all alike,' said one.

'And who will feed us while we are waiting for election day?' asked another, who had been listening silently.

The question was unanswerable, and Sybert sat frowning down at the table without speaking. The Neapolitan presently broke in again. There was something electric about his words and the force behind them. Every one bent forward to listen.

'Who is the King?' he demanded. 'He is only a man. So am I a man. Then what makes him so different from me? They may shoot me down if they like, but first I have work to do. The King shall know me before I die. And he is not all,' he added darkly. 'Do you know why the wheat's so scarce? Because of a forestiere here in Rome—Signor Copli—he that put down the Camorra in Naples and throws the beggars into prison.'

An angry mutter ran around the room.

'You're mistaken there,' Sybert interrupted. 'It's not this Signor Copli who bought the wheat; it's his brother in America. This Signor Copli is the friend of the poor people. Many, many thousand lire he gives away every year, and no one knows about it.'

A more friendly murmur arose, but the Neapolitan was still unconvinced.

'It is the same Signor Copli,' he affirmed stubbornly. 'He hides the wheat in America, where he thinks no one will know about it. And then, after stealing it all from the mouths of the poor, he gives a little back with a great show, thinking to blind us. But we know. The Grido del Popolo printed it out in black and white for all who can to read.'

40

'And the Grido del Popolo was stopped this morning and the editor put in jail for printing lies,' said Sybert sharply.

'Ah, you're a police spy! You pretend to be for us to make us talk.' His hand half instinctively went to his belt.

Sybert rose to his feet and dropped his hand roughly on the man's shoulder. 'The best thing you can do for your country is to put that stiletto into the fire.' He turned aside with an expression of disgust and tossed some silver coins on the table in payment for the wine. Then pausing a moment, he glanced about the circle of swarthy faces. Gradually his expression softened. 'I've tried to warn you. The police are on the watch, and I should advise you to stick pretty closely to your homes and not mix up in any riots. I will do what I can to get food and money for the poor people—I know of no other way to help. Heaven knows I would do it if I could!'

He nodded to them, and motioning Tarquinio to follow, passed into the front room. Closing the door behind them, he turned to the innkeeper.

'Tarquinio, I think you had better go up into the hills and attend to your vineyard for a few weeks.'

The young Italian's face was the picture of dismay. 'But the osteria, Signor Siberti; who will manage that?'

'Your wife can look after it. Let it be given out that you are tending vines in the Sabine hills. That is the safest profession these days. The police will be paying you a visit before long if I am not greatly mistaken—and whatever you do, keep out fellows like that Neapolitan.'

Tarquinio's face darkened with a quick look of suspicion. 'I am but a poor innkeeper, Signor Siberti. I must welcome those who come.'

Sybert shrugged. 'I was merely speaking for your own safety. Such guests are dangerous. Addio.' He turned toward the door, and then turned back a moment. 'Take my advice, Tarquinio, and visit your vineyard.'

Tarquinio followed him to the threshold, and bidding him a voluble good-bye in the face of the world, begged the signor Americano to honour his humble osteria again; so that any chance passer-by might regard the gentleman as but a casual visitor. Sybert smiled at the simple strategy. An Italian loves a plot better than his dinner, and is never happier than when engaged in an imaginary intrigue. But in this case it occurred to him that his host's caution might not be out of place; and he fervently assured Tarquinio that the wine had been excellent, and that in the future he would send his friends to the Osteria del Popolo Italiano.

CHAPTER IX

Sybert turned away from the wine-shop with a half-laugh at Tarquinio's little play, with a half-frown at the fierce words of the Neapolitan, which were still ringing in his head. He walked along with his eyes upon the ground, scarcely aware of his surroundings, until an excited medley of voices close at hand suddenly startled him from his thoughts. He glanced up for a moment with unseeing eyes, and then with an astonished flash of recognition as he beheld Marcia Copley backed against one of the dark stone arches in the substructure of the theatre of Marcellus. Her head was thrown back and there were two angry red spots in her cheeks, while a struggling crowd of boys pressed around her with shouts and gesticulations.

As he paused to take in the meaning of the scene, he heard Marcia—evidently so angry that she had forgotten her Italian—say in English: 'You beastly little cowards! You wouldn't dare hurt anything but a poor animal that can't hit back.' She accompanied this speech with a vigorous shake to a small boy whom she held by the shoulder. The boy could not understand her words, but he did understand her action and he kicked back vigorously. The crowd laughed and began to close around her. She took out her purse. 'Who owns this dog?' she demanded. At sight of the money they pressed closer, and in another moment

41

would have snatched it away; but Sybert stepped forward, and raising his cane, scattered them right and left.

'What in the world are you doing here? What is the meaning of this?' he asked.

'Oh, Mr. Sybert! I'm so glad to see you. Look! those horrible little wretches were killing this dog.'

Sybert glanced down at her feet, where a bedraggled cur was crouching, shivering, and looking up with pleading eyes. The blood was running from a cut on its shoulder, and a motley assortment of tin was tied to its tail by a cord. He took out his knife and cut the dog loose, and Marcia stooped and picked it up.

'Take care, Miss Marcia,' he said in a disgusted tone. 'He's very dirty, and you will get covered with blood.'

Marcia put her handkerchief over the dog's wound, and it lay in her arms, whimpering and shaking.

'What is the meaning of this?' he demanded again, almost roughly. 'What are you doing in this part of the city alone?'

His tone at another time would have been irritating, but just now she was too grateful for his appearance to be anything but cordial, and she hastily explained—

'I've been spending the afternoon at Tre Fontane with some friends. I left them at the English cemetery, and was just driving back to the station when I saw those miserable little boys chasing this dog. I jumped out and grabbed him, and they all followed me.'

'I see,' said Sybert; 'and it is fortunate that I happened by when I did, or you wouldn't have had any money left to pay your cab-driver. These Roman urchins have not the perfect manners one could wish.'

'Manners!' Marcia sniffed indignantly. 'I loathe the Italians! I think they are the cruellest people I ever saw. Those boys were stoning this poor dog to death.'

'I dare say they have not enjoyed your advantages.'

'They would have killed him if I hadn't come just when I did.'

'You are not going out to the villa alone?'

'No; Aunt Katherine and Gerald are going to meet me at the station.'

'Oh, very well,' he answered in a tone of evident relief, as they turned toward the waiting carriage. 'Let me take the dog and I will drop him a few streets farther on, where the boys won't find him again.'

'Certainly not,' said Marcia indignantly. 'Some other boys would find him. I shall take him home and feed him. He doesn't look as if he had had anything to eat for weeks.'

'In that case,' said Sybert resignedly, 'I will drive to the station with you, for he is scarcely a lap-dog and you may have trouble getting him into the train.' And while she was in the midst of her remonstrance he stepped into the carriage and put the dog on the floor between his feet. The dog, however, did not favour the change, and stretching up an appealing paw he touched Marcia's knee, with a whine.

'You poor thing! Stop trembling. Nobody's going to hurt you,' and she bent over and kissed him on the nose.

Marcia was excited. She had not quite recovered her equanimity since the scene with Paul Dessart in the cloisters, and the affair of the dog had upset her afresh. She rattled on now, with a gaiety quite at variance with her usual attitude toward Sybert, of anything and everything that came into her mind—Gerald's broken tooth, the departure of Marietta, the afternoon at Tre Fontane, and the episode of the dog. Sybert listened politely, but his thoughts were not upon her words.

He was too full of what he had left behind in the little café for him to listen patiently to Marcia's chatter. As he looked at her, flushed and smiling in her dainty clothes, which were faultless with the faultlessness that comes from money, he experienced a feeling almost of anger against her. He longed to face her with a few plain truths. What right had she to all her useless luxuries, when her father was—as the Neapolitan had truly put it—taking his money from the mouths of the poor? It was their work which made it possible for such as she to live—and was she worth it? The world had given her much: she was educated, she was cultured, she had trained tastes and sensibilities, and in return what did she do for the world? She saved a dog. He made a movement of disgust and for a moment he almost obeyed his impulse to throw the dog out. But he brought himself back to reason with a half-laugh. It was not her fault. She knew nothing of her father's transaction; she knew nothing of Italy's need. There was no reason why she should not be happy. And, after all, he told himself wearily, it was a relief to meet some one who had no troubles.

Marcia suddenly interrupted her own light discourse to look at her watch. 'Gracious! I haven't much time. Will you please tell him to hurry a little, Mr. Sybert?'

The driver obeyed by giving his horse a resounding cut with the whip, whereupon Marcia jerked him by the coat-tails and told him that if he whipped his horse again she would not give him any mancia.

The fellow shrugged his shoulders and they settled down into a walk.

'Isn't there any society for the prevention of cruelty to animals?' she asked. 'These Italians are hopeless.'

'You can scarcely expect them to expend more consideration on animals than they receive themselves,' Sybert threw off.

'Oh, dear!' she complained anew, suddenly becoming aware of their pace; 'I'm afraid we'll be late for the train. Don't you suppose he could hurry just a little without whipping the horse?'

Sybert translated her wishes to the driver again, and they jogged on at a somewhat livelier rate; but by the time they reached the station the train had gone, and there were no Mrs. Copley and Gerald in the waiting-room. Marcia's face was slightly blank as she realized the situation, and her first involuntary thought was a wish that it had been Paul Dessart instead of Sybert who had come with her. She carried off the matter with a laugh, however, and explained to her companion—

'I suppose Aunt Katherine thought I had decided to stay in the city with the Roystons. I told her I was going to, but I found they had a dinner engagement. It doesn't matter, though; I'll wait here for the next train. There is one for Palestrina before very long—Aunt Katherine went by way of Tivoli. Thank you very much, Mr. Sybert, for coming to the station with me, and really you mustn't think you have to wait until the train goes. The dog will be company enough.'

Sybert consulted his time schedule in silence. 'The next train doesn't leave till seven, and there won't be any carriage waiting for you. How do you propose to get out to the villa?'

'Oh, the station-man at Palestrina will find a carriage for me. There's a very nice man who's often driven us out.'

Sybert frowned slightly as he considered the question. It was rather inconvenient for him to go out to the villa that night; but he reflected that it was his duty toward Copley to get his niece back safely—as to letting her set out alone on a seven-mile drive with a strange Palestrina driver, that was clearly out of the question.

'I think I'll run out with you,' he said, looking at his watch.

She had seen his frown and feared some such proposition. 'No, indeed!' she cried. 'I shouldn't think of letting you. I've been over the same road hundreds of times, and I'm not in the least afraid. It won't be late.'

'The Sabine mountains are infested with bandits,' he declared. 'I think you need an escort.'

'Mr. Sybert, how silly! I know your time is precious, (this was intended for irony, but as it happened to be true, he did not recognize it as such), 'and I don't want you to come with me.'

Sybert laughed. 'I don't doubt that, Miss Marcia; but I'm coming, just the same. I am sorry, but you will have to put up with me.'

'I should a lot rather you wouldn't,' she returned, 'but do as you please.'

'Thank you for the invitation,' he smiled. 'There's about an hour and a half before the train goes—you might run out to the Embassy and have a cup of tea.'

'Thank you for the invitation, but I think I'll stay here. I don't wish to miss a second train, and I shouldn't know what to do with the dog.'

'Very well, if you don't mind staying alone, I will drive out myself and leave a business message for the chief, and then I can take a vacation with a clear conscience. I have a matter to consult your uncle about, and I shall be very glad to run out to the villa.' He raised his hat in a sufficiently friendly bow and departed.

When he returned, an hour later, he found Marcia feeding the dog with sausage amid an appreciative group of porters, one of whom had procured the meat.

'Oh, dear!' she cried. 'I hoped Marcellus would have finished his meal before you came back. But you aren't so particular about etiquette as the contessa,' she added, 'and don't object to feeding dogs in the station?'

'I dare say the poor beast was hungry.'

'Hungry! I had a whole kilo of sausage, and you should have seen it disappear.'

'These facchini look as if they would not be averse to sharing his meal.'

'Poor fellows, they do look hungry.' Marcia produced her purse and handed them a lira apiece. 'Because I haven't any luggage for you to carry, and because you like my dog,' she explained in Italian. 'Don't tell Uncle Howard,' she added in English. 'I don't believe one lira can make them paupers.'

'It would doubtless be difficult to pauperize them any more than they are at present,' he agreed.

'You don't believe in Uncle Howard's ideas of charity, do you?' she inquired tentatively.

'Oh, not entirely; but we don't quarrel over it.—Perhaps,' he suggested, 'we'd better go out and find an empty compartment while the guards are not looking. I fear they might object to Marcellus—is that his name?—occupying a first-class carriage.'

'Marcellus, because I found him by the theatre.'

'Ah—I hope he will turn out as handsome a fellow as his namesake. Come, Marcellus; it's time we were off.'

He picked the dog up by the nape of the neck and they started down the platform, looking for an empty carriage. They had their choice of a number; the train was not crowded, and first-class carriages in an Italian way-train are rarely in demand. As he was helping Marcia into the car, Sybert was amused to see Tarquinio, the proprietor of the Inn of the Italian People, hurrying into a third-class compartment, with a furtive glance over his shoulder as if he expected every corner to be an ambuscade of the secret police. The warning had evidently fallen on good ground, and the poor fellow was fleeing for his life from the wicked machinations of an omniscient premier.

'If you will excuse me a moment, I wish to speak to a friend,' Sybert said as he got Marcia settled; and without waiting for her answer, he strode off down the platform.

She had seen the young Italian, weighed down by a bundle tied up in a bed-quilt, give a glance of recognition as he passed them; and as she watched Sybert enter a third-class compartment she had not a doubt but that the Italian was the 'friend' he was searching. She leaned back in the corner with a puzzled frown. Why had Sybert so many queer friends in so many queer places, and why need he be so silent about them?

CHAPTER X

Sybert presently returned and dropped into the seat opposite Marcia; the guard slammed the door and the train pulled slowly out into the Campagna. They were both occupied with their own thoughts, and as neither found much pleasure in talking to the other, and both knew it, they made little pretence at conversation.

Marcia's excited mood had passed, and she leaned forward with her chin in her hand, watching rather pensively the soft Roman twilight as it crept over the Campagna. What she really saw, however, was the sunlit cloister of St. Paul Without the Walls and Paul Dessart's face as he talked to her. Was she really in love with him, she asked herself, or was it just— Italy? She did not know and she did not want to think. It was so much pleasanter merely to drift, and so very difficult to make up one's mind. Everything had been so care-free before, why must he bring the question to an issue? It was a question she did not wish to decide for a long, long time. Would he be willing to wait—to wait for an indefinite future that in the end might never come? Patience was not Paul's way. Suppose he refused to drift; suppose he insisted on his answer now—did she wish to give him up? No; quite frankly, she did not. She pictured him as he stood there in the cloister, with the warm sunlight and shadow playing about him, with his laughing, boyish face for the instant sober, his eager, insistent eyes bent upon her, his words for once stammering and halting. He was very attractive, very convincing; and yet she sighed. Life for her was still in the future. The world was new and full and varied, and experience was beckoning. There were many things to see and do, and she wanted to be free.

The short southern twilight faded quickly and a full moon took its place in a cloudless turquoise sky. The light flooded the dim compartment with a shimmering brilliancy, and outside it was almost dazzling in its glowing whiteness. Marcia leaned against the window, gazing out at the rolling plain. The tall arches of Aqua Felice were silhouetted darkly against the sky, and in the distance the horizon was broken by the misty outline of the Sabine hills. Now and then they passed a lonely group of farm-buildings set in a cluster of eucalyptus trees, planted against the fever; but for the most part the scene was barren and desolate, with scarcely a suggestion of actual, breathing human light. On the Appian Way were visible the gaunt outlines of Latin tombs, and occasionally the ruined remains of a mediaeval watch-tower. The picture was almost too perfect in its beauty; it was like the painted back drop for a spectacular play. Scarcely real, and yet one of the oldest things in the world—the rolling Campagna, the arches of the aqueducts, Rome behind and the Sabines before. So it had been for centuries; thousands of human lives were wrapped up in it. That was its charm. The picture was not inanimate, but pathetically human. As she looked far off across the plain so mournfully beautiful in its desolation, a sudden rush of feeling swept over her, a rush of that insane love of Italy which has engulfed so many foreigners in the waters of Lethe. She knew now how Paul felt. Italy! Italy! She loved it too.

A half-sob rose in her throat and her eyes filled with tears. She caught herself quickly and shrank back in the corner, with a glance at the man across to see if he were watching her. He was not. He sat rigid, looking out at the Campagna under half-shut eyelids. One hand was plunged deep in his pocket and the other lay on the dog's head to keep him quiet. Marcia noticed in surprise that while he appeared so calm, his fingers opened and shut nervously. She glanced up into his face again. He was staring at the picture before him as impassively as at a blank wall; but his eyes seemed more deep-set than usual and the under shadows darker. She half abstractedly fell to studying his face, wondering what was behind those eyes; what he could be thinking of.

He suddenly looked up and caught her gaze.

'I beg your pardon?' he asked.

'I didn't say anything.'

'You looked as if you did,' he said with a slight laugh, and turned away from the light. And now Marcia had the uncomfortable feeling that from under his drooping lids he was watching her. She turned back to the window again and tried to centre her attention on the shifting scene outside, but she was oppressively conscious of her silent companion. His face was in the shadow and she could not tell whether his eyes were open or shut. She tried to think of something to talk about, but no relevant subject presented itself. She experienced a nervous sense of relief when the train finally stopped at Palestrina.

The station-man, after some delay, found them a carriage with a reasonably rested-looking horse. As Sybert helped Marcia in he asked if she would object to letting a poor fellow with an unbeautifully large bundle sit on the front seat with the driver.

'We won't meet any one at this time of night,' he added. 'He's going to Castel Vivalanti and it's a long walk.'

'Certainly he may ride,' Marcia returned. 'It makes no difference to me whether we meet any one or not.'

'Oh, I beg your pardon,' Sybert smiled. 'I didn't mean to be disagreeable. Some ladies would object, you know. Tarquinio,' he called as the Italian with the bed-quilt shuffled past. 'The signorina invites you to ride, since we are going the same way.'

Tarquinio thanked the signorina with Italian courtesy, boosted up his bundle, and climbed up after it. Marcellus stretched himself comfortably in the bottom of the carriage, and with a canine sigh of content went peaceably to sleep. They set out between moonlit olive orchards and vineyards with the familiar daytime details of farm-buildings and ruins softened into a romantic beauty. Behind them stretched the outline of the Alban mountains, the moonlight catching the white walls of two twin villages which crowned the heights; and before them rose the more desolate Sabines, standing fold upon fold against the sky. It was for the most part a silent drive. Sybert at first, aware that he was more silent than politeness permitted, made a few casual attempts at conversation, and then with an apparently easy conscience folded his arms and returned to his thoughts. Marcia, too, had her thoughts, and the romance of the flower-scented moonlit night gave them their direction. Had Paul been there to urge his case anew, Italy would have helped in the pleading. But Paul had made a tiny mistake that day—he had taken her at her word and let her go alone—and the tiniest of mistakes is often big with consequences.

Once Sybert shifted his position and his hand accidentally touched Marcia's on the seat between them. 'Pardon me,' he murmured, and folded his arms again. She looked up at him quickly. The touch had run through her like an electric shock. Who was this man? she asked herself suddenly. What was he underneath? He seemed to be burning up inside; and she had always considered him apathetic, indifferent. She looked at him wide-eyed; she had never seen him like this. He reminded her of a suppressed volcano that would burst out some day with a sudden explosion. She again set herself covertly to studying his face. His character seemed an anomaly; it contradicted itself. Was it good or bad, simple or complex? Marcia did not have the key. She put together all the things she knew of him, all the things she had heard—the result was largely negative; the different pieces of evil cancelled each other. She knew him in society—he was several different persons there, but what was he when not in society? In his off hours? This afternoon, for example. Why should he be so at home by the Theatre of Marcellus? It was a long distance from the Embassy. And the man on the front seat, who was he? She suddenly interrupted the silence with a question. Sybert started at if he had forgotten she were there.

She repeated it: 'Is that man on the front seat Tarquinio Paterno who keeps a little trattoria in Rome?'

'Yes,' he returned, bringing a somewhat surprised gaze to rest upon her. 'How do you come to know his name?'

'Oh, I just guessed. I know Domenico Paterno, the Castel Vivalanti baker, and he told me about his son, Tarquinio. It's not such a very common name; so when you said this man was going to the village, and when I heard you call him Tarquinio, I thought—why were you surprised?' she broke off. 'Is there anything more to know about him?'

'You seem to have his family history pretty straight,' Sybert shrugged.

They lapsed into silence again, and Marcia did not attempt to break it a second time.

When they came to the turning where the steep road to Castel Vivalanti branches off from the highway, the driver halted to let Tarquinio get out. But Marcia remonstrated, that the bundle was too heavy for him to carry up the hill, and she told the man to drive on up to the gates of the town.

They jogged on up the winding ascent between orchards of olive and almond trees fringed with the airy leafage of spring. Above them the clustering houses of the village clung to the hilltop, tier above tier, the jagged sky-line of roofs and towers cut out clearly against the light.

Marcia had never visited Castel Vivalanti except in the unequivocal glare of day, which shows the dilapidated little town in all its dilapidation. But the moonlight changes all. The grey stone walls stretched above them now like some grim fortress city of the middle ages. And the old round tower, with its ruined drawbridge, looked as if it had seen dark deeds and kept the secret. It was just such a stronghold as the Cenci was murdered in.

They came to a stand before the tall arch of the Porta della Luna. While Tarquinio was climbing down and hoisting the bundle to his shoulder, Marcia's attention was momentarily attracted to a group of boys quarrelling over a game of morro in the gateway.

Suddenly, in the midst of Tarquinio's expressions of thanks to the signorina for helping a poor man on his journey, a frightened shriek rang out in a child's high voice, followed by a succession of long-drawn screams. The morro-players stopped their game and looked at each other with startled eyes; and then, after a moment of hesitation, went on with the play. At the first cry Sybert had leaped from the carriage, and seizing one of the boys by the shoulder, he demanded the cause.

The boy wriggled himself free with a gesture of unconcern.

'Gervasio Delano's mother is beating him. He always makes a great fuss because he is afraid.'

'What is it?' Marcia cried as she sprang from the carriage and ran up to Sybert.

'Some child's mother is beating him.'

The two, without waiting for any further explanations, turned in under the gate and hurried along the narrow way to the left, in the direction of the sounds. People had gathered in little groups in the doorways, and were shaking their heads and talking excitedly. One woman, as she caught sight of Marcia and Sybert, called out reassuringly that Teresa wasn't hurting the boy; he always cried harder than he was struck.

By the time they had reached the low doorway whence the sounds issued, the screams had died down to hysterical sobs. They plunged into the room which opened from the street, and then paused. It was so dark that for a moment they could not see anything. The only light came from a flickering oil-lamp burning before an image of the Madonna. But as their eyes became accustomed to the darkness they made out a stoutly built peasant woman standing at one end of the room and grasping in her hand an ox-goad such as the herdsmen on the Campagna use. For a moment they thought she was the only person there, until a low sob proclaimed the presence of a child who was crouching in the farthest corner.

'What do you want?' the woman asked, scowling angrily at the intruders.

'Have you been striking the child with that goad?' Sybert demanded.

'I strike the child with what I please,' the woman retorted. 'He is a lazy good-for-nothing and he stole the soup.'

Marcia drew the little fellow from the corner where he was sobbing steadily with long catches in his breath. His tears had gained such a momentum that he could not stop, but he clung to her convulsively, realizing that a deliverer of some sort was at hand. She turned him to the light and revealed a great red welt across his cheek where one of the blows had chanced to fall.

'It's outrageous! The woman ought to be arrested!' said Marcia, angrily.

Sybert took the lamp from the wall and bent over to look at him.

'Poor little devil! He looks as if he needed soup,' he muttered.

The woman broke in shrilly again to say that he was eleven years old and never brought in a single soldo. She slaved night and day to keep him fed, and she had children enough of her own to give to.

'Whose child is he?' Sybert demanded.

'He was my husband's,' the woman returned; 'and that husband is dead and I have a new one. The boy is in the way. I can't be expected to support him forever. It is time he was earning something for himself.'

Marcia sat down on a low stool and drew the boy to her.

'What can we do?' she asked, looking helplessly at Sybert. 'It won't do to leave him here. She would simply beat him to death as soon as our backs are turned.'

'I'm afraid she would,' he acknowledged. 'Of course I can threaten her with the police, but I don't believe it will do much good.' He was thinking that she might better adopt the boy than the dog, but he did not care to put his thoughts into words.

'I know!' she exclaimed as if in answer to his unspoken suggestion; 'I'll take him home for an errand-boy. He will be very useful about the place. Tell the woman, please, that I'm going to keep him, and make her understand that she has nothing to do with him any more.'

'Would Mrs. Copley like to have him at the villa?' Sybert inquired doubtfully. 'It's hardly fair——'

'Oh, yes. She won't mind if I insist—and I shall insist. Tell the woman, please.'

Sybert told the woman rather curtly that she need not be at the expense of feeding the boy any longer, the signorina would take him home to run errands.

The woman quickly changed her manner at this, and refused to part with him. Since she had cared for him when he was little, it was time for him to repay the debt now that she was growing old.

Sybert succinctly explained that she had forfeited all right to the child, and that if she made any trouble he would tell the police, who, he added parenthetically, were his dearest friends. Without further parleying, he picked up the boy and they walked out of the house, followed on the woman's part by angry prayers that 'apoplexies' might fall upon them and their descendants.

Curious groups of people had gathered outside the house, and they separated silently to let them pass. At the gateway the morro-players stopped their game to crowd around the carriage with shrill inquiries as to what was going to be done with Gervasio. The driver leaned from his seat and stared in stupid bewilderment at this rapid change of fares. But he whipped up his horse and started with dispatch, apparently moved by the belief that if he gave them time enough they would invite all Castel Vivalanti to drive.

As they rattled down the hill Sybert broke out into an amused laugh. 'I fear your aunt won't thank us, Miss Marcia, for turning Villa Vivalanti into a foundling-asylum.'

'She won't care when we tell her about it,' said Marcia, comfortably. She glanced down at the thin little face resting on Sybert's shoulder. 'Poor little fellow! He looks hungrier than Marcellus. The woman said he was eleven, and he's scarcely bigger than Gerald.'

Sybert closed his fingers around Gervasio's tiny brown wrist. 'He's pretty thin,' he remarked; 'but that can soon be remedied. These peasant children are hardy little things when they have half a chance.' He looked down at the boy, who was watching their faces with wide-open, excited eyes, half frightened at the strange language. 'You mustn't be afraid, Gervasio,' he reassured him in Italian. 'The signorina is taking you home with her to Villa Vivalanti, where you won't be whipped any more and will have all you want to eat. You must be a good boy and do everything she tells you.'

Gervasio's eyes opened still wider. 'Will the signorina give me chocolate?' he asked.

'He's one of the children I gave chocolate to, and he remembers it!' Marcia said delightedly. 'I thought his face was familiar. Yes, Gervasio,' she added in her very careful Italian. 'I will give you chocolate if you always do what you are told, but not every day, because chocolate is not good for little boys. You must eat bread and meat and soup, and grow big and strong like—like Signor Siberti here.'

Sybert laughed and Marcia joined him.

'I begin to appreciate Aunt Katherine's anxiety for Gerald—do you suppose there is any danger of malaria at Villa Vivalanti?'

For the rest of the drive they chatted quite gaily over the adventure. Sybert for the time dismissed whatever he had on his mind; and as for Marcia—St. Paul's cloisters were behind in Rome. As they turned into the avenue the lights of the villa gleamed brightly through the trees.

'See, Gervasio,' said Sybert. 'That is where you are going to live.'

Gervasio nodded, too awed to speak. Presently he whispered, 'Shall I see the little principino?'

'The little principino? what does he mean?' Marcia asked.

'The little principino with yellow hair,' Gervasio repeated.

'Gerald!' Sybert laughed. 'The 'principino' is good for a free-born American. Ah—and here is the old prince,' he added, as the carriage wheels grated on the gravel before the loggia and Copley stepped out from the hall to see who had come.

'Hello! is that you, Sybert?' he called out in surprise. 'And, Marcia! I thought you had decided to stay in town—what in the deuce have you brought with you?'

'A boy and a dog, O Prince,' said Sybert, as he set Gervasio on his feet. 'Miss Marcia must plead guilty to the dog, but I will take half the blame for the boy.'

Gervasio and Marcellus were conveyed into the hall, and it would be difficult to say which was the more frightened of the two. Marcellus slunk under a chair and whined at the lights, and Gervasio looked after him as if he were tempted to follow. Mrs. Copley, attracted by the disturbance, appeared from the salon, and a medley of questions and explanations ensued. Gervasio, meanwhile, sat up very straight and very scared, clutching the arms of the big carved chair in which Sybert had placed him.

'We thought he might be useful to run errands,' Sybert suggested as they finished the account of the boy's maltreatment.

'Poor child!' said Mrs. Copley. 'We can find something for him to do. He is small, but he looks intelligent. I have always intended to have a little page—or he might even do as a tiger for Gerald's pony-cart.'

'No, Aunt Katherine,' expostulated Marcia. 'I shan't have him dressed in livery. I don't think it's right to turn him into a servant before he's old enough to choose.'

'The position of a trained servant is a much higher one than he would ever fill if left to himself. He is only a peasant child, my dear.'

'He is a psychological problem,' she declared. 'I am going to prove that environment is everything and heredity's nothing, and I shan't have him dressed in livery. I found him, and he's mine—at least half mine.'

She glanced across at Sybert and he nodded approval.

'I will turn my share of the authority over to you, Miss Marcia, since it appears to be in such good hands.'

'Marcia shall have her way,' said Mr. Copley. 'We'll let Gervasio be an unofficial page and postpone the question of livery for the present.'

'He can play with Gerald,' she suggested. 'We were wishing the other night that he had some one to play with, and Gervasio will be just the person; it will be good for his Italian.'

'I suspect that Gervasio's Italian may not be useful for drawing-room purposes,' her uncle laughed.

'I shall send him to college,' she added, her mind running ahead of present difficulties, 'and prove that peasants are really as bright as princes, if they have the same chance. He'll turn out a genius like—like Crispi.'

'Heaven forbid!' exclaimed Sybert, but he examined Marcia with a new interest in his eyes.

'We can decide on the young man's career later,' Copley suggested. 'He seems to be embarrassed by these personalities.'

Gervasio, with all these august eyes upon him, was on the point of breaking out into one of his old-time wails when Mrs. Copley fortunately diverted the attention by inquiring if they had dined.

'Neither Mr. Sybert nor I have had any dinner,' Marcia returned, 'and I shouldn't be surprised if Gervasio has missed several. But Marcellus, under the chair there, has had his,' she added.

Mrs. Copley recalling her duties as hostess, a jangling of bells ensued. Pietro appeared, and stared at Gervasio with as much astonishment as is compatible with the office of butler. Mrs. Copley ordered dinner for two in the dining-room and for one in the kitchen, and turned the boy over to Pietro's care.

'Oh, let's have him eat with us, just for to-night.' Marcia pleaded. 'You don't mind, do you, Mr. Sybert? He's so hungry; I love to watch hungry little boys eat.'

'Marcia!' expostulated her aunt in disgust. 'How can you say such things? The child is barefooted.'

'Since my own son and heir is banished from the dinner-table, I object to an unwashed alien's taking his place,' Copley put in. 'Gervasio will dine with the cook.'

To Gervasio's infinite relief, he was led off to the kitchen and consigned to the care of François, who later in the evening confided to Pietro that he didn't believe the boy had ever eaten before. Marcia's and Sybert's dinner that night was an erratic affair and quite upset the traditions of the Copley ménage. To Pietro's scandalization, the two followed him into the kitchen between every course to see how their protégé was progressing.

Gervasio sat perched on a three-legged stool before the long kitchen table, his little bare feet dangling in space, an ample towel about his neck, while an interested scullery-maid plied him with viands. He would have none of the strange dishes that were set before him, but with an expression of settled purpose on his face was steadily eating his way through a bowl of macaroni. It was with a sigh that he had finally to acknowledge himself beaten by the Copley larder. Marcia called Bianca (Marietta's successor) and bade her give Gervasio a bath and a bed. Bianca had known the boy in his pre-villa days, and, if anything, was more wide-eyed than Pietro on his sudden promotion.

As Marcia was starting upstairs that night, Sybert strolled across the hall toward her and held out his hand.

'How would it be if we declared an amnesty,' he inquired—'at least until Gervasio is fairly started in his career?'

She glanced up in his face a second, surprised, and then shook her head with an air of scepticism. 'We can try,' she smiled, 'but I am afraid we were meant to be enemies.'

Her room was flooded with moonlight; she undressed without lighting her candle, and slipping on a light woollen kimono, sat down on a cushion beside the open window. She was too excited and restless to sleep. She leaned her chin on her hand, with her elbow resting on the low window-sill, and let the cool breeze fan her face.

After a time she heard some one strike a match on the loggia, and her uncle and Sybert came out to the terrace and paced back and forth, talking in low tones. She could hear the rise and fall of their voices, and every now and then the breeze wafted in the smell of their cigars. She grew wider and wider awake, and followed them with her eyes as they passed and repassed in their tireless tramp. At the end of the terrace their voices sank to a low murmur, and then by the loggia they rose again until she could hear broken sentences. Sybert's voice sounded angry, excited, almost fierce, she thought; her uncle's, low, decisive, half contemptuous.

Once, as they passed under the window, she heard her uncle say sharply: 'Don't be a fool, Sybert. It will make a nasty story if it gets out—and nothing's gained.'

She did not hear Sybert's reply, but she saw his angry gesture as he flung away the end of his cigar. The men paused by the farther end of the terrace and stood for several minutes arguing in lowered tones. Then, to Marcia's amazement, Sybert leaped the low parapet by the ilex grove and struck out across the fields, while her uncle came back across the terrace alone, entered the house, and closed the door. She sat up straight with a quickly beating heart. What was the matter? Could they have quarrelled? Was Sybert going to the station? Surely he would not walk. She leaned out of the window and looked after him, a black speck in the moonlit wheat-field. No, he was going toward Castel Vivalanti. Why Castel Vivalanti at this time of the night? Had it anything to do with Gervasio?—or perhaps Tarquinio, the baker's son? She recalled her uncle's words: 'Don't be a fool. It will make a nasty story if it gets out.' Perhaps people's suspicions against him were true, after all. She thought of his look that night in the train. What was behind it? And then she thought of the picture of him in the carriage with the little boy in his arms. A man who was so kind to children could not be bad at heart. And yet, if he were all that her uncle had thought him, why did he have so many enemies—and so many doubtful friends?

The breeze had grown cold, and she rose with a quick shiver and went to bed. She lay a long time with wide-open eyes watching the muslin curtains sway in the wind. She thought again of Paul Dessart's words in the warm, sleepy, sunlit cloister; of the little crowd of ragamuffins chasing the dog; of her long, silent ride with Sybert; of the moonlit gateway of Castel Vivalanti, with the dark, high walls towering above. Her thoughts were growing hazy and she was almost asleep when, mingled with a half-waking dream, she heard footsteps cross the terrace and the hall door open softly.

CHAPTER XI

Marcia was awakened the next morning by Bianca knocking at the door, with the information that Gervasio wished to get up, and that, as his clothes were very ragged, she had taken the liberty the night before of throwing them away.

For an instant Marcia blinked uncomprehendingly; then, as the events of the evening flashed through her mind, she sat up in bed, and solicitously clasping her knees in her hands, considered the problem. She felt, and not without reason, that Gervasio's future success at the villa depended largely on the impression he made at this, his first formal appearance. She finally dispatched Bianca to try him with one of Gerald's suits, and to be very sure that his face was clean. Meanwhile she hurried through with her own dressing in order to be the first to inspect his rehabilitation.

As she was putting the last touches to her hair she heard a murmur of voices on the terrace, and peering out cautiously, beheld her uncle and Sybert lounging on the parapet engaged with cigarettes. She had not been dreaming, then; those were Sybert's steps she had heard the night before. She puckered her brow over the puzzle and peered out again. Whatever had happened last night, there was nothing electrical in the air this morning. The two had apparently shoved all inflammable subjects behind them and were merely waiting idly until coffee should be served.

It was a beautifully peaceful spring morning that she looked out upon. The two men on the terrace appeared to be in mood with the day—careless, indifferent loungers, nothing more. And last night? She recalled their low, fierce, angry tones; and the lines in her forehead deepened. This was a chameleon world, she thought. As she stood watching them, Gervasio for the moment forgotten, Gerald ran up to the two with some childish prattle which called forth a quick, amused laugh. Sybert stretched out a lazy hand and drew the boy toward him. Carefully balancing his cigarette on the edge of one of the terra-cotta vases, he rose to his feet and tossed the little fellow in the air four or five times. Gerald screamed with delight and called for more. Sybert laughingly declined, as he resumed his cigarette and his seat on the balustrade.

The little play recalled Marcia to her duty. With a shake of her head at matters in general, she gave them up, and turned her face toward Gervasio's quarters. Bianca was on her knees before the boy, giving the last touches to his sailor tie, and she turned him slowly around for inspection. His appearance was even more promising than Marcia had hoped for. With his dark curls still damp from their unwonted ablutions, clad in one of Gerald's baggiest sailor-suits of red linen with a rampant white collar and tie, except for his bare feet (which would not be forced into Gerald's shoes) he might have been a little princeling himself, backed by a hundred noble ancestors.

Marcia sank down on her knees beside him. 'You little dear!' she exclaimed as she kissed him.

Gervasio was not used to caresses, and for a moment he drew back, his brown eyes growing wide with wonder. Then a smile broke over his face, and he reached out a timid hand and patted her confidingly on the cheek. She kissed him again in pure delight, and taking him by the hand, set out forthwith for the loggia.

'Ecco! my friends. Isn't he beautiful?' she demanded.

Mr. Copley and Sybert sprang to their feet and came forward interestedly.

'Who denies now that it's clothes that make the man?'

'I can't say but that he was as picturesque last night,' her uncle returned; 'but he's undoubtedly cleaner this morning.'

'Where's Gerald?' asked Sybert. 'Let's see what he has to say of the new arrival.'

Gerald, who had but just discovered Marcellus, was delightedly romping in the garden with him, and was dragged away under protest and confronted with the stranger. He examined him in silence a moment and then remarked, 'He's got my cloves on.' And suddenly, as a terrible idea dawned upon him, he burst out: 'Is he a new bruvver? 'Cause if he is you can take him away.'

'Oh, my dear!' his mother remonstrated in horror. 'He's a little Italian boy.'

Gerald was visibly relieved. He examined Gervasio again from this new point of view.

'I want to go wifout my shoes and socks,' he declared.

'Oh, but he's going to wear shoes and socks, too, as soon we can get some to fit him,' said Marcia.

'Do you want to see my lizhyards?' Gerald asked insinuatingly, suddenly making up his mind and pulling Gervasio by the sleeve.

Gervasio backed away.

'You must talk to him in Italian, Gerald,' Sybert suggested. 'He's like Marietta: he doesn't understand anything else. I should like to have another look at those lizards myself,' he added. 'Come on, Gervasio,' and taking a boy by each hand, he strode off toward the fountain.

Mrs Copley looked after them dubiously, but Marcia interposed, 'He's a dear little fellow, Aunt Katherine, and it will be good for Gerald to have some one to play with.'

'Marcia's right, Katherine; it won't hurt him any, and I doubt if the boy's Italian is much worse than Bianca's.'

Thus Gervasio's formal installation at the villa. For the first week or so his principal activity was eating, until he was in the way of becoming as rosy-cheeked as Gerald himself. During the early stages of his career he was consigned to the kitchen, where François served him with soup and macaroni to the point of bursting. Later, having learned to wield a knife and fork without disaster, he was advanced to the nursery, where he supped with Gerald under the watchful eye of Granton.

Taken all in all, Gervasio proved a valuable addition to the household. He was sweet-tempered, eager to please, and pitifully grateful for the slightest kindness. He became Gerald's faithful henchman and implicitly obeyed his commands, with only an occasional rebellion when they were over-oppressive. He was quick to learn, and it was not long before he was jabbering in a mixture of Italian and English with a vocabulary nearly as varied as Gerald's own.

The first week following Gervasio's advent was a period of comparative quiet at the villa, but one fairly disturbing little contretemps occurred to break the monotony.

The boy had been promised a reward of sweet chocolate as soon as he should learn to wear shoes and stockings with a smiling face—shoes and stockings being, in his eyes, an objectionable feature of civilization. When it came time for payment, however, Marcia discovered that there was no sweet chocolate in the house, and, not to disappoint him, she ordered Gerald's pony-carriage, and taking with her the two boys and a groom, set out for Castel Vivalanti and the baker's. Had she stopped to think, she would have known that to take Gervasio to Castel Vivalanti in broad daylight was not a wise proceeding. But it was a frequent characteristic of the Copleys that they did their thinking afterward. The spectacle of Gervasio Delano in a carriage with the principino, and in new clothes, with his face washed, very nearly occasioned a mob among his former playmates. The carriage was besieged, and Marcia found it necessary to distribute a considerable largess of copper before she could rid herself of her following.

As she laughingly escaped from the crowd and drove out through the gateway a man stepped forward from the corner of the wall and motioned her to stop. For a moment a remembrance of her aunt's rencontre with the Camorrist flashed through her mind, and then she smiled as she reflected that it was broad daylight and in full sight of the town. She pulled the pony to a standstill and asked him what he wanted. He was Gervasio's stepfather, he said. They were poor, hard-working people and did not have enough to eat, but they were very lonely without the boy and wished to have him back. Even American princes, he added, couldn't take poor people's children away without their permission. And he finished by insinuating that if he were paid enough he might reconsider the matter.

Marcia did not understand all that he said, but as Gervasio began to cry, and at the same time clasped both hands firmly about the seat in an evident determination to resist all efforts to dislodge him, she saw what he meant, and replied that she would tell the police. But the man evidently thought that he had the upper hand of the situation, and that she would rather buy him off than let the boy go. With a threatening air, he reached out and grasped Gervasio roughly by the arm. Gervasio screamed, and Marcia, before she thought of possible consequences, struck the man a sharp blow with the whip and at the same time lashed the pony into a gallop. They dashed down the stony road and around the corners at a perilous rate, while the man shouted curses from the top of the hill.

They reached the villa still bubbling with excitement over the adventure, and caused Mrs. Copley no little alarm. But when Marcia greeted her uncle's arrival that night with the story, he declared that she had done just right; and without waiting for dinner, he remounted his horse, and galloping back to Castel Vivalanti, rode straight up to the door of the little trattoria, where the fellow was engaged in drinking wine and cursing Americans. There he told him, before an interested group of witnesses, that Gervasio was not his child; that since he could not treat him decently he had forfeited all claim to him; and that if he tried to levy any further blackmail he would find himself in prison. Wherewith he wheeled his horse's head about and made a spectacular exit from the town. If anything were needed to strengthen Gervasio's position with Mr. Copley, this incident answered the purpose.

As a result of the adventure, Marcia, for the time, dropped Castel Vivalanti from her calling-list and extended her acquaintance in the other direction. She came to be well known as she galloped about the country-side on a satin-coated little sorrel (born and bred in Kentucky), followed by a groom on a thumping cob, who always respectfully drew up behind her when she stopped. As often as she could think of any excuse, she visited the peasants in their houses, laughing gaily with them over her own queer grammar. It was an amused curiosity which at first actuated her friendliness. Their ingenious comments and naïve questions in regard to America proved an ever-diverting source of interest; but after a little, as she understood them better, she grew to like them for their own stanch virtues. When she looked about their gloomy little rooms, with almost no furnishing except a few copper pots and kettles and a tawdry picture of the Madonna, and saw what meagre, straitened lives they led, and yet how bravely they bore them, her amusement changed to respect. Their quick sympathy and warm friendliness awakened an answering spark, and it was not long before she had discovered for herself the lovable charm of the Italian peasant.

She explored, in the course of her rides, many a forgotten little mountain village topping a barren crag of the Sabines, and held by some Roman prince in almost the same feudal tenure as a thousand years ago. They were picturesque enough from below, these huddling grey-stone hamlets shooting up from the solid rock; but when she had climbed the steeply winding path and had looked within, she found them miserable and desolate beyond belief. She was coming to see the under side of a great deal of picturesqueness.

Meanwhile, though life was moving in an even groove at Villa Vivalanti, the same could not be said of the rest of Italy. Each day brought fresh reports of rioting throughout the southern provinces, and travellers hurrying north reported that every town of any size was under martial law. In spite of reassuring newspaper articles, written under the eye of the police, it was evident that affairs were fast approaching a crisis. There was not much anxiety felt in the immediate neighbourhood of Rome, for the capital was too great a stronghold of the army to be in actual danger from mobs. The affair, if anything, was regarded as a welcome diversion from the tediousness of Lent, and the embassies and large hotels where the foreigners congregated were animated by a not unpleasurable air of excitement.

Conflicting opinions of every sort were current. Some shook their heads wisely, and said that in their opinion the matter was much more serious than appeared on the surface. They should not be surprised to see the scenes of the French Commune enacted over again; and they intimated further, that since it had to happen, they were very willing to be on hand in time to see the fun.

Many expressed the belief that the trouble had nothing to do with the price of bread; the wheat famine was merely a pretext for stirring up the people. It was well known that the universities, the younger generation of writers and newspaper men, even the ranks of the army, were riddled with socialism. What more likely than that the socialists and the church adherents had united to overthrow the government, intending as soon as their end was accomplished to turn upon each other and fight it out for supremacy? It was the opinion of these that the government should have adopted the most drastic measures possible, and was doing very foolishly in catering to the populace by putting down the dazio. Still others held that the government should have abolished the dazio long before, and that the people in the south did very well to rise and demand their rights. And so the affairs of the unfortunate Neapolitans were the subject of conversation at every table d'hôte in Rome; and the forestieri sojourning within the walls derived a large amount of entertainment from the matter.

Marcia Copley, however, had heard little of the gathering trouble. She did not read the papers, and her uncle did not mention the matter at home. He was too sick at heart to dwell on it uselessly, and it was not a subject he cared to discuss with his niece. His family, indeed, saw very little of him, for he had thrown himself into the work of the Foreign Relief Committee with characteristic energy, and he spent the most of his time in Rome. Marcia's interest in sight-seeing had come to a sudden halt since the afternoon of Tre Fontane. She had ventured into the city only once, and then merely to attend to the purchase of clothes for Gervasio. The Roystons, on that occasion, had been out when she called at their hotel, and her feeling of regret was mingled largely with relief as she left her card and retired in safety to Villa Vivalanti.

She had not analysed her emotions very thoroughly, but she felt a decided trepidation at the thought of seeing Paul. The trepidation, however, was not altogether an unpleasant sensation. The scene in the cloisters had returned to her mind many times, and she had taken several brief excursions into the future. What would he say the next time they met? Would he renew the same subject, or would he tacitly overlook that afternoon, and for the time let everything be as it had been before? She hoped that the latter would be the case. It would give a certain piquancy to their relations, and she was not ready—just at present—to make up her mind.

Paul, on his side, had also pondered the question somewhat. Events were not moving with the rapidity he wished. Marcia, evidently, would not come into Rome, and he could think of no valid excuse for going out to the villa. His pessimistic forecast of events had proved true. Holy Week found the Roystons still in the city, treating themselves to orgies of church-going. As he followed his aunt from church to church (there are in the neighbourhood of three hundred and seventy-five in Rome, and he says they visited them all that week) he indulged in many speculations as to the state of Marcia's mind in regard to himself. At times he feared he had been over-precipitate; at others, that he had not been precipitate enough.

His aunt and cousins returned from a flying visit to the villa, with the report that Marcia had adopted a boy and a dog and was solicitously engaged with their education. 'What did she say about me, Madge?' Paul boldly inquired.

'She said you were a very impudent fellow,' Margaret retorted; and in response to his somewhat startled expression she added more magnanimously: 'You needn't be so vain as to think she said anything about you. She never even mentioned your name.'

Paul breathed a meditative 'Ah!' Marcia had not mentioned his name. It was not such a bad sign, that: she was thinking about him, then. If there were no other man—and he was vain enough to take her at her word—nothing could be better for his cause than a solitary week in the Sabine hills. He knew from present—and past—experience that an Italian spring is a powerful stimulant for the heart.

On Tuesday of Holy Week Mrs. Royston wakened slightly from her spiritual trance to observe that she had scarcely seen Marcia for as much as a week, and that as soon as Lent was over they must have the Copleys in to luncheon at the hotel.

'Where's the use of waiting till Lent's over?' Paul had inquired. 'You needn't make it a function. Just a sort of—family affair. If you invite them for Thursday, we can all go together to the tenebræ service at St. Peter's. As this is Miss Copley's first Easter in Rome, she might be interested.'

Accordingly a note arrived at the villa on Wednesday morning inviting the family—Gerald included—to breakfast the next day with the Roystons in Rome. On Thursday morning an acceptance—Gerald excluded—arrived at the Hôtel de Lourdres et Paris, and was followed an hour later by the Copleys themselves.

The breakfast went off gaily. Paul was his most expansive self, and the whole table responded to his mood. It was with a sense of gratification that Marcia saw her uncle, who had lately been so grave, laughingly exchanging nonsense with the young man. She felt, though she would scarcely have acknowledged it to herself, a certain property right in Paul, and it pleased her subtly when he pleased other people. She sat next to him at the table, and occasionally, beneath his laughter and persiflage, she caught an undertone of meaning. So long as they were not alone and he could not go beyond a certain point, she found their relations on a distinctly satisfying basis.

In spite of Paul's manœuvres, he did not find himself alone with Marcia that afternoon. There was always a cousin in attendance. Mr. and Mrs. Copley, declining the spectacle of the tenebræ in St. Peter's—they had seen it before—left shortly after luncheon. As they were leaving, Mr. Copley remarked to Mrs. Royston—

'I will entrust my niece to your care, and please do not lose sight of her until you put her in my hands for the evening train. I wish no more such escapades as we had the other day.' And, to Marcia's discomfort, the adventures involving the rescue of Marcellus and Gervasio were recounted in detail. For an unexplained reason, she would have preferred the story of their origin to remain in darkness.

Paul's face clouded slightly. 'My objections to Sybert grow rapidly,' he remarked in an undertone.

Marcia laughed. 'If you could have seen him! He never spoke a word to me all the way out in the train. He sat with his arms folded and a frown on his brow, like—Napoleon at Moscow.'

Paul's face brightened again. 'Oh, I begin to like him, after all,' he declared.

Toward five o'clock that evening every carriage in the city seemed to be bent for the Ponte Sant' Angelo. A casual spectator would never have chosen a religious function as the end of all this confusion. In the tangle of narrow streets beyond the bridge the way was almost blocked, and such progress as was possible was made at a snail's pace. The Royston party, in two carriages, not unnaturally lost each other. The carriage containing Marcia, Margaret, and Paul, getting into the jam in the narrow Borgo Nuovo, arrived in the piazza of St. Peter's with wheels locked with a cardinal's coach. The cardinal's coachman and theirs exchanged an unclerical opinion of each other's ability as drivers. The cardinal advanced his head from the window with a mildly startled air of reproof, and the Americans laughed gaily at the situation. After a moment of scrutiny the cardinal smiled back, and the four disembarked and set out on foot across the piazza, leaving the men to sever the difficulty at their leisure. He proved an unexpectedly cordial person, and when they parted on the broad steps he held out of his hand with a friendly smile and after a moment of perplexed hesitation the three gravely shook it in turn.

'Do you think we ought to have kissed it?' Marcia inquired. 'I would have done it, only I didn't know how.'

Paul laughed. 'He knew we weren't of the true faith. No right-minded Catholic would laugh at nearly spilling a cardinal in the street.'

They stood aside by the central door looking for Mrs. Royston and Eleanor and watching the crowd surge past. Paul was quite insistent that they should go in without the others, but Marcia was equally insistent that they wait. She had an intuitive feeling that there was safety in numbers.

For a wonder they presently espied Mrs. Royston bearing down upon them, a small camp-stool clutched to her portly bosom, and Eleanor panting along behind, a camp-stool in either hand.

Mrs. Royston caught sight of them with an expression of relief.

'My dears, I was afraid I had lost you,' she gasped. 'We remembered, just as we got to the bridge, that we hadn't brought any chairs, and so we went back for them. Paul, you should have thought of them yourself. I suppose we'd better hurry in and get a good place.'

Paul patiently possessed himself of the chairs and followed the ladies, with a glance at Marcia which seemed to say, 'Is there this day living a more exemplary nephew and gentleman than I?'

The tenebræ service on Holy Thursday is the one time in the year when St. Peter's may be seen at night. The great church looms vaster and emptier and more solemn then than at any other time. The eye cannot penetrate to the distant dome hidden in shadows. The long nave stretches interminably into space, the chapels deepen and broaden until they are churches themselves. The clustered pillars reach upward till they are lost in the darkness. What the eye cannot grasp the imagination seizes upon, and the vast interior grows and widens until it seems to stretch out arms to inclose all Christendom itself. On this one night it does inclose all Rome—nobility and peasants, Italians and foreigners: those who are of the faith, and those who are merely spectators; those who come to worship; those who come to be amused—St. Peter's receives them all with the same impartiality.

Standing outside, it had seemed to them that the whole city had flowed through the doors; but within, the church was still approximately empty. As they walked down the broad nave in the dimness of twilight, Marcia turned to the young man beside her.

'At first I didn't think St. Peter's was impressive—that is, compared to Milan and Cologne and some of the other cathedrals—but it's like the rest of Rome, it grows and grows until——'

'It comes to be the whole world,' he supplied.

By the bronze baldacchino Mrs. Royston spread her camp-stools and sat down.

'This is the best place we could choose,' she said contentedly as she folded her hands. 'We shan't be very near the choir, but we can hear just as well, and we shall have an excellent view of the altar-washing and the sacred relics.' She spoke in the tone of one who is picking out a stall for a theatrical performance.

From time to time friends of either the Roystons or Marcia drifted up and, having paused to chat a few minutes, passed on, giving place to others. As one group left them with smiles and friendly bows, Marcia turned to Paul, who was standing beside her.

'It's really dreadful,' she said, 'the way the foreigners take possession of Rome. This might as well be a reception at the Embassy. If I were the pope, I would put up a sign on the door of St. Peter's saying, "No forestieri admitted."'

'Ah, but there are no forestieri in the case of St. Peter's; it belongs to all nations.'

Marcia smiled at the young man and turned away; and as she turned she caught, across an intervening stream of heads, a face, looking in her direction, wearing about the eyes a curiously quizzical expression. It was the face of a middle-aged woman—an interesting face—not exactly beautiful, but sparkling with intelligence. It seemed very familiar to Marcia, and as her eyes lingered on it a moment the quizzical expression gave place to one of amused friendliness. The woman smiled and bowed and passed on. Marcia bowed vaguely, and then it flashed through her mind who it was—the lady who wrote, the 'greatest gossip in Rome,' whom she had met at the studio tea so many weeks before. She had forgotten all about her unknown friend of that day, and now she turned quickly to Paul to ask her identity. Paul was engaged in answering some question of his aunt's, and before she could gain his attention again a hush swept over the great interior and everything else was forgotten in the opening chorus of the 'Miserere.'

The twilight had deepened, and the great white dome shone dimly far above the blackness of the crowd. The voices of the papal choir swelled louder and louder in the solemn chant, and high and separate and alone rose the clear, flute-like treble of the 'Pope's Nightingale.' And as an undertone, an accompaniment to the music, the shuffle and murmur of thirty thousand listeners rose and fell like the distant beat of surf.

The candles on the altar showed dimly above their heads. As the service continued, one by one the lights were extinguished. After half an hour or so, the waiting and intensity grew wearing. The crowd was pressing closer, and Margaret Royston craned her neck, vainly trying to discover how many candles remained. Paul, with ready imagination, was answering his aunt's questions as to the meaning of the ceremonies. Margaret turned to Marcia.

'Poke this young priest in front of me,' she whispered, 'and ask him in Italian how many candles are left.'

The young priest, overhearing the words, turned around with an amused smile, obligingly stood on his tiptoes to look at the altar, and replied in English that there were three.

'Thank you,' said Margaret; 'I didn't suppose you could talk English.'

'I was born in Troy, New York.'

'Really?' she laughed, and the two fell to comparing the rival merits of the Hudson and the Tiber.

He proved most friendly, carefully explaining to the party the significance of the service and the meaning of the different symbols. Mrs. Royston looked reproachfully at her nephew, whose stories, it transpired, did not accord with fact.

'You really couldn't expect me to know as much as a professional, Aunt Eleanor,' he unblushingly expostulated. My explanations were more picturesque than his, at any rate; and if they aren't true, they ought to be.'

The last candle was finally out, and for a moment the great interior remained in darkness. Then a noise like the distant rattle of thunder symbolized the rending of the veil, and in an instant lights sprang out from every arch and pier and dome. A long procession of cardinals, choristers, and acolytes wound singing to the high altar—the 'Altar of the World.' Marcia stood by the railing and watched their faces as they filed past. They were such thoughtful, spiritual, kindly faces that her respect for this great power—the greatest power in Christendom—increased momentarily. She felt a sort of shame to be there merely as a spectator. She looked about at the faces of the peasants, and thought what a barren, barren existence would be theirs without this church, which promised the only joy they could ever hope to have.

When the ceremony of washing the altar with oil and wine was ended, the young priest bade them a friendly good evening. He could not wait for the holy relics, he said; they had supper at the monastery at seven o'clock. He hastily added, however, in response to the smile trembling on Margaret's lips, 'Not that they are not the true relics and very holy, but I have seen them several times before.'

The relics were exhibited to the multitude from St. Veronica's balcony far above their heads. Paul whispered to Marcia with a little laugh:

'Our friend the cardinal would be gratified, would he not, to see his heretics bowing before St. Veronica's handkerchief? Look,' he added, 'at that peasant woman in her blue skirt and scarlet kerchief. She has probably walked fifty miles, with her baby strapped to a board. I suppose she thinks the child will have good fortune the rest of his life If he just catches a glimpse of a splinter of the true cross.'

Marcia looked at the woman standing beside her, a pilgrim from the Abruzzi, judging from her dress. She was raising an illumined face to the little balcony where the priest was holding above their heads the holy relic. In her arms she held a baby whose face she was turning upward also, while she murmured prayers in his ears. Marcia's glance wandered away over the crowd—the poor pilgrim peasants whose upturned faces, worn by work and poverty, were softened for the moment into a holy awe. Then she raised her eyes to the balcony where the priest in his white robes was holding high above his head the shining silver cross in which was incased St. Peter's dearest relic, the tiny splinter of the true cross. The light was centred on the little balcony; every eye in the great concourse was fixed upon it. The priest was fat, his face was red, his attitude theatrical. The whole spectacle was theatrical. A quick revulsion of feeling passed over her. A few moments before, as she watched the procession of cardinals, she had been ready to admit the spiritual significance of the scene; now she saw only its spectacular side. It was merely a play, a delusion got up to dazzle the poor peasants. This church was the only thing they had in life, and, after all, what did it do for them? What could St. Veronica's handkerchief, what could a splinter of the true cross, do to brighten their lives? It was superstition, not religion, that was being offered to the peasants of Italy.

She looked again across the sea of upturned faces and shook her head. 'Isn't it pitiful?' she asked.

'Isn't it picturesque?' echoed Paul.

'That priest up there knows he's deluding all these people, and he's just as solemn as if he believed in the relics himself. The church is still so hopelessly mediaeval!'

'That's the beauty of the church,' Paul objected. 'It's still mediaeval, while the rest of the world is so hopelessly nineteenth-century. I like to see these peasants believing in St. Veronica's handkerchief and the power of the sacred Bambino to cure disease. I think it's a beautiful exhibition of faith in a world where faith is out of fashion. I don't blame the priests in the least for keeping it up. It's a protest against the age. They're about the only artists left. If I were a priest I'd learn prestidigitation, and substantiate the efficacy of the relics with a miracle or so.'

'It's simply fostering superstition.'

'Take their superstition away and you deprive them of their most picturesque quality.'

'You don't care for anything but what's picturesque!' she exclaimed in a tone half scornful.

Paul did not answer. The ceremony was over and the crowd was beginning to pour out. They turned with the stream and wedged their way toward the right-hand entrance, near which their carriages were waiting. Paul manœuvred very adroitly so that the crowd should separate them from the rest of the party at the door.

'I will tell you what I care for most,' he said in her ear as they pushed out into the portico. 'I care for you.'

She perceived his drift too late and looked back with an air of dismay. The others were lost in the moving mass of heads.

Paul saw her glance and laughed. 'You're going to take good care that we shan't be alone together, aren't you?'

Marcia echoed his laugh. 'Yes,' she acknowledged frankly; 'I'm trying to.'

'It doesn't matter. My time's coming; you can't put it off.' His hand touched hers hanging at her side and he clasped it firmly. 'Come here; we'll get out of this crowd,' and he pushed on outside and drew back into a corner by one of the tall columns. The crowd surged past, flowing down the steps like a river widening to the sea. Below them the piazza was black with a tossing, moving mass of carriages and people. The mass of the Vatican at their left loomed a black bulk in the night, its hundreds of windows shining in the reflected lights of the piazza like the eyes of a great octopus. At another time Marcia might have looked very curiously toward the palace. She might have wondered if in one of those dark windows Leo was not standing brooding over the throng of worshippers who had come that day. How must a pope feel to see thirty thousand people go out from under his roof—go out freely to their homes—while he alone may not step across the threshold? At another time she would have paused to play a little with the thought, but now her attention was engaged. Paul still held her hand.

He squared himself in front of her, with his back to the crowd. 'Have you been thinking about what I asked you?'

Had she been thinking! She had been doing nothing else. She looked at him reproachfully. 'Let's not talk about it. The more I think, the more I don't know.'

'That's an unfortunate state to be in. Perhaps I can help you to make up your mind. Are you going to be in love with me some day, Marcia—soon?' he persisted.

'I—I don't know.'

He leaned toward her, with his face very close to hers. She shrank back further into the shadow. 'There they are!' she exclaimed, as she caught sight of Eleanor's head above the crowd, and she tried to draw her hand away.

'Never mind them. They won't be here for three minutes. You've got time enough to answer me.'

'Please, not now—Paul,' she whispered.

'When?' he insisted, keeping a firm hold of her hand. 'The next time I see you?'

'Yes—perhaps,' and she turned away to greet the others.

CHAPTER XII

The week following Easter proved rainy and disagreeable. It was not a cheerful period, for the villa turned out to be a fair-weather house. The stone walls seemed to absorb and retain the moisture like a vault, and a mortuary atmosphere hung about the rooms. Mr. Copley, with masculine imperviousness to mud and water, succeeded in escaping from the dampness of his home by journeying daily to the ever-luring Embassy. But his wife and niece, more solicitous on the subject of hair and clothes, remained storm-bound, and on the fourth day Mrs. Copley's conversation turned frequently to malaria.

Marcia, who had taken the villa for better, for worse, steadfastly endeavoured to approve of it in even this uncheerful mood. She divided her time between romping through the big rooms with Gerald, Gervasio, and Marcellus, and shivering over a brazier full of coals in her own room, to the accompaniment of dripping ilex trees and the superfluous splashing of the fountain. Her book was the Egoist, and the Egoist is an illuminating work to a young woman in Marcia's frame of mind. It makes her hesitate. She knew that Paul Dessart in no wise resembled the magnificent Sir Willoughby, and that it was unfair to make the comparison, but still she made it.

As she stood by the window, gazing down on the rain-swept Campagna, she pondered the situation and pondered it again, and succeeded only in working herself into a state of deeper indecision. Paul was interesting, attractive—as her uncle said, 'decorative'; but was he any more, or was that enough? Should she be sorry if she said 'no'? Should she be sorrier if she said 'yes'? So her mind busied itself to the dripping of the raindrops; and for all the thought she spent upon the question, she wandered in a circle and finished where she had started.

The Monday following Easter week dawned clear and bright again. Marcia opened her eyes to a bar of sunlight streaming in at the eastern window, and the first sound that greeted her was a joyful chorus of bird-voices. She sat up and viewed the weather with a sense of re-awakened life, feeling as if her perplexities had somehow vanished with the rain. She was no nearer making up her mind than she had been the day before, but she was quite contented to let it stay unmade a little longer. The sound of horses' hoofs beneath her window told her that her uncle had started for the station. When he was away and there were no guests in the house, Marcia and Mrs. Copley usually had the first breakfast served in their rooms. Accordingly, as she heard her uncle gallop off, she made a leisurely toilet, and then ate her coffee and rolls and marmalade at a little table set on the balcony. It was late when she joined her aunt on the loggia.

Mrs. Copley looked up from an intricate piece of embroidery. 'Good morning, Marcia,' she said, returning her niece's greeting. 'Yes, isn't it a relief to see some sunshine again!—I have a surprise for you,' she added.

'A surprise?' asked Marcia. 'My birthday isn't coming for two weeks. But never mind; surprises are always welcome. What is it?'

'It isn't a very big surprise; just a tiny one to break the monotony of these four days of rain. I had a note from Mrs. Royston this morning. It should have come yesterday, only it was so wet that Angelo didn't go for the mail.' She paused to rummage through the basket of silks. 'I thought it was here, but no matter. She says that owing to these dreadful riots they have changed all their plans. They have entirely given up Naples, and are going north instead, on a little trip of a week or so to Assisi and Perugia. She wrote to say good-bye and to tell me that they would get back to Rome in time for your party; though they are afraid they can't spend more than two or three days with us then, as the change of plan involves some hurry. They leave on Wednesday.'

'That is too bad,' said Marcia, and with the words she uttered a sigh of relief. Paul would go with them, probably; or, at any rate, she need not see him; it would postpone the difficulty. 'But where is the surprise?' she inquired.

'Oh, the surprise!' Mrs. Copley laughed. 'I entirely forgot it. I was afraid they might think it strange that I hadn't answered the note—though I really didn't get it in time—so I asked your uncle to stop at their hotel and invite them all to come out to the villa for the night. I thought that since we were planning to drive to the festa at Genazzano to-morrow, it would be nice to have them with us. I am sure they would be interested in seeing the festa.'

Marcia dropped limply into a chair and looked at her aunt. 'Is Mr. Dessart coming too?'

'I invited him, certainly. What's the matter? Aren't you pleased? I thought you liked him.'

'Oh, yes, I do; only—I wish I'd got up earlier!' And then she laughed. The situation was rather funny, after all. She might as well make the best of it. 'Suppose we send over to Palestrina and invite M. Benoit for dinner,' she suggested presently. 'I think he is stopping there this week, and it would be nice to have him. I suspect,' she added, 'that he is a tiny bit interested in Eleanor.'

A note was sent by a groom, who returned with the information that he had found the gentleman sitting on a rock in a field, painting a portrait of a sheep; that he had delivered the note, and got this in return.

'This' was a rapid sketch on bristol-board, representing the young Frenchman in evening clothes making a bow, with his hand on his heart, to the two ladies, who received him on the steps of the loggia, while a clock in the corner pointed to eight.

Marcia looked at the sketch and laughed. 'Here's an original acceptance, Aunt Katherine.'

Mrs. Copley smiled appreciatively. 'He seems to be a very original young man,' she conceded.

'Naturellement. He's a prix de Rome.'

'When Frenchmen are nice they are very nice,' said Mrs. Copley; 'but when they are not——' Words failed her, and she picked up her embroidery again.

At the mid-day breakfast Marcia announced rather hopefully that she did not think the Roystons would come.

'Why not?' her aunt inquired.

'They've lost their maid, and there won't be anybody to help them pack. If they come out to the villa to-night they won't be ready to start for Perugia on Wednesday. Besides, Mrs. Royston never likes to do anything on the spur of the moment. She likes to plan her programme a week ahead and stick to it. Oh, I know they won't come,' she added with a laugh. 'M. Benoit will be the only guest, after all.'

'And I've ordered dinner for eight!' said Mrs. Copley, pathetically. 'I am thinking of driving over to the contessa's this afternoon—I might invite her to join us.'

'Oh, no, Aunt Katherine! Please, not to-day. If the Roystons should come, there'll be a big enough party without her; and, anyway, she wouldn't be particularly interested—Mr. Sybert isn't here.'

'The contessa comes to see us, not Mr. Sybert,' Mrs. Copley returned, with a touch of asperity.

Marcia smiled into her cup of chocolate and said nothing.

While the sun was sunk in its noonday torpor, she stood by her window, gazing absently off toward the old monastery, engaged in a last valiant struggle to make up her mind. She finally turned away with an impatient shrug which banished Paul Dessart and his importunities to the bottom of the Dead Sea. There was no use in bothering any more about it now; Mrs. Royston's mind at least was no weathercock. Marcia clung tenaciously to the hope that they would not come.

It was a beautiful afternoon, fresh and sparkling from the week of rain, and she suddenly decided upon a horseback ride to brush from her mind all bothersome questions. She got out her riding-habit and jerked the bell-rope with a force which set bells jangling wildly through the house, and brought Granton as nearly on a run as was consonant with her dignity and years.

'It's nothing serious,' Marcia laughed in response to the maid's anxious face; 'I just made up my mind to go for a ride, and in the first flush of energy I rang louder than I meant. It's a great thing, Granton, to get your mind made up about even so unimportant a matter as a horseback ride.'

'Yes, miss,' Granton agreed somewhat vaguely as she knelt down to help with a boot.

'How in the world do those soldiers in the King's guard ever get their boots on?' Marcia asked.

'I don't know, miss,' said Granton, patiently.

Marcia laughed. 'Send word to the stables for Angelo to bring the horses in fifteen minutes. I'm going to take a long ride, and I must start immediately.'

'Very well, miss.'

'Immediately,' Marcia called after her. In dealing with Angelo reiteration was necessary. He was an Italian, and he had still to learn the value of time.

She tied her stock before the glass in a very mannish fashion, adjusted her hat—with the least perceptible tilt—and catching up her whip and gloves, started out gaily, humming a snatch of a very much reiterated Neapolitan street song.

"'Jammo 'ncoppa, jammo jà . . .
Funiculì—funiculà.'"

It ended in a series of trills; she did not know the words. At the head of the stairs she met Granton returning. Granton stood primly expressionless, waiting patiently for her to have done before venturing to speak.

Marcia completed her measure and broke off with a laugh. 'Well, Granton, what's the matter?'

'Angelo has taken Master Gerald's pony to Palestrina to be shod and both of the carriages are to be used, so the other men will be needed for them, and there isn't any one left to ride with you.'

Marcia's smile changed to a frown. 'How stupid! Angelo has no business to go off without saying anything.'

'Mr. Copley left orders for him to have the pony shod.'

'He's not Mr. Copley's groom; he's mine.'

'Yes, miss,' said Granton.

Marcia went on slowly downstairs, her frown gathering volume as she proceeded. She wished to take a horseback ride, and she wished nothing else for the moment. She foresaw that her aunt would propose that she ride into Tivoli and take tea with the contessa. If there was one thing she hated, it was to ride at a steady jog-trot beside the carriage; and if there was a second thing, it was to take tea with the contessa.

She heard Mrs. Copley's and Gerald's voices in the salon and she advanced to the doorway.

'Aunt Katherine! I'm furious! This is the first time in four days that it has stopped raining long enough for me to go out, and I'm dying to take a gallop in the country. That miserable Angelo has gone off with Gerald's pony, and there isn't another man on the place that can go with me. You needn't propose my riding into Tivoli to take tea with the contessa, for I won't do it.'

She delivered this outburst from the threshold, and as she advanced into the room she was slightly disconcerted to see Laurence Sybert lazily pulling himself from a chair to greet her—if she ever showed in a particularly bad light, Sybert was sure to be at hand. He bowed, his face politely grave, but there was the provoking suggestion of a smile not far below the surface; and as she looked at him Marcia had the uncomfortable feeling that her own face was growing red.

'I'm sorry about Angelo, my dear,' said Mrs. Copley. 'I didn't know that you wanted to ride this afternoon. But here is Mr. Sybert who has come out to see your uncle, and your uncle won't be back till evening. I'm sure he will be glad to go with you.'

Marcia glanced back at her aunt with an expression which said, 'Oh, Aunt Katherine, wait till I get you alone!'

'Certainly, Miss Marcia, I should be delighted to fill the recreant Angelo's place,' he affirmed, but in a tone which to her ear did not express any undue eagerness.

'Thank you, Mr. Sybert,' she smiled sweetly; 'you are very kind, but I shouldn't think of troubling you. I know that Aunt Katherine would like to have you go with her to call on the contessa.'

'If you will permit it. Miss Marcia, I will ride with you instead; for though I should be happy to call on Contessa Torrenieri with Mrs. Copley, I have just driven out from Tivoli, and by way of change I should prefer not driving back.'

'It's awfully kind of you to offer, but I don't really want to ride. I was just cross with Angelo for going off without saying anything.'

'Marcia,' remonstrated Mrs. Copley, 'that doesn't sound polite.'

Sybert laughed. 'There is nothing, Miss Marcia,' he declared, 'that would give me more pleasure this afternoon than a gallop with you; and with your permission——' he touched the bell.

Marcia shrugged her shoulders and gave the order as Pietro appeared.

'Send word to the stables for Kentucky Lil and Triumvirate to be saddled at once.'

'You may go upstairs and borrow as much of Howard's wardrobe as you wish,' said Mrs. Copley. 'I dare say you did not come prepared to play the part of groom.'

'I'll try not to get them muddier than necessary,' he promised as he turned toward the stairs. He reappeared shortly in corduroys and leather puttees. Marcia was leaning on the loggia balustrade, idly watching the hills, while a diminutive stable-boy slowly led the horses back and forth in the driveway. Sybert helped her to mount without a word, and they galloped down the avenue in silence. He appreciated the fact that she would have preferred staying at home to accepting his escort, and the situation promised some slight entertainment. A man inclined to be a trifle sardonic can find considerable amusement in the spectacle of a pretty girl who does not wish to talk to him, but finds herself in a position where she cannot escape. As Sybert had been passing a very hard week, he was the more willing to enjoy a little relaxation at Marcia's expense.

They pulled their horses to a walk at the gateway, and Sybert looked at her interrogatively. She took the lead and turned to the left along the winding roadway that led up into the mountains away from the Via Praenestina. He rode up beside her again, and they galloped on without speaking. Marcia did not propose to take the initiative in any conversation; he could introduce a subject if he wished, otherwise they would keep still. For the first mile or so he maintained the stolid reserve of a well-trained groom. But finally, as they slowed the horses to a walk on a steep hill-side, he broke the silence.

'Are we going anywhere, or just riding for pleasure?'

'Just for pleasure.'

He waited until they had reached the top of the hill before renewing the conversation. Then, 'It is a pleasant day,' he observed.

Marcia regarded the landscape critically.

'Very pleasant,' she acquiesced.

'Looks a little like rain, however,' he added, anxiously fixing his eye on a small cloud on the horizon.

Marcia studied the sky a moment with an heroic effort at seriousness, and then she began to laugh.

'I suppose we might as well make the best of it,' she remarked.

'Philosophy is the wisest way,' he agreed.

'Have you seen Gervasio?'

'I have not yet paid my respects to him. He is well, I trust?'

'He is simply a walking appetite!'

'I thought he showed a tendency that way. Mrs. Copley says that you have been suffering persecution for his sake.'

'Did she tell you about his stepfather? That's my story; she ought to have left it for me. I can tell it much more dramatically. It was quite an adventure, wasn't it?'

'It was. And you got off easily. It might have turned out to be more of an adventure than you would have cared for.'

'Oh, I like adventures.'

'When they're ended safely, yes. But these Italian peasants are a revengeful lot when they get it into their heads that they have been mistreated. I don't believe you ought to drive about the country that way.'

'I should think that two boys and a groom might be escort enough—the pony-carriage doesn't accommodate many more.'

'Nevertheless, joking apart, I don't think it is safe. The country's pretty thoroughly stirred up just at present.'

'You're as bad as Aunt Katherine with her tattooed man! As for being afraid of these peasants, I know every soul in Castel Vivalanti, and they're all adorable—with the exception of Gervasio's relatives.'

'If I were your uncle,' he observed, 'I should prefer a niece readier to take suggestions.'

'I am ready to take his suggestions, but you're not my uncle.'

'No,' said Sybert, 'I am not; and——'

'And what?' Marcia asked.

He laughed.

'I believe we declared an amnesty, did we not? Do you think it is best to reopen hostilities?'

'It strikes me that there has been more or less light skirmishing in spite of the amnesty.'

'At least there has been no serious damage done on either side. I would suggest, if heavy firing is to be recommenced, that we postpone it until the ride home.'

'Very well. Let's talk some more about the weather. It seems to be the only subject on which we can agree.'

Sybert bowed gravely.

'It's been rather rainy for the last week.'

'Very.'

'The villa must have been a little damp.'

'Very.'

'And rather monotonous?'

'Very!' Marcia laughed and gave the dialogue a new turn. 'I spent the time reading.'

'Indeed?'

'The Egoist.'

'Meredith? Don't you find him a trifle—er—for rainy weather, you know?'

'I found the Egoist,' she returned, 'a most suggestive work. It throws interesting side-lights on the men one knows.'

'Oh, come, Miss Marcia,' he remonstrated. 'That's hardly fair; you slander us.'

'You mustn't blame me—you must blame the author. It's a man who wrote it.'

'He should be regarded as a traitor. In case he is captured and brought into camp, I shall order him shot at sunrise.'

'He doesn't accuse all men of being Sir Willoughbys,' she returned soothingly. 'I hadn't thought of you in exactly that connexion. If you choose to wear the coat, you have put it on yourself.'

'We'll say, then, that it doesn't fit, and I'll resemble the other fellow—the Daniel Deronda one—what's his name, Whitfield, Whitford?' (Whitford, it will be remembered, was the dark horse who came in at the finish and captured the heroine.)

Marcia laughed. 'I really can't say that the other fits any better. I'm afraid you're not in the book, Mr. Sybert.'

They came to a fork in the roads and drew rein again.

'Which way?' he asked.

She paused and looked about. They were already far up in the mountains, and towering ahead, nearer and clearer now, on the crest of a still higher ridge, rose the old monastery she could see from her window. She pointed with her whip to the gaunt pile of grey stone against the sky.

'Is that your destination?' he asked.

'Is it too far? I've been wanting to see it closer ever since we came to the villa.'

He studied the distance. 'I should judge it's about seven kilometres in a straight line, but there's no telling how long the road takes to get there. We can try it, though; and if you're not in a hurry to get home, we may reach it.'

'At any rate, there's nothing to prevent our turning back if we find it's too far,' she suggested.

'Oh, yes; one can always turn back,' he agreed.

'One can always turn back.' The words caught Marcia's attention, and she repeated them to herself. They seemed to carry an inner meaning, and she commenced weighing anew her feelings toward Paul. Could she turn back? Was it not too late? No, if she were on the wrong road, the sooner the better; but was she on the wrong road? There were no guide-posts; the end was hidden by a turning. She rode on, forgetting to talk, with a shadow on her face and a serious light in her eyes.

'Well?' Sybert inquired, 'would you like my advice?'

'I'm afraid it's not a matter you can help me with,' she returned, with a quick laugh.

They pushed on farther up into the hills, between groves of twisted olive trees and sloping vineyards, through fields dyed blue and scarlet with forget-me-nots and poppies. All nature was green and glistening after the rain, and the mountain breeze blew fresh against their faces. Neither could be insensible to the influence of the day. Their talk was light and free and glancing—mere badinage; but it occasionally struck a deeper note, and holding it for an instant, half reluctantly let it go. Marcia had never known Sybert in this mood—she had not, as she realized, known him in any. In all their casual intercourse of the past few months they had scarcely exchanged a single idea. He was an unexplored country, and his character held for her the attraction of the unknown.

Sybert, on his side, glanced at her curiously from time to time as she flung back a quick reply. With him, first impressions died hard. He had first seen Marcia at a tea, the centre of a laughing group, with all the room paying court to her. She was pretty and attractive, faultlessly gowned, thoroughly at ease. He had, in his thirteen seasons, met many women who played many parts; and the somewhat cynical conclusion he had carried away from the experience was that if a woman be but young and fair she has the gift to know it. But as he watched her now he wondered suddenly if she were quite what he had thought her. It struck him that what he had regarded as over-sophistication was rather the pseudo-sophistication of youth; her occasional crudeness, but the crudeness that comes from lack of experience. She knew nothing of life outside the carefully closed confines of her own small world. And yet he recognized in her a certain reckless spirit of daring, of curiosity toward the world, that responded to a chord in his own nature. He had seen it the night they found Gervasio. It was in her face now as she galloped along against the wind, with her eyes raised to the half-ruined towers of the mediæval monastery. He had not been very lenient toward her, he knew; and her scarcely veiled antagonism had amused him. He felt now, as he watched her, a momentary impulse to draw her out, to mould the direction of her thoughts, to turn her face a new way.

After a wild gallop along the crest of a hill she drew up, laughing, to steady her hair, which threatened to come tumbling down about her ears. She dropped the rein loosely on the horse's neck in order to leave both hands free, and Sybert reached over and took it.

'See here, young lady,' he remonstrated, 'you're going to take a cropper some day if you ride like that.'

She glanced back with a quick retort on her lips, but his expression disarmed her. He was not watching her with his usual critical look. She changed the words into a laugh.

'Do you know what you make me feel like doing, Mr. Sybert? Giving Lil the reins and galloping down that hill there with my hands in the air.'

'Perhaps I would better keep the reins in my own hands,' was his cool proposition.

'I never knew any one who could rouse so much latent antagonism in a person as you can! You never say a word but I feel like doing exactly the opposite.'

'It's well to know it. I shall frame my future suggestions accordingly.'

Marcia settled her hat and stretched out her hand. He returned the reins with a show of doubt.

'Can I trust you to restrain your impulses?' he inquired, with his eyes on the declivity before them.

She gathered up the reins, but made no movement to go on. Instead she half-turned in the saddle and looked behind. .

They were on the shoulder of a mountain. Below them smaller foothills receded, tier below tier, until they sank imperceptibly into the level plain of the Campagna. Ahead of them the bare Sabines stretched in broken ridges, backed in the distance by two snow-peaks of the Apennines. Everywhere was the warmth of colouring, the brilliant hues of an Italian spring.

'Italy is beautiful, isn't it?' Marcia asked simply.

'Yes,' he agreed; 'Italy is cursed with beauty.'

She turned her eyes inquiringly from the landscape to him.

'A nation of artists' models!' he exclaimed half contemptuously. 'Because of their fatal good looks, the Italians can't be allowed to be prosperous like any other people.'

'Perhaps,' she suggested, 'their beauty is a compensation. They are poor, I know; but don't you think they know how to be happy in spite of it?'

'They are too easily happy. That's another curse.'

'But you surely don't want them to be unhappy,' she remonstrated. 'Since they have to be poor, shouldn't you rather see them contented?'

'Certainly not. They have nothing to be contented with.'

'But I don't see that it makes any difference what you are contented with so long as you are contented.'

He looked at her with a half-smile.

'Nonsense, Miss Marcia; you know better than that. When people are contented with their lot, does their lot ever improve? Do you think the Italian people ought to be happy? You have seen the way they live, or—no,' he broke off, 'you don't know anything about it.'

'Yes, I do,' she returned. 'I know they're poor—horribly poor—but they seem to get a good deal of pleasure out of life in spite of it.'

He shook his head. 'You can't convince me with that argument. Have you never heard of a holy discontent? That's what these people need—and,' he added grimly, 'some of them have got it.'

'A holy discontent,' she repeated. 'What a terrible thing to have! It's like living for revenge.'

'Oh, well,' he shrugged, 'a man must live for something besides his three meals a day.'

'He can live for his family,' she suggested.

'Yes, if he has one. Otherwise he must live for an idea.'

She glanced at him sidewise. She would have liked to ask what idea he lived for, but it was a question she did not dare to put. Instead she commented: 'It's queer, isn't it, how the ideas that men used to live for have passed away? Chivalry and crusading and going to war and living as hermits—I really don't see what's left.'

'The most of the old ideals are exploded,' he agreed. 'But we have new ones to-day—sufficiently bad—to meet the needs of the present century. A man can make a god of his business, for instance.'

Marcia shifted her seat a trifle uneasily as she thought of her father, who certainly did make a god of his business. It may have struck Sybert that it was not a propitious subject, for he added almost instantly—

'And there's always art to fall back upon.'

'But you don't object to that,' she remonstrated.

'No, it's good enough in its way,' he agreed; 'but it doesn't go very deep.'

'Artists would tell you then that it isn't the true art.'

'I dare say,' he shrugged; 'but at best there are a good many truer things.'

'What, for instance?'

'Well, three meals a day.'

Marcia laughed, and then she inquired—

'Suppose you knew a person, Mr. Sybert, who didn't care for anything but art—who just wanted to have the world beautiful and nothing else, what would you think?'

'Not much,' he returned; 'what would you?'

'I think that you go a great deal farther in the other extreme!'

'Not at all,' he maintained. 'I am granting that art is a very fine thing; only there are so many more vital issues in life that one doesn't have time to bother with it much. However, I suppose it's a phase one has to go through with in Italy. Oh, I've been through with it, too,' he added. 'I used to feel that Botticelli and Giorgione and the rest of them were really important.'

'But you got over it?' she inquired.

'Yes, I got over it—one does.'

Marcia laughed again. 'Mr. Sybert,' she said, 'I think you are an awfully queer man. You are so sort of unfeeling in some respects and feeling in others.'

'Miss Marcia, you strike me as an awfully queer young woman for exactly the same reasons.'

They had come to a curve in the road, and under an over-hanging precipice hollowed out of the rock was a little shrine to the Madonna, and beside it a rough iron cross.

'Some poor devil has met his fate here,' said Sybert, and he reined in his horse and leaned from his saddle to make out the blurred inscription traced on the bars. 'Felice Buconi in the year 1840 at this spot received death at the hand of an assassin. Pray for his soul,' he translated. 'Poor fellow! It's a tragedy in Italy to meet one's death at the hands of an assassin.'

'Why more in Italy than in any other place?'

'Because one dies without receiving the sacrament, and has some trouble about getting into heaven.'

'Oh!' she returned. 'I suppose when Gervasio's father wished that I might die of an apoplexy he was not only damning me for this world, but for the world to come.'

'Exactly. An apoplexy in Italy is a comprehensive curse.'

'I think,' she commented, 'that I prefer a religion which doesn't have a purgatory.'

'Purgatory,' he returned, 'has always struck me as quite superior to anything the Protestants offer. It really gives one something to die for.'

'I should think, for the matter of that, that heaven direct would give one something to die for.'

'What, for instance? Golden paving-stones, eternal sunshine, and singing angels!'

'Oh, not necessarily just those things. They're merely symbolical.'

'At least,' said Sybert, 'perfect peace and beauty and happiness, and nothing beyond. You needn't tell me, Miss Marcia, that you want to spend an eternity in any such place as that. It might do for a vacation—a villeggiatura—but for ever!'

'Probably angels' ideas of happiness are more settled than men's.'

'In that case angels must be infinitely lower than men. To be happy in a place that has reached the end, that stands still, would require a very selfish man—and I don't see why not a very selfish angel—to settle down contentedly to an eternity of bliss while there's still so much work to be done in the world.'

'I suppose,' she suggested, 'that when you get to be an angel, you forget about the world and leave all the sorrow and misery behind.'

'A fools' paradise!' he maintained.

They were suddenly aroused from their talk by a peal of thunder. They looked up to see that the sun had disappeared. Sybert's small cloud on the horizon had grown until it covered the sky.

'Well, Miss Marcia,' he laughed, 'I am afraid we are going to get a wetting to pay for our immersion in philosophy and art. Shall we turn back?'

'If we're going to get wet anyway,' she said, 'I should prefer seeing the monastery first, since we've come so far.' She looked across the valley in front of them, where, not half a mile away, the walls rose grim and gaunt amid a cluster of cypresses.

'You can see about as much from here as you could if you went any nearer,' he returned. 'I should advise you to look and run.'

As he spoke a cool wind swept up the valley, swaying the olive trees and turning their leaves to silver. A flash of lightning followed, and a few big drops splashed in their faces.

'We're in for it!' Marcia exclaimed, as she struggled to control Kentucky Lil, who was quivering and plunging.

Sybert glanced about quickly. The flying clouds overhead, and an ominous orange light that had suddenly settled down upon the landscape, betokened that a severe mountain storm was at hand. They would be drenched through before they could reach the monastery—which, after all, might not prove a hospitable order to ladies. He presently spied a low stone building nearer at hand on the slope of the hill they had just left behind. 'We'd better make for that,' he said, pointing it out with his whip. 'Though it hasn't a very promising look, it will at least be a shelter until the storm is over.'

CHAPTER XIII

The drops were falling fast by the time they reached the building. They hastily dismounted and pushed forward to the wide stone archway which served as entrance. A door of rudely joined boards swung across the opening, but it was ajar and banging in the wind. Sybert threw it open and led the horses into the gloomy interior. It proved to be a wine-cellar, probably belonging to the monastery. The room was low but deep, with a dirt floor and rough masonry walls; in the rear two huge vats rose dimly to the roof, and the floor was scattered with farming-implements. The air was damp and musty and pungent with the smell of fermenting grape-juice.

Sybert fastened the horses to a low beam by means of their bridles, while Marcia sat down upon a plough and pensively regarded the landscape. He presently joined her.

'This is not a very cheerful refuge,' he remarked; 'but at least it is drier than the open road.'

She moved along and offered him part of her seat.

'I think I can improve on that,' he said, as he rummaged out a board from a pile of lumber and fitted it at a somewhat precarious slope across the plough. They gingerly sat down upon it and Marcia observed—

'I suppose if you had your way, Mr. Sybert, we should be sitting on a McCormick reaper.'

'It would at least be more comfortable,' he returned.

The rain was beating fiercely by this time, and the lightning flashes were following each other in quick succession. Black clouds were rolling inland from across the Volscian mountains and piling layer upon layer above their heads. Marcia sat watching the gathering storm, and presently she exclaimed:

'This might be a situation out of a book! To be overtaken by a thunderstorm in the Sabine mountains and seek shelter in a deserted wine-cellar—it sounds like one of the "Duchess's" novels.'

'It does have a familiar ring,' he agreed. 'It only remains for you to sprain your ankle.'

She laughed softly, with an undertone of excitement in her voice.

'I've never had so many adventures in my life as since we came out to Villa Vivalanti—Marcellus, and Gervasio, and Gervasio's stepfather, and now a cloud-burst in the mountains! If they're going to rise to a climax, I can't imagine what our stay will end with.'

'Henry James, you know, says that the only adventures worth having are intellectual adventures.'

Marcia considered this proposition doubtfully.

'In an intellectual adventure,' she objected, 'you could never be quite sure that it really was an adventure; you'd always be afraid you'd imagined half of it. I think I prefer mine more visibly exciting. There's something picturesque in a certain amount of real bloodshed.'

Sybert turned his eyes away from her with a gesture of indifference.

'Oh, if it's merely bloodshed you're after,' he said dryly, 'you'll find as much as you like in any butcher's shop.'

She watched him for a moment and then she observed, 'I suppose you are disagreeable on purpose, Mr. Sybert. You have a—' she hesitated for a word, and as none presented itself, substituted a generic term—'horrid way of answering a person.'

He turned back toward her with a laugh. 'If I really thought you meant it, I should have a still "horrider" way.'

'Certainly I mean it,' she declared. 'I've always liked to read about fights and plots and murders in books. I think it's nice to have a little blood spattered about. It's a sort of concrete symbol of courage.'

'Ah—I saw a concrete symbol of courage the other day, but I can't say that it struck me as attractive.'

'What was it?'

'A fellow lying by the roadside, in a pool of dirty water and blood, with his mouth wide open, a couple of stiletto wounds in his neck, and his brains spattered over his face—brains may be useful, but they're not pretty.'

She looked at him gravely, with a slow expression of disgust.

'I suppose you think I'm horrider than ever now?'

'Yes, said Marcia; 'I do.'

'Then don't make any such absurd statement as that you think bloodshed picturesque. The world's got beyond that. Do you object if I smoke? I don't think it would hurt this place to have a bit of fumigating.'

She nodded permission, and watched him silently as he rolled a cigarette and hunted through his pockets for a match. The coat did not reward his search, and he commenced on the waistcoat. Suddenly she broke out with—

'What's that in your pocket, Mr. Sybert?'

A momentary shade of annoyance flashed over his face.

'It's a dynamite bomb.'

'It's a revolver! What are you carrying that for? It's against the law.'

'Don't tell the police' he pleaded. 'I've always liked to play with fire-arms; it's a habit I've never outgrown.'

'Why are you carrying it?' she repeated.

Sybert found his match and lighted his cigarette with slow deliberation. Then he rose to his feet and looked down at her. 'You ask too many questions, Miss Marcia,' he said, and he commenced pacing back and forth the length of the dirt floor.

She remained with her elbow resting on her knee and her chin in her hand, looking out at the storm. Presently he came back and sat down again.

'Is our amnesty off?' he asked.

Before she could open her mouth to respond a fierce white flash of lightning came, followed instantly by a deafening crash of thunder. A torrent of water came pouring down on the loose tiles with a roar that sounded like a cannonading. The air seemed quivering with electricity. The horses plunged and snorted in terror, and Sybert sprang to his feet to quiet them.

'Jove! It is a cloudburst,' he cried.

Marcia ran to the open doorway and stood looking out across the storm-swept valley. The water was coming down in an almost solid sheet; the clouds hung low and black and impenetrable except when a jagged line of lightning cut them in two. From the height across the valley the tall square monastery tower rose defiantly into the very midst of the

69

storm, while the cypress trees at its base swayed and writhed and wrung their hands in agony. Sybert came and stood beside her, and the two watched the storm in silence.

'There,' he suddenly flashed out, with a little undertone of triumph in his voice—'there is Italy!' He nodded toward the old walls rising so stanchly from the storm. 'That's the way the Italians have weathered tyranny and revolution and oppression for centuries, and that's the way they will keep on doing.'

She looked up at him quickly, and caught a gleam of something she had never seen before in his face. It was as if an internal fire were blazing through. For an imperceptible second he held her look, then his eyelids drooped again and his usual expression of reserve came back. 'Come and sit down,' he said; 'you're getting wet.'

They turned back to the plough again and sat side by side, looking out at the storm. The beating of the rain on the tiles above their heads made a difficult accompaniment for conversation, and they did not try to talk. But they were electrically aware of each other's presence; the wild excitement of the storm had taken hold of both of them. Marcia's breath came fast through slightly parted lips, her cheeks were flushed, her hair was tumbled, and there was a yellow glow in her deep grey eyes. Her face seemed to vivify the gloomy interior. Sybert glanced at her sidewise once or twice in half surprise; she did not seem exactly the person he had thought he knew. Her hand lay in her lap, idly clasping her gloves and whip. It looked white and soft against her black habit.

Suddenly Marcia asked a question.

'Will you tell me something, Mr. Sybert?'

'I am at your service,' he bowed.

'And the truth?'

'Oh, certainly, the truth.'

She glanced down in her lap a moment and smoothed the fingers of her gloves in a thoughtful silence. 'Well,' she said finally, 'I don't know, after all, what I want to ask you; but there is something in the air that I don't understand. Tell me the truth about Italy.'

'The truth about Italy?' He repeated the words with a slight accent of surprise.

'Last week in Rome, at the Roystons' hotel, everybody was talking about the wheat famine and the bread riots, and they all stopped suddenly when I asked any questions. Uncle Howard will never tell me a thing; he just jokes about it when I ask him.'

'He's afraid,' said Sybert. 'No one dares to tell the truth in Italy; it's lèse majesté.'

She glanced up at him quickly to see what he meant. His face was quite grave, but there was a disagreeable suggestion of a smile about his lips. She looked out of doors again with an angry light in her eyes. 'Oh, I think you are beastly!' she cried. 'You and Uncle Howard both act as if I were ten years old. I don't think that a wheat famine is any subject to joke about.'

'Miss Marcia,' he said quietly, 'when things get to a certain point, if you wish to keep your senses you can't do anything but joke about them.'

'Tell me,' she said.

There was a look of troubled expectancy in her face. Sybert half closed his eyes and studied the ground without speaking. Not very many days before he had felt a fierce desire to hurl the story at her, to confront her with a picture of the suffering that her father had caused; now he felt as strongly as her uncle that she must not know.

'Since you cannot do anything to help, why should you wish to understand? There are so many unpleasant things in the world, and so many of us already who know about them. It's—' he turned toward her with a little smile, but one which she did not resent—'well, it's a relief, you know, to see a few people who accept their happiness as a free gift from heaven and ask no questions.'

'I am not a baby. I should not care to accept happiness on any such terms.'

'And you want to know about Italy? Very well,' he said grimly; 'I can give you plenty of statistics.' He leaned forward with his elbows on his knees and traced lines in the dirt floor with his whip, speaking in the emotionless tone of one who is quoting a list from a catalogue.

'The poor people bear three-fourths of the taxes. Every necessity of life is taxed—bread and salt and meat and utensils—but such things as carriages and servants and jewels go comparatively free. When the government has squeezed all it can from the people, the church takes its share, and then the government comes in again with the state lotteries. The Latin races are already sufficiently addicted to gambling without needing any extra encouragement from the state. Part of the revenue thus collected is spent in keeping up the army—in training the young men of the country in idleness and in a great many things they would do better without. Part of it goes to build arcades and fountains and statues of Victor Emmanuel. The most of it stops in official pockets. You may think that politics are as corrupt as they can be in America, but I assure you it is not the case. In Italy the priests won't let the people vote, and the parliament is run in the interests of a few. The people are ignorant and superstitious; more than half of them can neither read nor write, and the government exploits them as it pleases. The farm labourer earns only from twenty-five to thirty cents a day to support himself and his family. Fortunately, living is cheap or there would soon not be any farm labourers alive.

'Last year—' he paused and an angry flush crept under his dark skin—'last year in Lombardy, Venetia, and the Marches—three of the most fertile provinces in Italy—fifteen thousand people went mad from hunger. The children of these pellagrosi will be idiots and cripples, and ten years from now you will find them on the steps of churches, holding out maimed hands for coppers. At this present moment there are ten thousand people in Naples crowded into damp caves and cellars—practically all of them stricken with consumption and scrofula, and sick with hunger.'

He leaned forward and looked into her face with blazing eyes.

'Marcia, in this last week I've seen—God!' he burst out, 'what things I've seen!'

He got up and strode to the door, and Marcia sat looking after him with frightened eyes. The air seemed charged with his words. She felt herself trembling, and she caught her breath quickly with a half-gasp. She closed her eyes and pictures rose up before her— pictures she did not wish to see. She thought of the hordes of poor people in Castel Vivalanti, of the bony, wrinkled hands that were stretched out for coppers at every turn, of the crowds of children with hungry faces. She thought of the houses that they lived in— wretched little dens, dark and filthy and damp. And it wasn't their fault, she repeated to herself; it wasn't their fault. They were honest and frugal, they wanted work; but there was not enough to go around.

She sat quite still for several moments, feeling acutely a great many things she had scarcely divined before. Then presently she glanced over her shoulder at the great vats towering out of the darkness behind her. They suddenly presented themselves to her imagination as a symbol, a visible sign of the weight of society bearing down upon the poor, crushing out goodness and happiness and hope. As she watched them with half-fascinated eyes, they seemed to swell and grow until they dominated the whole room with the sense of their oppressiveness. She rose with a little shiver and almost ran to the door.

'Let's go!' she cried.

'What's the matter?' he asked, looking at her face.

'Nothing. I want to go. It's stopped raining.'

He led out the horses and helped her to mount.

'What's the matter?' he asked again, 'Your hand is trembling. Did I say anything to frighten you?'

She shook her head without answering, and when they reached the road she drew a long breath of fresh air and glanced back with a nervous laugh.

'I had the most horrible feeling in there! I felt as if something were going to reach out from those vats and grab me from behind.'

'I think,' he suggested, 'that you'd better take some of your aunt's quinine when you get home.'

'Mr. Sybert,' she said presently, 'I told you one day that I thought poor people were picturesque, I don't think so any more.'

'I didn't suppose that you meant it.'

'But I did!' said Marcia. 'I've merely changed my mind.' She touched Kentucky Lil with her whip and splashed on ahead down the road that led toward the monastery, while Sybert followed with a slightly perplexed frown.

The storm had passed as quickly as it had come. Loose, flying clouds still darkened the sky, but the heavy black thunder-clouds were already far to the eastward over the Apennines. In its brief passage, however, the storm had left havoc behind it. The vines in the wayside vineyards were stripped of their leaves, and the bamboo poles they were trained upon broken and bent. Branches torn from the olive trees were strewn over the grass, and in the wheat fields the young grain was bowed almost to the ground. A fierce mountain torrent poured down the side of the road through a gully that an hour before had been dry.

The mountain air was fresh and keen, and the horses, excited by the storm, plunged on, recklessly irrespective of mud and water. They crossed the little valley that lay between the hill of the wine-cellar and the higher hill of the monastery, clattered through the single street of the tiny hamlet which huddled itself at the base of the hill, and wound on upward along the narrow walled roadway that turned and unturned upon itself like the coils of a serpent. They passed through the dark grove of cypresses that skirted the outer walls, and emerged for a moment on a small plateau which gave a wide view of receding hills and valleys and hills again. Below them, at a precipitous angle, lay the valley they had just come through and the clustering brown-tiled roofs of the little Noah's Ark village.

As they rode out from the shadow of the trees, by a common impulse they both drew rein and brought their horses to a standstill at the edge of the grove. Away to the eastward the sky was black, but the western sky was a blaze of orange light, and the sun, an orange ball, was dropping into the purple Campagna as into a sea. The shadows were settling in the valley beneath them, but the hills were tinged with a shimmering light, and the tower above their heads was glowing in a sombre, softened beauty.

They had scarcely had time, however, to more than glance at the wide-spread picture before them when they became aware of a little human drama that was being enacted under their eyes.

A young monk in the brown cassock of the Franciscans, probably a lay brother in the monastery, was standing in the vineyard by the roadside, resting for a moment from his task of tying up the vines that had been beaten down by the storm. He had not seen the riders— his back was turned toward them, and his gaze was resting on the field across the way, where scarlet poppies were growing among the wheat. But his eyes were not for the flowers, nor yet for the light on the hills beyond—these he had seen before and understood. He was watching a dark-haired peasant girl and a man dressed in shepherd's clothes, who were strolling side by side along the narrow pathway that led diagonally through the wheat. The man, strong-limbed and brown and muscular, in sheepskin trousers and pointed hat, was bending toward her, talking insistently with vehement Italian gestures. She appeared to listen, and then she shrugged her shoulders and half drew back, while her mocking laugh rang out clearly on the still evening air. For a moment he hesitated, then he boldly put his arm around her, and the two passed down the hill and out of sight in the direction of the hamlet. The poor young frate, his work forgotten, with hands idly hanging at his sides, stared at the spot where they had disappeared. And as he looked, the monastery bells in the campanile above him slowly rang out the 'Ave Maria.' He started guiltily, and with a hasty sign of the cross caught up his rosary and bowed his head in prayer.

At the unexpected sound of the bells the horses broke into a quick trot. The monk, startled at the clatter of hoofs so near, turned suddenly and looked in their direction. As he caught sight of Marcia's and Sybert's eyes upon him, and knew that they had seen, a quick flush spread over his thin dark face, and turning away he bowed his head again.

Marcia broke the silence with a low laugh as they rode on into the shade of the cypresses. 'He thought we were——' and then she stopped.

'Lovers too,' said Sybert. 'Poor devil! I suppose he thinks the world is full of lovers outside his monastery walls. There,' he added, 'is a man who is living for an idea.'

'And is beginning to suspect that it is the wrong one.'

He shot her a quick glance of comprehension. 'Ah, there's the rub,' he returned, a trifle soberly—'when you begin to suspect your idea's the wrong one.'

They rode on down the hill into the darkening valley. They were going the straight way home now, and the horses knew it. They were still in the hills when the twilight faded, and a young moon, just beyond the crescent, took its place, riding high in a sky scattered thick with flying clouds. It was a wild, wet, windy night, though on the lower levels the roads were fairly dry: the storm had evidently wasted its fury on the heights.

It was too fast a pace to admit much talking, and they both contented themselves with their thoughts. Only once did Marcia break the silence.

'I feel as if we were carrying the good news from Ghent to Aix!'

Sybert laughed and quoted softly:—

'Behind shut the postern, the lights sank to rest,
And into the midnight we galloped abreast.
Not a word to each other; we kept the great pace—
Neck by neck, stride by stride, never changing our place——

Kentucky Lil would make quite a Roland,' he broke off.

'She's the nicest horse I ever rode,' said Marcia.

As they turned in at the villa gates she said contritely, 'I didn't know it would take so long; I'm afraid, Mr. Sybert, that I've made you very late!'

'Perhaps I like adventures too,' he smiled; 'and you and I, Miss Marcia, have travelled far to-day.'

CHAPTER XIV

As they galloped up the long avenue under the arching trees, the villa presently came into view. The sound of laughing voices floated out from the open windows. Marcia drew rein with a half-involuntary cry of dismay. The Roystons had come.

'I'd forgotten!' she explained to her companion. 'We're giving a dinner-party to-night.'

At the sound of the clattering hoofs on the gravel of the driveway a gay group poured out on to the loggia, welcoming the dilatory riders with laughter and questions and greetings.

'My dear child! Where have you been?'

'Here, Pietro; call some one to take the horses.'

'Is this the way you welcome guests? I shall never——'

'Dinner's been waiting half an hour. We were beginning to think——'

'I've been worried to death! You haven't caught cold, have you?'

'No, Aunt Katherine,' she laughed as she pulled off her gloves and shook hands with the visitors. 'But we've been nearly drowned! We should have been wholly drowned if Mr. Sybert hadn't spied a very leaky ark on the top of a hill.'

'I'm relieved!' sighed her uncle as they passed into the hall. 'I was beginning to fear that you had had a disagreement on the way, and that it was another case of the Kilkenny cats.'

'Marcia, how you look! You're covered with mud!' cried Mrs. Copley.

With a slightly apprehensive glance toward the mirror, Marcia straightened her hat and rubbed a daub of mud from her cheek. 'Kentucky Lil and Triumvirate were in too much of a hurry to get home to turn out for puddles,' she said. 'How much time may we have to dress, Aunt Katherine?'

'Just fifteen minutes,' returned her uncle; 'and that is a quarter of an hour more than you deserve. If you are not down then, we shall eat without waiting for you.'

'Fifteen minutes, remember!' cried Marcia to Sybert as they parted at the top of the stairs. 'I'll race with you,' she added; 'though I think myself that a girl ought to have a handicap.'

She found Granton, a picture of prim disapproval, waiting with her dress spread out on the bed. Marcia dropped into a wicker chair with a tired sigh.

'You've ridden a long way,' Granton remarked as she removed a muddy boot.

'Yes, Granton, I have; and dinner's already been waiting half an hour, and Pietro looks like a thunder-cloud, and Mrs. Copley looks worried, and the guests look hungry—what François looks like I don't dare to think. We must fly; our reputations depend on it.'

'Am I ready?' she inquired, not much more than fifteen minutes later, as she twisted her head to view the effect in the mirror.

'You'll do very well,' said Granton.

'I'm terribly tired,' she sighed; 'and I feel more like going to bed than facing guests—but I suppose, in the natural order of events, dinner must be accomplished first.'

'To be sure,' said the maid, critically adjusting her train.

'Your philosophy is so comfortable, Granton! As we have done yesterday, so shall we do to-day and also to-morrow. It saves one the trouble of making up one's mind.'

She reached the salon just in time to take Paul Dessart's silently offered arm to the dining-room. Sybert did not appear until the soup was being removed. He possessed himself of the empty chair beside Eleanor Royston, with a murmured apology to his hostess.

'It's excusable, Sybert,' said Copley, with a frown. 'You should not allow a woman to beat you.'

'The furniture in that room you gave me,' he complained gravely, 'was built as a trap for collar-buttons. The side of the bed comes to within three inches of the floor—I couldn't crawl under.'

'What did you do?' Eleanor Royston asked.

'I borrowed one of our host's—and I had a hard time finding it.'

'I shall put my wardrobe under lock and key the next time you visit us,' Copley declared.

Sybert was curiously inspecting a small white globule he found by his plate.

Marcia laughed and called from the other end of the table: 'It's your own prescription, Mr. Sybert; drop it in your wine-glass and drink it like a man. I've taken my dose.'

During this exchange of badinage Paul Dessart said never a word. He sat with his eyes fixed moodily on the table-cloth, and—one hates to say it of Paul—he sulked. For the first time since she had known him, Marcia found him difficile. He started no subject himself, and those that she started, after a brief career, fell lifeless. It may have been that she herself was somewhat ill at ease, but in any case several awkward silences fell between them, which the young man made no attempt to break. Mr. Copley would never have said of him to-night that he was an ornament to any dinner-table. It fell to the Frenchman across the way to keep the ball rolling.

In an errant glance toward the other end of the table, Marcia saw Sybert laughing softly at something Eleanor had said. She stayed her glance a second to note involuntarily how well they went together. Eleanor, with her white shoulders rising from a cloud of pale-blue gauze, looked fair and distinguished; and Sybert, with his dark face and sullen eyes, made an esthetically satisfying contrast. He was bending toward her with that air of easy politeness, that superior self-sufficiency, which had always exasperated Marcia so. But Eleanor knew how to take it; she had been out nine seasons, and the smile with which she answered him was quite as mocking as his own.

He looked to-night, through and through, what Marcia had always taken him for—the finished cosmopolitan—the diplomat—the diner-out. But he was not just that, she knew; she had seen him off his guard in the midst of the storm that afternoon, and she was still tingling with the surprise of it. She recalled what Mr. Melville had said that afternoon in the

74

ilex grove—she was always recalling what people said about Sybert. The things seemed to stick in one's mind; he was a subject that gave rise to many mots. 'You think you are very broad-minded because you see the man underneath the peasant. Don't you think you could push your broad-mindedness one step further and see the man underneath the man of the world?' She had caught a glimpse that afternoon. It seemed now as if his air of super civilization were only a mask to conceal—she did not know what, underneath. She was searching for an apt description when she heard the young Frenchman laughingly inquire: 'Mademoiselle Copley est un peu distraite ce soir, n'est-ce pas?'

With a little start, she became aware that some one had asked her a question. For the remainder of the dinner she kept her eyes at her end of the table, and exerted herself to be gracious to her taciturn companion. Paul's bad temper was not unbecoming, and he scarcely could have adopted a wiser course. Marcia had expected to find him sparkling, enthusiastic, convincing; and she had come down prepared to withstand his charm. Mais voilà! there was no charm to withstand. He was sullen, moody, with a frown scarcely veiled enough for politeness. Some one had once compared him, not very originally, to a Greek god. He looked it more than ever to-night, if one can imagine a Greek god in the sulks. What was the matter with him, Marcia could only guess. Perhaps, as his cousin had affirmed, he was like a cat and needed stroking the right way of the fur. At any rate, she found the new mood rather taking, and she somewhat weakly allowed herself to stroke him the right way. By the time they rose from the table he was, if not exactly purring, at least not showing his claws.

At the Royston girls' suggestion, they put on evening wraps and repaired to the terrace—except the two elder ladies, who preferred the more tempered atmosphere of the salon. Mrs. Copley delegated her husband and Sybert to act as chaperons—a position which Sybert accepted with a bow, to the accompaniment of a slightly puzzled smile on Eleanor's part. She could not exactly make out the gentleman's footing in the household. They seated themselves in a group about the balustrade, with the exception of Eleanor and Sybert, who strolled back and forth the length of the flagging. Eleanor was doing her best to-night, and her best was very good; she appeared to have wakened a spark in even his indifference. Marcia, with her eyes on the two, thought again how well they went together, and M. Benoit was a second time on the verge of calling her distraite.

The two strollers after a time joined the group, Eleanor humming under her breath a little French chanson that had been going the rounds of the Paris cafés that spring.

'Oh, sing something we all know,' said Margaret, and with a laughing curtesy toward Sybert she struck into 'Fair Harvard.' The other girls joined her. Their voices, rising high and clear, filled the night with the swinging melody. It seemed strangely out of place there, in the midst of the Sabine hills, with the old villa behind them and the Roman Campagna at their feet. As their voices died away Sybert laughed softly.

'I swear I'd forgotten it!'

Margaret shook her head in mock reproof. 'Forgotten it!' she cried. 'A man ought to be ashamed to acknowledge it if he had forgotten his Alma Mater song. It's like forgetting his country.'

'I suspect,' said Eleanor, 'that it's time for you to go back to America and be naturalized, Mr. Sybert.'

'Oh, well, Miss Royston,' he objected, 'I suppose in time one outgrows his college, just as one outgrows his kindergarten.'

'And his country,' Marcia added, as much for Paul Dessart's benefit as for his own.

Margaret, searching for diversion, presently suggested that they visit the ghost. Marcia objected that the ghost was visible only during the full moon, but the objection was overruled. There was some moon at least, and a wild night like this, with flying clouds and waving branches, was just the time for a ghost to think of his sins. Mr. Copley, in the office of chaperon, remonstrated that the grass would be damp; but there were rubbers, he was told. Marcia acquiesced in the expedition without any marked enthusiasm; she foresaw a possible tête-à-tête with Paul Dessart. As they set out, however, she found herself walking beside M. Benoit, with Paul contentedly strolling on ahead at the side of his younger cousin, while Eleanor and the two chaperons brought up the rear. As they came to the end of the laurel path and approached the region of the ruins, Margaret paused with her finger on her lips and in a conspiratorial whisper impressed silence on the group. They laughingly fell into the spirit of the play, and the whole party stole along with the elaborate caution of ten-year-old boys ambuscading Indians.

The ruins in the dim light looked a fit harbour for ghosts. The crumbling piles of masonry were almost hidden by the dark foliage, but the empty fountain stood out clearly in a little open space between the trees.

The group paused on the edge of the trees and stood with eyes turned half expectantly toward the fountain. As they looked, they saw, with a tremor of surprise, the dim figure of a man rise from the coping and dissolve into the surrounding shadows. For a moment no one uttered a sound beyond a quick gasp of astonishment, and an excited giggle from Margaret Royston. Paul was the first to rise to the occasion with the muffled assertion that he recognized the fair and warlike form in which the majesty of buried Denmark did sometime march. Before any of them had recovered sufficiently to follow the apparition, a second ghost rose from the coping and stood wavering in apparent hesitancy whether to recede or advance. This was more than tradition demanded, and with a quick exclamation both Copley and Sybert sprang forward to solve the mystery.

A babble of noisy expostulation burst forth. The ghost was vociferous in his apologies. He had finished his work and had desired to take the air. It was a beautiful night. He came to talk with a friend. He did not know that the signore ever came here, or he would never have ventured.

The tones were familiar, and a little sigh of disillusionment swept through the group. The two men came back laughing, and Paul apostrophized tragically:

'Another lost illusion! If all the ghosts turned out to be butlers, how unromantic the world would be!'

The young Frenchman took up the tale of mourning.

'But the true ghost, Monsieur le Prince, whom I was preparing to paint; after this he will not deign to poke his nose from the grave. It is an infamy! An infamy!' he declared.

They laughingly turned back toward the villa, and Marcia discovered that she was walking beside Paul. It had come about quite naturally, without any apparent interposition on his part; but she did not doubt, since he had the chance, that he would take advantage of it to demand an answer, and she prepared herself to parry what he might choose to say. He strolled along, whistling softly, apparently in no hurry to say anything. When he did break the silence it was to remark that the tree-toads were infernally noisy to-night. He went on to observe that he wasn't particularly taken with her butler; the fellow protested too much in the wrong place, and not enough in the right. From that he passed to a flying criticism of villa architecture. Villa Vivalanti was a daisy except for the eastern wing, and that was 'way off in style and broke the lines. Those gingerbread French villas at Frascati, he thought, ought to be razed to the ground by act of parliament.

Marcia responded rather lamely to his remarks, as she puzzled her brains to think whether she had done anything to offend him. He seemed entirely good-humoured, however, and chatted along as genially as the first time they had met. She could not comprehend this new attitude, and though it was just what she had wished for—such is the contrariness of human nature—she vaguely resented it. Had M. Benoit seen her just then he might have accused her, for the third time, of being distraite.

The ghost-hunters, upon their return, shortly retired for the night, as the festa at Genazzano would demand an early start. Before going upstairs, Marcia waited to give orders about an open-air breakfast-party she was planning for the morrow. In searching for Pietro she also found her uncle. Mr. Copley, very stern, was engaged in telling the butler that if it occurred again he would be discharged; and the butler, very humble, was assuring the signore that in the future his commands should be implicitly obeyed.

'Uncle Howard,' Marcia remonstrated, 'you surely aren't scolding the poor fellow because of to-night? What difference does it make if he does entertain his friends in the grounds of the old villa? We never go near the place.'

'It is this particular friend I am objecting to.'

'Who was it?'

'Gervasio's stepfather.'

'Oh, you don't suppose,' she cried, 'that he is trying to steal the child back again?'

'I should like to see him do it!' said Mr. Copley, with decision. 'He doesn't want the boy,' he added. 'What he wants is money, but he isn't going to get any. I won't have him hanging about the place, and the servants may as well understand it first as last.'

Marcia, having outlined her plan for the breakfast to a somewhat unresponsive Pietro, finally gained her room; and setting her candle down on the table, she dropped into the first chair she came to with a sigh of relief that the evening was over. She was tired, not only in body, but in mind as well.

The evening was not quite ended, however. A gentle tap came on the door, and she opened it to find Eleanor and Margaret in loose silk dressing-gowns. 'Let us in quick,' said Margaret. 'We've just met a man in the hall.'

'The ubiquitous Pietro shutting up windows,' added Eleanor. 'If I were you, I'd discharge that man and get a more companionable butler. It's uncanny for an Italian servant to be as grave as an English one.'

'Poor Pietro has just had a scolding, which, I suppose, accounts for his gravity. It's funny,' she added, 'that's exactly the advice that Paul gave me to-night.' The 'Paul' was out before she could catch it, and she reddened apprehensively, but the girls let it pass without challenging.

'We've come to talk,' said Margaret, possessing herself of the couch and settling the cushions behind her. 'I hope you're not sleepy.'

'Very,' said Marcia; 'but I dare say I shan't be ten minutes from now.'

'You needn't worry; this isn't going to be an all-night session,' drawled Eleanor from the lazy depths of an easy-chair. 'We start at nine for the Madonna's festa.'

'You'd better appreciate us now that you've got us,' added Margaret. 'We should by rights have slept in Rome to-night.'

'How did you manage it?'

'Paul took mamma down to the Forum to look at some inscriptions they've just dug up; and while she was gone Eleanor and I scrambled around and packed the trunks for Perugia. By the time she came back we had everything ready to come out here, and our hats on waiting to start. She didn't recover her breath until we were in the train, and then she couldn't say anything before Mr. Copley. When it comes to starting on journeys,' Margaret added, 'mamma is not what you'd call impulsive.'

'Not often,' assented Eleanor; 'but there have been instances. By the way,' she added, 'I wish you'd explain about Mr. Sybert; I confess I don't quite grasp his standing in the family. How do you come to be taking such lengthy horseback rides with a young man and no groom? You never did that when my mother was chaperoning you.'

'No,' acquiesced Marcia; 'I didn't. But Mr. Sybert's a little different. He's not exactly a young man, you know; he's a friend of Uncle Howard's. He happened to be available this afternoon, and Angelo didn't happen to be, so he came instead.'

'As a sort of sub-groom?' Eleanor asked. 'I should think he might object to the position.'

'He couldn't help himself!' she laughed. 'Aunt Katherine forced him into it.'

Eleanor regarded Marcia with a still puzzled smile. 'You talk about Mr. Sybert as if he were a contemporary of your grandfather. How old is he, may I ask?'

'I don't know. He's nearly as old as Uncle Howard. Thirty-five or thirty-six, I should say.'

'A man isn't worth talking to under thirty-five.'

'Oh, nonsense!' Margaret objected. 'I never heard any one in my life talk better than Paul, and he's exactly twenty-five.'

'Paul talks words; he doesn't talk ideas,' said her sister.

There was a pause, in which Eleanor leaned forward to examine some bits of green and blue iridescent glass lying in a little tray on the table. 'What are these?' she inquired.

'Pieces of perfume-bottles that the grave-digger in Palestrina found in an old Etruscan tomb. There were some bronze mirrors, and the most wonderful gold necklace—I wanted it dreadfully, but he didn't dare sell it; it's gone to a museum in Rome. Aren't these pieces of glass lovely, though? I am going to have them set in gold and made into pins.'

'Here's a little bottle that's scarcely broken.' Eleanor held it up before the candle and let the light play upon its surface. 'Who do you suppose owned it before you, Marcia?'

'Some girl who turned to dust centuries ago.'

'And her necklaces and mirrors and perfume-bottles still exist. What a commentary!'

'Thank goodness, they don't put such things in one's coffin nowadays,' said Marcia; 'or twenty-five hundred years from now some other girl would be saying the same of us.'

'Twenty-five hundred years,' Eleanor murmured. 'I declare, my nine seasons sink into insignificance!' She dropped the bottle into its tray and leaned back in her chair with a little laugh. 'America is a bit tame, isn't it, after Italy? One doesn't get so many emotions.'

'I'm not sure but one gets too many in Italy,' said Marcia.

'How long are you going to stay over?'

'I don't know. It's so much easier not to make up one's mind. I shall probably stay a year or so longer with Uncle Howard.'

'I like your uncle, Marcia. He has a very taking way of saying funny things without smiling.'

'Ah,' sighed Marcia, 'he has!'

'And as for Mr. Sybert——' Margaret put in mockingly.

'I think he's about the most interesting man I've met in Europe,' Eleanor agreed imperturbably.

'The most interesting man you've met in Europe?' Marcia opened her eyes. The statement was sweeping, and Eleanor had had experience. 'How do you mean?' she asked.

'Well,' said Eleanor, with the judicial air of a connoisseur, 'for one thing, he has a striking face. I don't know whether you ever noticed it, but he has eyes exactly like that portrait of Filippino Lippi in the Uffizi. I kept thinking about it all the time I was talking to him—sleepy sort of Italian eyes, you know—and an American mouth. It makes an interesting combination; you keep wondering what a man like that will do.'

As Marcia made no comment, she continued:

'He has an awfully interesting history. We met him at a reception last week, and Mr. Melville told me all about him afterward. He was born in Genoa—his father was United States consul—and he was brought up in the midst of the excitement during the fight for Italian unity. Politics was in the air he breathed. He knows more about the Italians than they know about themselves. He speaks the language like a native, and he never——'

'Oh, I know what Mr. Melville told you,' Marcia interrupted. 'He likes him.'

'Don't most people?'

'Ask your cousin about him. Ask Mr. Carthrope, the English sculptor. Ask anybody you please—barring my uncle—and see what you'll hear.'

'What shall I hear?'

'A different story from every person.'

'Well, really! He's worth knowing.'

'I detest him!' Marcia made the statement as much from habit as conviction.

Eleanor regarded her a moment rather narrowly, and then she observed: 'I will tell you one thing, Marcia Copley; and that is, that interesting men are mighty scarce in this world. I don't remember ever having met more than half a dozen.'

'And you've had experience,' suggested Marcia.

'Nine seasons.'

'Who were they—the half-dozen?'

'One was a Kansas politician who wrote poetry. A most amazing mixture of crudeness and tact—remarkably bright in some ways, but unexpectedly lacking in others. He'd never read Hamlet; said he'd heard of it, though. Another was a super-civilized Russian. I met him in Cairo. He spoke seven languages, and didn't find any of them full enough to express his thoughts. Another was——'

'The engineer,' suggested Marcia. She had heard of the engineer both from Eleanor and her mother.

'Yes,' agreed Eleanor, 'the chief engineer on the Claytons' yacht. I cruised around with them two years ago on the Mediterranean, and the only interesting man on board was the engineer. He was English, and he'd lived in India and Burma, and in—oh, hundreds of nameless places. I couldn't get much out of him at first; he was pretty shy. English people are, you know. But when he saw that one was really interested he would tell the most astonishing tales. I didn't have much chance to talk to him—he didn't appeal to mamma. That was one of the times that mamma was impetuous,' she added with a laugh. 'Instead of keeping on to Port Said with the boat, we disembarked at Alexandria and ran up to Cairo for the rest of the winter. It was there I met the Russian. He was stopping at Shepheard's.'

Eleanor paused, and her gaze became reminiscent as she sat toying with the little Etruscan perfume-bottle.

'And the others?' Marcia prompted.

'Well, let me see,' Eleanor laughed. 'I once knew a professor of psychology in a little speck of a New England college. He spent his whole life in thinking, and he'd arrived at some very queer conclusions. He was most entertaining—he knew absolutely nothing about the world.' A shade of something like remorse crossed her face, and she hastily abandoned the professor. 'Did I say there were any more? I can't think who the fifth can be, unless I include the blacksmith who married my maid. I never knew him personally; I merely judge from her report of him. He beats her, I believe, when he gets angry; but he's so apologetic afterward that she enjoys it. If you've ever read Wuthering Heights he's exactly like Heathcliff. I'd really like to know him. He'd be worth studying.'

'That's the trouble,' complained Marcia. 'If you're a man you can go around and get acquainted with any one you please, whether he's a blacksmith or a prince; but if you're a girl you have to wait till you're introduced at a tea. And the interesting ones never are introduced at teas.'

'Yes,' agreed Eleanor; 'that's partly true. But, on the other hand, I think you really get to know people better if you're a girl—what they're really like inside, I mean. Men are remarkably confidential creatures.'

'Did you find Mr. Sybert confidential?'

'N-no. I can't say that I did. He's queer, isn't he? You have the feeling that he doesn't talk about what he thinks about—that's why I should like to know him. It's not what a man does that makes him interesting; it's what he thinks. It's his potentialities.'

Margaret rose with something of a yawn. 'If you're going to discuss potentialities, I'm going to bed. Come on, Eleanor. To-morrow's the festa of Our Lady of Good Counsel, and we start at nine o'clock.'

Eleanor rose reluctantly. 'I wish we weren't going to Perugia on Wednesday. I should much rather stay here with Marcia.'

'And Mr. Sybert,' Margaret laughed.

'Oh, yes, Mr. Sybert,' Eleanor acquiesced. 'He annoys you until you get him settled.'

'He's like one of those problems in algebra,' suggested Marcia. 'Given a lot of things, to find the value of x. You work it exactly right and x won't come.'

Margaret paused by the door and gathered her wrapper around her like a toga.

'While you're talking about interesting people,' she threw back, 'I know one who isn't appreciated, and that's Paul. He's a mighty nice boy.'

'That's just what he is,' said Eleanor. 'A nice boy—et c'est tout. Good night, Marcia. When we come back from Perugia we'll sit up all night talking about interesting men. It's an interesting subject.'

CHAPTER XV

Villa Vivalanti was astir early in the morning—early, that is, for the villa. Castel Vivalanti had been at work two hours and more when Pietro went the rounds of the bedroom doors with his very obsequious, 'Buon giorno, Excellency; if it suits your convenience, coffee will be served in the ilex grove in half an hour.' Coffee in the ilex grove was a new departure in accordance with Marcia's inspiration of the night before. And the ilex grove to-day, as Bianca exclaimed with clasped hands, reminded one of paradise. The week of rain had left it a study in green; the deep, rich tone of ilex leaves arching overhead, the blue green moss on dark tree trunks, the tender tint of young grass sprouting in the paths, and the yellow flickering sunlight glancing everywhere. Out on the terrace the peacock was trailing his feathers over the marble pavement with a conscious air of being in tune with the day.

Marcia was first to appear. She stepped on to the loggia with a little exclamation of delight at the beauty of the morning. In a pale summer gown, her hair burnished by the sun, she herself was not out of touch with the scene. She crossed the terrace and stood by the balustrade, looking off through a golden and purple haze to the speck on the horizon of Rome and St. Peter's. The peacock called her back, strutting insistently with wide-spread tail.

'You ridiculous bird!' she laughed. 'I suppose you have been posing here for two hours, waiting for some one to come and admire,' and she hurried off to the grove to make sure that Pietro had carried out her orders.

The table was spread by the fountain, where the green arched paths converged and the ilexes grew in an open circle. The sunlight flickering through on dainty linen and silver and glass and on little cakes of golden honey—fresh from a farm in the Alban hills—made a feast which would not have been out of place in a Watteau painting. Marcia echoed Bianca's enthusiasm as her eyes fell upon the scene, and Pietro flew about with an unprecedented ardour, placing rugs and cushions and wicker chairs.

'It is perfect,' she cried, as she retreated down one of the paths to get a perspective. 'But there are no flowers,' she added. 'That will never do; we must have some lilies-of-the-valley, Pietro. You fix a bowl in the centre, while I run and pick them,' and she started off toward the garden borders.

Here Paul Dessart found her five minutes later. He greeted her with a friendly, 'Felicissimo giorno, signorina!' The transient clouds of yesterday had disappeared from his brow as well as from the sky, and he joined gaily in her task.

'There!' said Marcia as she rose to her feet and shook back the stray hair from her eyes. 'Could anything be more in keeping with a sylvan breakfast than these?' She held at arm's length for him to admire a great bunch of delicate transparent bells sheathed in glistening green. 'Come,' she cried; 'the artist must arrange them'; and together they turned toward the fountain.

A spray of bluest forget-me-nots hung over one of the garden borders. The young man stooped and, breaking it, presented it with his hand on his heart.

'Signorina,' he begged in a tone of mock-Italian sentiment—'dearest signorina, I am going where duty calls—far, far away to Perugia. Non-te-scordar-di-me!'

She laughed as she put the flowers in her belt, but with a slightly deeper tinge on her cheek. Paul, in a mood like this, was very attractive.

As they entered the grove they heard the prattle of childish voices, and presently Gerald and Gervasio appeared down the walk, carrying each a saucer of crumbs for their scaly friends of the fountain. They stopped with big eyes at the sight of the table spread for breakfast.

'Oh, Cousin Marcia!' Gerald squealed delightedly, 'are we doin' to eat out uv doors? May Gervas' an' me eat wif you? Please! Please!'

Marcia feigned to consider.

'Yes,' said she finally, 'this is my party, and if you'll be good boys and not talk, I'll invite you. And when you've finished your bread and milk, if you've been very good, you may have some—' she paused and lowered her voice dramatically while the two hung upon her words—'honey!'

Paul Dessart laughed at what struck him as an anticlimax, but the boys received the assurance with acclamation. Gervasio was presented to the young painter, and he acknowledged the introduction with a grace equal to Gerald's own. He had almost forgotten that he was not born a prince. As Gerald shook hands he invited the guest, with visible hesitancy, to throw the crumbs; but Paul generously refused the invitation, and two minutes later the little fellows were kneeling side by side on the coping of the fountain, while the arching pathways rang with their laughter.

The rest of their excellencies soon appeared in a humour to fit the morning, and the usually uneventful 'first breakfast' partook of the nature of a fête. Gerald's and Gervasio's laughter rang free and unchecked. The two were sitting side by side on a stone garden-seat (the broken-nosed bust of a forgotten emperor brooding over them), engaged for the present with twin silver bowls of bread and milk, but with speculative eyes turned honeyward. The ghost of overnight was resurrected and jeered at, while the ghost himself gravely passed the cups. The sedately stepping peacock, who had joined the feast uninvited, became the point of many morals as he lowered his feathers in the dust to scramble for crumbs. Before the party ended, Sybert and Dessart engaged in a good-natured bout on Sybert's theme of yesterday concerning Italy's baneful beauty.

'Paul has missed his calling!' declared Eleanor Royston. 'He should have been a ward politician in New York. It is a pity to see such a gift for impromptu eloquence wasted in private life.'

For a time Paul subsided, but their controversy closed with the laugh on his side. Apropos of riots, his thesis was that they were on the whole very jolly. And he upheld this shockingly barbaric view with the plea that he always liked to see people having a good time, and that next to sleeping in the sun and eating macaroni the Italians were never so happy as when engaged in a row. For his part, he affirmed, he expected to find them tearing up the golden paving-stones of paradise to heave at each other!

The image wrung a smile from even Sybert's gravity; It contained just enough of truth, and not too much, to make it funny. Pietro's announcement, at this point, that the carriages were ready to drive their excellencies to the festa dissolved the party in a scurry for hats and wraps. Sybert at first had declined the festa, on the plea that he had business in Rome. Marcia had accepted his excuse with the simply polite statement that they would be sorry not to have him, but Eleanor Royston had refused to let him off.

'I've known a great many diplomats,' she affirmed; 'and though they are supposed to be engaged with the business of nations, I have never yet seen one who was too busy to attend a party. We shan't let you off on that score.'

Somewhat to Paul's secret annoyance, and not entirely to Marcia's gratification, he finally consented to change his mind. As the carriage started, Marcia glanced back toward the loggia steps, where the two little boys, one with yellow curls and one with black, were standing hand in hand, wistfully watching the departure.

'Good-bye, Gerald and Gervasio,' she called. 'If you are very good, I'll bring you something nice from the festa.'

The Copley pilgrimage was not the only one bound for Genazzano that day. They passed on the road countless bands of contadini, both on foot and on donkey-back, journeying toward the festa, their babies and provisions in baskets on their heads. Genazzano, on St Mark's day, wisely unites pleasure and piety, with masses in the cathedral and jugglers in the piazza. The party from the villa devoted the larger share of their time to the piazza, laughing good-naturedly at the 'Inglese! which was shouted after them at every turn. They lunched on the terrace of the very modest village inn, in company with a jovial party of young Irish students from the Propaganda who seemed to treat the miracles of the wonder-working Madonna in the light of an ecclesiastical joke. The afternoon found the sight-seeing ardour of the two elder ladies somewhat damped. There was to be a function in the cathedral at three, and they stated their intention of stopping quietly in the low-raftered parlour of the inn until it should commence. Eleanor Royston issued a frank invitation to Sybert to explore the old Colonna castle which surmounted the town, and he accepted with what struck Marcia as a flattering show of interest.

In regard to Laurence Sybert she herself was of many minds. A very considerable amount of her old antagonism for him remained, mixed with a curiosity and interest in his movements out of all proportion to the interest he had ever expended upon her. And to-day she was experiencing a fresh resentment in the feeling that his attitude toward Eleanor was more deferential than toward herself. It was a venturesome act for any man to awaken Marcia's pique.

Meanwhile she had Paul; and the slight cloud upon her brow vanished quickly as she and Margaret and the young man turned toward the piazza. Paul was in holiday humour, and the contagion of his fun was impossible to escape. He wore a favour in his hat and a gilt medal of the Madonna in his buttonhole; he laughed and joked with the people in the booths; he offered his assistance to a prestidigitator who called for volunteers; he shot dolls with an air-rifle and carried off the prize, a gaudily decorated pipe, which he presented with a courtly bow to a pretty peasant girl who, with frank admiration, had applauded the feat. Finally he brought to a triumphant close a bargain of Marcia's. She had expressed a desire for a peculiar style of head-dress—a long silver pin with a closed fist on the end—worn by the women from the Volscian villages. Paul readily agreed to acquire one for her. The spillo was plucked from an astonished woman's head and the bargaining began.

Sell it! But that was impossible. It was an heirloom! it had been in the family for many generations; she could not think of parting with it—not perhaps for its weight in silver?—the money was jingled before her eyes. She wavered visibly. Paul demanded scales. They were brought from the tobacco-shop, the tobacconist importantly presiding. The spillo was placed on one side; lire on the other—six—seven—eight. The woman clasped her hands ecstatically as the pile grew. Nine—ten—the scales hesitated. At eleven they went down with a thud, and the bargain was completed. A pleased murmur rippled through the crowd, and some one suggested, 'Now is the signorina sposata.' For, according to Volscian etiquette, only married woman might wear the head-dress.

Marcia shook her head with a laugh. She and Paul, standing side by side, made an effective couple, and the peasants noted it with pleased appreciation. Italians are quick to sympathize with a romance. 'Promessi sposi,' some one murmured, this time with an accent of delighted assurance. Paul cast a sidewise glance at Marcia to see how she would accept this somewhat public betrothal. She repudiated the charge again, but with a slightly heightened colour, and the crowd laughed gaily. As the two turned up the steep street toward the cathedral, Paul held out his hand.

'Give me the pin,' he said. 'I will carry it in my pocket for you, since you are not entitled—as yet—to wear it.'

Marcia handed it over, trying not to look conscious of the undertone in his voice. He was very convincing to-day; she was reconsidering her problem.

In the crowded little piazza before the cathedral they found the rest of the party. They all mounted the steps and stood in a group, watching the processions of pilgrims with votive offerings. They came in bands of fifty and a hundred, bearing banners and chanting litanies. As they approached the church they broke off their singing to shout 'Ave Marias,' mounting on their knees and kissing the steps as they came. Marcia, looking down over the tossing mass of scarlet and yellow kerchiefs, compared it with the great function she had witnessed in St. Peter's. These peasants approaching the Madonna's shrine on their knees, shouting themselves hoarse, their faces glowing with religious ardour, were to her mind far the more impressive sight of the two. She turned into the church, half carried away by the movement and colour and intensity of the scene. There was something contagious about the simple energy of their devotion.

The interior was packed with closely kneeling peasants, the air filled with a blue haze of incense through which the candles on the altar glowed dimly. The Copley party wedged their way through and stood back at the shadow of one of the side chapels, watching the scene. Paul dropped on his knees with the peasants, and, sketch-book in hand, set himself surreptitiously to copying the head of a girl in front. Marcia watched him for a few moments with an amused smile; then she glanced away over the sea of kneeling figures. There was no mechanical devotion here: it came from the heart, if any ever did. Ah, they were too believing! she thought suddenly. Their piety carried them too far; it robbed them of dignity, of individuality, of self-reliance. Almost at her feet a woman was prostrate on the floor, kissing the stones of the pavement in a frenzy of devotion. She turned away in a quick revulsion of feeling such as she had experienced in St. Peter's. And as she turned her eyes met Laurence Sybert's fixed upon her face. He was standing just behind her, and he bent over and whispered:

'You've seen enough of this. Come, let's get out,' and he made a motion toward the sacristy entrance behind them. They stepped back, and the crowd closed into their places.

Out in the piazza he squared his shoulders with a little laugh. 'The church must make itself over a bit before I shall be ready to be received into the fold. How about you, Miss Marcia?'

'It seemed so beautiful, their simple faith; and then suddenly—that horrible woman—and you realize the ignorance and superstition underneath. Everything is alike!' she added. 'Just as you begin to think how beautiful it is, you catch a glimpse below the surface. It's awful to begin seeing hidden meanings; you can never stop.'

'Look at that,' he laughed, nodding toward a house where a pig was stretched asleep in the doorway. 'He's evidently been left to keep guard while the family are at the festa. I suppose you've noticed that every house is Genazzano has a separate door for the chickens cut in the bottom of the big door. It's rather funny, isn't it?'

Marcia regarded the pig with a laugh and a sigh.

'Yes, it's funny; but then, the first thing you know, you begin to think what a low standard of life the people must have who keep their pigs and their chickens in the house with them, and it doesn't seem funny any more.'

'Ah,' he said. 'You're coming on.'

'I'm afraid I am!' she agreed.

As they strolled toward the upper part of the town, they came upon a group of men and boys talking and smoking and throwing dice in a prolonged noonday rest. It was a part of the pilgrimage from the village of Castel Vivalanti, and the group instantly recognized Marcia. The festal spirit of the day, joined to a double portion of wine, had made them more boisterous than usual; and one ragged little urchin, who had been playing the part of buffoon for the crowd, fell upon the two signori as a fresh subject for pleasantries. He set up the usual beggar's whine, asking for soldi. The two paying no attention, he changed the form of his petition.

'Signorina,' he implored, running along at Marcia's side and keeping a dirty hand extended impudently in front of her, 'I have hunger, signorina; I have hunger. Spare me, for the love of God, a few grains of wheat.'

'That's a new formula,' Marcia laughed. 'It's usually bread they want; I never heard them ask for wheat before.'

Sybert turned on the boy, with an air of threatening, and he hastily scrambled out of reach, though he still persevered in his petition, to the noisy amusement of the crowd.

Marcia spread out empty hands.

'I have no wheat,' she said, with a shake of her head.

The youngster turned to his following, mimicking her.

'The signorina has no wheat,' he cried. 'Will no one give to the signorina? She is poor and she has hunger.'

Some one tossed a soldo. The boy pounced upon it and extended it toward her.

'Behold, signorina! This good man is poor, but he is generous. He offers you money to get some wheat.'

Marcia laughed at the play in thorough enjoyment, while Sybert, with an angry light in his eye, seized the boy by the collar and cuffed him soundly.

'Mr. Sybert,' she cried, 'take care; you'll hurt him!'

'I mean to hurt him,' he said grimly, as with a final cuff he dropped him over the side of the bank.

The crowd jeered at his downfall as loudly as they had jeered at his impudence, and the two turned a corner and left them behind.

'You needn't have struck him,' Marcia said. 'The boy didn't mean anything beyond being funny. He is one of my best friends; his name is Beppo, and he lives next door to the baker's shop.'

'If that is a specimen of your friends,' Sybert answered dryly, 'my advice is that you shake their acquaintance.'

'I don't mind a little impertinence,' she said lightly. 'It's at least better than whining.'

'I told you yesterday, Miss Marcia, that I didn't think you ought to be running about the country alone—I think it even less to-day. It isn't safe up here in the mountain towns, where the people aren't used to foreigners.'

'Why don't you suggest to Uncle Howard that he engage a nurse for me?'

'I begin to think you need one!'

Marcia laid a light hand on his arm.

'Mr. Sybert, please don't speak to me so harshly.'

'I'll speak to your uncle—that's what I'll do,' he retorted.

They had by this time reached the castle, and having crossed the drawbridge and the stone courtyard, they came out on the other side, with the noisy little town left suddenly behind. The mountains rose above them, the valley lay beneath, and before them a straight, grassy road stretched into the hills, bordered by the tall arches of an old aqueduct. They strolled along, talking idly, Marcia well in command of the situation. There was a touch of audacity, even of provocation, underneath her glance, and Sybert was amusedly aware of the fact that he was being flirted with. Quite to Marcia's astonishment, he met her on her own ground; he accepted the half-challenge in her manner and was never the first to lower his eyes. They had come to a bank starred pink with cyclamen and backed by one of the tall arches of the aqueduct.

'Suppose we sit down and look at the view,' he suggested.

Marcia seated herself on a projecting block of masonry, while Sybert lounged on the grass at her side.

'Mr. Melville told me the other day,' he remarked presently, 'that he remembers having seen your mother when she was a little girl.'

Marcia nodded and laughed. 'He told me about it—he says she was the worst tom-boy he ever saw.'

'It was a very pretty picture he drew—I wonder if you ever rode the colts bareback?'

'My mother was brought up on a Southern plantation; I, in a New York house and a Paris convent—there weren't any colts to ride.'

'And your mother died when you were a little girl?'

'When I was twelve.'

'Ah, that was hard,' he said, with quick sympathy.

She glanced up in half surprise. It was the first time she had ever heard him say anything so kindly.

'And the convent in Paris?' he asked. 'How did that happen?'

'Some one suggested it to my father, and I suppose it struck him as an excellent way to dispose of me. Not that he isn't an appreciative parent,' she added quickly, in response to an expression on his face; 'but the education of a daughter is a problem to a business man.'

'I should think it might be,' he agreed. 'And how did the convent go?'

'Not very well. I didn't learn anything but prayers and French, and I was dreadfully homesick.'

'And then?'

'Oh, one or two governesses and a boarding-school, and after that college.' Marcia laughed. 'You should have seen my father when I suggested the college. He clutched at the idea like a drowning man; it was another four years' reprieve.'

'It's a pity,' he remarked, 'that the French method of marrying one's daughter offhand as soon as she gets out of school doesn't prevail in America.'

'I really did feel guilty when I graduated, the poor man looked so dazed through it all. He asked me if I would like to take a little trip into Venezuela with him to look into some mines. It would have been fun, wouldn't it?' she asked. 'I should have liked to go.'

'But, being charitable, you declined?'

'Yes, and having another plan in my head. It had been years since I had seen Uncle Howard, and I thought it would be nice to come over and live with him for a while.'

'And so here you are in Genazzano.'

'Here I am,' she agreed. 'But as soon as papa is ready to settle down respectably like other people, I am going back to keep house for him, and I shall take with me some fourteenth-century Italian furniture, and some nice Italian servants, and give nice little Italian dinners.'

'And shall you invite me sometimes?'

'Drop in whenever you wish.'

Marcia began to laugh.

'Well?' he inquired. 'What is so funny?'

'To be talking to you this way—I shouldn't have issued that invitation a week ago. You couldn't help yourself yesterday,' she added; 'Aunt Katherine made you come; but really it's your own fault to-day.'

'Is that the impression I gave you? I am afraid I must have very bad manners.'

'You have—rather bad,' she agreed.

'You hit straight,' he laughed. 'No,' he added presently; 'Aunt Katherine had nothing to do with our walk to-day. If you care to know, I'll tell you why I wanted to come. Yesterday afternoon I took a ride with a most charming young woman, and I thought I'd like to renew the acquaintance.'

'If that's intended for a compliment, it's of a very doubtful nature. You have known this same charming young woman for the last three months, and have never shown any marked desire for her company before.'

'I was blind, but I have been made to see.'

He commenced rolling a cigarette in a lazy, half-amused fashion, while Marcia occupied an interval of silence by checking the progress of a black beetle who found himself on the stone beside her, and who seemed in a great hurry to get somewhere else. In whichever way he turned, a mountain of a green leaf sprang up in his path. He ran wildly in a circle, vainly seeking an outlet, his six little legs twittering with anxiety.

Sybert stretched out a sympathetic hand and dropped him over the bank to a place of safety.

'Now why must you do that?' Marcia inquired.

'A sense of fellow-feeling—I've watched too many women playing with too many men not to know how the poor beast felt. His progress was thwarted at every turn, without his being able to comprehend any underlying motive or reason or law.'

'It was good for him,' she affirmed. 'I was giving him a new experience—was widening his horizon. When I finally let him go he would have been so thankful to think of the danger he had escaped, that he would have been twice as happy a beetle as ever before.'

'That is one way of looking at it,' Sybert agreed.

Marcia watched him a moment speculatively. She was thinking about the Contessa Torrenieri.

'Mr. Sybert,' she suggested, 'there are a lot of things I should like to know about you.'

'I can think of nothing in my past that ought to be hidden.'

'These are things that you wouldn't tell me.'

'Try me and see.'

'Anything I choose to ask?'

'I am at your disposal.'

'Have you ever been in love with any one?'

He glanced up from his cigarette with an amused stare. 'What's this—a confessional?'

'Oh, no—only you don't look as if you'd ever done such a foolish thing, and I just wondered——'

'Half a dozen times.'

'Really?'

'Oh, I dare say not—really,' he laughed. 'In my cub days I used to be—well, interested sometimes.'

'But you outgrew it?'

'It would be a rash man who would affirm that! You never can tell what's waiting for you around the next corner.'

She would have liked to put a question or so in regard to the contessa, but instead she remarked, 'There are some other things I'd like to ask you.'

'I'm not so sure I'll answer if that's a specimen.'

'Why were you carrying a revolver yesterday?'

'You strike me as a very inquisitive young woman, Miss Marcia.'

'You strike me as a very mysterious man, Mr. Sybert.'

'Why was I carrying a revolver? For a very simple reason. I have been travelling through the south, helping to quiet the rioters; and as that is not a popular occupation, I thought it wisest to go armed. A revolver is an excellent thing with which to persuade people, though in all probability I shall never have any occasion to use it. I hope you are satisfied.'

'Thank you,' said Marcia. 'Not that I believe you at all,' she added with a laugh.

He regarded her a moment with a slightly perplexed frown. 'What on earth do you take me for, Miss Marcia? An anarchist, a bandit, a second Fra Diavolo in disguise? I am nothing so picturesque, I assure you—merely a peaceful private citizen of the United States.'

'How do you come to know the baker's son, Tarquinio, so well?'

'I think I've answered questions enough. Suppose we have a confession from you, Miss Marcia. Have you ever been in love?'

Marcia rose. 'It's a quarter past four, and we ought to be going back. The Roystons have to catch the evening train into Rome.'

Marcia drove to the station with the travellers, leaving the rest of the party to return to the villa in the other carriage. She had a slight feeling of compunction in regard to Paul, and it made her more responsive to his nonsense than she might otherwise have been. In the rôle of cicerone he naïvely explained the story of the ruins they passed on the way, and the entire history of Rome, from Romulus and Remus to Garibaldi, unfolded itself upon that nine-mile stretch of dusty road. Marcia gave herself up gaily enough to the spirit of the play, forgetting for the time any troubling questions lurking in the background. When she bade him good-bye she smiled back, half laughingly, half seriously, at his parting speech—a repetition of the morning's pretty phrase—'non-te-scordar-di-me!'

As the carriage turned homeward she smiled to herself over her yesterday's state at the prospect of meeting Paul. The actuality had not been so disconcerting. She did not quite comprehend his new attitude, but she accepted it as a tacit recognition of her desire to let matters stand, and was grateful. She felt very kindly toward him this evening. He was such a care-free, optimistic young fellow; and even supposing he were too ready to look on the bright side of things, was not Laurence Sybert, she asked herself, too ready also to look on the dark side? Since his words of yesterday, in the old wine-cellar, she had felt an undertone of sadness to her thoughts which she vaguely resented. As she rode along now between the fresh fields, glowing in the soft light of the April sunset, she was dimly conscious of a struggle, a rebellion, going on within her own nature.

She seemed pulled two ways. The beautiful sunshiny world of dreams was calling to her. And Paul stood at the crossways—laughing, careless, happy Paul—holding out his hand with a winning smile to show the way to Cytherea. But deep within her heart she felt the weight of the real world—the world which means misery to so many people—dragging on her spirits and holding her back. And in the background she saw Sybert watching her with folded arms and a half-quizzical smile—Sybert making no move either to lure her on or to turn her back—merely watching with inscrutable eyes.

Happiness seemed to be her portion. Why could she not accept it gladly, and shut her eyes to all else? If she once commenced seeing the misery in the world, there would be no end. Until a few weeks before she had scarcely realized that any existed outside of books, but she knew it now; she had seen it face to face. She thought of the crowded, squalid little houses of Castel Vivalanti; of the women who went out at sunrise to work all day in the fields, of the hordes of children only half fed. Oh, yes, she knew now that there was misery outside of books, but she asked herself, with an almost despairing cry, why need she know? Since she could do nothing to help, since she was not to blame, why not close her eyes and pretend it was not there? It was the shrinking cry of the soul that for the first time has tasted of knowledge; that with open eyes is hesitating on the threshold of the real world, with a longing backward glance toward the unreal world of dreams. But in life there is no going back; knowledge once gained may not be cancelled, and there was further knowledge waiting for Marcia not very far ahead.

Two little boys turning somersaults by the side of the carriage suddenly recalled to her mind the boys at the villa, and her promise to bring them a present from the festa. Not once had she thought of them during the day, and the only possible present now was the inevitable sweet chocolate of Castel Vivalanti. She glanced at her watch; there was still an hour before dinner, and she ordered Giovanni to drive up the hill to the town. Giovanni respectfully begged her pardon, with the suggestion that the horses were tired; they had had a long journey and the hill was steep. Marcia replied, with a touch of sharpness, that the horses could rest all day to-morrow. They wound up the gradual ascent at a walk, in company with the procession coming home for the night. It was a sight which Marcia always watched with fresh interest: field-workers with mattocks on their shoulders trudging wearily back to supper and bed; washerwomen, their clothes in baskets on their heads, calling cheery goodbyes to one another; files of ragged little donkeys laden with brush, sheep and pigs and goats, and long-horned oxen—where they were all to be stowed for the night was an ever-recurring mystery.

Under the smiling moons of the Porta della Luna the carriage came to a halt, and the crowd of Castel Vivalanti boys, who were in the habit of scouring the highway for coppers, fell upon it vociferously. Marcia had exhausted her soldi in Genazzano, and with a laughing shake of her head she motioned them away. But the boys would not be shaken off; they swarmed about the carriage like little rats, shrilly demanding money. She continued to shake her head, and instantly their cries were transferred to the taunts of the afternoon. 'Grano! Grano!' they shouted in chorus; and Giovanni raised his whip and drove them away.

Marcia paused with her foot on the carriage-step, puzzling over this new cry which was suddenly assailing her at every turn.

'What is the matter, Giovanni? Why are they always shouting "Wheat"?'

He waved his whip disdainfully. 'Chi sa, signorina? They are of no account. Do not listen to their foolishness.'

They were the same children to whom she had given chocolate not many days before. 'They forget quickly!' she said to herself, 'perhaps, after all, Paul was right, and beauty is their strongest virtue.'

The 'Ave Maria' was ringing as she turned into the crooked little streets, and the town was buzzing like a beehive over its evening affairs. Copper water-jars were coming home from the well, blue smoke was pouring out of every chimney, and yellow meal was being sifted outside the doors. Owing to the festa, the streets were crowded with loungers, and in the tiny piazza groups of men were gathered about the door of the tobacco-shop, arguing and quarrelling and gesticulating in their excitable Italian fashion. It had been a week or more since Marcia had visited the village, and now, as she threaded her way through the crowd, it struck her suddenly that the people's usual friendly nods were a trifle churlish; she had the uncomfortable feeling that group after group fell silent and turned to stare after her as the passed. One little boy shouted 'Grano!' and was dragged indoors with a box on his ears.

'Madonna mia!' cried his anxious mother. 'Are we not poor enough already, that you would bring down foreign curses upon the house?'

In the bake-shop Domenico served her surlily, answering her friendly inquiries as to the health of his family and the progress of his vineyard with grunts rather than words. Amazed and indignant, she shrank within herself; and with head erect and hotly burning cheeks turned back toward the gate, not so much as glancing at the people, who silently made way for her.

'Ah, you see,' they murmured to one another, 'the foreign signorina played at having a kind heart for amusement. But what does she care for our miseria? No more than for the stones beneath her feet.'

Laurence Sybert, coming out from the village, was somewhat astonished to find Giovanni drawn up before the gate. Giovanni hailed him with an anxious air.

'Scusi, signore; have you seen the signorina? She is inside.' He nodded toward the porta. 'She has gone to the bake-shop alone. I told her the horses were tired, but she paid no attention; and the ragazzi called "Wheat!" but she did not understand.'

'They shouted "Wheat!" did they?'

'Si, signore. They read the papers. The Avanti yesterday——'

Sybert nodded. 'I know what the Avanti said.'

He turned back under the archway and set out for the baker's—the place, as it happened, from which he had just come. He had been entertained there with some very plain comments on his friends in the villa—as Giovanni suggested, they read their papers, and the truth of whatever was stated in printer's ink was not to be doubted. It was scarcely the time that Marcia should have chosen for an evening stroll through Castel Vivalanti; and

Sybert was provoked that she should have paid so little heed to his warning of the afternoon. The fact that she was ignorant of the special causes for his warning did not at the moment present itself as an excuse. He had not gone far when he heard shouts ahead. The words were unmistakable.

'Wheat! Wheat! Signorina Wheat!'

The volume of sound sent him hurrying forward in quick anxiety, almost fearing a riot. But his first glance, as he came out into the piazza, showed him that it was scarcely as serious as that. Marcia, looking hurt and astonished and angry, was standing in the midst of a fast-increasing crowd of dirty little street urchins, who were shrieking and jumping and gesticulating about her. She was in no possible danger, however; the boys meant no harm beyond being impudent. For a second Sybert hesitated, with the grim intention of teaching her a lesson, but the next moment he saw that she was already thoroughly frightened. She called out wildly to a group of men who had paused on the outskirts of the crowd; they laughed insolently, and made no move to drive the boys away. She closed her eyes and swayed slightly, while Sybert in quick compunction hurried forward. Pushing into the midst of the tumult, he cuffed the boys right and left out of the way. Marcia opened her eyes and regarded him dazedly.

'Mr. Sybert!' she gasped. 'What's the matter? What are they saying?'

'Can you walk?' he asked, stretching out a hand to steady her. 'Come, we'll get out of the piazza.'

By this time other men had joined the crowd, and low mutterings ran from mouth to mouth. Many recognized Sybert, and his name was shouted tauntingly. 'Wheat! Wheat!' however, was still the burden of the cry. One boy jostled against them impudently—it was Beppo of the afternoon—and Sybert struck him a sharp blow across the shoulders with his cane, sending him sprawling on the pavement. Half the crowd laughed, half called angrily, 'Hit him, Beppo, hit him. Don't let him knock you down,' while a half-drunken voice in the rear shouted, 'Behold Signor Siberti, the friend of the poor!'

'Here, let's get out of this,' he said. And clearing an opening with a vigorous sweep of his cane, he hurried her down a narrow alley and around a corner out of sight of the piazza. Leading the way into a little trattoria, he drew a chair forward toward the door.

'Giuseppe,' he called, 'bring the signorina some wine.'

Marcia dropped into the chair and leaned her head on the back. She felt dazed and bewildered. Never before had she been treated with anything but friendliness and courtesy. Why had the people suddenly turned against her? What had she done that they should hate her? In the back of the room she heard Sybert explaining something in a low tone to Giuseppe, and she caught, the words, 'she does not know.'

'Poverina, she does not know,' the woman murmured.

Sybert came across with a glass of wine.

'Here, Marcia, drink this,' he said peremptorily.

She received the glass with a hand that trembled, and took one or two swallows and then set it down.

'It's nothing. I shall be all right in a moment. They pressed around me so close that I couldn't breathe.'

The wine brought some colour back to her face, and after a few minutes she rose to her feet.

'I'm sorry to have made so much commotion. I feel better now; let's go back to the carriage.'

Skirting the piazza, they returned to the porta by a narrow side-street, the boys behind still shouting after, but none approaching within reach of Sybert's stick. They had regained the carriage and reached the bottom of the hill before either of them spoke. Marcia was the first to break the silence.

'What is it, Mr. Sybert, that I don't know?'

'A good many things, apparently,' he said coolly. 'For one, you don't know how to take a piece of friendly advice. I told you this afternoon that the country-side was too stirred up to be safe, and I think you might have paid just a little attention to my warning. Respectable Italian girls don't run around the streets alone, and they particularly don't choose the evening of a festa for a solitary walk.'

'If you have quite finished, Mr. Sybert, will you answer my question?—Why do they call me "Signorina Wheat"?'

He was apparently engaged with his thoughts and did not hear.

'Mr. Sybert, I asked you a question.'

'Why do they shout "Wheat"?' His tone was still sharp. 'Well, I suppose because just at present wheat is a burning question in Italy, and the name of Copley is somewhat unpleasantly connected with it. Your uncle has just bought a large consignment of American wheat, which is on its way to Italy now. His only object is to relieve the suffering—he loses on every bushel he sells—but, as is usually the case with disinterested people, his motives have been misjudged. The newspapers have had a great deal to say about the matter, and the people, with their usual gratitude toward their benefactors, have turned against him.'

'Mr. Sybert, you are not telling me the truth.'

Sybert did not see fit to answer this charge; he folded his arms and leaned against the cushions, with his eyes fixed on the two brass buttons on the back of Giovanni's coat. And Marcia, the colour back in her cheeks, sat staring at the roadway with angry eyes. Neither spoke again till the carriage came to a stand before the loggia.

'Well, Miss Marcia, are we friends?' said Sybert.

'No,' said Marcia, 'we are not.'

She turned up to her room and set about dressing in a very mingled frame of mind. She was still excited and hurt from her treatment in the village—and very much puzzled as to its motive. She was indignant at Sybert's attitude, at his presuming to issue orders with no reason attached and expecting them to be obeyed. Instead of being grateful for his timely assistance, she was irritated that he should have happened by just in time to see the fulfilment of his warning. His superior 'I told you so!' attitude was exasperating to a degree. She ended by uniting her various wounded sensibilities into a single feeling of resentment toward him. The desire that was uppermost in her mind was a wish to pay him back, to make him feel sorry—though for exactly what, she was not quite clear.

She hung up in the wardrobe the simple dinner-dress that Granton had laid out on the bed, and chose in its place a particularly dignified gown with a particularly long train. Having piled her hair on the top of her head, she added a diamond star and a necklace with a diamond pendant. She did not often wear jewels, but they were supposedly 'American' and irritating to a man of Sybert's cosmopolitan sensibilities.

'Quite stately,' she murmured, critically surveying the effect in the mirror. 'One might almost say matronly.'

As she started downstairs she was waylaid at the nursery door by a small figure in a white nightgown.

'Cousin Marcia, what did you bwing me from ve festa?'

'Oh, Gerald! I brought you some chocolate and I left it in the carriage. But never mind, dear; it's too late, anyway, for you to eat it to-night. I will send and get it, and you shall have it with your breakfast to-morrow morning. Be a good boy and go to sleep.'

She went downstairs with her mind bent upon chocolate, and crossed the empty salon to the little ante-room at the rear. She had opened the door and burst in before she realized that any one was inside; then before the apology had risen to her lips she had heard her uncle's words.

'Good heavens, Sybert, what can I do? You know my hands are tied. Willard Copley would let the last person in Italy starve if he could make one more dollar out of it!'

Marcia stood still, looking at her uncle in horror while the meaning of his words sank into her mind. He whirled around upon her. His face was whiter and sterner than she had ever seen it.

'What do you want, Marcia?' he asked sharply. 'Why don't you knock before you come into a room?'

Marcia's face flushed hotly. 'I am sorry, Uncle Howard; I was in a hurry, and didn't know any one was in here.'

'Oh, I beg your pardon, Marcia! I spoke hastily.'

She hesitated in the doorway and then faced him again.

'I heard what you said. Will you please tell me what you mean?'

Copley cast an annoyed glance at Sybert, who was standing in the embrasure by the window with his hands in his pockets and his eyes bent upon the floor. Sybert glanced up with a little frown, and then with a half-perceptible shrug turned away and looked out of the window.

'I might as well tell you, I suppose—you appear to be hearing it from other sources. Your father has been the originator this spring of a very successful corner in wheat. He is, as you know, a keen judge of markets; and foreseeing that wheat for a number of reasons was likely to be scarce, he and one or two of his friends have purchased the whole of the visible supply. As Italy has had to import more than usual—and pay for it in gold when she hasn't much but paper at her command—you can readily see that it places her in an awkward position. America is a great country, Marcia, when a single one of her citizens can bankrupt a whole kingdom.'

'You don't mean, Uncle Howard,' she cried, aghast, 'that my father has caused the wheat famine?'

'There may be one or two minor causes, but I think he is deserving of most of the credit. The name of Copley, I assure you, is not beloved in Italy just now.'

'And that is what the boys meant when they shouted "Grano"?'

'Oh, it's no secret. We're celebrities in our small way. Two continents are ringing with the name of the American Wheat King, and we come in for a share of his fame. When you think about it,' he added, 'there is something beautifully fitting about our taking Villa Vivalanti this spring. We appear to be American editions of the "Bad Prince." I fancy the old gentleman turned in his grave and smiled a trifle when I signed the lease.'

'But, Uncle Howard, he doesn't understand. He does it like a mathematical problem, just to show what he can do, just for the pleasure of winning. Why don't you write to him? Why didn't you tell him?'

'Tell him!' Copley laughed. 'You have not been acquainted with your father for so many years as I have, Marcia. Why should he care for a lot of Italian peasants? There are too many of them in existence already. The food in this world has to be fought for, and those who are beaten deserve to die.'

Marcia's face turned white as the meaning of a hundred petty incidents flashed through her mind that before had had no significance. She knew now why the people in Rome had stopped talking about the wheat famine when she entered the room. She understood Sybert's attitude toward her all the year—his quizzical expression once or twice when she spent money over-lavishly. She recalled the newspaper the workman in Rome had thrust in her face—the Grido del Popolo—the Cry of the People. She did not have to ask now what it meant. The very beggars in the street had known of her shame, while she alone was ignorant.

'Why didn't you tell me?' she cried.

'I did not wish to spoil your pleasure; there is no reason why you shouldn't be happy. If all goes well, a year from now you will be one of the notable heiresses of America. I only hope, when you're enjoying your wealth, that you'll not think of the poor starving wretches in Italy who gave it to you.'

Copley's tone was as brutal as his words. He had forgotten the girl before him; he was talking to the man in America.

Marcia turned away and, with a deep sob, sank down by the table and buried her face in her arms. Sybert threw up his head quickly with a glance of anger, and Copley suddenly came to his senses. He sprang forward and laid his hand on her shoulder.

'For Heaven's sake, Marcia, don't cry about it! I don't know what I'm saying. I'm nervous and excited and worried. It isn't as bad as I told you.'

Marcia had a pitiable sense that she was acting like a child when, of all times, she ought to be calm and think. But the sudden revulsion of feeling had swept her away. She had indeed been living in a fools' paradise the past few months! The poor people Sybert had told her of yesterday—the starving thousands in Naples—her own father was the cause. And the peasants of Castel Vivalanti—no wonder they hated her; while she distributed chocolate with such graceful condescension, her father was taking away their bread. She thought over her uncle's words, and then, as she realized their content, she suddenly rose, and faced the two men.

'Uncle Howard,' she said, 'I think you've done very wrong not to tell me this before. I had a right to know, and I could have helped it. My father loves his business, but he loves me better. It's true, as I say, he's just doing it as a sort of problem. He doesn't see the suffering he causes, and he doesn't really believe there is any. Of course he knows that some people lose when he gains, but he thinks that they go into it with their eyes open, and that they must accept the chances of war. He's exactly as good a man as either of you.' And then, as a sudden recollection flashed across her, she whirled about toward Sybert, her glance divided between indignation and contempt. 'And you called me the "Wheat Princess" before every one in Paul Dessart's studio. You knew that it wasn't my fault; you knew that I didn't even know about the trouble, and you laughed when I told the story of the Vivalanti ghost.'

Her voice broke slightly, and, turning her back, she drew a piece of paper toward her on the table and began to write.

'There,' she said, holding out a scrawled sheet toward her uncle. 'There is a cablegram. Please see that it is sent immediately.'

Copley ran his eyes over it in silence, and his mouth twitched involuntarily into a smile.

'Well, Marcia, I'll see that it goes. I don't know—it may do some good, after all.' He paused awkwardly a moment and held out his hand. 'Am I forgiven?' he asked. 'I shouldn't have said anything against your father; but he's my brother, remember, and while I abuse him myself I wouldn't let an outsider do it. You are right; he doesn't know what he is doing. You must forget what I said. I have thought about it too much. Every one in Italy believes that I have an interest in the deal; and when I am doing my best to help things along, it is a little hard, you know, to be accused—by the very people I am giving to—of being the cause of their distress.'

'Yes, Uncle Howard, I understand; I don't blame you,' she returned, with a note of weariness in her voice; 'but—papa is really the kindest man in the world.'

'Ah, Marcia, a very kind-hearted man nowadays can do a great deal of harm by telegraph without having to witness the results.'

Sybert crossed the room toward her with a curious deep look in his eyes. He half held out his hand, but Marcia turned away without appearing to notice, and picking up her uncle's cheque-book from the table, she tore out a leaf and scrawled across the face.

'There's some money for the Relief Committee,' she said, as she tossed the slip of paper across the table toward him. 'That's all I have in the bank just at present, but I will give some more as soon as I get it.'

Sybert's face was equally impassive as he glanced from the paper back to her.

'Thirteen thousand lire is a good deal. Do you think you ought——'

'I do as I please with my own money—this is my own,' she added in parenthesis. 'My mother left it to me.'

'As you please,' he returned, pocketing the slip with a half-shrug. 'I know a village in Calabria that will be very grateful for a little help until the olives ripen again.'

'Dinner is served,' announced Pietro in the doorway.

Marcia nodded to the two men.

'I don't want any dinner to-night,' and she turned upstairs to her room. She sat for half an hour staring out at the darkening Campagna; then she rose and lighted the candles, and commenced a letter to her father. Her pen she dipped in blood. She told him everything she had heard or seen or imagined about Italy—of the 'hunger madness' in the north and the starving peasants in the south; of the poor people of Castel Vivalanti and little Gervasio. She told him what the people said about her uncle; that they called her the 'Wheat Princess'; and that the children in the streets taunted her as she went past. She told him that the name of Copley was despised from end to end of Italy. All the crimes that have ever been laid at the door of the government and the church and the ignorance of the people, Marcia heaped upon her offending father's shoulders, but with the forgiving assurance that she knew he didn't mean it. And would he please prove that he didn't mean it, by stopping the corner immediately and sending wheat to Italy? It was a letter to wring a father's heart—and a financier's.

CHAPTER XVII

For the next week or so Marcia steadfastly avoided meeting people. There were no visitors at the villa, and it was easy to find pretexts for not going into Rome. She felt an overwhelming reluctance to meeting any of her friends—to meeting any one, in truth, who even knew her name. It seemed to her that beneath their smiles and pleasant speeches she could read their thoughts; that the words 'wheat, wheat, wheat' rang as an undertone to every sentence that was spoken. Her horseback rides were ridden in the direction away from Castel Vivalanti, and if, by chance, she did meet any of her former friends the villagers, she galloped past, looking the other way.

Mrs. Copley was engaged with preparations for the coming ball. It was to be partially in honour of the Roystons, partially in honour of Marcia's birthday, and all of Rome—or as much of it as existed for the Copleys—was to be asked to stop the night either at Villa Vivalanti or at the contessa's villa in Tivoli. Marcia, her aunt complained, showed an inordinate lack of interest in these absorbing preparations. She was usually ready enough with suggestions, and her listlessness did not pass unnoticed. Mr. Copley's eyes occasionally rested upon her with a guiltily worried expression, and if she caught the look she immediately assumed an air of gaiety. Neither had made the slightest reference to the subject of that evening's scene, except upon the arrival of a characteristic cablegram from Willard Copley, in which he informed his daughter that he was sending her a transport of wheat as a birthday present.

'You see, Uncle Howard,' she had said as she handed him the message, 'it is possible to do good as well as harm by telegraph.'

Copley read it with a slight smile. 'After all, I'm afraid he's no worse than the rest of us!' and with that, wheat was a tabooed subject.

For the future, however, he was particularly thoughtful toward his niece to show that he was sorry, and she met his advances more than half-way to show that she had forgiven; and, all in all, they came to a better understanding because of their momentary falling out. Mrs. Copley accounted for Marcia's apathy (and possibly nearest the truth) on the ground that she had taken a touch of malaria in the old wine-cellar, and she dosed her with quinine until the poor girl's head rang. It happened therefore that when the evening came to attend a musicale at the Contessa Torrenieri's villa, Marcia could very gracefully decline. The occasion of the function was the count's return from the Riviera; and although Marcia had some little curiosity in regard to the count, still it did not mount to such proportions that she was ready to face the rest of the world for its sake.

Tivoli and Villa Torrenieri were a long nine miles away, and Villa Vivalanti that evening dined earlier than usual. As Marcia came downstairs in response to Pietro's summons, she paused a moment on the landing; she had caught the sound of Sybert's low voice in the salon. She had not seen him since the tempestuous ending of the San Marco festa, and she had not yet determined on just what footing their relations were. She stood hesitating with a very slight quickening of the pulse, and then with a decided thrill of annoyance as an explanation for his unexpected visit presented itself—he had returned from Naples and come out to Villa Vivalanti for the purpose of attending the contessa's musicale. Marcia went on downstairs more slowly, and entered the salon with a none too cordial air. Sybert's own greeting was in his usual vein of polite indifference. His manner contained not the slightest suggestion of any misunderstanding in the past. It transpired that he knew nothing of the impending party; he was clothed in an unpretentious dinner-jacket. But he expressed his willingness to attend, in spite of the lack of invitation—it was doubtless waiting for him in Naples, he declared—provided his host would lend him a coat. His host grumblingly assented, and Sybert inquired, with a glance from Mrs. Copley's velvet and jewels to Marcia's simple white woollen gown, what time they were planning to start.

'About eight; it takes almost two hours to get there,' said Mrs. Copley. 'Marcia is not going,' she added.

'Why not, Miss Marcia?'

She looked a trifle self-conscious as she put forth her excuse. 'I've been having a little touch of malaria, and Aunt Katherine thought perhaps the night air——'

'I remember, when I was a boy in school, I used frequently to have headaches on Monday mornings,' said Sybert, with a show of sympathy.

Marcia sat in her room till she heard the carriage drive away, then she dragged a wicker chair out to the balcony which overlooked the eastern hills, already darkened into silhouettes against the sky. She sat leaning back with her hands clasped in her lap, watching the outlines of the old monastery fade into the night. She thought of the pale young monk with his questioning eyes, and wondered what sort of troubles people who lived in monasteries had. They were at least not her troubles, she smiled, as she thought of Paul Dessart.

Suddenly she leaned over the railing and sniffed the light breeze as it floated up from the garden. Mingled with the sweet scent of lilies and oleanders was the heavy odour of a cigar. Her pulses suddenly quickened. Could——? She pushed her chair back and rose with an impatient movement. Pietro was holding a rendezvous with his friends again, and entertaining them with her uncle's tobacco. The night was chilly and she was cold. She turned into the dark room with a little laugh at herself: she was staying away from the contessa's musicale to avoid the night air?

She groped about the table for a book and started downstairs with the half-hearted intention of reading out the evening in the salon. A wood fire had been kindled that afternoon, to dispel the slight dampness which the stone walls seemed to exude at the slightest suggestion of an eastern wind. It had burned low now, and the embers gave out a slight glow which was not obliterated by the two flickering candles on the table—Pietro's frugal soul evidently looked upon the lamp as unnecessary when Mr. and Mrs. Copley were away. Marcia piled on more sticks, with a shake of her head at Italian servants. The one thing in the world that they cannot learn is to build a fire; generations of economy having ingrained within them a notion that fuel is too precious to burn.

The blaze once more started, instead of ringing for a lamp and settling down to her book, she dropped into a chair and sat lazily watching the flames. Italy had got its hold upon her, with its spell of Lethian inertia. She wished only to close her eyes and drift idly with the current.

Presently she heard the outer door open and close, and steps cross the hall. She looked up with a start to see Laurence Sybert in the doorway.

'What's the matter—did I surprise you?' he inquired.

'Yes; I thought you had gone to the party.'

'I was in the wine-cellar just as much as you,' he returned, with a little laugh, as he drew up a chair beside her. 'Why can't I have malaria too?'

His sudden appearance had been disconcerting, and her usual self-assurance seemed to be wandering to-night. She did not know what to say, and she half rose.

'I was just going to ring for the lamp when you came. Pietro must have forgotten it. Would you mind——'

Sybert glanced lazily across the room at the bell. 'Oh, sit still. We have light enough to talk by, and you surely aren't intending to read when you have a guest.' He stretched out his hand and took possession of her book.

'I don't flatter myself that you stayed away from the contessa's to talk to me,' she returned as she leaned back again with a slight shrug.

'Why else should I have stayed?' he inquired. 'Do you think, when it came to the point, your uncle wouldn't give me a coat?'

'Probably you found that it didn't fit.'

Sybert laughed. 'No, Miss Marcia; I didn't even try. I stayed because—I wanted to talk with you.'

She let the statement pass in silence, and Sybert addressed himself to a careful rearrangement of the burning wood. When he finally laid down the tongs he remarked in a casual tone, 'I owe you an apology—will you accept it?'

'What for?'

'You appear to have several counts against me—suppose we don't go into details. I offer a collective apology.'

'Because you called me "the Wheat Princess"? Oh, yes, I'll excuse it; I dare say you were justified.'

He leaned forward with a slight frown.

'Certainly I was not justified; it was neither kind nor gentlemanly, and I am sorry that I said it. I can only promise to have better manners in the future.'

Marcia dismissed the subject with a gesture.

'Let me tell you about the good your money has done.'

'No, please don't! I don't want to hear. I know that it's horrible, and that you did the best with it possible. I'm glad if it helped. My father is sending some wheat that will be here in a few weeks.'

'Miss Marcia,' he said slowly, 'I wish you wouldn't take this matter so badly. Your uncle was out of his senses when he talked to you, and he didn't realize what he was saying. He feels awfully cut up about it. He told me to-night that he was afraid he had spoiled your summer, and that he wouldn't have hurt you for the world.'

Marcia's eyes suddenly filled with tears and she bit her lip. Sybert leaned forward and poked the fire.

'I should like to talk to you about your uncle,' he said, with his eyes fixed on the embers. 'He is one of the finest men I have ever known. And it is not often that a man in his position amounts to much—that is, as a human being; the temptations are all the other way. Most men, you know, with leisure and his tastes would—well, go in for collecting carved ivory and hammered silver and all that rubbish. Nobody understands what he is trying to do, least of all the people he is doing it for. He does it very quietly and in his own way, and he doesn't ask for thanks. Still, just a little appreciation would be grateful; and, instead of that, he is abused at every turn. This wheat business increased the feeling against him, and naturally he feels sore. The other evening he'd just been reading some articles about the trouble in a Roman paper, and I had been telling him about your encounter with the village people when you came in. It was an unfortunate moment you chose, and he forgot himself. I wish you would be as kind to him as you can, for he has a good many critics outside, and—' Sybert hesitated an instant—'he needs a little sympathy at home.'

Marcia drew a deep breath.

'I understand about Uncle Howard,' she said. 'I used to think sometimes—' she hesitated too—'that he wasn't very happy, but I didn't know the reason. Of course I don't blame him for what he said; I know he was worried, and I know he didn't mean it. In any case, I should rather know the truth. But about the wheat,' she continued, 'my father is not to blame the way you think he is. He and Uncle Howard don't understand each other, but I understand them both, and if I had known sooner I could have stopped it. He didn't have the remotest idea of harming Italy or any other country. He just thought about getting ahead of a lot of others, and—you know what men are like—making people look up to him. He's very quick; he sees things faster than other men; he knows what's going to happen ahead of time, and you can't expect him not to take advantage of it. Of course'— she flushed—'he wants to make money, too; but it isn't all that, for he doesn't use it after he gets it made. It's the beating others that he likes—the power it gives him. I'm afraid,' she added, with a slightly pathetic smile, 'that I shall have to go home and look after him.'

'Oh, certainly, Miss Marcia, we all know that your father had no thought of deliberately harming Italy or any other country. And, as a matter of fact, the American wheat corner has not had so much to do with the trouble as the Italian government would have us believe. The simple truth is that your father has been used as a scapegoat. While the Roman papers have been suggestively silent on many points, they have had much to say of the American Wheat King.'

'Have the things they said been very bad?'

Sybert smiled a trifle.

'There's not been much, to tell the truth, that he will care to cut out and paste in his scrapbook.'

'Our party, next week, seems heartless, doesn't it—sort of like giving a ball while the people next door are having a funeral? I wanted to give it up, but Uncle Howard looked so hurt when I proposed it that I didn't say anything more about it.'

'No, certainly not. That would be foolish and useless. Because some people have to be unhappy is no reason why all should be.'

'I suppose not,' she agreed slowly; and then she added, 'The world used to be so much pleasanter to live in before I knew there was any misery in it—I wish I didn't have to know!'

'Miss Marcia, I told you the other day that it was a relief sometimes to see people who are thoroughly, irresponsibly happy; who dance over the pit without knowing it's there. A man who has been in the pit, who knows all its horrors—who feels as if he reeked with them— likes occasionally to see some one who doesn't even know of its existence. And yet in the end do you think he can thoroughly respect such blindness? Don't you feel that you are happier in a worthier sense when you look at life with your eyes open; when you honestly take the bad along with the good?'

She sat silent for a few minutes, apparently considering his words. Presently he added—

'As for your party, I think you may dance with a free conscience. You've done what you could to help matters on, and you'll do a great deal more in the future.'

'I'm afraid that my conscience didn't have much to do with wanting to give up the ball,' she acknowledged, with a slightly guilty laugh. 'It's simply that I can't bear to meet people, and feel that all the time they're talking to me they're calling me in their minds "the Wheat Princess."'

'That, I suppose you know, is very silly. It's the price you have to pay, and I haven't much sympathy to offer. However, you need not let it bother you; for, as a matter of fact, there will not be many men here, who would not be wheat kings themselves if they had the chance—even knowing beforehand all the suffering it was going to bring to this trouble-ridden country. And now, suppose we don't talk about wheat any more. You've thought about it a good deal too much.'

'You're not very optimistic,' she said.

'Oh, well, I'm not blind. It takes an Italian to be optimistic in this country.'

'Do you like the Italians, or don't you?' she asked. 'Sometimes you seem to, and sometimes you act as if you despised them.'

'Yes, certainly I like them; I was born in Italy.'

'But you're an American,' she said quickly.

He laughed at her tone.

'You surely want to be an American,' she insisted.

'As Henry James says, Miss Marcia, one's country, like one's grandmother, is antecedent to choice.'

She studied the fire for some time without speaking, and Sybert, leaning back lazily, studied her. Her next observation surprised him.

'You said the other day, Mr. Sybert, that every man lived for some idea, and I've been wondering what yours was.'

A curious expression flashed over his face.

'You couldn't expect me to tell; I'm a diplomatist.'

'I have an idea that it is not very much connected with diplomacy.'

'In which case it would be poor diplomacy for me to give it away.'

'Mr. Sybert, you give a person a queer impression, as if you were acting a part all the time, and didn't want people to know what you were really like.'

'An anarchist must be careful; the police——'

'I believe you are one!' she cried.

'Don't be alarmed. I assure you I am not. But,' he added, with a little flash of fire, 'I swear, in a country like this, one would like to be—anything for action! Oh, I'm not a fool,' he added, in response to her smile. 'We're living in the nineteenth century, and not in the thirteenth. Anarchy belongs to the dark ages as much as feudalism.'

'You're so difficult to place! I like to know whether people are Democrats or Republicans, and whether they are Presbyterians or Episcopalians. Then one always knows where to find them, and is not in danger of hurting their feelings.'

'I'm afraid I can't claim any such respectable connexions as those,' Sybert laughed.

'Half the time one would think you were a Catholic by the way you stand up for the priests; the other half one would think you weren't anything by the way you abuse them.'

'This mania for classifying! What difference if a person calls himself a Catholic or a Baptist, a Unitarian or a Buddhist? It's all one. A man is not necessarily irreligious because he doesn't subscribe to any cut-and-dried formulae.'

'Mr. Sybert,' she dared, 'I used to be terribly suspicious of you. I knew you weren't just the way you appeared, and I thought you were really rather bad; but I'm beginning to believe you're unusually good.'

'Oh, I say, Miss Marcia! What are you trying to get at? Do you want me to confess to a hair shirt underneath my dinner-jacket?—I am afraid you must leave that to our friend the monk, up on his mountain-top.'

'No, I didn't mean just that. Flagellations and hair shirts strike me as a pretty useless sort of goodness.'

'It does seem a poor business,' he agreed, 'for a strong young fellow like that to give up his whole life to the work of getting his soul into paradise.'

'Still, if he wants paradise that much, and is willing to make the sacrifice——'

'It's setting a pretty high value on his own soul. I should never rate mine as being worth a lifetime of effort.'

'I suppose a person's soul is worth whatever price he chooses to set.'

'Oh, of course, if a man keeps his soul in a bandbox he can produce it immaculate in the end; but what's a soul for if it's not for use? He would much better live in the world with his fellow-men, and help them keep their souls clean, even at the risk of getting his own a little dusty.'

'Yes, perhaps that's true,' she conceded. 'Such dust will doubtless brush off in the end.'

'It certainly ought, if things are managed right.'

'I can't help feeling sorry, though, for the poor young monk; he will be so disappointed, when he brings out his shiny new soul, to find that it doesn't rank any higher than some of the dusty ones that have been dragged through the world.'

'It will serve him right,' Sybert declared. 'He ought to have been thinking of other people's souls instead of his own.'

'"'Tis a dangerous thing to play with souls, and matter enough to save one's own,"' quoted Marcia.

'Oh, well,' he shrugged, 'I won't argue, with the poet and the priests both against me; but still——'

'You think that your speckled soul is exactly as good at other people's white souls?'

'It all depends,' he demurred, 'upon how they kept theirs white and how I got mine speckled.'

'Our frate has afforded a long moral,' she laughed.

'Ah—and I suspect he didn't deserve it. He looks, poor devil, as if his heart were still in the world, in spite of the fact that he himself is in the cloister.'

'In that case,' she returned, 'he's lost the world for nothing, for his prayers will not be answered unless his heart is in them.'

'There's a tragedy!' said Sybert—'to have lost the world, and then, in spite of it, to turn up in the end with a dusty soul!'

They looked at each other soberly, and then they both laughed.

'Philosophy is a queer thing,' said Marcia. 'You may go as far as you please, but you always end where you started.'

'"Bubbles that glitter as they rise and break on vain philosophy's aye-bubbling spring,"' he repeated softly, with his eyes on the fire; and then he leaned toward her and laughed again. 'Miss Marcia, do you know I have an idea?'

'What is it?' she asked.

'It's about you and me—I have a theory that we might be pretty good friends.'

'I thought we'd been friends for some time,' she returned evasively. 'I am sure my uncle's friends are mine.'

'Really, I hadn't suspected it! But it's the same with friends as with politics and religion: they don't amount to much until you find them for yourself.'

She considered this in silence.

'I should say,' he added, 'that we'd been pretty good enemies all this time. What do you say to our being friends, for a change?'

Marcia glanced away in a sudden spasm of shyness.

'Shall we try it?' he asked in a low tone, bending toward her and laying his hand palm upward on the arm of her chair.

She dropped her hand into his hesitatingly, and his fingers closed upon it. He looked at the fire a moment, and then back in her face.

'Marcia,' he said softly, 'did you ever hear the Tuscan proverb, "The foes of yesterday become the friends of to-day and the lovers of to-morrow"?'

A quick wave of colour swept over her face, and a faint answering flush appeared in his. She drew her hand away and rose to her feet, with a light laugh that put the last few minutes ages away.

'I'm afraid it's getting late, and Aunt Katherine would be scandalized if she found her malaria patient waiting up for her. I will leave you to smoke in peace.'

Sybert rose and followed her into the hall. He chose a tall brass candlestick from the row on the chimney-piece, lighted it, and handed it to her with a silent bow.

'Thank you,' said Marcia, with a brief glance at his face. She paused on the landing and looked down. He was standing on the rug at the foot of the stairs, watching her with an amused smile.

'Buona notte, Signor Siberti,' she murmured.

'Buona notte, signorina,' he returned, with a little laugh. 'Pleasant dreams!'

CHAPTER XVIII

'Shall I do it high or low, ma'am?'

Marcia, who was sitting before the mirror in a lace camisole, fidgeted impatiently.

'Oh, do it any way you please, Granton, only hurry—low, I think. That will look best with my gown. But do be quick about it. I have to go downstairs.'

'There's plenty of time,' replied the maid, imperturbably. 'But I would be a little faster if you would kindly sit still.'

'Very well, Granton; I won't move for five minute. I'm really getting excited, though; and I didn't care a bit for the party until it began.'

'Yes, ma'am. If you'll just turn your head a little more this way. It's very early.'

'I know, but I have to go down and be sure that Pietro understands about the lights. He's so stupid, he has to be watched every minute. And, Granton, as soon as you get through with Mrs. Copley please go and help Bianca dress Miss Royston. Bianca doesn't know anything more about fixing hair than a rabbit.'

Granton's silence breathed acquiescence in this statement, and under impulse of the implied compliment she became more sprightly in her movements as she skilfully twisted Marcia's yellow-brown hair into a seemingly simple coil at the nape of her neck.

For the past three days the house had been full of guests and though Marcia had been somewhat cold in her anticipations of the time, she found herself thoroughly enjoying it when it came. The days had been filled with rides and drives and impromptu gaiety. Paul Dessart had been master of the revels, and he filled the office brilliantly. He had supplied the leaven of fun on every occasion, and had been so thoroughly tactful that his host and hostess had gratefully blessed him, and Marcia had cast him more than one involuntary glance of approval. And this was her birthday and the night of the ball. All day long she had been the centre of a congratulatory group, the recipient of prettily worded felicitations; and she not unnaturally found it pleasant. The afternoon train had brought still more guests from Rome, and Villa Vivalanti's nineteen bedrooms were none too many. Five o'clock tea on the terrace had in itself been in the nature of a festa, with gaily dressed groups coming and going amid the sound of laughter and low voices; while the excitable Italian servants scurried to and fro, placing tea-tables and carrying cups.

Marcia had been secretly disappointed that afternoon by the non-arrival of one guest whom she had half expected—and Eleanor Royston had been frankly so.

'Mr. Copley,' Eleanor had inquired of her host, as he offered her a cup of tea, 'where's that friend of yours, Mr. Laurence Sybert?'

'Quelling rioters, I presume. It's more in his line just now than attending balls.'

'As if anything could be more in a diplomat's line than attending balls! With all the other diplomats here and off their guard, it's just the time to learn state secrets. And he's the most interesting man in Rome,' she complained. 'I wanted to add him to my collection.'

'Your collection?' Mr. Copley's startled expression approached a stare.

'Of interesting men,' she explained. 'Oh, don't be alarmed; I don't scalp them. The collection is purely mental—it's small enough, so far, to be carried in my head. It's merely that I am a student of human nature and am constantly on the alert for fresh specimens. Your Mr. Sybert is puzzling; I don't know just how to classify him.'

'Ah, I see! It is merely a scientific interest you take in him.' Mr. Copley's tone was one of relief. 'If I can be of any assistance with the label—I am sure that he would feel honoured to grace your collection.'

'I am not so sure,' said Marcia. 'Wait till you hear the others, Uncle Howard! A Kansas politician who wants to be a poet, an engineer on the Claytons' yacht, a Russian prince who talks seven languages and can't express his thoughts in any, and—who were the others, Eleanor? Oh, yes! the blacksmith who married the maid and beats her.'

'You don't do them justice,' Eleanor remonstrated, 'Those are merely their accidental, extrinsic qualities. That which makes them interesting is something intrinsic.'

Mr. Copley shot her an amused glance, and drawing up a chair, sat down beside her, prepared to argue it out.

'The list has possibilities, Miss Royston,' he assured her, 'though of course one can't judge without knowing the gentlemen personally. With which one, may I ask, are you going to classify Mr. Sybert?'

'Oh, in a separate pigeonhole by himself. That is just what makes my collection interesting.' It was evidently a subject that she discussed with some relish. 'Most men, you know—you look them over and immediately assign them to a group with a lot of others; but once in a while you come across a man who goes entirely by himself—is what the French call an original—and he is worth studying.'

Mr. Copley took out a cigarette and regarded it speculatively. 'I see,' he said. 'The best study of mankind is man—and so you think Sybert a specimen who deserves a pigeonhole by himself?'

'Yes, I think he does, though I haven't quite decided on the hole yet. That's why it worries me that he didn't come to the party. One hates to leave these little matters unsolved.'

'I am sincerely sorry for you to have lost the opportunity. I must tell him your opinion.'

'No, indeed!' remonstrated Eleanor. 'I may meet him again some day, and if you tell him I shall never learn the truth. One's only chance is to catch them unawares.'

'You're a very penetrating person, Miss Royston.'

'I've been out nine seasons,' she laughed. 'You can trust me to know a man when I see one!'

'I wish you'd teach Marcia some of your lore,' he murmured, as he turned toward the loggia to greet a fresh carriageful of guests.

Even though one man were missing, still a great many others were there, and it had only been an undercurrent of Marcia's consciousness in any case that had considered the matter. The laughter and babel of voices, the gay preparations and hurrying servants, had had their effect. As Granton clasped about her neck Mr. Copley's expiatory gift—a copy of an old Etruscan necklace in pearls and uncut emeralds set in hammered gold—she was as pleasurably excited as a young woman may legitimately be on the eve of a birthday ball.

'There, Granton; that's all,' she cried, catching up her very Parisian skirts and flying for the door. 'Hurry with the others, please, for it won't be long before the guests begin coming.'

She started downstairs, pulling on her gloves as she went. She paused a moment on the landing to view the scene below, and she blinked once or twice as it dawned upon her that Laurence Sybert was standing at the foot of the stairs watching her, just as he had stood the last time she had seen him when he bade her good-night. For a moment she felt an absurd tremor run through her, and then with something like a gulp she collected herself and went on down to greet him.

'Mr. Sybert! We were afraid you weren't coming. When did you get here?'

'On the late train. I have been in the south, and I didn't get back to the city till this afternoon.'

'Your arrivals are always so spectacular,' she said. 'We entirely give you up, and then the first thing we know you are quietly standing before us on the rug.'

'I should call that the reverse of spectacular.'

'Have you seen Uncle Howard? Did they find any place to put you? The house is cram full.'

'Oh, yes, I've been officially welcomed. I have a bed in your uncle's dressing-room.'

'You may be thankful for that. The next comer, I am afraid, will be put in the cellar.'

Sybert did not choose to prolong these amenities of welcome any further, and he stood quietly watching her while she buttoned her gloves. She looked very radiant to-night, with the candle-light gleaming on her hair and her hazel eyes shining with excitement. Her gown was the filmiest, shimmering white with an undertone of green. About her neck the pearls gleamed whitely, each separate jewel a pulsing globe of light. Marcia glanced up and touched the necklace with her hand.

'This is Uncle Howard's birthday present,' she said. 'Isn't it lovely? It's a copy of an old, old necklace in Castellani's collection. My uncle gives me pearls, and my father is sending wheat.'

She turned aside into the long salon, and Sybert followed her. If Marcia had been momentarily jostled from her self-possession by his sudden appearance, she had completely regained her poise. She was buoyantly at her ease again. There was a touch of intimacy, almost of coquetry, about her manner as she talked; and yet—Sybert noted the fact with a sub-smile of comprehension—she avoided crossing eyes with him. That moment by the fireside was still too vivid. They returned to the hall, and Marcia stepped to the door leading on to the loggia. The cornice was outlined with tiny coloured lamps, while a man was lighting others by the terrace balustrade. She glanced back at Sybert, who was standing still in the hall.

'You aren't going out?' he asked.

'Just a moment. I want to see how it looks.'

He looked at her bare shoulders with a slight frown. 'Bring the signorina a wrap,' he said to the servant at the door.

'I don't need a wrap,' said Marcia; 'it's a warm night.'

Sybert shook his head with an expression that was familiar.

'Oh, if you wish to say anything, say it!' she cried. 'Only please don't look at me with that smile. It's the way you looked the first time I saw you—and I don't like it.'

'I have nothing to say. When a young woman threatened with malaria proposes to go out into an Italian night, bare-shouldered, a mere man is left speechless.'

'Pride would keep me warm.'

'I haven't a doubt of it; but in case it should for the moment fail——' He took the long white cloak from the man's arm and glanced at it with another expression as he placed it on her shoulders. It was composed mostly of chiffon and lace.

'All is vanity that comes from a Paris shop!' laughed Marcia.

Sybert lit a cigarette and followed her. 'Well?' he asked, as they paused by the terrace balustrade. 'Does it meet with your approval?'

'It's lovely, isn't it?' she replied as she looked back at the broad, white façade with its gleaming windows. There was no moon, but a clear, star-sprinkled sky. In all the dark landscape the villa alone was a throbbing centre of life and light. Rows of coloured lanterns were beginning to outline the avenue leading to the gate, and in the ilex grove tiny red and blue and white bulbs glowed among the branches like the blossoms of some tropical night-blooming cereus. Servants were hurrying past the windows, musicians were commencing to tune their instruments; everywhere was the excitement of preparation.

'And this is your birthday,' he said. 'I suppose you have received many pretty speeches to-day, Miss Marcia; I hope they may all come true.' She glanced up in his face, and he looked down with a smile. 'Twenty-three is a great age!'

A shadow flitted across her face. 'Isn't it?' she sighed. 'I thought twenty-two was bad enough—but twenty-three! It won't be many years before I'll be really getting old.'

Sybert laughed. 'It's been a long time since I saw twenty-three—when I first came back to Rome.'

'Twelve years,' said Marcia.

'It's an easy enough problem if you care to work it out. I don't care to, any more.'

'It's not bad for a man,' she said; 'but a woman grows old so young!'

'You need not worry over that just now. The grey hairs will not come for some time yet.'

'I'm not worrying,' she laughed. 'I was just thinking—it isn't nice to grow old, is it?'

'Certainly not. It's the great tragedy of life; and it comes to all, Miss Marcia—to you as well as to the poorest peasant girl in Castel Vivalanti. Life, after all, contains some justice.'

Marcia turned her back to the shining villa and looked down over the great Campagna stretching away darkly under the stars, with here and there the gleam of a shepherd's fire, built to ward off the poison in the air.

'Things are not very just,' she said slowly.

'Not very,' he agreed; 'and one has little faith that they ever will be—either in this world or the next.'

'It would be comfortable, wouldn't it, if you could only believe that people are unfortunate as a punishment—because they deserve to be.'

'It would be a beautiful belief, but one which you can scarcely hold in Italy.'

'Poor Italy!' she sighed.

'Ah—poor Italy!' he echoed.

With a sudden motion he threw away his cigarette over the balustrade and immediately lit another. Marcia watched his face in the flare of the match. The eyes seemed deeper-set than usual, the jaw more boldly marked, and there were nervous lines about the mouth. His face seemed to have grown thinner in the last few weeks.

They turned away and sauntered toward the ilex grove.

'There are, however, compensations,' he went on presently. 'Our poor peasants do not have all the pleasures, but they do not have all the pains, either. There are a great many girls in Castel Vivalanti who will never have a birthday ball'—he glanced from the lighted villa behind them to the glowing vista in front, the green stretch of the ilex walk with the shimmering fountain at the end—'whose lives will be very bare, indeed. They will work and eat and sleep, and love and perhaps hate, and that is all. You have many other pleasures which they could never understand. You enjoy the Egoist, for instance. But also'—he paused—'you can suffer many things they cannot understand. You are an individual, while they are merely human beings. Gervasio's stepmother married a husband, and doubtless loved him very much and cried for him a week after he was dead. Then she married another, and saw no difference between him and the first. She may have to work hard, and she may be hungry sometimes, but she will escape the worst suffering in life, which you, with all your privileges, may not escape, Marcia.'

'One would rather not escape it,' she answered. 'I should rather feel what there is to feel.'

'Ah!' he breathed, 'so should we all! And these poor devils of peasants, who can't feel anything but their hunger and weariness, lose the most of life. They are not even human beings; they are merely beasts of burden, hard-working, patient, unthinking oxen, who go the way they are driven, not dreaming of their strength. That is the unfairness; that is where society owes them a debt; they have no chance to develop. However,' he broke off with a short laugh, 'it's not the time to bother you with other people's troubles—on your birthday night. We will hope, after all, that you may not have any very grave ones of your own.'

They had reached the fountain and they paused. They were alone in a fairy grove, with a nightingale pouring out his soul in the branches above their heads. Marcia stood looking down the dim, green alley they had come by, breathing deeply. She knew that Sybert's eyes were on her, and slowly she raised her head and looked up in his face. For a moment they stood in silence; then, as the sound of carriage wheels reached them from the avenue, she started and turned away.

'The people are beginning to come. I am afraid that Aunt Katherine will be wondering where I am,' she said in a voice that trembled slightly.

Sybert followed her in silence.

Some one had once said to her that Sybert's silences meant more than other men's words, and as they turned back she tried to think who it had been. Ah—she remembered! It was the contessa.

CHAPTER XIX

Throughout the evening while she was laughing and talking with the stream of guests, Marcia kept a sub-conscious notion of Sybert's movements. She saw him in the hall exchanging jokes with the English ambassador. She saw him talking to Eleanor Royston and bending over the Contessa Torrenieri. And once, as she whirled past in a waltz, she caught sight of his dark face in a doorway with his eyes fixed on her, and she forgave him Eleanor and the contessa. She was conscious all the time of a secret amazement at herself. Sybert had suddenly become for her the only person in the room, and while she was outwardly intent upon what other men were saying, her mind was filled with the picture of his face as he had looked during that silent moment by the fountain. She went through the evening in a maze, conscious only of the approach of the one dance she had with him.

When the evening was nearing its end she was suddenly brought to her senses by the realization that she was strolling down one of the ilex walks with Paul Dessart at her side. She had been rattling on unheedingly, and she scarcely knew how they had come there. Her first instinct was one of self-preservation; she felt what was coming, and she wanted to ward it off. Anything to get back to the crowd again! She paused and looked back at the lighted villa, listening to the sound of the violins rising above the murmur of voices and laughter. For a moment she almost felt impelled to turn and run. Since she had stopped, Paul stopped perforce, and looked at her questioningly.

'I—I think we'd better go back,' she stammered. 'This dance is almost over, and——'

'We won't go back just yet,' he returned. 'I want to talk to you. You owe me a few moments, Marcia. Come here and sit down and listen to what I have to say.'

He turned into the little circle by the fountain and motioned toward a garden seat. Marcia dropped limply upon it and looked at him with an air of pleading. There was no circumlocution; both knew that the time had come when everything must be said, and Paul went to the point.

'Well, Marcia, are you going to marry me?'

Marcia sat opening and shutting her fan nervously, trying to frame an answer that would not hurt him.

'I've been patient; I haven't bothered you. You surely ought to know your own mind now. You've had a month—it hasn't been exactly a happy month for me. Tell me, please, Marcia. Don't keep me waiting any longer.'

'Oh, Paul!' she said, looking back with half-frightened eyes. 'It's all a mistake.'

'A mistake! What do you mean? Marcia, I trusted you. You can't throw me over now. Tell me quickly!'

'Forgive me, Paul,' she faltered miserably. 'I—I was mistaken. I thought, that day in the cloister——'

He realized that, somehow, she was slipping away from him and that he must fight to get her back. He bent toward her and took her hand, with his glowing, eager face close to hers, his words coming so fast that he fairly stuttered.

'Yes, that day in the cloister. You did care for me then, didn't you, Marcia—just a little bit? You let me hope—you told me there wasn't any other man—you've been kind to me ever since. That's what I've lived on this whole month—the memory of that afternoon. Tell me what the trouble is—don't let anything come between us. We've had such a happy spring— let it keep on being happy. We've lived in Arcady, Marcia—you and I. Why should we ever leave it? Why must we go back—why not go forward? If you cared that afternoon, you can care now. I haven't changed. Tell me why you hesitate. I don't want to force you to make up your mind, but this uncertainty is simply hell.'

Marcia listened, breathing fast, half carried away by the impetuous flow of his words. She sat watching him with troubled eyes and silent lips in a sort of stupor. She could not collect her thoughts sufficiently to answer him. What had she to say? she asked herself wildly. What could she say that was adequate?

Paul, bending forward, his eyes close to hers, was waiting expectantly, insistently, for her to speak, when suddenly they were startled by a step on the gravel path before them, and they both looked up to see Laurence Sybert, cigarette in hand, stroll around the corner of the ilex walk. As his eye fell upon them he stopped like a man shot, and for a breathless instant the three faced one another. Then, with a quick rigidity of his whole figure, he bowed an apology and wheeled about. Marcia turned from red to white and snatched her hand away.

Paul watched her a moment with an angry light growing in his eyes. 'You are in love with Laurence Sybert!' he whispered.

Marcia shrank back in the corner and hid her face against the back of the seat. Paul bent over her.

'Look at me,' he cried; 'tell me it's not true. You can't do it! You've been deceiving me. You've been lying! Oh, yes, I know you've been very careful not to make any promises in so many words, but you've made them in other ways, and I believed you. I've been fool enough to think you in earnest, and all the time you've been amusing yourself!'

Marcia raised her eyes to his. 'Paul, I haven't. You are mistaken. I don't know how I've changed; I can't explain. That day in the cloister I thought I liked you very much. And if Margaret hadn't come in, perhaps—I wouldn't have deceived you for a moment, and you know it.'

'Tell me you don't love Sybert.'

'Paul, you have no right——'

'I have no right! You said there was no one else, and I believed you; and now, when I ask for an explanation, you tell me to go about my business. I suppose you were beginning to get tired of me these last few days, and thought——'

'You have no right to talk to me this way! I haven't meant to deceive you. You asked me if there were any one else, and I told you there was not, and it was true. I'm sorry—sorry to hurt you, but it's better to find it out now.'

Paul rose to his feet with a very hard laugh.

'Oh, yes, decidedly it's better to find it out now. It would have been still better if you had found it out sooner.'

He turned his back and kicked the coping of the fountain viciously. Marcia crossed over to him and touched him on the arm.

'Paul,' she said, 'I can't let it end so. I know I have been very much to blame, but not as you think. I liked you so much.'

He turned and saw the tears in her eyes, and his anger vanished.

'Oh, I know. I've no business to speak so—but—I'm naturally cut up, you know. Don't cry about it; you can't help it. If you don't love me, you don't, and that ends the matter. I'll get over it, Marcia.' He smiled a trifle bleakly. 'I'm not the fellow to sit down and cry when I can't have what I want. I've gone without things before.' He offered her his arm. 'We'll go back now; I'm afraid you're missing your dances.'

Marcia barely touched his arm, and they turned back without speaking. He led her into the hall, and bowing with his eyes on the floor, turned back out of doors. She laughed and chatted her way through two or three groups before she could reach the stairs and escape to her own room, where she locked the door and sank down on the floor by the couch. Trouble was beginning for her sooner than she had thought, and underneath the remorse and pity she felt for Paul, the thing that lay like lead on her heart was the look on Sybert's face as he turned away.

104

A knock presently came on the door, followed by a rattling of the knob.

'Marcia, Marcia!' called Eleanor Royston. 'Are you in there?' Marcia raised her head and listened in silence.

The knock came again. She rose and went to the door.

'What do you want?' she asked.

'I want to come in. It's I—Eleanor. Open the door. Why don't you come down?'

Marcia shook out her rumpled skirts, pushed back her hair, and opened the door.

'Everybody's asking for you. The ambassador says you were engaged to him for a—— Why, what's the matter?'

Marcia drew back quickly into the shadow, and Eleanor stepped in and closed the door behind her.

'What's the matter, child?' she inquired again. 'You've been crying! Has Paul——?' she asked suddenly. Eleanor's intuitive faculties were abnormally developed. 'I suppose he was pretty nasty,' she proceeded, taking Marcia's answer for granted. 'He can be on occasion. But, to tell you the truth, I think he has some cause to be. I think you deserve all you got.'

Marcia sank into a chair with a gesture of weariness, and Eleanor walked about the room handling the ornaments.

'Oh, I knew he was in love with you. There's nothing subtle about Paul. He wears his heart on his sleeve, if any one ever did. But if you don't mind my saying so, Marcia, I think you've been playing with rather a high hand. It's hardly legitimate, you know, to deliberately set out to make a man fall in love with you.'

'I haven't been playing. I didn't mean to.'

'Oh, nonsense! Men don't fall in love without a little encouragement; and I'm not blind— I've been watching you. If you want my honest opinion, I think you've been pretty unfair with Paul.'

'I know it,' Marcia said miserably; 'you can't blame me any worse than I blame myself. But you just can't love people if you don't.'

'I'm not blaming you for not loving him; it's for his loving you. That, by using a little foresight, might have been avoided. However, I don't know that I'm exactly the person to preach.' Eleanor dropped into a chair with a short laugh, and leaned forward with her chin in her hand and her eyes on Marcia's face. 'I have a theory, Marcia—it's more than a theory: it's a superstition,—that some day we'll be paid in our own coin. I'm twenty-eight, and a good many men have thought they were in love with me, while I myself have never managed to fall in love with any of them. But I'm going to, some day—hard—and then either he's not going to care about me or something's going to be in the way so that we can't marry. It's going to be a tragedy. I know it as well as I know I'm sitting here. I'm going to pay for my nine seasons, and with interest. It makes me reckless; the score is already so heavy against me that a few more items don't count. But I know my tragedy's coming, and the longer I put it off the worse it's going to be. It's a nice superstition; I'll share it with you, Marcia.'

Marcia smiled rather sorrily. It was not a superstition she cared to have thrust upon her just then. She was divining it for herself, and did not need Eleanor to put it into words.

'As for Paul, you couldn't do anything else, of course. You're not fitted to each other for a moment, and you'll grow more unfitted every day. Paul needs some one who is more objective—who doesn't think too much—some one like—well, like Margaret, for instance. In the meantime, you needn't worry; he'll manage to survive it.' She rose with another laugh and stood over Marcia's chair. 'It's over and done with, and can't be helped; there's nothing to cry about. But mark my words, Marcia Copley, you'll be falling in love yourself some day, and then I—Paul will be avenged. Meanwhile there are several years before you in which you can have a very good time. Come on; we must go downstairs. The people will be leaving in a little while. Bathe your eyes, and I'll fix your hair.'

Marcia went downstairs and laughed and danced and talked again, and once she almost stopped in the middle of a speech to wonder how she could do it. It was finally with heartfelt thankfulness that she watched the people beginning to leave. Once, as she was bidding a group good night, she caught sight of Sybert in the hall bending over the contessa's hand. She covertly studied his face, but it was more darkly inscrutable than ever. She slipped upstairs as soon as the last carriage had rolled away; it was not until long after the sunlight had streamed into her windows, however, that she finally closed her eyes. Eleanor Royston's pleasant 'superstition' she was pondering very earnestly.

CHAPTER XX

The ball ended, the guests gone, Villa Vivalanti forgot its one burst of gaiety, and settled down again to its usual state of peaceful somnolence. The days were growing warmer. White walls simmering in the sunshine, fragrant garden borders resonant with the hum of insects, the cool green of the ilex grove, the sleepy, slow drip of the fountain—it was all so beautifully Italian, and so very, very lonely! During the hot mid-days Marcia would sit by the ruins of the old villa or pace the shady ilex walks with her feelings in a tumult. She had seen neither Paul Dessart nor Laurence Sybert since the evening of her birthday, and that moment by the fountain when the three had faced each other silently was not a pleasant memory. It was one, however, which recurred many times a day.

Of Sybert Marcia heard no news whatever. In reply to her casual question as to when he would be at the villa again, her uncle had remarked that just at present Sybert had more important things to think of than taking a villeggiatura in the Sabine hills. But of Paul Dessart and the Roystons most unexpected news had come. Paul's father had had an 'attack' brought on by overwork, and they were all of them going home. The letters were written on the train en route for Cherbourg; a long letter from Margaret, a short one from Eleanor. The latter afforded some food for reflection, but the reflection did not bring enlightenment.

'Dear Marcia' (it ran):

'I am sorry not to see you again, and (to be quite frank) I am equally sorry not to have seen Mr. Sybert again. I feel that if I had had more time, and half a chance, I might have accomplished something in the interests of science.

'Margaret told you, of course, that Paul is going back with us. We hope his father's illness isn't serious, but he preferred to go. There is nothing to keep him in Rome, he says. Poor fellow! you must write him a nice letter. Don't worry too much about him, though; he won't blow his brains out.

'I could tell you something. I have just the tiniest suggestion of a suspicion which—granted fair winds and a prosperous voyage—may arrive at the dignity of news by the time we reach the other side. However, you don't deserve to hear it, and I shan't tell. Have I aroused your curiosity sufficiently? If so, c'est tout.

'I shall hope to see you in Pittsburg this autumn. That, my dear Marcia, is merely a polite phrase and is not strictly true. I shall hope, rather, to see you in Paris or Rome or Vienna. I am afraid that I have the wander-habit to the end. The world is too big for one to settle down permanently in one place—and that place Pittsburg; is it not so? One can never be happy for thinking of all the things that are happening in all of the places where one is not.

'Au revoir, then, till autumn; we'll play on the Champs-Elysées together.

'Eleanor.'

A letter had come also from Marcia's father, which put her in an uncomfortably unsettled frame of mind. It was written in the Copley vein of humorous appreciation of the situation; but, for all that, she could see underneath that she had hurt him. He disavowed all knowledge and culpability in the Triple Alliance and the Abyssinian war. He regretted the fact that the taxes were heavy, but he had had no hand in making up Italy's financial budget.

As to wheat, there were many reasons why Italy could not afford it, aside from the fact that it was dear. Marcia could give what she wished to the peasants to make up for her erring father, and he inclosed a blank cheque to her order—surely an excessive sign of penitence on the part of a business man. The letter closed with the statement that he was lonely without her, and that she must come back to America next winter and keep her old father out of mischief.

She read the last few sentences over twice, with a rising lump in her throat. It was true. Poor man, he must be lonely! She ought to have tried to take her mother's place, and to have made a home for him before now. Her duty suddenly presented itself very clearly, and it appeared as uninviting as duties usually do. A few months before she would not have minded, but now Italy had got its hold upon her. She did not wish to go; she wished only to sit in the sunshine, happy, unthinking, and let the days slip idly by. A picture flashed over her of what the American life would be—a brownstone house on Fifth Avenue in the winter, a country place in the Berkshires in the summer; an aunt of her mother's for chaperon, her father's friends—lawyers and bankers and brokers who talked railroads and the Stock Exchange; for interests she would have balls and receptions, literary clubs and charities. Marcia breathed a doleful sigh. Her memories of the New York house were dreary; it was not a life she cared to renew. But nothing of all this did she let her father know. She sent a gracefully forgiving letter, with the promise that she would come home for the winter, and not a hint that the home-coming was not her own desire.

It seemed that, things having once commenced to change, everything was going. Mr. Copley himself exploded the next bombshell. He came back from Rome one night with the announcement that the weather was getting pretty hot, and the family ought to leave next week for Switzerland.

'Oh, Uncle Howard, not yet!' Marcia cried. 'Let us wait until the end of June. It isn't too hot till then. Up here in the hills it's pleasant all summer. I don't want to leave the villa.'

'Rome is hot just now in more ways than one,' he returned. 'I'd feel safer to have you in Switzerland or up in the Tyrol during the excitement. Goodness only knows what's going to happen next. I'm expecting to wake up in the middle of a French revolution every morning, and I should like to have you out of the country before the beheading begins.'

'There isn't really any danger of a revolution?' she asked breathlessly.

'Not in a country where every other man's a soldier and the government's in command. But there have been houses broken into and a good many acts of lawlessness, and we're rather lonely off here.'

'I hate to think of going away,' Marcia sighed. 'We'll come back in the autumn, won't we, Uncle Howard?'

'Oh, yes, if you like. I dare say we could manage a month or so out here before we go into the palazzo for the winter.'

'And I'll be going back to America for the winter,' she sighed.

He looked at her with a slight smile.

'Are you the girl, Marcia, who used to preach sermons to your uncle about Americans living abroad?'

Marcia reflected his smile somewhat wanly.

'And I'm practising my own preaching, am I not?'

'Oh, well,' he said, 'when the time comes you can do as you please. Your father can get along without you one year more.'

'No, I think I ought to go, for of course he must be lonely but—I should like to stay! It seems more like home than any place I've ever been in. I've really never belonged anywhere before, and I like so much to be with you.'

'Poor little girl! You have had a chequered career.'

'Yes, Uncle Howard, I have; and it keeps on being chequered! I haven't been in the villa three months, but really I don't remember ever having lived so long in one place before. It's been nice, hasn't it? I hate dreadfully to have it end. It seems like shutting away a whole part of my life that can never come back.'

'Oh, well, if you feel that way about it, I'll buy the villa and we can come out every spring. You can bring your father over, and we will dip him in the waters of Lethe, too.'

'I'm afraid he wouldn't be dipped,' she laughed. 'He'd be running a cable connexion out here and setting up a ticker on the terrace, so that he could watch the stock market as well as the view.'

Mr. Copley's mouth twitched slightly at the picture.

'We must all ride our hobbies, I suppose, or the world would be a very dreary world indeed.'

She looked up at him and hesitated.

'Uncle Howard, do you and papa—that is—do you mind my asking?—are you very good friends?'

Mr. Copley frowned a moment without replying. 'Well Marcia, he's a good deal older than I, and we're not particularly congenial.' He straightened his shoulders with a laugh. 'Oh, well, there's no use concealing disagreeable truths. It appears they will out in the end. As a matter of fact, your father and I haven't had anything to do with each other for the past ten years. The first move was on his part, when he wrote about you last fall—you didn't know that you came as an olive-branch, did you?'

'I didn't know; he didn't tell me anything about it, but I—well, I sort of guessed. I'm sorry about it, Uncle Howard. I'm sure that it's just because you don't understand each other.'

'I'm afraid we never have understood each other, and I doubt if we ever can, but we'll make another effort.'

'It's so hard to like people when you don't understand them, and so easy when you do,' said Marcia.

'It facilitates matters,' he agreed.

'I think I'm beginning to understand Mr. Sybert,' she added somewhat vaguely. 'He's different, when you understand him, from the way you thought he was when you didn't understand him.'

'Ah, Sybert!' Mr. Copley raised his head and brought his eyes back from the edge of the landscape. 'I thought I knew him, but he's been a revelation to me this spring.'

'How do you mean?' Marcia asked, striving to keep out of her tone the interest that was behind it.

'Oh, the way he's taken hold of things. It seems an absurd thing to say, but I believe he's had almost as much influence as the police in quieting the trouble. He has an unbelievably strong hold on the people—how he got it, I don't know. He understands them as well as an Italian, and yet he is a foreigner, which gives him, in some ways, a great advantage. They trust him because they think that, being a foreigner, he has nothing to make out of it. He's a marvellous fellow when it comes to action.'

'You never would guess it to look at him!' she returned. 'Why does he pretend to be so bored?'

'Be so bored? Well, I suppose there are some things that do bore him; and the ones that don't, bore other people. His opinions are not universally popular in Rome, and being a diplomatist, I dare say he thinks it as well to keep them to himself.'

'What are his opinions?' she asked tentatively. 'I don't like to accuse him of being an anarchist, since he assures me that he's not. But when a man wants to overthrow the government——'

'Nonsense! Sybert doesn't want to overthrow the government any more than I do. Just at present it's under the control of a few corrupt politicians, but that's a thing that's likely to happen in any country, and it's only a temporary evil. The Italians will be on their feet again in a year or so, all the better for their shaking-up, and Sybert knows it. He's got more real faith in the government than most of the Italians I know.'

'But he talks against it terribly.'

'Well, he sees the evil. He's been looking at it pretty closely, and he knows it's there; and when Sybert feels a thing he feels it strongly. But,' Copley smiled, 'while he says things himself against the country, you'll find he'll not let any one else say them.'

'What do people think about him now—being mixed up in all these riots?'

'Oh, just now he's mixed up in the right side, and the officials are very willing to pat him on the back. But as for the populace, I'm afraid he's not making himself over-liked. They have a most immoral tendency to sympathize with the side that's against the law, and they can't understand their friends not sympathizing with the same side. It's a pretty hard thing for him to have to tell these poor fellows to be quiet and go back to their work and starve in silence.' Copley sighed and folded his arms. 'I am sorry, Marcia, you don't like Sybert better. There are not many like him.'

Marcia let the observation pass without comment.

The next morning, as Mrs. Copley and Marcia were sitting on the loggia listlessly engaged with books and embroidery, there came whirring down the avenue the contessa's immaculate little victoria, with the yellow coronet emblazoned on the sides, with the coachman and footman in the Torrenieri livery, green with yellow pipings. It was a gay little affair; it matched the contessa. She stepped out, pretty and debonair, in a fluttering pale-green summer gown, and ran forward to the loggia with a little exclamation of distress.

'Cara signora, signorina, I am desolated! We must part! Is it not sad? I go with Bartolomeo' (Bartolomeo was the count) 'to plant olive orchards on his estate in the Abruzzi. Is it not lonely, that—to spend the summer in an empty castle on the top of a mountain, with only a view for company? And my friends at the baths or the lakes or in Switzerland, or—oh, everywhere except on my mountain-top!'

Marcia laughed at the contessa's despair.

'But why do you go, contessa, if you do not like it?' she inquired.

'But my husband likes it. He has a passion for farming; after roulette, it it his chief amusement. He is very pastoral—Bartolomeo. He adores the mountain and the view and the olive orchards. And in Italy, signorina, the wife has to do as the husband wishes.'

'I'm afraid the wives have to do that the world over, contessa.'

'Ah, no, signorina, you cannot tell me that; I have seen. In America the husband does as the wife wishes. It is a beautiful country, truly. You have many charming customs. Yes, I will give you good advice: you will be wise to marry an American. They do not like mountain-tops. But perhaps you will visit me on my mountain-top?' she asked. 'The view—ah, the beautiful view! It is not so bad.'

'I'm afraid not, contessa. We are leaving for the Tyrol ourselves a week from to-morrow.'

'So soon! Every one is going. Truly, the world comes to an end next week in Rome.'

Marcia found herself growing unexpectedly cordial toward their guest; even the contessa appeared suddenly dear as she was about to be snatched away. She bade her an almost affectionate farewell, and stood by the balustrade waving her handkerchief until the carriage disappeared.

'Will marvels never cease?' she asked her aunt. 'I think—I really think that I like the contessa!'

CHAPTER XXI

The next day—it was just a week before their proposed trip to the Tyrol—Marcia accompanied her uncle into Rome for the sake of one or two important errands which might not be intrusted to a man's uncertain memory. Mr. Copley found himself unready to return to the villa on the train they had planned to take, and, somewhat to Marcia's consternation, he carried her off to the Embassy for tea. She mounted the steps with a fast-beating heart. Would Laurence Sybert be there? She had not so much as seen him since the night of her birthday ball, and the thought of facing him before a crowd, with no chance to explain away that awful moment by the fountain, was more than disconcerting.

Her first glance about the room assured her that he was not in it, and the knowledge carried with it a mingled feeling of relief and disappointment. The air was filled with an excited buzz of conversation, the talk being all of riots and rumours of riots. Marcia drifted from one group to another, and finally found herself sitting on a window-seat beside a woman whose face was familiar, but whom for the moment she could not place.

'You don't remember me, Miss Copley?' her companion smiled.

Marcia looked puzzled. 'I was trying to place you,' she confessed. 'I remember your face.'

'One day, early this spring, at Mr. Dessart's studio——'

'To be sure! The lady who writes!' she laughed. 'I never caught your name.'

'And the worst gossip in Rome? Ah, well, they slandered me, Miss Copley. One is naturally interested in the lives of the people one is interested in—but for the others! They may make their fortunes and lose them again, and get married, and elope and die, for all the attention I ever give.'

Marcia smiled at her concise summary of the activities of life, and put her down as a Frenchwoman.

'And the villa in the hills?' she asked. 'How did it go? And the ghost of the Wicked Prince? Did Monsieur Benoit paint him?'

'The ghost was a grievous disappointment. He turned out to be the butler.'

'Ah—poor Monsieur Benoit! He has many disappointments. C'est triste, n'est-ce pas?'

'Many disappointments?' queried Marcia, quite in the dark.

'The Miss Roystons, Mr. Dessart's relatives,' pursued the lady; 'they are friends of yours. I met them at the Melvilles' a few weeks ago. They are charming, are they not?'

'Very,' said Marcia, wondering slightly at the turn the conversation had taken.

'And this poor Monsieur Benoit—he has gone, all alone, to paint moonlight in Venice. Ce que c'est que l'amour!'

'Ah!' breathed Marcia. She was beginning to have an inkling. Had he been added to the collection? It was too bad of Eleanor!

'Miss Royston is charming, like all Americans,' reiterated the lady. 'But, I fear, a little cruel. Mais n'importe. He is young, and when one is young one's heart is made of india-rubber, is it not so?' Her eyes rested on Marcia for a moment.

Marcia's glance had wandered toward the door. Laurence Sybert had just come in and joined the group about her uncle, and she noted the fact with a quick thrill of excitement. Would he come and speak to her? What would he say? How would he act? She felt a strong desire to study his face, but she was aware that the eyes of 'the greatest gossip in Rome' were upon her, and she rallied herself to answer. Monsieur Benoit was commiserated for the third time.

'Ah, well,' finished the lady, philosophically, 'perhaps it is for the best. A young man avec le cœur brisé is far more interesting than one who is heart-whole. There is that Laurence Sybert over there.' She nodded toward the group on the other side of the room. 'For the last ten years, when the forestieri in Rome haven't had anything else to talk about, they've talked about him. And all because they think that under that manner of his he's carrying around a broken heart for the pretty little Contessa Torrenieri.'

Marcia laughed lightly. 'Mr. Sybert at least carries his broken heart easily. One would never suspect its presence.'

The lady's eyes rested upon her an appreciable instant before she answered: 'Che vuole? People must have something to talk about, and a good many girls—yes, and with dots— have sighed in vain for a smile from his dark eyes. Between you and me, I don't believe the man's got any heart—either broken or whole. But I mustn't be slandering him,' she laughed. 'I remember he's a friend at Casa Copley.'

'Mr. Sybert is my uncle's friend; the rest of us see very little of him,' Marcia returned as she endeavoured to think of a new theme. Her companion, however, saved her the trouble.

'And were you not surprised at Mr. Dessart's desertion?'

'Mr. Dessart's desertion?' Marcia repeated the question with a slight quiver of the eyelids.

'Exchanging Rome for Pittsburg. You Americans do things so suddenly! One loses one's breath.'

'But his father was ill and they sent for him.'

'Yes; but the surprising part is that he goes for good. The pictures and carvings and curios are packed; there is a card in the window saying the studio is for rent—he is giving up art to mine coal instead.'

Marcia laughed. 'It is a seven-league step from art to coal,' she acknowledged. 'I had thought myself that he was an artist to the end.'

'Ah—he was an artist because he was young, not because he was called, and I suppose he got tired of the play. The real artist for you—it is that poor young man painting moonlight in Venice.' The lady tapped Marcia's arm gently with her fan. 'But you and I know, Miss Copley, that Paul Dessart never went back to America just from homesickness; when a young man hasn't reached thirty yet, you may be pretty sure of finding a woman behind most of his motives.'

Marcia had the uncomfortable feeling that the lady's eyes were fixed upon her with a speculative light in their depths. She endeavoured to look disinterested as she again cast about for a more propitious topic. Glancing up, she saw that her uncle, accompanied by Laurence Sybert and Mr. and Mrs. Melville, was crossing the room in their direction. Sybert, who was laughing and chatting easily with Mrs. Melville, apparently did not feel that there was any awkwardness in the moment. He delivered a cordially indifferent bow which was evidently meant to be divided between Marcia and her companion. After a moment or so of general greetings, Marcia found herself talking with Mrs. Melville, while her uncle and the consul-general still discussed riots, and the lady who wrote appropriated Sybert.

'We are sorry to hear you are leaving the villa so early, though I suppose we shall all be following in a week or so,' said Mrs. Melville. 'One clings pretty closely to the shady side of the street even now. Aren't these riots dreadful?' she rambled on. 'Poor Laurence Sybert is working himself thin over them. It is the only subject one hears nowadays.'

Marcia achieved an intelligent reply, while at the same time she found herself listening to the conversation on the other side. To her intense discomfort, it was still of Paul Dessart.

'Yes, I heard that he had been suddenly called home; that was hard luck,' said Sybert quietly. 'Between you and me, Paul Dessart never gave up art and went back to Pittsburg because he was tired of Rome. As I told Miss Copley, when a young man decides to settle down and be serious, you may mark my words there's a woman in the case. Oh, I knew it all the time.' She lowered her tone. 'We'll be reading of an engagement in the Paris Herald one of these days.'

'I dare say, as usual, you're right,' Sybert said dryly; while Marcia, inwardly raging and outwardly smiling, gave ear to Mrs. Melville again.

'Oh, did I tell you,' Mrs. Melville asked, 'that we are coming out to the villa next Saturday for "week-end"? It's a long-standing invitation, that we've never found a chance to accept. But it's so charming out there that we can't bear to miss it, and so we are throwing over all our other engagements in order to get out this week before you break up.'

Marcia murmured some polite phrases while she tried to catch the gist of the conversation on the other side. It was not of Paul Dessart, she reassured herself. The woman who wrote was narrating an adventure with some 'bread-tickets' of the anti-begging society, and the two men—Melville and Sybert—were chaffing her uncle. The point of the story appeared to be against him. He finally broke away, and with a glance at his watch turned back to his niece.

'Well, Marcia, if we are to catch that six-o'clock train, I think it is time that we were off.'

111

Sybert accompanied them to the door, talking riots to her uncle, while she went on ahead, feeling forgotten and overlooked. Melville joined them again in the vestibule, and the three fell to discussing barricades and soldiers until Copley, with another look at his watch, laughingly declared that they must run.

Sybert for the first time, Marcia thought, gave any sign of being aware of her presence.

'Well, Miss Marcia,' he said, turning toward her with a friendly smile. 'Your uncle says that you are talking of going back to America next winter. That is too bad, but we shall hope to see a little of you in the autumn before you leave. You are going to the Tyrol for the summer, I hear. That will be pleasant, at least.'

'You talk as if America were a terrible hardship,' said Marcia, taking her tone from him.

Sybert laughed, with his old shrug. 'Ah, well, it depends on where one's interests are, I suppose.'

She suddenly flushed again, with the thought that he was referring to Paul Dessart, and she plunged blindly into another subject to cover her confusion.

'Did Uncle Howard tell you that we have decided to take Gervasio with us for the summer? He wanted to find a home for him in Rome; I wanted to take him with us; Aunt Katherine hadn't made up her mind until Gerald cried at the thought of parting with him, and, as usual, Gerald's tears decided the matter.'

'It was a most fortunate whipping for Gervasio the night that we drove by,' he returned as he held out his hand. 'Well, Miss Marcia, as you break up next week, I shall probably not see you again. I hope that you will have a delightful summer.'

Marcia shook hands smilingly, with her heart sunk fathoms deep.

He followed them to the carriage for a last word with her uncle.

'You'd better change your mind, Sybert, and come out to the villa Saturday night with the Melvilles,' Copley called as the carriage started.

'I'm sorry, but I'm afraid there's too much excitement elsewhere for me to afford a vacation just now,' and he bowed a smiling good-bye to Marcia.

CHAPTER XXII

The next few days were anxious ones for Italy. The straw-weavers of Tuscany were marching into Florence with the cry, 'Pane o lavore!'—'Bread or work!'—and in the north not bread, but revolution was openly the watchword. Timid tourists who had no desire to be mixed up in another '49 were scurrying across the frontiers into France and Switzerland; adventurous gentlemen from the Riviera, eager to enjoy the fun and not unwilling to take advantage of a universal tumult, were gaily scrambling in. The ministry, jostled from its usual apathy, had vigorously set itself to suppressing real and imaginary plots. Opposition newspapers were sequestered and the editors thrown into jail; telegrams and letters were withheld, public meetings broken up, and men arrested in the streets for singing the 'Hymn of Labour.' The secret police worked night and day. Every café and theatre and crowd had its spies disguised as loungers; and none dared speak the truth to his neighbour for fear his neighbour was in the pay of the premier.

In Milan the rioters had been lashed into a frenzy by their first taste of blood, and for three days the future of United Italy looked dark. Wagons and tramcars were overturned in the streets to make barricades. Roofs and windows rained down tiles and stones, and the soldiers obeyed but sullenly when ordered to fire upon the mob. In their hearts many of them sympathized. The socialists were out in force and working hard, and their motto was, 'Spread the discontent!' Priests and students from the universities were stirring up the peasants in the fields and urging them on to revolt. All dissatisfied classes were for the moment united in their desire to overthrow the existing government; what should take its place could be decided later. When Savoy was ousted, then the others—the republicans, the priests, the socialists, the hungry mob in the streets—could fight it out among themselves.

And as each faction in its heart believed itself to be the strongest, the fight, if it should come, was like to prove the end of Italy.

While the rest of the kingdom was filled with tumult, only faint echoes reached Villa Vivalanti dozing peacefully in the midst of its hills. Marcia, sitting with folded hands, fretted uselessly at her forced inaction. She scarcely left the villa grounds; she was carrying out Sybert's suggestion far more literally than he had meant it. She had not the moral courage to face the countryside; it seemed as if every peasant knew about the wheat and followed her with accusing eyes. Even the villa servants appeared to her awakened sensibilities to go about their duties perfunctorily, as if they too shared the general distrust in their employers. The last week dragged slowly to its end. There were only four more days to be spent in the villa, and Marcia now was impatient to leave it. She wanted to get up into the mountains—anywhere out of Italy—where she need never hear the word 'wheat' again.

Saturday—the week-end that the Melvilles were to spend at the villa—dawned oppressively hot. It was a foretaste of what Rome could do in midsummer. Not a leaf was stirring; there was no suggestion of mist on the hills, and the sun beat down glaringly upon a gaudily coloured landscape. The outer walls of the villa fairly sizzled in the light; but inside the atmosphere was respectably tempered. The green Venetian blinds had been dropped over the windows, the rugs rolled back, and the floors sprinkled with water. The afternoon sun might do its worst outside, but the large airy rooms were dark and cool—and quiet. Half an hour before, the walls had echoed Gerald's despairing cry, 'I won't go to sleep! I won't go to sleep!' for Gerald was a true Copley and he took his siestas hardly. But he had eventually dropped off in the midst of his revolt; and all was quiet now when Marcia issued from her room, garden hat in hand.

She paused with a light foot at Gerald's door. The little fellow was spread out, face downward, on the bed, his arms and legs thrown to the four winds. Marcia smiled upon the little clenched fists and damp yellow curls and tiptoed downstairs. On a pile of rugs in the lower hall Gervasio and Marcellus were curled up together, sleeping peacefully and happily. She smiled a blessing on them also. Next to Gerald, Gervasio was the dearest little fellow in the world, and Marcellus the dearest and the homeliest dog.

She raised the blind and stepped on to the loggia. A blast of hot air struck her, and she hesitated dubiously. It was scarcely the weather for an afternoon stroll, but the ilex grove looked cool and inviting, and she finally made a courageous dash across the terrace and plunged gratefully into its shady fastnesses. The sun-beaten world outside the little realm of green was an untempered glare of heat and colour. The only sounds which smote the drowsy air were the drip, drip of the fountain and the murmurous drone of insects in the borders of the garden. Marcia paused by the fountain, and dropping down upon the coping, dipped her fingers idly in the water.

Shaking the drops of water from her fingers, she rose and stood a moment looking down the green alley she had come by toward the sunny blaze of terrace at the end. She closed her eyes and pictured it as it had looked on her birthday night, a fairy scene, with the tiny bulbs of coloured light glowing among the branches. She pictured Sybert's face as he had stood beside her. It seemed almost as if the moment would come back again, if she only thought about it hard enough. And then the remembrance of that other moment followed, and the expression on Sybert's face as he had turned away. What did he think? she asked herself for the hundredth time; and she turned her back upon the fountain and hurried down the laurel walk as if to shut the memory out.

The wheat field to-day was ablaze with flaming poppies. The reds and yellows were so crude that no artist would have dared to paint them in their untoned brilliancy. Marcia paused to study the effect. Her eyes wandered from this daring foreground across scarcely less brilliant olive groves and vineyards to Castel Vivalanti on its mountain-top, an irregular mass of yellow ochre against a sky of cobalt blue. There was no attempt at shading. The colours were as unaffectedly primary as an illumination from some old manuscript, or as the outlines a child fills in from his tin box of half a dozen little cakes of paint. This Italy was so uncompromising in her moods. No variant note was allowed to creep in to mar the effect she was striving for. Marcia recalled the sudden storm of the mountain, how fiercely untamed, how intense it had been; she thought of the moonlight nights of the spring, when the mood was lyrical—the soft outline of tower and rain, the songs of nightingales, the heavy odours of acacia and magnolia blossoms. Italy was an impressionist, and her children were like her. There were no half-tones in the Italian nature any more than in the Italian landscape. There were many varying moods, but each in itself was concentrated. Just now there were storms, perhaps, but before long there would be moonlight and singing and love-making again, and the clouds would be forgotten.

She strolled on to the ruins of the old villa and sat down among the crumbling arches. She was in a very different mood herself than on that other afternoon of the early spring when Paul Dessart had found her there. She thought of the little sketch he had painted, and recalled her own words as he gave it to her: 'I will keep it to remember you and the villa by when I go home to America.' The words had been spoken lightly, but now they sounded prophetic. Everything had seemed before her then; now all seemed behind. A few months more and she would be back in America, with possibly nothing more than the sketch to remember her life in Italy by—and it had meant so much to her; now that it was slipping away, she realized how much. She seemed to have grown more, to have felt more, than in all her life before; and she hated inexpressibly to leave it behind.

Crossing to the little grotto that had formed the subject of the picture, she stood gazing pensively at the dilapidated moss-grown pile of stones. The afternoon when Paul had sketched it seemed years before; in reality it was not two months. She thought of him as he had looked that day—so enthusiastic and young and debonair—and she thought of him without a tremor. Many things had changed since then, and she had changed with them. If only Eleanor's suspicion might be true, that he would come to care for Margaret! She clung to the suggestion. Eleanor's 'superstition' need trouble her no more; Paul would not need to be avenged.

She turned aside, and as she did so something caught her eyes. She leaned over to look, and then started back with an exclamation of alarm. A man was lying asleep, almost at her feet, hidden by the tall weeds that choked the entrance to the grotto. The first involuntary thought that flashed to her mind was of Gervasio's stepfather, but immediately she knew that he was not the sleeper. Gervasio's stepfather was old, with a grizzled beard; it was evident that this man was young, in spite of the fact that his hat was pulled across his eyes. She laughed at her own fear; it was some peasant who had come from the fields to rest in the shade.

She leaned over to look again, and as she did so her heart suddenly leaped into her mouth. The man's shirt was open at the throat, and there was a dark-purple crucifix tattooed upside down upon his breast. For a second she stood staring, powerless to move; the next, she was running wildly across the blazing wheat field toward the shelter of the villa, with a frightened glance behind at the shadow of the cypresses.

CHAPTER XXIII

Marcia passed the afternoon in a state of nervous impatience for her uncle's return. She said nothing to Mrs. Copley of the man she had found asleep in the grotto, and the effort to preserve an outward serenity added no little to her inner trepidation. In vain she tried to reason with her fear; it was not a subject which responded to logic. She assured herself over and over again that the man could not be the same Neapolitan who had warned her uncle; that he was safely in prison; and that the tattooed crucifix was only the general mark of a secret society. The assurance did not carry conviction. Her first startled impression had been too deep to be thrown off lightly, and coming just then, in the midst of the rioting and lawlessness, the incident carried additional force. She had lately heard many stories of lonely villas being broken into, of travellers on the Campagna being waylaid and robbed, of the vindictiveness of the Camorra, which her uncle had opposed. The stories were not reassuring; and though she resolutely put them out of her mind, she found herself thinking of them again and again. Italy's elaborate police system, she knew, was not merely for show. Mr. Copley and the Melvilles were due at five, but as they had not appeared by half-past, Mrs. Copley decided that they had missed their train, and she and Marcia sat down to tea— or, more accurately, to iced lemonade—without waiting. The table was set under the shade of the ilex trees where the grove met the upper end of the terrace, and where any slight breeze that chanced to be stirring would find them out. Gerald and Gervasio swallowed their allotted glassful and two brioches with dispatch, and withdrew to the cool shadows of the ilex grove to play at horse with poor, patient Bianca and the streaming ribbons of her cap. Mrs. Copley and Marcia took the repast in more leisurely fashion, with snatches of very intermittent conversation. Marcia's eyes wandered in the pauses to the poppy-sprinkled wheat field and the cypresses beyond.

'I believe they are coming, after all!' Mrs. Copley finally exclaimed, as she shaded her eyes with her hands and looked down across the open stretch of vineyards to where the Roman road, a yellow ribbon of dust, divided the fields. 'Yes, that is the carriage!'

Marcia looked at the moving speck and shook her head. 'Your eyes are better than mine, Aunt Katherine, if you can recognize Uncle Howard at this distance.'

'The carriage is turning up our road. I am sure it is they. Poor things! I am afraid they will be nearly dead after the drive in this heat. Rome must have been unbearable to-day.' And she hastily dispatched Pietro to prepare more iced drinks.

Ten minutes later, however, the carriage had resolved itself into a jangling Campagna wine-cart, and the two resigned themselves to waiting again. By half-past seven Marcia was growing frankly nervous. Could anything have happened to her uncle? Should she have told her aunt and sent some one to meet him with a warning message? Surely no one would dare to stop the carriage on the open road in broad daylight. A hundred wild imaginings were chasing through her brain, when finally, close upon eight, the rumble of wheels sounded on the avenue.

Both Mrs. Copley and Marcia uttered an exclamation of relief. Mrs. Copley had been worried on the score of the dinner, and Marcia for any number of reasons which disappeared with the knowledge that her uncle was safe. They hurried out to the loggia to meet the new-comers, and as the carriage drew up, not only did the Melvilles and Mr. Copley descend, but Laurence Sybert as well. At sight of him Marcia hung back, asking herself, with a quickly beating heart, why he had come.

Mrs. Copley, with the first glance at their faces, interrupted her own graceful words of welcome to cry: 'Has anything happened? Why are you so late?'

They were visibly excited, and did not wait for greetings before pouring out their news—an attempted assassination of King Humbert on the Pincian hill that afternoon—Rome under martial law—a plot discovered to assassinate the premier and other leaders in control.

The two asked questions which no one answered, and all talked at once—all but Sybert. Marcia noticed that he was unusually silent, and it struck her that his face had a haggard look. He did not so much as glance in her direction, except for a bare nod of greeting on his arrival.

'Well, well,' Copley broke into the general babel, 'it's a terrible business. You should see the excitement in Rome! The city is simply demoralized; but we'll give you the particulars later. Let us get into something cool first—we're all nearly dead. Has it been hot out here? Rome has been a foretaste of the inferno.'

'And this young man,' Melville added, laying a hand on Sybert's arm, 'just got back from the Milan riots. Hadn't slept, any to speak of for four days, and what does he do this afternoon but sit down at his desk, determined to make up his back work, Sunday or no Sunday, with the thermometer where it pleases. Your husband and I had to drag him off by main force.'

'Poor Mr. Sybert! you do look worn out. Not slept for four days? Why, you must be nearly dead! You may go to bed immediately after dinner, and I shall not have you called till Monday morning.'

'I've been sleeping for the last twenty-four hours, Mrs. Copley, and I really don't need any more sleep at present,' he protested laughingly, but with a slight air of embarrassment. It was a peculiar trait of Sybert's that he never liked to be made the subject of conversation, which was possibly the reason why he had been made the subject of so many conversations. This reticence when speaking of himself or his own feelings, struck the beholder as somewhat puzzling. It had always puzzled Marcia, and had been one reason why she had been so persistent in her desire to find out what he was really like.

The party shortly assembled for dinner, the women in the coolest of light summer gowns, the men in white linen instead of evening dress. They went into the dining-room without affording Marcia a chance to catch her uncle alone. The meal did not pass off very gaily. Assassinations were served with the soup, bread riots with the fish, and hypothetical robberies and plots with the further courses; while Pietro presided with a sinister obsequiousness which added darkly to the effect. In vain Mrs. Copley tried to turn the conversation into pleasanter channels. The men were too stirred up to talk of anything else, and the threatened tragedy of the day was rehearsed in all its bearings.

The assassin had dashed out from the crowd that lined the driveway and sprung to the side of the royal carriage before any of the bystanders had realized what was happening. The white-haired aide-de-camp sitting at his Majesty's side was the first to see, and springing to his feet, he struck the man fiercely in the face just as he raised his arm. Had it not been for the aide-de-camp's quick action, the man would have plunged his stiletto into the King's heart.

Mrs. Copley and Mrs. Melville shuddered, and Marcia leaned forward listening with wide eyes.

'Right on the Pincio, mind you.' Melville in his excitement thumped the table until the glasses rang. 'Not a chance of the fellow's getting off. Scarcely a chance of his accomplishing his purpose. He knew he would be taken. Shouted, "Viva libertà!" as the soldiers grabbed him—I swear it beats me what these fellows are after. "Viva libertà!" That's what they cried when they put the House of Savoy on the throne, and now they're trying to pull it off again with the same cry.'

'I fear the seeds of revolution are sown pretty thick in Italy,' said Copley.

'Where aren't there the seeds of revolution to-day?' Melville groaned. 'Central Africa is only waiting a government in order to overturn it.'

'By the way,' interpolated Copley, 'the assassin is a friend of Sybert's.'

'A friend of Sybert's!' Marcia echoed the words before she considered their form.

Sybert caught the expression and smiled slightly.

'Not a very dear friend, Miss Marcia. I first made his acquaintance, I believe, on the day that you discovered Marcellus.'

'How did that happen?' Mrs. Copley asked.

'I heard him talking in a café.'

'It's a pity you didn't hand him over,' said Melville. 'You would have saved the police considerable trouble. It seems they have been watching him for some time.'

'I wasn't handing people over just then,' Sybert returned dryly. 'However, I don't see that the police need complain. It strikes me that he has handed himself over in about as effectual a way as he possibly could; he won't go about any more sticking stilettos into kings. The Italians are an excitable lot when they once get aroused; they talk more than is wise—but when it comes to doing they usually back down. It seems, however, that this fellow had the courage of his convictions. After all, it was, in a way, rather fine of him, you know.'

116

'A pretty poor way,' Melville frowned.

'Oh, certainly,' Sybert acquiesced carelessly. 'Umberto's a gentleman. I don't care to see him knifed.'

'What I can't understand,' reiterated Melville, 'is the fellow's point of view. No matter how much he may object to kings, he must know that he can never rid the country of them through assassination; as soon as one king is out of the way, another stands in line to take his place. No possible good could come to the man through Humbert's death, and he must have known that he had not one chance in a hundred of escaping himself—I confess his motive is beyond me. The only thing that explains it to my mind is that the fellow's crazy, but the police seem to think he's entirely sane.'

Sybert leaned back in his chair and studied the flowers in the centre of the table with a speculative frown.

'No,' he said slowly, 'the man was not crazy. I understand his motive, though I don't know that I can make it clear. It was probably in part mistaken patriotism—but not entirely that. I heard him state it very clearly, and it struck me at the time that it was doubtless, at bottom, the motive for most assassinations. His words, as I remember them, were something like this: "Who is the King? He is only a man. Why is he so different from me? Am I not a man, too? I am, and before I die the King shall know it."'

Sybert raised his eyes and glanced about the table. Copley nodded and Melville frowned thoughtfully. The two elder ladies were listening with polite attention, and Marcia was leaning forward with her eyes on his face. Sybert immediately dropped his own eyes to the flowers again.

'There you have the matter in a nutshell. Why did he wish to assassinate the King? As an expression of his own identity. Through a perfectly natural egotistical impulse for self-assertion. The man had been oppressed and trampled on all his life. He was conscious of powers that were undeveloped, of force that he could not use. He was raging blindly against the weight that was crushing him down. The weight was society, but its outward symbol was the King. The King had only one life to lose, and this despised, obscure Neapolitan peasant, the very lowest of the King's subjects, had it in his power to take that life away. It was the man's one chance of utterance—his one chance of becoming an individual, of leaving his mark on the age. And, in acting as he did, he acted not for himself alone, but for the people; for the inarticulate thousands who are struggling for some mode of expression, but are bound by cowardice and ignorance and inertia.'

Sybert paused and raised his eyes to Melville's with a sort of challenge.

'If that man had been able to obtain congenial work—work in which he could take an interest, could express his own identity; if he could have become a little prosperous, so that he need not fear for his family's support; why, then—the King's life would not have been in danger to-day. And as long as there is any man left in this kingdom of Italy,' he added, 'who, in spite of honest endeavour, cannot earn enough to support his family, just so long is the King's life in danger.'

'And there are thousands of such men,' put in Copley.

Melville uttered a short laugh. 'By heavens, it's true!' he said. 'The position of American consul may not carry much glory, but I don't know that I care to trade it with Umberto for his kingdom.'

'Do you suppose the King was scared?' inquired Marcia. 'I wonder what it feels like to wake up every morning and think that maybe before night you'll be assassinated.'

'He didn't appear to be scared,' said her uncle. 'He shrugged his shoulders when they caught the man, and remarked that this was one of the perquisites of his trade.'

'Really?' she asked. 'Good for Umberto!'

'Oh, he's no coward,' said Sybert. 'He knows the price of crowns these days.'

'It's terrible!' Mrs. Melville breathed. 'I am thankful they caught the assassin at least. Society ought to sleep better to-night for having him removed.'

'Ah,' said Sybert, 'Society can't be protected that way. The point is that he leaves others behind to do his work.'

'The man was from Naples, you say?' Mrs. Copley asked suddenly.

Her husband read her thoughts and smiled reassuringly. 'So far as I have heard, my dear, there was no crucifix tattooed upon his breast.'

Marcia raised her head quickly. 'Uncle Howard,' she asked, 'is that the mark of a society or of just that special man?'

'I can't say, I'm sure, Marcia,' he returned with a laugh. 'I suspect that it's an original piece of blasphemy on his part, though it may belong to a cult.'

'When is his time up?' she persisted. 'To get out of prison, I mean.'

'I don't know; I really haven't figured it up. There are enough things to worry about without troubling over him.'

In her excitement over the King's attempted assassination she had almost forgotten the man of the grotto, but her uncle's careless laugh brought back her terror. The man might at that very moment be watching them from the ilex grove. She cast a quick glance over her shoulder toward the open glass doors which led to the balcony. It was moonlight again. In contrast to the soft radiance of the marble-paved terrace, the ilex shadows were black with the sinister blackness of a pall. She looked down at her plate with a little shiver, and she sat through the rest of the meal in an agony of impatience to get up and move about.

Once she roused herself to listen to the conversation. They were talking of the soldiers; a large detachment of carabinieri had been stationed at Palestrina, and the mountain roads were being patrolled. The carriage that night had passed two men on horseback stationed at the turning where the road to Castel Vivalanti branches off from the Via Prænestina. Mrs. Copley said something about its giving them a feeling of security at the villa to have so many soldiers near, and Melville replied that whatever the crimes of the Italian government, it at least looked after the safety of its guests, Marcia listened with a sigh of relief, and she rose from the table with an almost easy mind. They all adjourned to the salon for coffee, and as soon as she could speak to her uncle without attracting attention she touched him on the arm.

'Come out on the loggia just a moment, Uncle Howard; I want to tell you something.'

He followed her in some surprise. She went down the steps and paused on the terrace, well out of ear-shot of the salon windows.

'Uncle Howard, I saw the tattooed man to-day.'

Mr. Copley paused with a match in one hand and a cigar in the other. 'Whereabouts?' he asked.

'Asleep in the ruined grotto.'

'Are you sure?'

'There was a crucifix tattooed upside down on his breast.'

'So!'

He examined the pavement in silence a moment, then he raised his head with an excited little laugh such as a hunter might give when hot on the scent.

'Well! I thought I had done for him, but it appears not.' He strode over to the salon windows. 'Sybert—ah, Sybert,' he called in a low tone, 'just step out here a moment.'

Sybert joined them with a questioning look. Copley very deliberately scratched his match on the balustrade and lighted his cigar. 'Tell your story, Marcia,' he said between puffs.

She felt a load of anxiety roll from her shoulders; if he could take the information as casually as this, it could not be very serious. She repeated the account of what she had seen, and the two men exchanged a silent glance. Copley gave another short laugh.

'It appears that his Majesty and I are in the same boat.'

'I warned you that if you let that wheat be sold in your name you could expect the honour,' Sybert growled.

'What do you mean?' Marcia asked quickly.

118

'Just at present, Miss Marcia, I'm afraid that neither your uncle nor myself is as popular as our virtues demand.'

'Oh, there's no danger,' said Copley. 'They wouldn't dare break into the house, and of course I sha'n't be fool enough to walk the country-side unarmed. The first thing in the morning, I shall send into Palestrina for some carabinieri to patrol the place. And on Monday the family can move into Rome instead of waiting till Wednesday. There's nothing to be afraid of,' he added, with a reassuring glance at Marcia. 'Forewarned is forearmed—we'll see that the house is locked to-night.'

'Can you trust the servants?' Sybert asked.

Copley looked up quickly as a thought struck him.

'By Jove! I don't know that I can. Come to think of it, I shouldn't trust that Pietro as far as I could see him. He's been acting mighty queer lately.'

Marcia's eyes suddenly widened in terror, and she recalled one afternoon when she had caught Pietro in the village talking to Gervasio's stepfather, as well as a dozen other little things that she had not thought of at the time, but which now seemed to have a secret meaning.

Sybert saw her look of fear and he said lightly: 'There's not the slightest danger, Miss Marcia. We'll get the soldiers here in the morning; and for to-night, even if we can't put much trust in the butler, there are at least three men in the house who are above suspicion and who are armed.' He touched his pocket with a laugh. 'When it comes to the point I am a very fair shot, and so is your uncle. You were wishing a little while ago that something exciting would happen—if it gives you any pleasure, you can pretend that this is an adventure.'

'Oh, yes, Marcia,' her uncle rejoined. 'Don't let the thought of the tattooed man disturb your sleep. He's more spectacular than dangerous.'

The others had come out on to the loggia and were exclaiming at the beauty of the night.

'Howard,' Mrs. Copley called, 'don't you want to come and make a fourth at whist?'

'In a moment,' he returned. 'We won't say anything to the others,' he said in a low tone to Marcia and Sybert.

'There's no use raising any unnecessary excitement.'

'Marcia, if you and Mr. Sybert would like to play, we can make it six-handed euchre instead of whist.'

Sybert glanced down to see that her hand was trembling, and he decided that to make her sit through a game of cards would be too great a test of her nerves.

'Thank you, Mrs. Copley,' he called back; 'it's too fine a night to pass indoors. Miss Marcia and I will stay out here.'

The proposal was a test of his own nerves, but he had schooled himself for a good many years to hide his feelings; it was an ordeal he was used to.

With final exclamations on the beauty of the night, the whist party returned to the salon. Sybert brought a wicker chair from the loggia for Marcia, and seated himself on the parapet while he lighted a cigar with a nonchalance she could not help but admire. Did she but know it, his nonchalance was only surface deep, though the cause for his inward tumult had nothing to do with the man of the ruined grotto. They sat in silence for a time, looking down on the shimmering Campagna. The scene was as beautiful as on that other night of the early spring, but now it was full summer. It was so peaceful, so idyllic, so thoroughly the Italy of poetry and romance, that it seemed absurd to think of plots and riots in connexion with that landscape. At least Marcia was not thinking of them now; she was willing to take her uncle at his word and leave the responsibility to him. The thing that was still burning in her mind was that unexplained moment by the fountain. It was the first time she had been alone with Sybert since. How would he act? Would he simply ignore it, as if it had never happened? He would, of course; and that would be far worse than if he apologized or congratulated her, for then she would have a chance to explain. What did he think? she asked herself for the hundredth time as she covertly scanned his dark, impassive face. Did he think her engaged to Paul Dessart, or did he divine the real reason why the young man had so suddenly sailed for America? Even so, it would not put her in a much better light in his eyes. He would think she had been playing with Paul and—her face flushed at the thought—had tried to play with him.

Sybert was the one who broke the silence. 'I think,' he said slowly, 'that I could spot your man with the crucifix this very moment.' He pointed with his cigar toward the hill above them, where little stone-walled Castel Vivalanti was outlined against the sky. 'If I am not mistaken, he is in the back room of a trattoria up there, in company with our friend Tarquinio of the Bed-quilt, who,' he added meditatively, 'is a fool. Those carabinieri are not guarding the roads for nothing. A number of Neapolitans have come north lately who might better have stayed at home—Camorrists for the most part—and the government is after them. This fellow with the crucifix is without doubt one of them, and in all probability he just happened into the ruins this afternoon to rest, without having an idea who lived here. At any rate, I strongly suspect that your uncle it not the hare he's hunting. Italy is too busy just at present to take time for private revenge—though,' he smiled, 'I have no wish to spoil your adventure.'

Marcia breathed a little sigh by way of answer, and another silence fell between them. 'On such a night as this,' he said dreamily, 'did you and I, Miss Marcia, once take a drive together.'

'And we didn't speak a word!'

'I don't know that we did,' he laughed. 'At least I don't recall the conversation.'

From the valley below them there came the sound of a man's voice singing a familiar serenade. Only the tune was audible, but the words they knew:

'Open your casement, love.
I come as a robber to steal your heart.'

Sybert, listening, watched her from under drooping lids. He was struggling with a sudden temptation which almost overmastered him. He thought her engaged to another man, but—why not come as a robber and steal her heart? In the past few weeks he had seen lifelong hopes come to nothing; he was wounded and discouraged and in need of human sympathy, and he had fought his battles alone. During that time of struggle Marcia had come to occupy a large part of his consciousness. He had seen in her character undeveloped possibilities—a promise for the future—and the desire had subtly taken hold of him to be the one to watch and direct her growth. The new feeling was the more intense, in that it had taken the place of hopes and interests that were dying. And then that, too, had been snatched away. Since the night of her birthday ball he had not doubted for a moment that she was engaged to Paul Dessart. It had never occurred to him that the scene he had interrupted was merely her sympathetic fashion of dismissing the young man. A dozen little things had come back to him that before had had no significance, and he had accepted the fact without questioning. It seemed of a piece with the rest of his fate that this should be added just when it was hardest for him to bear. It was the final touch of Nemesis that made her work rounded and complete.

And now, as he watched her, he was filled with a sudden fierce rebellion, an impulse to fight against the fate that was robbing him, to snatch her away from Paul Dessart. Every instinct of his nature urged him forward; only honour held him back. He turned away and with troubled eyes studied the distance. She had chosen freely—whether wisely or not, the future would prove. He knew that he could not honourably stretch out so much as his little finger to call her back.

Presently he pulled himself together and began to talk fluently and easily on purely impersonal themes—of the superiority of the Tyrol over the Swiss lakes as a summer resort, of the character of the people in Sicily, of books and art and European politics, and of a dozen different subjects that Marcia had never heard him mention before. It was the small talk of the diplomat, of the man who must always be ready to meet every one on his own ground. Marcia had known that Sybert could talk on other subjects than Italian politics when he chose, for she had overheard him at dinners and receptions, but he had never chosen when with her. In their early intercourse he had scarcely taken the trouble to talk to her in any but the most perfunctory way, and then suddenly their relations had no longer demanded formal conversation. They had somehow jumped over the preliminary period of getting acquainted and had reached the stage where they could understand each other without talking. And here he was conversing with her as politely and impersonally as if they had known each other only half an hour. She kept up her end of the conversation with monosyllables. She felt chilled and hurt; he might at least be frank. Whatever he thought of her, there was no need for this elaborate dissimulation. She had no need to ask herself to-night if he were watching her. His eyes never for a moment left the moonlit campagna.

After half an hour or so Mrs. Copley stepped to the window of the salon to ask Marcia if she did not wish a wrap. It was warm, of course, but the evening dews were heavy. Marcia scoffed at the absurdity of a wrap on such an evening, but she rose obediently. They strolled into the house and paused at the door of the salon. The whist-players were studying their cards again with anxious brows; it appeared to be a scientific game.

Marcia shook her head and laughed. 'On such a night as this to be playing whist!'

Melville glanced up at her with a little smile. 'Ah, well, Miss Marcia, we're growing old— moonlight and romance were made for the young.'

Sybert smiled rather coldly as he turned away. It struck him that the remark was singularly malapropos.

Marcia went on up to her room, and throwing about her shoulders a chiffon scarf, an absurd apology for a wrap, she paused a moment by the open glass doors of the balcony and stood looking down upon the moonlit landscape. She felt sore and bruised and hopeless. Sybert was beyond her; she did not understand him. He had evidently made up his mind, and nothing would move him; he would give her no chance to put herself right. She suddenly threw back her head and stiffened her shoulders. If that were the line he chose to take—very well! She would meet him on his own ground. She turned back, and on her way downstairs paused a second at Gerald's door. It was a family habit to look in on him at all hours of the night to make sure that he was sleeping and duly covered up, though to-night it could scarcely be claimed that cover was necessary. She glanced in, and then, with a quickening of her breath, took a step farther to make sure. The bed was empty. She stood staring a moment, not knowing what to think, and the next she was hurrying down the hall toward the servants' quarters. She knocked on Bianca's door, and finding no one within, called up Granton.

There was no cause for worry, Granton assured her. Master Gerald and that little Italian brat were probably in the scullery, stealing raisins and chocolate.

'Oh,' said Marcia, with a sigh of relief; 'but where's Bianca? She ought to sit by Gerald till he goes to sleep.

Bianca!—Granton sniffed disdainfully—no one could make head or tail of Bianca. Her opinion was that the girl was half crazy. She had been in there that night crying, and telling her how much she liked the signora and the signorina, and how she hated to leave them.

'But she isn't going to leave,' said Marcia. 'We've decided to take her with us.'

Granton responded with a disdainful English shrug and the reiterated opinion that the girl was crazy. Marcia did not stop to argue the point, but set out for the kitchen by way of the 'middle staircase,' creeping along quietly, determined to catch the marauders unawares. Her caution was superfluous. The rear of the house was entirely deserted. No sign of a boy, no sign of a servant anywhere about. The doors were open and the rooms were vacant. She hurried upstairs again in growing mystification, and turned toward Gervasio's room. The little fellow was in bed and sound asleep. What did it mean? she asked herself. What could have become of Gerald, and where had all the servants gone?

121

Suddenly a horrible suspicion flashed over her. Gervasio's stepfather—could he have stolen Gerald by way of revenge? That was why Bianca was crying! It was a plot. She had overheard, and they had threatened to kill her if she told. Perhaps they would hold him for a ransom. Perhaps—as the sound of her uncle's careless laugh floated up from below she caught her breath in a convulsive sob and stretched out her hand against the wall to steady herself.

CHAPTER XXIV

Collecting herself sufficiently to know that she must not cry out or alarm her aunt, Marcia hurried to the front staircase and stood a moment on the landing, hesitating what to do. Sybert was lounging in the doorway leading on to the loggia. She leaned over the balustrade and called to him softly so as not to attract the attention of the others. He turned with a start at the sound of his name, and in response to her summons crossed the hall in his usual leisurely stroll. But at the foot of the stairs, as he caught sight of her face in the dim candle-light, he came springing up three steps at a time.

'What's the matter? What's happened?' he cried.

'Gerald!' Marcia breathed in a sobbing whisper.

'Gerald!' he repeated, anxious lines showing in his face. 'Good heavens, Marcia! What's happened?'

'I don't know; he's gone,' she said wildly. 'Come up here, where Aunt Katherine won't hear us.' She led the way up into the hall again and explained in broken sentences.

Sybert turned without a word and strode back to Gerald's room. He stood upon the threshold, looking at the empty little crib and tossed pillows.

'It will simply kill Uncle Howard and Aunt Katherina if anything has happened to him,' Marcia faltered.

'Nothing has happened to him,' Sybert returned shortly. 'The scoundrels wouldn't dare steal a child. Every police spy in Italy would be after them. He must be with Bianca somewhere.'

He turned away from the room and went on down the stone passage toward the rear of the house. He paused at the head of the middle staircase, thinking the matter over with frowning brows, while Marcia anxiously studied his face. As they stood there in the dim moonlight that streamed in through the small square window over the stairs they suddenly heard the patter of bare feet in the passage below, and in another moment Gerald himself came scurrying up the winding stone stairway, looking like a little white rat in the dimness.

Marcia uttered a cry of joy, and Sybert squared his shoulders as if a weight had dropped from them. Their second glance at the child's face, however, told them that something had happened. His little white nightgown was draggled with dew, his face was twitching nervously, and his eyes were wild with terror. He reached the top step and plunged into Marcia's arms with a burst of sobbing.

'Gerald, Gerald, what's the matter? Don't make such a noise. Hush, dear; you will frighten mamma. Marcia won't let anything hurt you. Tell me what's the matter.'

Gerald clung to her, crying and trembling and pouring out a torrent of unintelligible Italian. Sybert bent down, and taking him in his arms, carried him back to his own room. 'No one's going to hurt you. Stop crying and tell us what's the matter,' he said peremptorily.

Gerald caught his breath and told his story in a mixture of English and Italian and sobs. It had been so hot, and the nightingales had made such a noise, that he couldn't go to sleep; and he had got up very softly so as not to disturb mamma, and had crept out the back way just to get some cherries. (A group of scrub trees, cherry, almond, and pomegranate, grew close to the villa walls in the rear.) While he was sitting under the tree eating cherries, some men came up and stopped in the bushes close by, and he could hear what they said, and one of them was Pietro. Here he began to cry again, and the soothing had to be done over.

'Well, what did they say? Tell us what they said, Gerald,' Sybert broke in, in his low, insistent tones.

'Vey said my papa was a bad man, an' vey was going to kill him 'cause he had veir money in his pocket—an' I don't want my papa killed!' he wailed.

Marcia's eyes met Sybert's in silence, and he emitted a low breath that was half a whistle.

'What else did they say, Gerald? You needn't be afraid. We won't let them hurt your papa, but you must remember everything they said, so that we can catch them.'

'Pietro said he was going to kill you, too, 'cause you was here an' was bad like papa,' Gerald sobbed.

'Go on,' Sybert urged. 'What else did they say?'

'Vey didn't say nuffin more, but went away in ve grove. An' I was scared an' kept still, an' it was all nero under ve trees; an' ven I cwept in pianissimo an' I found you—an' I don't want you killed, an' I don't want papa killed.'

'Don't be afraid. We won't let them hurt us. And now try to remember how many men there were.'

'Pietro an''—some uvers, an' vey went away in ve trees.'

They questioned him some more, but got merely a variation of the same story; it was evidently all he knew. Marcia called Granton to sit with him and tremulously explained the situation. Granton received the information calmly; it was all she had ever expected in Italy, she said.

Out in the hall again, Marcia looked at Sybert questioningly; she was quite composed. Gerald was safe at least, and they knew what was coming. She felt that her uncle and Sybert would bring things right.

'What shall we do?' she asked.

Sybert, with folded arms, was considering the question.

'It's evidently a mixture of robbery and revenge and mistaken patriotism all rolled into one. It would be convenient if we knew how many there were; Pietro and Gervasio's stepfather and your man with the crucifix we may safely count upon, but just how many more we have no means of knowing. However, there's no danger of their beginning operations till they think we're asleep.' He looked at his watch. 'It is a quarter to ten. We have a good two hours still, and we'll prepare to surprise them. We won't tell the people downstairs just yet, for it won't do any good, and their talk and laughter are the best protection we could have. You don't know where your uncle keeps his revolver, do you?'

'Yes; in the top drawer of his writing-table.' She stepped into Mr. Copley's room and pulled open the drawer. 'Why, it's gone!'

'I say, the plot thickens!' and Sybert, too, uttered a short, low laugh, as Copley had done on the terrace.

'And the rifle's gone,' Marcia added, her glance wandering to the corner where the gun-case usually stood.

'It's evident that our friend Pietro has been helping himself; but if he thinks he's going to shoot us with our own arms he's mistaken. We must get word to the soldiers at Palestrina— did you tell me the servants were gone?'

'I couldn't find any one but Granton. The whole house is empty.'

'It's the Camorra!' he exclaimed softly.

'The Camorra?' Marcia paled a trifle at the name.

'Ah—it's plain enough. We should have suspected it before. Pietro is a member and has been acting as a spy from the inside. It appears to be a very prettily worked out plot. They have waited until they think there's money in the house; your uncle has just sold a big consignment of wheat. They have probably dismissed the servants with their usual formula: "Be silent, and you live; speak, and you die." The servants would be more afraid of the Camorra than of the police.—How about the stablemen?'

123

'Oh, I can't believe they'd join a plot against us,' Marcia cried. 'Angelo and Giovanni I would trust anywhere.'

'In that case they've been silenced; they are where they won't give testimony until it is too late. I dare say the fellows are even planning to ride off on the horses themselves. By morning they would be well into the mountains of the Abruzzi, where the Camorrists are at home. We'll have to get help from Palestrina. If we could reach those guards at the cross-roads, they would ride in with the message. It's only two miles away, but——' He frowned a trifle. 'I suppose the house is closely watched, and it will be difficult to get out unseen. We'll have to try it, though.'

'Whom can we send?'

He was silent a moment. 'I don't like to leave you,' he said slowly, 'but I'm afraid I'll have to go.'

'Oh!' said Marcia, with a little gasp. She stood looking down at the floor with troubled eyes, and Sybert watched her, careless that the time was passing.

Marcia suddenly raised her eyes, with an exclamation of relief. 'Gervasio!' she cried. 'We can send Gervasio.'

'Could we trust him?' he doubted.

'Anywhere! And he can get away without being seen easier than you could. I am sure he can do it; he is very intelligent.'

'I'd forgotten him. Yes, I believe that is the best way. You go and wake him, and I'll write a note to the soldiers.' Sybert turned to the writing-table as he spoke, and Marcia hurried back to Gervasio's room.

The boy was asleep, with the moonlight streaming across his pillow. She bent over him hesitatingly, while her heart reproached her at having to wake him and send him out on such an errand. But the next moment she had reflected that it might be the only chance for him as well as for the rest of them, and she laid her hand gently on his forehead.

'Gervasio,' she whispered. 'Wake up, Gervasio. Sh—silenzio! Dress just as fast as you can. No, you haven't done anything; don't be frightened. Signor Siberti is going to tell you a secret—un segreto,' she repeated impressively. 'Put on these clothes,' she added, hunting out a dark suit from his wardrobe. 'And never mind your shoes and stockings. Dress subito, subito, and then come on tiptoe—pianissimo—to Signor Copley's room.'

Gervasio was into his clothes and after her almost before she had got back. When undirected by Bianca, his dressing was a simple matter.

Sybert drew him across the threshold and closed the door. 'What shall we tell him?' he questioned Marcia.

'Tell him the truth. He can understand, and we can trust him.' And dropping on her knees beside the boy, she laid her hands on his shoulders. 'Gervasio,' she said in her slow Italian, 'some bad, naughty men are coming here to-night to try to kill us and steal our things. Pietro is one of them' (Pietro had that very afternoon boxed Gervasio's ears for stealing sugar from the tea-table), 'and your stepfather is one, and he will take you back to Castel Vivalanti, and you will never see us again.'

Gervasio listened, with his eyes on her face and his lips parted in horror. Sybert here broke in and explained about the soldiers, and how he was to reach the guard at the corners, and he ended by hiding the note in the front of his blouse. 'Do you understand?' he asked, 'do you think you can do it?'

Gervasio nodded, his eyes now shining with excitement. 'I'll bring the soldiers,' he whispered, 'sicure, signore, sicurissimo! And if they catch me,' he added, 'I'll say the padrone has whipped me and I'm running away.'

'You'll do,' Sybert said with a half-laugh, and taking the boy by the hand, he led the way back to the middle staircase, and the three crept down with as little noise as possible.

They traversed on tiptoe the long brick passageway that led to the kitchen, and paused upon the threshold. The great stone-walled room was empty and quiet and echoing as on the first day they had come to the villa. The doors and windows were swinging wide and the moonlight was streaming in.

Sybert shook his head in a puzzled frown. 'What I can't make out,' he said in a low tone, 'is why they should leave everything so open. They must have known that we would find out before we went to bed that the servants were missing. Who usually locks up?'

'Pietro.'

'You and I will lock up to-night.' He considered a moment. 'We mustn't let him out within sight of the grove. A window on the eastern side of the house would be best, where the shrubbery grows close to the walls.'

Marcia led the way into a little store-room opening from the kitchen, and Sybert gave Gervasio his last directions.

'Keep well in the shadow of the trees across the driveway and down around the lower terrace. Creep on your hands and knees through the wheat field, and then strike straight for the cross-roads and run every step of the way. Capisci?'

Gervasio nodded, and Marcia bent and kissed him and whispered in his ear, 'If you bring the soldiers, Gervasio, you may live with us always and be our little boy, just like Gerald.'

He nodded again, fairly trembling with anxiety to get started. Sybert carefully swung the window open, and the little fellow dropped to the ground and crept like a cat into the shadows. They stood by the open window for several minutes, straining their ears to listen, but no sound came back except the peaceful music of a summer night—the murmur of insects and the songs of nightingales. Gervasio had got off safely.

'Now we'll lock the house,' Sybert added in an undertone, 'so that when our friends come to call they will have to come the front way.'

He closed the window softly and examined with approval the inside shutters. They were made of solid wood with heavy iron bolts and hinges. The villa had been planned in the old days before the police force was as efficient as now, and it was quite prepared to stand a siege.

'It will take considerable strength to open these, and some noise,' he remarked as he swung the shutters to and shot the bolts.

They groped their way out and went from room to room, closing and bolting the windows and doors with as little noise as possible. Sybert appeared, to Marcia's astonished senses, to be in an unusually light-hearted frame of mind. Once or twice he laughed softly, and once, when her hand touched his in the dark, she felt that same warm thrill run through her as on that other moonlight night.

They came last to the big vaulted dining-room which had served as chapel in the devotional days of the Vivalanti. The three glass doors at the end were open to the moonlight, which flooded the apartment, softening the crude outlines of the frescoes on the ceiling to the beauty of old masters. Sybert paused with his back to the doors to look up and down approvingly.

'Do you know, it isn't half bad in this light,' he remarked casually to Marcia. 'That old fellow up there,' he nodded toward Bacchus reclining among the vines in the central panelling, 'might be a Michelangelo in the moonlight, and in the sunlight he isn't even a Carlo Dolci.'

Marcia stared. What could he be thinking of to choose this time of all others to be making art criticisms? Never had she heard him express the slightest interest in the subject before. She had been under so great a strain for so long, such a succession of shocks, that she was nearly at the end of her self-control. And then to have Sybert acting in this unprecedented way! She looked past him out of the door toward the black shadow of the ilexes, and shuddered as she thought of what they might conceal. The next moment Sybert had stepped out on to the balcony.

'Mr. Sybert!' she cried aghast. 'They may be watching us. Come back.'

125

He laughed and seated himself sidewise on the iron railing. 'If they're watching us, they're doubtless wondering why we're closing the house so carefully. We'll stop here a few minutes and let them see we're unsuspicious; that we're just shutting the doors for fear of draughts and not of burglars.'

'They'll shoot you,' she gasped, her eyes upon his white suit, which made a shining target in the moonlight.

'Nonsense, Miss Marcia! They couldn't hit me if they tried.' He marked the distance to the grove with a calculating eye. 'There's no danger of their trying, however. They won't risk giving their plot away just for the sake of nabbing me; I'm not King Humbert. They don't hate me as much as that.' He leaned forward with another laugh. 'Come out and talk to me, Miss Marcia. Let me see how brave you are.'

Marcia flattened herself against the wall. 'I'm not brave. Please come back, Mr. Sybert. We must tell Uncle Howard.'

If Marcia did not know Sybert to-night, he did not know himself. He was under a greater strain than she. He had sworn that he would not see her again, and he had weakly come to-night; he had promised himself that he would not talk to her, that he would not by the slightest sign betray his feelings, and he found himself thrown with her under the most intimate conditions. They shared a secret; they were in danger together. It was within the realms of possibility that he would be killed to-night. The Camorrists had attempted it before; they might succeed this time. He actually did not care; he almost welcomed the notion. Ambition was dead within him; he had nothing to live for and he was reckless. He thought that Marcia was in love with another man, but he dimly divined his own influence over her. Once at least, he told himself—once, before she went back to the boy she had chosen, she should acknowledge his power; she should bend her will to his. He knew that she was frightened, but she should conquer her fear. She should come out into the moonlight and stand beside him, hand in hand, facing the shadows of the ilex grove.

He bent forward, watching her as she stood in her white evening gown outlined against the dark tapestry of the wall, her face surrounded by glowing hair, her grey eyes big with amazement and fear. He stretched out his hand toward her. 'Marcia,' he called in a low, insistent tone. 'Come here, Marcia. Come out here and stand beside me, or I shall think you are a coward.'

She turned aside with a little shuddering gasp and hid her head against the wall. What if they should shoot him in the back as he sat there?

Sybert suddenly came to himself and sprang forward with an apology. 'Oh, I beg your pardon, Miss Marcia; I didn't mean to frighten you. I don't know what I'm saying.'

He began closing the doors and shutters farthest away. As he reached her side he paused and looked at her. Her eyes were shut and she did not move. He closed and barred the last shutter, and they stood silent in the dark. Marcia was struggling to control herself. 'I shall think you a coward,' was ringing in her ears. She had borne a great deal to-day, from the moment when she had first seen the man asleep in the grass; and now, as she opened her eyes in the darkness, a sudden rush of fear swept over her such as she had experienced in the old wine-cellar. It was not fear of any definite thing; she could be as brave as any one in the face of visible danger. It was merely a wild, unreasoning sensation of physical terror, bred of the dark and overwrought nerves. She stretched out her hand and touched Sybert to be sure he was there. The next moment she was beyond herself. 'I'm afraid,' she sobbed out, and she clung to him convulsively.

She felt him put his arm around her. 'Marcia! My dear little girl. There's nothing to be afraid of. When they find we are on our guard they won't dare molest us. Nothing can hurt you.' It was so exactly his tone to Gerald, she would have laughed had she not been crying too hard to stop. Then suddenly his arms tightened about her. 'Marcia,' he whispered hoarsely, 'Marcia,' and he bent his head until his lips touched hers. They stood for an instant without moving; then she felt him become quickly rigid as he dropped his arms and gently loosened her hands. They groped their way into the hall without a word, and neither looked at the other. They were both ashamed. The tears still stood in Marcia's eyes, but her cheeks were scarlet. And Sybert was pale beneath the olive of his skin.

He stepped to the threshold of the salon. 'Ah, Copley,' he said in a low tone. 'Are you nearly through? I want to tell you something.'

Copley waved him off without looking up. 'Sh—it's a crucial moment. Don't interrupt. The scores are even and only one hand more to play. I'll be out in a few minutes.'

Marcia sat down in a chair on the loggia. It was on the opposite side of the house from the ilex grove, and besides, her spasm of fear had passed. Everything was blotted out of her mind except what had just happened. Her thoughts, her feelings, were in wild commotion; but one thing stood out clearly. She had thrown herself into his arms and he had kissed her; and then—he had unloosed her hands. She shut her eyes and winced at the thought; she felt that she could never face him again.

And on the other end of the loggia Sybert was pacing up and down, lighting cigarettes and throwing them away. He, too, was fiercely calling himself names. He had frightened her when he knew that she was beside herself with nervousness; he had taken advantage of the fact that she did not know what she was doing; he knew that she was engaged to Paul Dessart, and he had forgotten that he was a gentleman. With a quick glance toward the salon, he threw away his cigarette, and crossing the loggia, he sat down in a chair at Marcia's side. She shrank back quickly, and he leaned forward with his elbows on his knees and his eyes on the brick floor.

'Marcia,' he said in a tone so low that it was barely audible, 'I love you. I know you don't care for me; I know you are engaged to another man. I didn't mean to see you again; most of all I didn't mean to tell you. I had no right to take advantage of you when you were off your guard, but—I couldn't help it; I'm not so strong as I thought I was. Please forgive me and forget about it.'

Marcia drew a deep breath and shut her eyes. Her throat suddenly felt hot and dry. The rush of joy that swept over her made her feel that she could face anything. She had but to say, 'I am not engaged to another man,' and all would come right. She raised her head and looked back into Sybert's deep eyes. It was he this time who dropped his gaze.

'Mr. Sybert——' she whispered.

A shadow suddenly fell between them, and they both sprang to their feet with a little exclamation. A man was standing before them as unexpectedly as though he had risen from the earth or dropped from the sky. He was short and thick-set, with coarsely accentuated features; he wore a loose white shirt and a red cotton sash, and though the shirt was fastened at the throat, Marcia could see the mark of the crucifix on his brown skin as plainly as if it were visible.

'It's the tattooed man!' she gasped out, but as she felt Sybert's restraining touch on her arm she calmed herself.

The man took off his hat with a polite bow and an impertinent smile.

'Buona sera, signorina,' he murmured. 'Buona sera, Friend of the Poor. I'm sorry to interrupt you, but I come on business molto urgente.'

'What is your business?' Sybert asked sharply.

'My business is with Signor Copley.'

'What is this? Some one to see me?' Copley asked, appearing in the doorway. 'Well, my man,' he added in Italian, 'what can I do for you?'

'Uncle Howard, don't speak to him! It's the tattooed man,' Marcia cried. 'There's a plot. He wants to kill you.'

An expression approaching amusement flitted over Mr. Copley's face as he looked his visitor over.

127

'I wish to speak to the signore alone, in private, on urgent business,' the man reiterated, looking scowlingly from one face to the other. He did not understand the foreign language they spoke among themselves, and he felt that it gave them an advantage.

'Don't speak to him alone,' Sybert warned. 'He's dangerous.'

'Well, what do you want?' Copley demanded peremptorily. 'Say whatever you have to say here.'

The man glanced at Marcia and Sybert, and then, shrugging his shoulders in true Italian fashion, turned to Copley.

'I wish the money of the poor,' he said.

'The money of the poor? I haven't any money of the poor.'

'Si, si, signore. The money you stole from the mouths of the poor—the wheat money.'

Marcia shuddered at the word 'wheat.' It seemed to her that it would follow her to her dying day.

'Ah! So it's the wheat money, is it? Well, my good man, that happens to be my money. I didn't steal it from the mouths of the poor. I bought the wheat myself to give to the poor, and I sold it for half as much as I paid for it; and with the money I intend to buy more wheat. In the meantime, however, I shall keep it in my own hands.'

'You don't remember me, signore, but I remember you. We met in Naples.'

Copley bowed. 'On which occasion I put you in jail—a pleasure I shall avail myself of a second time if you trouble me any further.'

'I have come for the money.'

'You fool! Do you think I carry thirty thousand lire around in my pockets? The money is in the Banca d'Italia in Rome. You may call there if you wish it.'

The man put his hands to his mouth and whistled.

'Ah! It's a plot, is it!' Copley exclaimed.

'Si, signore. It is a plot, and there are those who will carry it out.'

He turned with an angry snarl, and before Sybert could spring forward to stop him he had snatched a stiletto from his girdle. Copley threw up his arm to protect himself, and received the blow in the shoulder. Before the man could strike again, Sybert was upon him and had thrown him backward across the balustrade. At the same moment half a dozen men burst from the ilex grove and ran across the terrace; and one of them—it was Pietro—levelled the stolen rifle as he ran.

'Back into the house!' Sybert shouted, 'and bar the salon windows.' He himself sprang back to the threshold and snatched out his revolver. 'You fools!' he cried to the Italians in front. 'We're all armed men. We'll shoot you like dogs.'

For answer Pietro fired the rifle, and the glass of an upper window crashed.

Sybert closed the door and dropped the bar across it. He faced the excited group in the hall with a little laugh. 'If that's a specimen of his marksmanship, we haven't much to fear from Pietro.'

He glanced quickly from one to the other. Marcia, in the salon, was slamming the shutters down. Mrs. Melville and Mrs. Copley were standing in the doorway with white faces, too amazed to move. Copley, in the middle of the hall, with his right arm hanging limp, was dripping blood on the marble pavement while he loudly called for a pistol; and Melville was standing on a chair hastily tearing from the wall a collection of fourteenth-century Florentine arms.

'Pietro's got your pistol,' Sybert said. 'But I've got five shots in mine, and we'll do for the sixth man with one of those bludgeons. I ought to have shot that tattooed fellow when I had the chance—he's the leader—but I'll make up for it yet.'

A storm of blows on the door behind him brought out another laugh. 'That door is as solid as the side of the house. They can hammer on it all night without getting in.'

The assailants had evidently arrived at the same conclusion, for the blows ceased while they consulted. A crash of glass in the salon followed, and Sybert sprang in there, calling to

Melville to guard the hall window. The shutters held against the first impact of the men's bodies, and they drew off for a minute and then redoubled the blows. They were evidently using the butt of the rifle as a battering-ram, and the stoutest of hinges could not long withstand such usage. With a groan one side of the shutter gave way and swung inward on a single hinge.

'Put out the lights,' Sybert called over his shoulder to Marcia, and he fired a shot through the aperture. The assailants fell back with groans and curses, but the next moment, raising the cry, 'Avanti! Avanti!' they came on with a rush, the Camorrist leading with the stolen revolver in his hand. Sybert took deliberate aim and fired. The man slowly sank to his knees and fell forward on his face. His comrades dragged him back.

Marcia, in the darkness behind, shut her eyes and clenched her hands. It was the first time she had ever seen a person die, and the sight was sickening. The men withdrew from the window and those waiting inside heard them consulting in low, angry guttural tones. The next moment there was a crash of glass at the hall window which opened into the loggia, and again the rifle as a battering-ram.

'Ah!' said Sybert under his breath, and he thrust the revolver into Marcia's hand. 'Quick, take that to Melville and bring me one of those spiked truncheons. We'll make 'em think we've got a regular arsenal in here.'

Marcia obeyed without a word, and the next moment shots and cries rang out in the hall. She had scarcely placed the unwieldy weapon in Sybert's hands when another man thrust himself into the salon opening. They had evidently determined to divide their forces and attack the two breaches at once. Both Marcia and Sybert recognized the man instantly. It was Tarquinio, the son of Domenico, the baker of Castel Vivalanti.

'Tarquinio! You fool! Go back,' Sybert cried.

'Ah-h—Signor Siberti!' the young fellow cried as he lunged forward with a stiletto. 'You have betrayed us!'

Sybert shut his lips, and reversing the truncheon, struck him with the handle a ringing blow on the head. Tarquinio fell forward into the darkness of the room, and the moonlight streamed in on his bloody face.

Sybert bent over him a moment with white lips. 'You poor fool!' he muttered. 'I had to do it.'

The next moment Marcia uttered a joyous cry that rang through the rooms.

'Listen!'

A silence of ten seconds followed, while both besieged and besiegers held their breath. The sound was unmistakable—a shout far down the avenue and the beat of galloping hoofs.

'The soldiers!' she cried, and the men outside, as if they had understood the word, echoed the cry.

'I soldati! I soldati!'

The next moment a dozen carabinieri swept into sight, the moonlight gleaming brightly on their white cross-belts and polished mountings. The men on the loggia dropped their weapons and dashed for cover, while the soldiers leaped from their horses and with spiked muskets chased them into the trees.

Sybert hastily bent over Tarquinio and dragged him back into the shadow.

'Is he alive?' Marcia whispered.

'He's only stunned. And, poor fellow, he doesn't know any better; he was nothing but their dupe. It's a pity to send him to the galleys for life.'

They dropped a rug over the man and turned into the hall, which was hot with the smell of powder and smoking candles. Sybert threw the door wide and let the moonlight stream in. It was a queer sight it looked upon. Copley, weak from his wound, had collapsed into a tall carved chair, while the two ladies, in blood-stained evening dresses, were anxiously bending over him. Melville, with the still smoking revolver in his hand and a jewelled dagger sticking from his pocket, was frenziedly inquiring, 'For the Lord's sake, has any one got any whisky?' Gerald, in his white nightgown and little bare legs, was howling dismally on the stairway; while Granton, from the landing, looked grimly down upon the scene with the air of an avenging Nemesis. The next moment the soldiers had come trooping in, and everything was a babel of cries and ejaculations and excited questions. In the midst of the confusion Mrs. Copley suddenly drew herself up and pronounced her ultimatum.

'On the very first steamer that sails, we are going back to America to live!'

Marcia uttered a little hysterical laugh, and Melville joined in.

'And I think you'd better go with them, my boy,' he said, laying a grimy hand on Sybert's arm. 'I suspect that your goose is pretty thoroughly cooked in Italy.'

Sybert shook the elder man's hand off, with a short laugh that was not very mirthful.

'I've suspected that for some time.' And he turned on his heel and strode out to the loggia, where he began talking with the soldiers.

'Poor fellow!' Melville glanced at Marcia and shook his head. 'It's a bad dose!' he murmured. 'I have a curiosity to see with what grace he swallows it.'

Marcia looked after Sybert with eyes that were filled with sympathy. She realized that it was a bitter time for him, though she did not know just why; but she had seen the spasm that crossed his face at Tarquinio's cry, 'You have betrayed us!' She half started to follow him, and then she drew back quickly. Through the open door she had caught a glimpse of Sybert and a soldier bending over the Camorrist's body. They had opened his shirt in front, and she had seen the purple crucifix covered with blood. She leaned back against the wall, faint at the sight. It seemed as if the impressions of this dreadful day could never leave her!

CHAPTER XXV

Mr. Copley's wounded arm was bandaged the best that they could manage and a soldier dispatched to Palestrina for a doctor. Gerald was put to bed and quieted for the third time that night, and the excitement in the house was subsiding to a murmur when Marcia came downstairs again. Melville met her by the door of the loggia, evidently anxious that she should not go out. She had no desire to; she had seen more than she cared to see.

'We have caught two of the men,' he said; 'but I am afraid that the rest have got off—that precious butler of yours among them.'

'Where is Mr. Sybert?' she asked. The thought of Tarquinio had suddenly occurred to her; she had forgotten him in the distraction of helping with her uncle.

'He's locking the house.'

'I will see if I can help him,' and she turned into the salon.

Melville looked after her with a momentary smile. He had a theory which his wife did not share.

Marcia passed through the empty salon and the little ante-room, and hesitated with her hand on the dining-room door. She had a premonition that he was within; she turned the knob softly and entered.

Sybert sprang up with a quick exclamation. 'Oh, it's you!' he said. 'I thought I had locked the door. Draw the bolt, please. I brought him in here and I'm trying to bring him round. If they find him he'll be sent to the galleys, and it seems a pity. He's got a wife and child to support.'

Marcia looked down on the floor where Tarquinio was lying. Sybert had thrown the glass doors open again and the moonlight was flooding the room. A towel, folded into a rough bandage, was wrapped around the young Italian's head, and his pale face beneath it had all the dark, tragic beauty of his race.

'Poor man!' she exclaimed as she bent over him. 'Are you sure he's alive?' she asked, starting back.

'Heavens, yes! It takes more than that knock to kill one of these peasants. He groaned when I carried him in. Here, let me give him some whisky.'

He raised the man's head and pressed the flask to his lip. Tarquinio groaned again, and presently he opened his eyes. Sybert raised him to a sitting posture against the wall. For a moment his glance wandered about the room, uncomprehendingly, dully. Then, as it fixed upon Sybert, a wild, fierce light suddenly sprang into his eyes. 'Traitor!' he gasped out, and he struggled to his feet.

Again Marcia saw that quick look of pain shoot over Sybert's face; he swallowed a couple of times before speaking, and when he did speak his voice was hard and cold.

'Can you walk? Then climb over that railing and get away as fast as you can. The soldiers are here, and if they find you they will send you to the galleys—not that it would be any great loss,' he added with a contemptuous laugh. 'Italy has no need of such men as you.'

Something of the fierceness faded from the young fellow's face, and he looked back with the pleading, child-like eyes of the Italian peasant. The two men watched each other a moment without speaking, then Tarquinio turned to the open door with a shrug of the shoulders—Young Italy's philosophy of life.

They stood silently looking after him as he let himself down to the ground and unsteadily crossed the open space to the shadow of the grove. Sybert was the first to move. He turned aside with a tired sigh that was half a groan, and dropping into a chair, rested his elbows on his knees and his head in his hands. All the wild buoyancy that had kept him through the evening had left him, and there was nothing in its place but a dull, unreasoning despair. For the last few weeks he had been glancing at the truth askance. To-night he was looking it full in the face. The people no longer trusted him; he could do no more good in Italy; his work was at an end. Why had they not killed him? That would have been the appropriate conclusion.

Marcia, watching his bowed figure, dimly divined what was going on within his mind. She hesitated a moment, and then with a quick impulse laid her arm about his neck. 'There isn't any one but you,' she whispered.

He sat for a moment, motionless, and then he slowly raised his eyes to hers. 'What do you mean, Marcia?'

'I love you.'

'And—you're free to marry me?'

She nodded.

He sprang to his feet with a deep, shuddering breath of relief. 'I've lost Italy, Marcia, but I've found you!'

She smiled up at him through her tears, and he looked back with sombre eyes.

'You aren't getting much of a man,' he said brokenly. 'I—was just thinking of shooting myself.'

A quick tremor passed over her, and she drew his face down close to hers and kissed it.

They stood for a long time on the little balcony, hand in hand, facing the shadows of the ilex grove; but the shadows no longer seemed black, because of the light in their own souls. He talked to her of his past—frankly, freely—and of Italy, his adopted land. He told her what he had tried to do and wherein he had failed. And as she listened, many things that had puzzled her, that had seemed enigmas in his character, assumed their right relations. The dark glass that had half hidden his motives, that had contorted his actions, suddenly cleared before her eyes. She saw the inherent sweetness and strength of his nature beneath his reserve, his apparent indifference. And as he told the story of Italy, of the sacrifices and valour and singleness of purpose that had gone to the making of the nation, there crept involuntarily a triumphant ring into his voice. The note of despondency that had dominated him for the past few months disappeared; for, as he dwelt upon the positive things that had been accomplished, they seemed to take shape and stand out clearly against the dimmer background of unaccomplished hopes. The remembrance of the nation's smaller mistakes and faults and crimes had vanished in the larger view. The story that he had to tell was the story of a great people and a great land. There had been patriots in the past; there would be

131

patriots in the future. The same strength that had made the nation would build it up and carry it on.

'Ah, Sybert! Miss Marcia!' Melville's voice rang through the house.

'I'd forgotten there was any one in the world but us,' Marcia whispered as they turned back into the hall.

'Here's a young gentleman calling for you, Miss Marcia.' Melville's hand rested on the shoulder of a barefooted little figure covered with the white dust of the Roman road.

'Gervasio!' Marcia cried, with a quick spasm of self-reproach. She had forgotten him.

The boy drew himself up proudly and pointed through the open door to the soldiers pacing the length of the terrace.

'Ecco! signorina. I soldati!'

Marcia dropped on her knees beside him with a little laugh. 'You darling!' she cried as she gathered him into her arms and kissed him.

Sybert bent over him and shook his hand. 'You're a brave boy, Gervasio,' he said; 'and you've probably saved our lives to-night.'

'Am I going to live with you now,' he asked, 'like Gerald?'

'Always,' said Marcia, 'just like Gerald.'

He opened his eyes wide. 'And will I be an Americano then?'

'No, Gervasio,' said Sybert, quickly. 'You'll never be an Americano. You were born Italiano, and you'll be Italiano till you die. You should be proud of it—it's your birthright. We are Americani, and we are going—home. You may come with us and study and learn, but when you get to be a man you must come back to your own country. It will need you—and now run to bed. And you too, Miss Marcia,' he added. 'You are tired and there's nothing to be done. Melville and I will attend to locking up.'

'Locking up!' cried Melville. 'Good Lord, man, how many locking-ups does this house require?' He watched them a moment in silence, and then he added bluntly: 'Oh, see here, what's the good of secrets between friends? I've known it all along.' He held out a hand to each of them. 'It's eminently fitting; my congratulations come from my heart.'

'You're too discerning by far,' Sybert retorted, his hands fast in his pockets.

Marcia, with a laugh and a quick flush, held out both of hers. 'It's a secret,' she said. 'I don't know how you guessed it, but you must promise on your honour as a gentleman and a diplomat not to tell a single soul!'

'I must tell my wife,' he pleaded. 'It's a case of "I told you so," and she usually comes out ahead in such cases. You can't ask me to hide what little light I have under a bushel.'

'I don't care so much about Mrs. Melville,' Marcia gave a reluctant consent. 'But promise me one thing: that you'll never, never breathe a word to—I don't know her name—the Lady who Writes.'

'The Lady who Writes? Who on earth is she talking about, Sybert?'

'The greatest gossip in Rome,' appended Marcia.

'Madame Laventi!' Melville laughed. 'You're too late, Miss Marcia. She knows it already. Madame Laventi does not get her news by word of mouth; the birds carry it to her. Good night,' he added, and he strolled discreetly into the salon. But his caution was unnecessary; their parting was blatantly innocent.

Sybert chose a tall brass candlestick from the row on the mantelpiece and handed it to her with a bow.

'Thank you,' said Marcia.

She paused on the landing and smiled down.

'Buona notte, Signor Siberti,' she murmured.

He smiled back from the foot of the stairs.

'Buona notte, signorina. Pleasant dreams!'

Hearing the sound of voices within, Marcia paused at Mrs. Copley's door to ask about her uncle. She found the room strewn with the contents of several wardrobes, and her aunt and Granton kneeling each before an open trunk.

'Good gracious, Aunt Katherine!' she exclaimed in amazement. 'What are you doing? It's one o'clock.'

'We are packing, my dear.'

Marcia sat down on the bed with a hysterical giggle. 'Aunt Katherine, if I didn't know the contrary, I should swear you were born a Copley.'

Mrs. Copley withdrew her head from the trunk and looked about for something further to fit in. In passing she cast her niece a reproachful glance. 'I don't see how you can be so flippant, Marcia, after what we've been through to-night—and with your uncle lying wounded in the next room! It's only one chance in a hundred that we aren't all in our graves by now. I shall not draw an easy breath until we have landed safely in the streets of New York. Just hand me that pile of things on the chair there.' Her gaze rested upon a parti-coloured assortment of ribbons and laces and gloves.

Marcia suppressed another smile. 'I know it isn't the time to laugh, Aunt Katherine, but I can't help it. You're so—sort of businesslike. It never would have occurred to me to pack to-night.'

'We are going into Rome the first thing to-morrow morning, and with only Granton to help there is no time to lose. We might as well begin while we are waiting for the doctor—he surely ought to be here by now,' she added, her anxiety coming to the fore. 'What do you suppose takes him so long? It's been an hour since we sent.'

'It's four miles to Palestrina, Aunt Katherine. And you must remember it's the middle of the night; the man was probably in bed and asleep. It will be another half hour at least before he can get here.'

'Yes, I suppose so'—Mrs. Copley turned back to her packing—'but I can't help being worried! One suspects everybody after an experience like this. I am really feeling very nervous over your uncle's arm; he makes light of it, but it may be more serious than any of us think. There's always so much danger of lockjaw or blood-poisoning from a wound of that sort. I shall not feel satisfied about it until we can get into Rome and consult an American doctor.'

'May I see him?' Marcia asked, 'or is he asleep?'

'No, he's awake; but you must not excite him.'

Marcia tapped lightly on Mr. Copley's door and entered. He was propped up on pillows, his arm in a sling. She crossed over and sat down on the edge of the bed. 'I'm so sorry, Uncle Howard,' she murmured.

'Oh, it's nothing to make a fuss over. I got off very easily.'

'I don't mean just your arm—I mean—everything.'

'Ah,' said Copley, and shut his eyes.

'But, after all,' she added, 'it may be for the best. The Italians don't understand what you are doing. I don't believe two such different races can understand each other.'

He opened his eyes with a humorous smile. 'It's rather a comic-opera ending,' he agreed. 'I have a feeling that before the curtain goes down I should join hands with the bandits and come out and make my bow.'

'There are lots of things to be done in America, and they'll appreciate you more at home.'

'I think I'll buy a yacht and go in for racing, as your aunt suggests. I may come off in that—if I have a captain.'

Marcia sat silent a moment, looking down on his finely lined, sensitive face.

'Uncle Howard,' she said slowly, 'it seems as if the good you do is some way cast up to the credit side of the world's account and helps just so much to overcome the bad, whether any one knows about it or not. You may go away and leave it all behind and never be appreciated, but it's a positive quantity just the same. It's so much accomplished on the right side.'

Her uncle smiled again.

'I'm afraid that's rather too idealistic a philosophy for this generation. We're living in a material age, and it takes something more solid than good intentions to make much impression on it. I have a sneaking suspicion that I wasn't born to set the world to rights. Many men are reformers in their youth, but I'm reaching the age when a club and a good dinner are excellent anodynes for my own and other people's troubles.'

A shadow fell over her face and she looked down in her lap without answering.

After a moment he asked suddenly, 'Where's Sybert, Marcia?'

'I think he's downstairs waiting for the doctor.'

'Ah!' said Copley again, with a little sigh.

Marcia slipped down on her knees beside the bed. 'Uncle Howard,' she whispered, 'I want to tell you something. I'm—going to marry Mr. Sybert.'

Copley raised himself on his elbow and stared at her.

'You are going to marry Sybert?' he repeated incredulously.

'Yes, uncle,' she smiled. 'He asked me to.'

'Sybert!' Copley repeated, with an astonished laugh. 'Holy St. Francis! What a change is here!'

'I thought you would be pleased,' she said a little tremulously.

He stretched out his hand and laid it over hers. 'My dear Marcia, nothing could have pleased me more. He's the finest man I have ever known, and I begin to suspect that you are the finest girl. But—good gracious! Marcia, I must be blind and deaf and dumb. I had a notion you didn't like each other.'

'We've changed our minds,' she said; 'and I wanted you to know it because I thought it would make you feel better.'

'And so it does, Marcia,' he said heartily. 'The year has accomplished something, after all; and I'm glad for Sybert's sake that he's got this just now, for, poor fellow, he's in a deeper hole than I.'

Marcia pressed his hand gratefully as her aunt came bustling in with her arms full of clothes.

'Howard,' she asked, 'shall I have Granton pack your heavy flannels, or shall you want them on the steamer?'

Her husband attempted a shrug and found the bandages would not permit it.

'I think perhaps I'd better leave them out. It's June, of course; but I've known very cold crossings even in July.'

Copley turned on his side and wrenched his arm again.

'Oh, for heaven's sake! Katherine,' he groaned, 'pack them, throw them away, burn them, do anything you please.'

Mrs. Copley came to the bedside and bent over him anxiously. 'What's the matter, dear? Is your arm very painful? You don't suppose,' she added in sudden alarm, 'that the stiletto was poisoned, do you?'

'Lord, no!' he laughed. 'Poisoned daggers went out two centuries ago—it's a mere scratch, Katherine; don't worry about it. Go on with your packing—I should hate to miss that first steamer.'

His wife patted the pillows and turned toward the door. 'Marcia,' she called over her shoulder, 'go to bed, child. You will be absolutely worn out to-morrow—and don't talk to your uncle any more. I'm afraid you will get him excited.'

Marcia bent over and lightly kissed him on the forehead. 'Good night,' she whispered. 'I hope you will feel better in the morning,' and she turned back to her own room.

She sat down on the couch by the open window and drew the muslin curtains back. The moon was low in the west, hanging over Rome. A cool night breeze was stirring, and the little chill that precedes dawn was in the air. She drew a rug about her and sat looking out, listening to the shuffling tramp of the soldiers and thinking of the long day that had passed. When she waked that morning it had been like any other day, and now everything was changed. This was her last night in the villa, and her heart was full of happiness and sorrow—sorrow for her uncle and Laurence Sybert and the poor peasants. It was Italy to the end—beauty and moonlight and love, mingled with tragedy and death and disappointment. She had a great many things to think about, but she was very, very tired, and with a half-sigh and a half-smile her head drooped on the cushions and she fell asleep.

CHAPTER XXVI

Marcia woke at dawn with the sun in her eyes. She started up dazedly at finding herself dressed in her white evening gown, lying on the couch instead of in bed. Then in a moment the events of yesterday flashed back. The floor was covered with broken glass, and on the wall opposite a dark spot among the rose-garlands showed where Pietro's misaimed bullet had lodged. On the terrace balustrade below her window two soldiers were sitting, busily throwing dice. They lent an absurd air of unreality to the scene. She stepped to the open doors of the balcony and drew a deep, delighted breath of the fresh morning air. Rome in the west was still sleeping, but every separate crag of the Sabines was glowing a soft pink, and the newly risen sun was hanging like a halo behind the old monastery. It was a day filled with promise.

The next moment she had brought her thoughts back from the distant horizon to the contemplation of homelier matters nearer at hand. Mingled with the early fragrance of roses and dew was the subtly penetrating odour of boiling coffee. Marcia sniffed and considered. Some one was making coffee for the soldiers, who were to be relieved at the 'Ave Maria.' She reviewed the possible cooks. Not Granton. The soldiers were Italians, and, for all Granton cared, they could perish from hunger on their way back to Palestrina. Not her aunt. In all probability, she did not know how to make coffee. Not her uncle. He was hors de concours with his wounded arm. The Melvilles! They would not have known where to look for the kitchen. She interrupted her speculations to exchange last night's evening gown for a fresh blue muslin, and her hasty glance at the mirror as she stole out on tiptoe told her that the slight pallor which comes from three hours' sleep was not unbecoming. She crept downstairs through the dim hall and paused a second by the open door of the loggia; her eyes involuntarily sought the spot outside the salon window. The rug was back in its place again, and everything was in its usual order. She felt thankful to some one; it was easier so to throw the matter from her mind.

She approached the kitchen softly and paused on the threshold with a reconnoitring glance. The big stone-floored room, with its smoky rafters overhead, was dark always, but especially so at the sunrise hour; its deep-embrasured windows looked to the west. In the farthest, darkest corner, before the big, brick-walled stove, some one was standing with his back turned toward her, and her heart quickened its beating perceptibly. She stood very still for several minutes, watching him; she would hypnotise him to turn around; but before she had fairly commenced with the business, he had picked up the poker by the wrong end and dropped it again. The observation which he made in Italian was quite untranslatable. Marcia tittered and he wheeled about.

'That's not fair,' he objected. 'I shouldn't have said anything so bad if I had known you were listening.'

'Do you know what we do with Gerald when he swears in Italian?'

He shook his head.

'We wash his mouth with soap.'

'I hope it doesn't happen often,' he shuddered.

'He speaks very fluent Italian—nearly as fluent as yours.'

'Suppose we change the subject.'

135

'Very well,' she agreed, advancing to the opposite side of the long central table. 'What shall we talk about?'

'We haven't said good morning.'

She dropped him a smiling curtsy. 'Good morning, Mr. Sybert.'

'Mr. Sybert! You haven't changed your mind overnight, have you?'

Her eyes were more reassuring than her speech. 'N-no.'

'No what?'

'Sir!' She laughed.

He came around to her side of the table, and faced her with his hands in his jacket pockets. 'You've never in your life pronounced my name. I don't believe you know it!'

She whispered.

'Say it louder.'

'It sounds too familiar,' she objected, backing against the wall with impudently laughing eyes. 'You're so—so sort of old—like Uncle Howard.'

'Oh, I know you're young, but you needn't put on such airs about it. You don't own all the youth in the world.'

'Thirty-five!' she murmured, with a wondering shake of her head.

'Ah—thirty-five. A very nice age. Just the right age, in fact, to make you mind me. Oh, you needn't laugh; I'm going to do it fast enough. And right here we'll begin.' He folded his arms with a very fierce frown, but with a smile on his lips, quizzical, humorous, comprehending, kindly—the finished result of so many smiles that had gone before. 'The business in hand, my dear young woman, is to find out whether or not you happen to know the name of the man you've promised to marry. Come, let me hear it; say it out loud.'

Marcia looked back tantalizingly a moment, and then, after an inquiring glance about the room as if she were searching to recall it, she dropped her lids and pronounced it with her eyes on the floor.

'Laurence.'

He unfolded his arms.

'The coffee's boiling over!' Marcia exclaimed.

'Kiss me good morning.'

'The coffee's boiling over.'

'I don't care if it is.'

The coffee boiled over with an angry spurt that deluged the stove with hissing steam. Marcia was patently too anxious for its safety to give her attention to anything else. Sybert stalked over and viciously jerked it back, and she picked up the plate of rolls and ran for the door. He caught up with her in the hall.

'I know why you discharged Marietta,' he threw out.

'Why?'

'If I were a French cook with a moustache and a goatee and a fetching white cap, and you were a black-eyed little Italian nursemaid with gold ear-rings in your ears, I should very frequently let things burn.'

'Oh,' Marcia laughed. 'And I should probably let the little boy I ought to be looking after fall over the balustrade and break his front tooth while I was sitting on the door-step smiling at you.'

'And so we should be torn apart—there was a tragedy!' he mused compassionately. 'I hadn't realized it before. It proves that you must suffer yourself before you can appreciate the sufferings of others.'

'French cooks with fetching caps have elastic hearts.'

'Ah,' said he, 'and so have black-eyed little Italian nursemaids—I'm glad you're not an Italian nursemaid, Marcia.'

'I'm glad you're not a French cook—Laurence.' And then she laughed. 'Will you tell me something?'

'Anything you wish.'

'Were you ever in love with the Contessa Torrenieri?'

'I used to fancy I was something of the sort nine or ten years ago. But, thank heaven, she was looking for a count.'

'I'm glad she found him!' Marcia breathed.

As they crossed the terrace to the little table at the corner of the grove where the afternoon before—it seemed a century—Mrs. Copley and Marcia had taken tea, one of the soldiers came hastily forward. 'Permit me, signorina,' he said with a bow, taking the plate from her hands. Marcia relinquished it with a 'Grazia tanto' and a friendly smile. They were so polite, so good-natured, these Italians! Cups were brought, the table was spread, and Marcia poured the coffee with as much ceremony as if she were presiding at an afternoon reception. The two, at the soldiers' invitation, stayed and shared the meal with them. Marcia never forgot that sunrise breakfast-party on the terrace—it was Villa Vivalanti's last social function.

She watched Sybert's intercourse with these men with something like amazement, feeling that she had still to know him, that, his character was in the end the mystery it had seemed. With his hand on their shoulders, he was chatting to the group as if he had known them all his life, cordial, friendly, intimate, with an air of good-comradeship, of perfect comprehension, that she had never seen him employ toward even his staunchest friends of the Embassy. One of the soldiers, noticing the direction of her glance, informed her that the signore had been up all night, alternately talking to them and pacing the walks of the ilex grove, and he added that the signore was a galantuomo—a gentleman and a good fellow.

'What did he talk about?' she asked.

'Many, many things,' said the man. 'Italia, and the people's miseria, and the priests, and the wine of Sicily, and the King and the Camorra, and (he looked a trifle conscious) our sweethearts. He is not like other forestieri, the signore; he understands. He is a good fellow.' And then the young soldier—he was most confiding—told her about his own sweetheart. Her name was Lucia and she lived in Lucca. She was waiting for him to finish his service, and then they would be married and keep a carved-wood shop in Florence. That was his trade—carving wood to sell to the forestieri. It was a beautiful trade; he had learned it in Switzerland, and he had learned it well. The signorina should judge if she ever came to Florence. How much longer did he have to serve? Four months, and then!—He rolled his eyes in the direction where Lucca might be supposed to lie.

Marcia smiled sympathetically. Lucia was a beautiful name, she said.

Was it not a beautiful name? he returned in an ecstasy. But the signorina should see Lucia herself! Words failed him at this point. 'Santa Lucia,' he murmured softly, and he hummed the tune under his breath.

Marcia unclasped a chain of gold beads from her neck and slipped it into his hand. 'When you go back to Lucca give this to Lucia from me—con amore.'

'Here, here! what is this?' said Sybert in English, coming up behind. 'Do I find you giving love-tokens to a strange young man?'

Marcia flushed guiltily at the detection. 'It's for a friend of mine in Lucca,' she said, nodding over her shoulder to the young soldier as they turned back toward the loggia.

Sybert laughed softly.

'What are you laughing at?' she asked.

'I sent a wedding present to Lucia myself.'

They strolled to the end of the loggia and stood by the balustrade, looking off into the hills. The fresh, dewy scents of early morning were in the air, and all the world seemed beautiful and young. Marcia thought of Sybert pacing up and down the dark ilex walks while the villa slept, and of the dreadful thing he had spoken last night in that wild moment of despair. She searched his face questioningly. There were shadows under his eyes, the marks of last night's vigil; but in his eyes a steady calm. He caught the look and read her thoughts.

137

'That's all over, Marcia,' he said quietly. 'I've fought it out. You mustn't think of it again. I don't very often lose control of myself, but I did last night. Once in thirty-five years,' he smiled, 'a man ought to be forgiven for being a little melodramatic.'

'Will you—really be happy?' she asked.

'Marcia, America is for me, as for so many poor Italians, the promised land. I'm going home to you.'

She shook her head sadly. 'That—won't be enough.'

'It's all I have, and it's all I want. There's not room in my heart for anything but you, Marcia.'

'Don't say that,' she cried. 'That's why I love you—because there's room in your heart for so many other people. America is your own country. Let it take the place of Italy.'

He studied the Campagna, silent, a moment, while a shadow crossed his face. He shook his head slowly and looked back with melancholy eyes.

'I don't know, Marcia. That may come later—but—not just now. You can't understand what Italy means to me. I was born here; I learned to speak the language before I did English; all that other men feel for their country, for their homes, I feel for Italy. And these poor, hard-working, patient people—I've done them harm instead of good. Oh, I see the truth; Italy must do for herself. The foreigners can't help, and I'm a foreigner like the rest.'

'Ah, Laurence,' she pleaded, 'don't you see that you're an American, and that nothing, nothing can stamp it out? It's all a mistake; your place isn't here—it's at home. Every man can surely do his best work in his own country, and America needs good men. Do you remember what you said at Uncle Howard's dinner that last night we were in Rome? That to be a loyal citizen of the world was the best a man could do? But you can't be a loyal citizen of the world unless you are first of all a loyal citizen of your own country. America may be crude and it may have a good many faults, but it's our country just the same, and we ought to love it better than any other. You do love it, don't you? Tell me you do. Tell me you're glad that you're an American.'

She put her hands on his shoulders and looked up with glowing eyes and cheeks that burned.

As he watched her a picture flashed over him of what it meant. He thought of the vast country, with its richness, its possibilities, its contrasts. He thought of its vitality and force; its energy and nervousness and daring. And for a brief instant he felt himself a part of it. A sudden wave swept over him of that strange, irrational, romantic love of fatherland which is fundamental underneath the polish, underneath the wickedness, in every man in every land. For a second he thrilled with it too; and then, as his eye wandered to the great plain beneath them, the old love—his first love—rushed back. He bent over and kissed her with sudden tears in his eyes.

'Some day, Marcia, I will tell you that I'm proud to be an American. Don't ask me just yet.'

And as they stood there, hand in hand, there was borne to them from the mountain-top above the sweet, prophetic sound of the bells of Castel Vivalanti ringing the Angelus; while below them on the horizon, like a great, far-reaching sea, stretched the Campagna, haunting, mysterious, insatiable—the Roman Campagna, that has demanded as sacrifice the lives of so many miserable peasants, that has lured from distant homes so many strangers and held them prisoners to its spell—the beautiful, deadly, desolate land that has inspired more passionate love than any land on earth.

Note from the Editor

Odin's Library Classics strives to bring you unedited and unabridged works of classical literature. As such, this is the complete and unabridged version of the original English text unless noted. In some instances, obvious typographical errors have been corrected. This is done to preserve the original text as much as possible. The English language has evolved since the writing and some of the words appear in their original form, or at least the most commonly used form at the time. This is done to protect the original intent of the author. If at any time you are unsure of the meaning of a word, please do your research on the etymology of that word. It is important to preserve the history of the English language.

Taylor Anderson

Printed in Great Britain
by Amazon

17639619R00088